He hesitated before he spoke, as if unsure of what he meant to say. "If any more pictures turn up—"

"Yes?" she said tightly as he paused. "You want a private viewing?"

The sensuous lines of his mouth tightened. "It's possible they could be traced, though the contact paper and envelope seem fairly generic."

"Forget it. This isn't your problem."

"Oh, I think it is. The good name of my wife is a matter of supreme importance to me."

"I am not your wife," she declared hotly.

"But you will be." Swinging around on the heel of his handmade Italian leather shoe, he walked away into the darkness. . . .

By Jennifer Blake
Published by Fawcett Books:

TIGRESS

Jennifer Blake

FAWCETT GOLD MEDAL • NEW YORK

A Fawcett Gold Medal Book
Published by Ballantine Books
Copyright © 1996 by Patricia Maxwell

http://www.randomhouse.com

Library of Congress Catalog Card Number: 95-96180

ISBN 0-449-14954-4

Manufactured in the United States of America

First Edition: July 1996

10 9 8 7 6 5 4 3 2 1

For the ladies of Brazil,
with warm appreciation for reading my books,
and for writing to me.

Author's Note

Writers are often asked where they get their ideas. With many books it's really not possible to say. A story may come so gradually and in such bits and pieces that it has no particular starting point. Not so with *Tigress*; I know exactly how it began.

I was at a cocktail party in the New Orleans French Quarter hosted by Louisiana author Beth Dubus. Conversation turned, not unnaturally, to Mardi Gras, then moved on from there to the pre-Lenten celebration in South America. When I said I had always wanted to visit Rio during carnival, one of the other guests, a Brazilian businessman, turned to me and said in the most serious of tones that I must be careful if I go at that time. There might be invitations for carnival parties extended to an attractive woman that would be dangerous to accept. Midway through these particular parties, he said, the lights would suddenly go out. When that happened, any unprotected female would be considered fair game for the sexual advances of any man.

The possibilities for a story of some kind using this situation were instantly apparent. I put the idea on a back burner of my mind where it simmered quietly for several years. *Tigress* is the result. I would like to take this opportunity, then, to extend a special thank-you to Beth Dubus for her part in setting me off on this story trail.

Anyone at all familiar with the southwest corner of Louisiana will recognize at once the chenier country below Lake Charles that is used in the book. Lying back from the gulf a distance of three to five miles, these landmark ridges of ancient shell and silt rise above the wetland paradise of the marsh. The prototype for Oak Ridge in my story is *Chenier Perdue*, or Lost Chenier, which has been the home place of the Theriot family for generations. I am supremely grateful to Loretta Theriot, who still lives on the old home chenier, for sharing with me the wonderful lore of this special place and of her family's long residence there. Though the family that I created for my story bears no resemblance to hers, the book still could not have been written without her.

As always, I am indebted to my husband Jerry for his inexhaustible understanding and patience with a wife who may appear to be at his side but is often miles, and even ages, away. In addition, this story is in large part the result of his expertise in the area of business, and I herewith go on record with my appreciation for 5:00 A.M. conferences on corporate practices, company ethics, and legal entanglements. There's nothing like having your research close at hand.

I am grateful, also, to Guy Baudier of the U.S. Customs Service for time spent in giving me a grand tour of the port of New Orleans. His knowledge, insight, and fascinating anecdotes about the many aspects of the shipping industry in Louisiana added immeasurably to the background of the book.

Publicist Pat Landry of New Orleans was instrumental in gathering material on import and export in the city. I appreciate her efforts, and also her company while climbing over boats and inspecting the back reaches of the New Orleans docks.

Thanks are also due to Mary Behlar of Bourbon French Parfum, New Orleans, for providing introductions, food, and relaxation for a working writer.

Research of many kinds was cheerfully ferreted out by librarian Faye Hood and the staff of the Jackson Parish Library, Jonesboro, Louisiana. My heartfelt appreciation to the whole crew, as usual.

I also would like to express my gratitude to Rosemary Prado of Colorado Springs, Colorado, for answering a writer's SOS, for canvassing her Brazilian friends on my behalf, and for introducing me to the wonderful book called *Behaving Brazilian* by Phyllis A. Harrison. The collected insight from all these sources added immeasurably to my understanding and appreciation for Brazil and its warm and fascinating people.

To my assistant Janis Murphy go beaucoup thanks as well. In the best tradition of a Woman Friday, she smooths my way and saves me from the maddening details, while at the same time helping me remember there is an outside world. Writing would be much harder without her.

Finally, I'd like to note the inclusion of two real people in *Tigress*. Because of a family connection with the University of Northwestern Louisiana, I responded a couple of years ago to a plea for a donation to a charity auction in association with the school. The prize to be auctioned off was an autographed book and lunch with the author, plus the dubious honor of being included as a character in a future work. The package was bidded in by Lena "Debbie" Ciaccio of Natchitoches, Louisiana, who subsequently became the character of the sister to the hero in my book *Silver-Tongued Devil*. In the spirit of fun and university profit, Debbie again battled her way to victory at the following year's auction. Since my next book up was scheduled to be *Tigress*, a contemporary story, I decided to present her as herself in this book, complete with husband Mike and their "golden arch" franchises. Here you are, then, Deb, along with a special thanks for charitable impulses, patience with the vagaries of the publishing industry, and friendship.

—Jennifer Blake
Sweet Briar
Quitman, LA
June 1995

Chapter One

▧ ▧ ▧ *The party was a mistake.*

Jessica Meredith suspected it within seconds of walking into the ultramodern mansion built on the grounds of an old coffee plantation high above Rio. At the end of a half hour, she knew it beyond a doubt.

It was just a feeling however; there was no obvious cause for her unease. The host and hostess seemed pleasant enough, not exactly upper-echelon Rio society, but far from its dregs. Their house with its space-age roof angles and soaring ceilings was furnished with the sleek opulence that comes from professional talent and copious amounts of money. The champagne being circulated by white-coated waiters was vintage Veuve Clicquot. The alternative, the potent and ubiquitous *caipirinhas*, a Brazilian cocktail made with fermented cane juice, was being passed around in crystal goblets. Extravagant and splendidly grotesque *fantasias* of jewels and feathers masked the faces of guests who wore small fortunes in designer clothes and jewelry. The scent of expensive perfume competed with the fragrance of tropical floral arrangements. The gathering was expensive, exotic, and not at all threatening.

Yet something was not right. Tension hung above the crowd as thick and choking as the blue cloud of cigarette smoke that grazed the ceiling. Alcohol was being consumed at a frantic pace. The buzz of conversation was more than a little loud, while laughter came in reckless, out-of-control bursts. The band was strong on drums, bongos, and tambourines meshing in a samba

1

that assaulted the eardrums and pounded against the walls in near-savage rhythm. The dancers gyrating to its exaggerated beat moved with each other in wild, barely contained sensuality.

It was the time of *Carnaval*, of course, the crazy-wild, sexually charged pre-Lenten "farewell to the flesh," which corresponded to Mardi Gras in Jessica's own New Orleans. Allowances had to be made for the license of the festival season. Regardless, she felt so jittery it was hard not to break and run for the door.

A part of her edginess could be called normal. Parties weren't high on her list of favorite things, and she really hadn't felt up to a night of drinking and dancing with strangers after the meeting this afternoon. She had planned an early dinner and a night curled up in her bed at the hotel with files and papers in neat stacks around her. That was before Keil appeared at her door.

Her cousin, who was also her business partner, had met a nice Brazilian couple in the hotel lounge. They were on their way to a party and had extended an invitation to come along. The chance was too good to pass up, Keil said; he and Jessica could see something of Rio other than a business office. She could relax for once and forget Sea Gull Transport & Charter, Inc., and the takeover bid looming over the company. Face flushed and blue eyes earnest, he had insisted that she needed to get out, needed to have a little fun for a change. She had done nothing except work and worry for weeks, even years. It was turning her into an old woman before her time.

Keil had a point and Jessica knew it, which was the reason she had finally agreed to attend the party. Now she wished she had sent him off alone with her blessing. She might as well have, since he had disappeared immediately after bringing her a drink. She suspected he was keeping out of sight because he knew the first words out of her mouth when she saw him again would be, "Are you ready to go?"

Raised voices caught Jessica's attention. Only a few steps from where she stood, a man and woman exchanged words with a vicious undertone in rapid-fire Portuguese. Abruptly the man snapped his fingers in the woman's face, then turned and walked away. The woman gazed after him with tears glazing her eyes and a miserable twist to her lips below her sequined mask.

Disturbed, reluctant to offend by staring, Jessica turned away. Her gaze was caught for an instant by that of a burly, barrel-chested man on the far side of the room. His eyes glittered behind a mask of brown and red feathers, which gave him the look of a lecherous turkey. Detaching himself from the group where he stood, the man moved purposefully in her direction.

Something in the man's swaggering stride and the curl of his moist, full lips made the skin at the back of Jessica's neck tingle in primitive alarm. She looked around hurriedly for Keil or escape, whichever presented itself first.

At that moment a tall man pushed away from where he had been propping up the wall with his broad shoulders. Dark-haired, wearing a silk-lined cape and a bandit's half mask of black velvet over his face, he stepped in smoothly to block the turkey's path. The bandit spoke to the big man behind the feathered turkey mask, a low and succinct suggestion. For an instant it appeared there would be a fight as the turkey balled a fist, but his protest was cut off by a swift, slicing gesture of dismissal from the man in black. The turkey lurched around and moved off, shouldering through the crowd in the direction of the bar.

The bandit turned his head to stare at Jessica. His gaze was intent, appraising. Beneath his mask the chiseled curves of his mouth were set in grim lines that might have indicated disapproval.

The heat of a flush rose to Jessica's cheekbones. She had not felt any need for a disguise until that moment. Keil had been told that it was not really a costume party. Now she felt naked with her face uncovered. She swung sharply to put her back to the room, facing the wide window just behind her.

Her head swam a little with the swift movement, and

she put out her hand to touch the cool plate glass. She was so hot, the effect of too many people and an air-conditioning system not quite up to the tropical climate, not to mention alcohol well above 100 proof. With no one to talk to and no inclination to force herself into any of the groups, she must have drunk too much of her *caipirinhas* too fast. Something to eat from the hors d'oeuvre trays wouldn't hurt; breakfast that morning had consisted of coffee and a bite or two of roll, and she had skipped lunch, since she was too nervous to eat before the business meeting. The normal dinner hour in Rio being some time after ten o'clock, it had still been too early to expect a decent meal in the local restaurants when she and Keil left the hotel.

Leaving to find something to eat would make a good excuse to go when she saw Keil. In the meantime she was more thirsty than hungry. She drained the melted ice water that was left in the bottom of her goblet before setting it on the table beside her.

As she shifted her stance, the dark surface of the window reflected the pale oval of her face and pure lines of her features, the clear green of her eyes, the tawny gleam of her hair in its shoulder-length cut, and the gold tracery of embroidery on her evening suit of beige linen. She thought, suddenly, that she looked a little like a ghost set apart from dazzle and life shifting behind her. It was unsettling and even a little depressing. No matter where she went, it seemed, she was always a little out of her element, always isolated, solitary.

The view beyond the wide expanse of glass was one seen in a thousand travel magazines: the lights of Rio gleaming in a splendid crescent around the bay while Sugarloaf and its attendant hills rose beyond like great bombe desserts from the glazed black platter of the water. Beautiful Rio. Its reputation was rather like that of New Orleans, a city of sinful pleasures where the only moment that counted was the one in your hands. She had arrived here with such hope, such plans for seizing that moment. Precious little of either was left.

Down there in one of the glass-encased high-rises

along the bay were the offices of CMARC, the Companhia Maritima Castelar, where she and Keil had kept their afternoon appointment. They had been ushered into the suite belonging to CMARC's president, Rafael Castelar y Torres. It had been an impressive space where stark expanses of glass let in the view of the sea, and modern, faintly erotic free-form sculptures were displayed on antique tables inlaid with old ivory and rare tropical woods. A Cézanne had shared a wall with an ancient map in a heavy gold frame, and silk cushions in rich colors brightened a sofa and chairs of cordovan leather.

The man who rose to greet them from behind a rosewood desk the size of a small island had been something of a surprise. Jessica had expected someone older, perhaps because the president and CEO of CMARC had been dealing with her grandfather for some time. Castelar, in his mid-thirties, had been darkly handsome with a personable smile and manners that bordered on courtly. He looked, in fact, as if he would be more at home on a polo field than in a business office; he had that air of sun-bronzed, upper-class privilege allied to a wide-shouldered, athletic form and a bearing with a dangerous competitive edge. In another age he might have been a conquistador rather than head of the largest shipping company in South America, one of the largest in the world. Astute, incisive, Castelar concealed his predatory instincts under layers of charm while he went all out for what he wanted, Jessica thought.

What he wanted now was Sea Gull Transport & Charter.

Castelar had been in no hurry to get down to business. While an elderly waiter served *cafezinho*, tiny cups of shudderingly strong, sweet coffee, he talked of a multitude of other things, sitting in easy relaxation as if he had no other appointments, nothing better to do than enjoy a cordial visit. Only when half an hour had passed did he lead the conversation to the subject Jessica and Keil had come so far to discuss.

Gaze intent and expression polite, he leaned back in

his chair while Jessica marshaled the arguments that would convince him to give Sea Gull Transport more time to consider his takeover bid. At the same time, however, his attention wandered. His gaze rested for long, disconcerting moments on her hair, her mouth, her hands, and the smooth shape of her knee that was exposed as her suit skirt retreated from her crossed legs. There was nothing idle in the inspection, but rather a careful noting of information about her, everything from the clothing she wore to the shape of her body under it.

Jessica had been warned of the extreme appreciation for women of the Brazilian male, and also of their tendency toward close inspection that could feel like staring to those unaccustomed to it. Regardless, it was unnerving to be on the receiving end. It made her feel oddly vulnerable and far more aware of herself as a woman than was comfortable.

Once she came to a faltering halt as she noticed that Castelar's concentration was centered on a spot a few inches below her chin. Glancing down, she saw that a button of her blouse had slipped from its hole. The silk gaped open, revealing the curve of her breast above her lace-edged bra. Her fingers were not quite steady as she hastily fastened the errant button.

As she looked up at the Brazilian again, his gaze caught and held hers for what seemed like endless aeons of time. It weighed, measured, penetrating deep as though to discover who and what she was inside. With breath suspended in her throat, she sustained the invasion. She even returned it in a brief moment of curiosity and bravado.

His eyes, she discovered, were not just brown, but the clear amber of some jungle creature such as the fabled Mayan jaguar. And something she saw in their rich depths made her heart kick into a suffocating rhythm.

She lowered her thick lashes in concealment, compelled by an abrupt instinct for self-preservation. Still, she caught the instant when he finally looked away from her, and she thought there was a trace of color under the olive bronze of his skin.

That minor byplay had no effect whatever on the mission entrusted to her and Keil. Castelar was diplomatic in the extreme. He fully understood their reasons for requesting a delay in the ongoing negotiations. He regretted the stroke that had felled her grandfather, recognized Jessica's need to become familiar with her new position as acting CEO in the older man's place, saw the necessity of assessing the strength of the company now that Claude Frazier, its primary founder, was no longer at the helm. Nevertheless, he made no promises she and Keil could carry back to her grandfather or the other family members on the company's board of directors. For all the good the two of them had done, they might as well have stayed at home.

If she had done that, if she had not come to Rio, Jessica thought, she would have at least been spared this party. She would also have avoided the noise and excesses of carnival.

The acres of bare brown skin and the uninhibited flaunting of sexual attributes that was carnival madness had not left her unaffected, no matter how much she might pretend. She could not ignore the blatantly assessing stares or frank comments on her looks and abilities in bed that followed her on the streets. The music of the samba that played everywhere made her feel restless and far too aware of her body. The urge to move to it, to fling off her clothes and dance half-naked to its sensual rhythm was a half-acknowledged temptation. It was as if there was something missing from her life, something she wanted with a bone-deep yearning but could not quite grasp. At the same time, the uninhibited sexual awareness around her made her acutely embarrassed.

Sex. That part of her nature had been repressed for so long that the deprivation had become second nature. Being reminded of it now was the last thing she needed. Rio's relentless celebration of the physical aspect of love set her nerves on edge, especially in the midst of the pressure-cooker heat and tension of this party, where everyone wore disguises in order to hide their true selves, their true inclinations.

She felt as if she were suffocating. She wanted desperately to be outside in the night air, where she could breathe, where there was only darkness and silence, the stars in the night sky and the sea that whispered on the horizon. She needed these things far more than she needed people or loud music or the strained gaiety that she felt around her.

Glancing over her shoulder, she traced a path with her gaze toward the heavy double doors leading into the room. Beyond them lay the entrance hall where she and Keil had been admitted to the house. That way out was blocked by several dozen people, however, including more than one man who watched her with what appeared to be speculation.

To her right, just down from where she stood, was a pair of tall French doors set back in the wall. They led into a walled patio. It might have an exit from it. She swung in that direction with abrupt decision.

The lights began to blink before she had taken two steps. Flashing like lightning among the crystal stalactites that made up the enormous chandelier high overhead, they flickered once, twice, three times. A murmur of excitement swept through the room like a moaning wind. The glittering lightbulbs winked once more, then abruptly went out. Total darkness descended.

Jessica froze in place. For the space of a breath, there was silence around her. Even the band stopped playing.

Then a woman laughed, a high-pitched, nervous giggle. In a far corner a man gave a grunt with the sound of triumph and a female voice cried out in a protest that was abruptly cut off. Scuffling noises broke out in half a dozen places. There came the hissing slide, quiet but unmistakable, of a zipper being lowered.

The band began again, but with only the percussion of drums and bongos. The beat was primitive, driving, with a cadence as steady as a metronome and just as relentless. The darkness seemed to pulse with it as faint, moving shadows began to dance over the walls.

With the slow precision of a camera focusing, Jessica's eyes adjusted to the dimness. Her breath caught in her throat. Her gaze widened in horrified disbelief as she pressed back against the long window behind her.

In the faint radiance of the distant city lights coming through the window, men and women were moving together like dark brutish shadows. Kissing, groping indiscriminately, they stripped off their clothing as they leaned against the walls or settled down to lie, body against writhing body, on the thick carpet. Small smacking, sucking noises came from all directions, along with soft moans.

The party guests were making love—if it could be called that—coupling promiscuously there in the darkness.

She had to get out of here. She had to get out now.

Where was Keil? She strained her eyes, but could not make out his tall form anywhere around her. She opened her mouth to call out to him, then snapped it shut again. Attracting attention to herself seemed like a very bad idea.

It was impossible to thread her way to the front entrance through the seething couples. The darkness made it difficult to see who anyone was, or if they were reaching for her. She might be caught, pulled down, her clothes . . .

No. She would not think of it. It was too incredible, too impossible.

If she could not get to Keil, she would have to find her way out of the house by herself. He would be all right. He was a man, after all.

Had he known this would happen? Could he have been told?

No, never. Surely her cousin would not have come anywhere near the place if he had guessed. He wasn't that kind of man. More than that, he was too well aware of how his uncle loathed such lack of self-control. Keil would be in just as much trouble as she with Claude Frazier if it ever came out he had been present at what amounted to an orgy. To Claude Frazier, immorality had no gender.

The patio. It could still be her best way out.

The doors should be just ahead of her. The lights must have been extinguished outside, too, for she could barely make out the rectangular glints of the panes in the French doors. She groped for a doorknob, found the cool metal of a curved brass handle. Pushing the door open with care, she slipped quietly from the room. As she breathed fresh air scented with sea salt, relief moved over her in a shivering wave.

The tall palms growing in the corners of the enclosed space blocked the little reflected light from the sky, making it even darker out here than inside the house. A wedge of black shadow marked the overhang of a balcony at the far end. She seemed to have the patio to herself, for nothing moved under the gently waving palm fronds.

She made a quick circuit of the walls that were cloaked in the white stars of night-blooming jasmine, skirting a trickling fountain that was inset into an alcove and flanked by cushioned stone benches. There was no exit that she could find. The only door other than the one she had used was one of sliding glass set in the window wall, which led from underneath the balcony into a different wing of the house.

The sliding-glass door was locked. She was trapped.

The French doors behind her opened again with a soft click. She whipped around toward the sound. One door panel stood ajar, and she thought she caught a slight movement, like a shadow in the darkness. Retreating swiftly beneath the balcony, she flattened herself against the rough brick of a square pillar. Eyes closed, breath suspended in her chest, she listened.

Nothing.

No, wait. Had that been the faint scrape of a footstep?

Long seconds passed. The space within the enclosing

patio walls was silent, though faint, disquieting sounds still came from the room Jessica had left. A shudder rippled over her, and she began to take in air again in quick, shallow breaths. With clenched teeth she fought down the peculiar combination of dread and fascination that assailed her.

How could the party guests pair off in that way, stranger with stranger in the dark? What reckless abandon made it possible? What rules applied? Or were there any beyond the deep, primal instinct of the moment? How could they reach out to touch, hold . . .

She wouldn't, couldn't, think about it.

The faint noise she had heard might have been a palm frond moving in the night wind, brushing against the wall. Or possibly a bird disturbed by her presence. A leaf drifting across the stone floor.

It could have been anything. Or nothing at all.

She could not stand there forever. Each passing moment made it more likely that she would have company, if only some couple seeking privacy. She had to retrace her steps, then find a way to run the gauntlet of moving bodies and snatching hands in order to get out of the house. Steeling her nerves, she stepped from behind the pillar.

She was grabbed from behind, snatched backward into a crushing hold. She tried to scream, but the sound was muffled in her throat as a hand clamped over her mouth. Kicking, struggling, she felt herself lifted against a hip and half carried, half dragged into the blackness farther back under the balcony.

Blind rage crashed through her brain. With the strength of pumping adrenaline, she jerked an elbow free and jabbed it backward as hard as she could into the man's ribs. The arm around her squeezed tighter.

She flailed behind her, clawing, but her blows lacked purchase and strength. Her chest burned. Dimness gathered at the edges of her vision. Her heartbeat sounded in her ears with a hard pounding like running footsteps.

Abruptly she was dropped. She caught herself on her hands and knees, breath whistling as she drew air back

into her lungs. Above her came the thud of a hard fist
on bone, followed by a rasping curse. Wrenching her
head around, she saw the wrestling shadows of two
men. Arms jerked and blows thudded. The pair broke
apart as one went stumbling backward, sprawling to the
stone floor. He heaved himself to a swaying crouch.
The other man moved toward him again in a lithe glide
with menace behind it.

The first man pushed upright, then staggered back before whirling into a broken run. A blast of drums and
soft, grunting cries poured into the patio as he snatched
the French doors open. The fleeing man plunged inside.
The doors slammed shut behind him.

The tall man swung and came toward Jessica, looming over her. A low exclamation of concern sounded in
his throat, then he swept the cape he wore aside and
knelt with supple strength. His face was shadowed, the
upper half covered by a velvety black mask. She
flinched as he reached out to touch her shoulder.

The man drew back his hand. "Your pardon, *senhorita*. I mean you no harm."

The words were deep and quiet, hardly more than a
whisper. In spite of the Portuguese form of address, she
thought they carried very little accent. She could not be
sure, however. She could hardly hear above her own la-
bored breathing and the sickening beat of her heart.
That her rescuer was unaffected by the fight he had
been in seemed unfair.

"I—thank you," she managed finally. Pushing upward, she tried to stand, but swayed as her head swam
with a sickening, disoriented sensation. Cane liquor and
terror definitely did not mix.

The stranger caught her, steadying her with a firm
arm around her shoulders. His manner was concerned
yet a shade critical as he stared into the bloodless oval
of her face there in the darkness. In tones of command
he said, "You must sit down."

"No, really, I'll be all right."

He paid no attention, but swung to stare into the

night shadows. His gaze fastened on the cushioned benches near the wall fountain. "Come."

She allowed herself to be led, since it was easier than protest, easier than finding her way alone. As she dropped down onto the padded softness, however, the trembling of reaction surged over her in a wave, abruptly becoming hard shudders. She wrapped her arms around her and held tight as she clenched her teeth to keep them from chattering.

With a soft curse the man sat down and drew her to him, closing her in the strong circle of his arms. Pressing her head to his shoulder with one hand, he held her while he rocked her as gently as a child.

For brief, confused seconds, Jessica sat rigid even as she jerked with the tremors tearing through her. But the arms that held her were warm and firm without being confining; they offered comfort, reassurance, infinite protection, all the things she needed so desperately. And touch—close, compelling human touch such as she had not known in long years. She allowed herself to relax by degrees until she was resting against the firm shoulder under her cheek. Though the shaking still rippled over her, she gave a soft sigh.

Her rescuer's hold tightened, while his warm exhalation feathered across the silk of her hair. She accepted the closer bodily contact as naturally as breathing. He was not quite as calm as he appeared, she discovered; she could feel his heartbeat pulsing against her breasts. The hard, steady throb matched that of her own heart, blending with it so the two seemed perfectly synchronized. Her trembling slowed, subsiding by degrees.

There grew upon her an odd sense that was very like recognition. Somewhere deep inside, she felt its slow unfurling, as if the imprint of his body, like the electronic identification of a handprint, had unlocked some inviolable recess of her being. She felt open, supersensitive, dangerously exposed, yet exhilarated at the same time.

She lifted her head and drew back in the circle of his arms to search the disguised planes of his face. He gazed down at her. The heat of his body surrounded her, enveloping her in the scents of clean male, warm silk from his shirt and suit, and the aromatic wood and musk of an expensive aftershave. They blended with her own linen and Parma violet fragrance plus that of the patio's night-blooming jasmine in mind-swimming combination.

The breeze sighed in that quiet, dark oasis. The night deepened. Male and female, they were perfectly still for long suspended seconds while between them rose an affinity of body, mind, and spirit so intense it had the feel of an ancient bond. Somewhere within herself, Jessica was aware of the defenses of years receding, dwindling to the vanishing point. Finally they were gone, and all that was left was shattering impulse.

The man who held her made a quiet sound of wordless amazement. Lifting his hand, he cupped her cheek, then traced a tingling path with one knuckle over the smooth and delicate turn of her jaw to the center of her pointed chin. He brushed the tender molding of her lower lip, testing the pulse that fluttered beneath the warm and fragile surface.

Dipping his head toward her a fraction, he hesitated as if constrained by internal doubts, or perhaps to give her time to avoid his intention. She did not move, could find no cause or will for it. His hold tightened while the shadows of his lashes flickered. Then abruptly he lowered his mouth to seek blindly for her own.

The contact jolted through her with the force of an electrical linkage. Stunned by its power, she clenched her fingers on the silky material of his suit, clinging to him as her senses whirled. The last vestiges of her shivering faded, ceased.

Under the searching fire of his mouth, her chill lips grew warm. He tasted their moist and sweet surfaces, traced the fine texture and the sensitive line where they joined. Deliberate, unhurried, he molded them to the firm, sensual contours of his own, increasing the delicate friction and pressure until they adhered to follow his slightest movement.

With slow care, he smoothed his hand downward along the curve of her neck, leaving a vibrant stirring in its wake. Easing lower, he spread his fingers and closed them over the full globe of her breast in a definite yet careful gesture of possession.

Jessica's lips parted for a stunned intake of air. He took instant advantage to deepen the kiss, yet the incursion was a smooth and subtle glide, an incitement rather than an invasion. Like an invitation to dance, he touched her tongue with his, each swirling flick a movement of artful and sinuous persuasion. She followed his lead, twining, advancing, retreating, while her blood ran ever faster and more molten in her veins. At the same time she felt the rise of a rich, debilitating languor.

Turning his fingers, he slipped them under the low neckline of her embroidered jacket to caress the swell of her breast with his knuckles. As he brushed the nipple, the exquisite reaction from the touch rippled through her, spiraling downward to ignite sensations as compelling as they were incredible.

Alarm skittered across her mind. What was she doing? How had she come to be lying in the arms of a stranger behind a mask? It was scandalous. It was depraved. More than that, it was deadly dangerous. A low protest sounded in her throat.

"Don't be afraid," he said softly against her lips. "I won't hurt you. I would never hurt you."

"Let me go." The words were a plea instead of a demand.

For long seconds he was quiet, then he tilted his head. "Are you sure that is what you want? The moment for love is in our hands. Once gone, it may never come again. All you have to do is take it."

Her eyes were wide and unseeing as she hesitated. She should push away from him and run for her life. It was unthinkable that she should do otherwise, unbelievable that she could even dream of descending to the same lewd coupling that was taking place inside the house.

Yet the feel of his arms around her was so right. The touch of his mouth was searing magic. The distant samba throbbed in her blood with an insistence that would not be denied. The need to be generous in her gratitude for his intervention was vital and reinforced by the steady rise of something far beyond mere lust.

It had been so long since she had felt any emotion other than family affection, so long since she had allowed herself to feel at all. She had not known she was capable of such wild inclinations, of such heedless, wanton rapture. She had not dreamed that her skin could hunger to be stroked, that she could ache to be touched as a man dying of thirst aches for life-giving water.

This was not New Orleans but Brazil. No one knew who or what she was, not a soul cared what was happening to her. There was only this stranger and herself, and she was not Jessica Meredith to him but only some faceless woman in the dark. If she took the love he was offering and made a memory of it to add joy and gladness to her barren days, who would ever know?

"It's insanity," she whispered.

"Yes, God guard us. It's also carnival, which may be the same thing. Yet it makes a fine excuse for following where the heart leads."

Her lips trembled into a smile. "I'm not sure the heart has anything to do with it."

"No? Then follow the sweet craving of the flesh. Afterward you can say farewell. If you must."

Had there been an accent to his words, after all? Or was it just the sequence of them, their deep intonation, that made her think so? She didn't know, and it didn't matter while her body pulsed with unimaginable need, while the warm wind stirred the palms overhead and the rich and haunting perfume of jasmine drifted in the air like a natural aphrodisiac.

She didn't intend to lean toward him; the impulse was never there in her conscious mind. In fact, a part of it hovered, astonished and aghast, as she swayed closer. Then such constraints were banished as her lashes drifted shut. She accepted the warm possession of his kiss as it came, allowing her lips to part under his in mute, helpless acquiescence.

His chest swelled with the depth of his breath, then he drew her down with him upon the bench. Settling her against the stone wall, he faced her on his side, shielding her from any possible view with his broad shoulders. His warm lips grazed her forehead, the space between her dark winged brows, the tip of her nose, her cheekbones. Then he took her mouth again as he carefully released the buttons of brushed gold circled with brilliants that closed the front of her suit jacket.

There was nothing hurried about his explorations, no sense of urgency in his touch. It was as if time had no meaning, or else he meant to drain the moments of their last breath of pleasure. Spreading the edges of her jacket, he pressed his palm between her breasts, smoothing in slow circles as he felt the gentle thunder of her heart. Stroking her tongue with his in time to its steady throb, he sought her nipples under their covering of lace with his fingertips, caressing them with the care he might use with warm, sun-ripened berries. As they budded under his close attention, he transferred the heat of his mouth to the tight sweetness of one, wetting the webbing of lace that covered it. Then pushing the lace aside, he drew the nipple into his mouth with painstakingly gentle suction.

His care and courtesy breached the last fastness of Jessica's self-protection. Freed of it, she arched toward him in giving surrender. Purest sensation ran rampant in her veins. Her skin seemed to expand under it, while its bright glory shone behind her closed eyelids.

The front closure of her bra parted to his sure manipulation. Pressing his lips to the valley he had uncovered, he spread his hand over her abdomen, then shifted it lower to smooth his palm over the tender mound at the juncture of her thighs. Through the heavy, lined linen of her skirt, she could feel the tensile strength of his fingers and their sure probing. He touched the tiny, ultrasensitive peak of flesh that nestled there. Centering his ministrations on it, he swept his middle finger around it in small concentric circles that closed to a smooth, delicate friction upon the exact core of her being.

With a soft gasp she convulsed against him, burying her face in the turn of his neck. She pressed her mouth to his skin, inhaling his scent, letting it fill her brain while she took it into deepest memory. With a low sound he caught her hips, dragging her against him. In place of his touch, she felt his hard, scorching arousal. He moved against her, a slow stroking of his full length, as if he could not help himself.

With trembling fingers she reached for the black tie at his throat, pulling the bow of his formal wear free before she began to unfasten the studs holding his tucked dress shirt. Beneath it, the muscles of his chest were firm and precisely sculpted. Her questing fingertips threaded through soft, curling hair, found a flat gold disk suspended from a heavy chain, and moved on. She touched the nub of his pap, which was already taut with anticipation and passion. Bending her head, she tasted it, laving it with her tongue for the pleasure of the abrasion, applying suction to return some small semblance of the piercing delight he had given her.

Intent on her own explorations, she barely noticed the movement as he slipped off her shoes, then gathered her skirt in his hand to draw it upward. His touch at the turn of her knee, as he lifted it and placed it over his own taut thigh, went almost unheeded. It was his hand upon her once more, the slide of his fingers over the edges of her garter belt and under the scrap of lace she wore for panties that stopped her breath. At his probing invasion she squeezed her eyes shut and was still, half in sheer enthrallment, half in fear of his discovery and what he would do about it.

But he sensed the clamp of internal muscles upon his knuckle, and the incursion of his finger was shallow as he diverted his attention to her moist and tender folds. Tracing them, separating them, he untangled the soft and silky curls around them, easing them aside for freer access, giving her more positive sensation. Returning to her tightness then, he centered his attention upon relaxing the ring of inner constriction.

Such searing magic seemed almost unendurable. Emboldened by his example and his instant response to her touch, she brushed her hand over the tautness of his abdomen, following the kite string of chest hair down and under the edge of his cummerbund. She smoothed around the wrapped cloth to its Velcro fastening and pulled it loose with a ripping sound. As it fell away, she released the clips of his suspenders and let them dangle, then unfastened his pants. The zipper was more difficult, impeded by his tumescence beneath his silk underwear. Her knuckles brushing against him as she followed the metal slide downward made the muscles of his belly ripple in reaction, even as hard ridges of goose flesh bristled over his skin.

Instinct and a shading of embarrassment made her draw her hand away. Feverishly she slid her palm over his arm to his shoulder, smoothing the roughness there, before she pressed her fingertips into his flesh until they were numb.

She was on fire. There was not enough air in her lungs. Her breasts were swollen, her flesh engorged. A haze filled her mind to obliterate all thought. Her heartbeat made a soft pounding in her ears. She felt a deep internal suspension, like a clock spring wound so tight it might well stop movement, freeze time.

Release was an abrupt, silent clamor, an unwinding so swift and violent her every muscle clenched with it. He expected it, was waiting for it, and so took her mouth to stifle and taste her cry of shocked joy. Immediately he guided his manhood to her and entered, pressing deep in a hot, liquid glide.

He came up against the internal barrier. His own shock stiffened him, while the cold sweat of sudden, desperate control broke over his skin. His curse was unrecognizable, but virulent. Shuddering, he began to draw back, away from her.

Through waves of surging desire and burning

discomfort, Jessica felt his withdrawal. Desolation gripped her. She could not bear to be left as she was, left alone. Her arm and leg muscles tensed. "No," she whispered in frantic protest. "Please, no."

He paused. It was all she needed. Driven by exacting desire and years of denial, she caught her breath against the stinging pain and lunged against him. His heated force broke through the agony, sounded her, came up against the warm satin wall of her depths. He filled her emptiness, routed her loneliness, made her whole. Tears pressed behind her nose and crowded her lashes. She felt their hot slide as they escaped to track backward into her hair.

From somewhere in the distance, yet not too far away, there was a red glow followed by a click and whir. The noise intruded, bringing a flicker of unease. Then the man in her arms was moving, a cautious advance and retreat that brought a surge of white-hot ecstasy. Her mind and her lungs expanded with it. With her breath caught in her chest, she matched his tentative rhythm, encouraged it as best she could by opening herself further to it, moving against it.

He needed no more. With a ragged whisper that might have been an apology or an endearment, he let go of his restraint.

Wondrous. It was a divine plundering, an amazing attrition, a stunning upheaval of the senses. Locked together, they strove to its demanding cadence.

His muscles flexed and hardened, bunched and stretched with effort. The feel of them under her hands fueled her own exertion. His hand at the narrow turn of her waist assisted her, compelled her. Supple in his strength, he held her so that the tight nipples of her breasts drove into his chest. Pressing upon him, receding to plunge again, she was transfigured by exquisite stimulation and the effortless glory of it.

She wanted him infinitely deep inside her. She craved the utmost limit of his power and skill and endurance. As if sensing her need, he heaved over and drew her beneath him. Pressing her knees wide, he settled between them, then began again.

"Yes," she whispered. With his every sounding stroke, he propelled her away from her narrow existence and into a wider world than any she had ever known. She felt her spirit expanding, felt the constriction of long years tearing free. The deliverance of it vibrated through her in an endless, throbbing refrain. Her heart felt full, expanding with aching and passionate joy.

Abruptly every atom of her being coalesced around the man who held her. Pressing close, she offered him everything that was in her while inside she caressed him with deep internal contractions. He gave a last, wrenching lunge, then was still while his own body pulsed to the same eternal cadence.

Long moments later, he subsided upon her and, holding her in a firm embrace, turned to his side once more. Locked together, they struggled for breath. And also for the composure necessary to look each other in the eyes if and when the lights came on again.

Chapter Two

▓ ▓ ▓ *That same faint red light flickered again,* dim yet definite. It was followed by the distant, mechanical click and whir. Jessica frowned in disturbance as recognition teased her brain. Beside her, the stranger raised himself on one elbow and turned his head to stare toward the sliding-glass doors underneath the balcony. The pinpoint of red light gleamed again, though the accompanying noise was lost in the harsh exclamation of the man who held her.

In that same instant Jessica understood. Infrared flashes of light. The sound of a camera's shutter. Someone was taking pictures.

Set-up!

The phrase screamed in her head. It drowned out fear and embarrassment, leaving only rage and pain such as she had never dreamed possible. Then came revulsion so strong that she felt sick with it.

The stranger beside her surged to his feet in silent, catlike grace. Skimming into his pants, fastening them as he moved, he stalked toward the expanse of glass.

Jessica did not wait for more. She snatched her skirt down, pushed the buttons of her jacket into their holes with trembling fingers. Scrambling from the bench, she stepped into her shoes. Her hair was disheveled, and she thrust her fingers through the tangled strands to smooth it. As her hand brushed across her ear, she paused with a soft sound of dismay.

She had lost an earring. The pair was special, a match in brushed gold and diamonds for her suit buttons. She searched over the bench cushions with her hands in trembling haste, but could not locate the missing piece of jewelry in the dark.

She straightened with a jerk. What difference did it make? Nothing really mattered now except getting away.

Whirling, she ran. Her footsteps clicked and grated on the tiles. She thought she heard a low call behind her, but did not look back. Snatching open the French doors, she propelled herself through them and into the dark room beyond.

Someone swung around to step in front of her. She swerved, stumbling over a chair where a seated figure caught her wrist. She struck out, and the edge of her hand caught something fleshy, perhaps a man's nose or lips. He gave a curse of surprised pain and fell back. She stumbled over a discarded shirt or blouse, side-stepped a sprawl of arms and legs. Near the door, the squat shape of a man loomed in front of her. She shied away as she snapped out, "Leave me alone!"

Then she was outside and running down the sidewalk toward the gate in the wall that surrounded the house. As she neared the wide entry, she scanned the parked cars that lined the street.

She slowed to a walk, stopped in confusion. She and Keil had arrived by taxi, but none would be cruising in this residential area. How was she to get back to the hotel? She might possibly call a cab if she could surmount the language barrier, but she couldn't stand the thought of going back inside. Clasping her arms around her, she held tight to keep the panic and the humiliation inside.

"Jessica?"

It was a familiar voice. She swung around with tears crowding behind her eyes. "Keil?"

"Where the hell have you been? I've been looking everywhere."

"Oh, Keil—" Her voice cracked in her pain and relief. "Please get me out of here. Get me out of here now!"

* * *

In the patio courtyard, the man whirled as he heard the swift tapping of feminine high heels in retreat. He took a long stride after the woman he had just made love to, then stopped in tense indecision.

What was the point of following, after all? She didn't want to face him, didn't want him to know her, didn't want his help or his comfort. If any of those things had been acceptable, she would have stayed.

He moved after her anyway, then stood listening at the French doors she had left wide open. She was crossing the room, he thought; he could just make out her fast-moving form, the glint of gold embroidery from her jacket. She should be safe enough. The lights would be coming on again at any second. That was her voice in sharp, breathless protest near the door. Now she was slamming from the house.

He sighed and rubbed a hand across his eyes. God, but what had he done? He should never have gone so far; it had not been what he intended. An excuse—any excuse at all—would be comforting. He had none.

He had acted at first from sheer instinct, obeying the drive to protect what he had staked out as his property. Then, in the best tradition of the country, he had succumbed to the ultimate machismo challenge, the conquest of the woman.

It wasn't like him. He had no use for that kind of strutting performance, certainly had no time for it. To succumb to it now when so much was at stake was criminally stupid.

He could say he had not expected even an instant of cooperation, and that would be true. It did not absolve him. The lady had asked him to stop, and he had used logic and persuasion to get what he wanted. He had never dreamed she might not be experienced—and the reason for that was also stupidity.

He felt like a bastard. And should, for it was how he had acted.

Nothing could change that now. It was past time for regret. All that was left was damage control.

The sliding-glass doors on the far side of the patio

had been locked when he reached them. The man with the camera was gone. He could tear the house apart, but he was fairly sure it would do no good. The pictures that had been taken were something he would deal with when the time came. For now he needed to think how he could repair the harm he had caused. It would be difficult, but it was necessary. He must hope that it was not impossible.

Dear God, but Jessica Meredith had felt good. To be inside her had been so right. Perfect, in fact. She fit his body as she fit the empty niche in his soul, settling like a revered saint in a specially constructed shrine. Except that he was too carnal to leave her in such unmolested grace. God help him.

Swinging back toward the bench, he picked up his shirt and coat. Something fell from among the folds to rattle on the tiles. He bent to pick it up.

It was a circle of diamonds fixed around the edges of a disk of brushed gold. It winked up at him in the starlight from overhead. He stared at it a long second, then he laughed, a low sound of wonder and satisfaction.

Her earring.

It was a token, a talisman, and, just possibly, a promise.

He closed his fingers on the piece of jewelry with great care, holding it trapped in his hand.

Chapter Three

■ ■ ■ *"Look what just came for you,"* Jessica's secretary said as she strode into the office. "Can you believe?"

Jessica looked up from the contract she was reading with a smile of anticipation. Sophie, attractive, black, and supremely blasé, refused to be impressed by anything or anybody on general principles. If there was awe in her tone, it was a put-on; there was sure to be a wisecrack of some kind to follow.

Sophie was carrying an enormous bouquet of at least two dozen perfect orchids. Jessica felt her amusement congeal on her face.

"Exactly," the secretary drawled. "Looks like somebody ripped off a prom."

Dread tightened Jessica's chest, constricting her voice as she asked, "Who sent them?"

"Search me." Sophie set the arrangement on Jessica's desk with exaggerated care. "I looked all over for a card, but there isn't one."

The Raku vase that held the orchids qualified as a work of art with its glazed luster in swirls of copper, gold, rich turquoise, and vivid fuchsia. The blossoms themselves were a rare salmon-gold with green and purple throats. A drop of dew hung from each fringed lip and a delicate, sweet scent like that of an iris drifted in the air around them.

Once refrigerated, orchids lost their natural perfume. These exotic blooms had been clipped from the plants scant hours, if not minutes, ago.

"Which florist delivered them?"

Sophie shrugged slim, expressive shoulders. "The man wore a business suit, not a uniform. He asked if this was your office and, when I said it was, he just plunked down the vase and walked out."

Orchids grew wild in Brazil.

Jessica closed her eyes and pressed the lids with her thumb and forefinger. It didn't help. In her mind rose a scene that had seldom left her mind, sleeping or waking, since her return from Rio two days ago. It was made up of a thousand flashing images, among them a dark and scented patio, the rhythm of a samba, and the warm caresses of a stranger with magic in his touch.

Were the orchids from him? If they were, how had he known where to send them? Were they intended as a reminder? Or were they, just possibly, a threat?

"You all right?" Concern threaded Sophie's voice.

"Yes, fine," Jessica said. With a supreme effort she straightened, glancing once more at the contract in her hand. "Check downstairs, will you? See if anyone saw a florist's van."

"I'll do that." The secretary paused, as if she meant to say something more. Apparently she thought better of it, for she turned and walked out of the room, closing the door behind her.

Jessica tossed the contract she still held to her desk and leaned back in her chair. Her hands were cold and trembling. She clasped them together so hard the knuckles turned white. At the same time her face felt hot and her lips tingled. Humiliation and rage burned in her brain, and she shook her head from side to side as if they might be physically dislodged. It wasn't possible.

How was she supposed to work like this? When was she going to get over what had happened? When was she was going to know, finally, what the outcome would be?

So far there had been no call, no sign of the pictures that had been taken. She had received no hint of a blackmail note of any kind. Nothing.

Until now.

What if the orchids were the first move in the game? She stared at them with stinging eyes.

The thing that disturbed her most about that night in Rio, she had concluded after close examination, was her own betrayal of everything she had worked so long and hard to gain. Other people had failed her, and she had managed to survive it. She had never expected to fail herself.

It would be easy to blame someone else, such as the people who gave the party, Keil for insisting she attend, or the man in the dark patio for taking advantage of her weakness. Her strict code wouldn't allow that. She was at fault. The consequences were on her own head.

And yet, it was so hard to believe what she had done. In the bright light of day, sitting in her office at Sea Gull Transport & Charter on Poydras, it seemed so irrational and out of character.

So dangerous.

So sordid.

What on earth had possessed her?

Had she been that drunk? Or had she felt some sense of indebtedness for her rescue? Had she been swept away by the combination of anonymity and natural urges too long repressed? Was it, perhaps, just Rio and the whole sexual fantasy, *Wild Orchid* mystique of carnival time? Or was it only chemistry, the unexpected physical response to a man her body recognized as being a perfect match for her own?

She didn't understand exactly what had happened to her. All she knew was that it had seemed right at the moment. Then it had gone so very wrong.

A quick knock sounded, and her office door swung open again. Keil stuck his head inside. His blue gaze quizzical, he said, "You about ready for a break? I've got the coffee."

She summoned a smile as she nodded. She might as well. Her concentration was in such tatters she was unlikely to accomplish anything else.

"Getting pretty fancy, aren't we?" Keil nodded in the

direction of the orchids as he put her cup on her desk then deposited himself with his own in the rust leather chair across from her. "You got a rich boyfriend I don't know about?"

"Not likely," she said in clipped tones as she pushed the flowers as far away as possible. "I don't know who sent them."

"A secret admirer, huh?" An auburn highlight glinted in his sandy blond hair as he leaned back in his chair.

"I expect the card just got lost."

"Or maybe it's a funeral offering from Castelar," her cousin returned with a grimace. "We might as well hold a wake over Sea Gull. You know, I thought the whole thing went okay—until I got home and realized that the Latin Attila the Hun didn't give an inch."

He was joking, but he had a point. She picked up her coffee, holding the mug to warm her chill fingers while she struggled to bring her mind to the business of the day. "Have you spoken to Grandpapa?"

Keil nodded. "Called bright and early yesterday morning, wanted to hear everything Castelar had to say."

"I'm sure." Jessica had made her own report, but she fully expected her grandfather would double-check it.

Keil took a sip from his cup. "Uncle Claude also asked what I thought of Castelar. Seems he wanted to compare my view with the one he formed from talking to him on the phone. Also from a report he had compiled on him. You know anything about that?"

"What kind of report?" She gave her cousin a brief glance, her pellucid gaze troubled.

"A thorough one, from what I saw when I glanced over it after talking to the old man. Seems the guy's rich as sin, has a penthouse in Rio, plus keeps up a big family estate at Recife in northern Brazil that dates from the 1600s. Quite a lady-killer: The girl he was engaged to some years back wound up killing herself the day before the wedding, then the high-fashion model he was going around with last spring almost overdosed on sleeping pills and alcohol—would have if Castelar hadn't found her. The affair ended when he pulled strings to get the woman an audition for some Brazilian soap opera. So far he hasn't replaced her."

Jessica made no attempt to conceal her distaste. "We're supposed to be able to use that kind of stuff?"

"Don't ask me. But what Uncle Claude was getting at, I think, was whether I thought Castelar was a certified bastard, had bad luck with his women, or just preferred the unstable type. In short, if he had any weakness—since nothing much showed up in the report."

"What did you tell him?"

"That I sure didn't see any. How about you?" The look Keil gave her was keen.

Jessica considered the question while the angles and planes of Rafael Castelar's face rose in her mind. The thing she remembered most, she realized, was his eyes with their amber intensity. There had been intelligence in them, she thought, and a will of tempered steel. Still, anything more had been concealed by humor, charm, and polite reserve.

"Who can tell?" she said finally. "He could be hiding anything."

"I suppose the answer might tell us something about how likely—or unlikely—Castelar is to be bluffed out of what he wants. Anyway, you know Uncle Claude, always figuring every angle."

"He's never hired a report done on a business opponent before that I know of." The words were tentative. Jessica was well aware that she was not privy to all of her grandfather's business practices.

"Maybe the deal was never important enough," Keil pointed out.

"And now it is, which is the reason for the stroke that's keeping him beached while the two of us steer the ship," she said, masking her concern with a display of irritation. "He'll worry himself into another one if he doesn't watch out."

A derisive snort was Keil's comment. "The only thing that will stop the old man from worrying is for

him to pass on. Of course, it would help if Castelar
went away and made like a shark around somebody
else's company."

Jessica could only agree.

"Anyway, the report on Castelar is in the private file
in Uncle Claude's desk, if you want to look at it. The
background is pretty interesting. Old Portuguese ex-
plorer blood runs in the family—which seems to be
about on a par with coming over on the *Mayflower*. One
great-grandaddy was a sugar baron with a place the size
of Vermont, another turned into some kind of revolu-
tionary in the nineteenth century. Apparently Castelar's
related, directly or by marriage, to everybody who matters in Brazil, or the rest of South America for that matter. He even has ties of some kind to the States."

"It might have been nice to see the details before we
went down to Rio," she commented dryly.

"Yeah, well, Uncle Claude didn't want to influence
us. We were supposed to use our own judgment—such
as it is. And now we have to justify the results. You
know he'll want a blow-by-blow description come Sunday?"

"You'll be there, too?" She gave him a direct look as
she waited for his answer.

"Lord, yes. It's a command performance, isn't it?"

Her smile in agreement was wry. Her grandfather had
always been something of a patriarch. He liked gathering his family around him at least once a month, the
better to keep tabs on them. This Sunday would be the
first time they had all been to the Landing, the home
place down in the marshlands of southwest Louisiana,
since he had been released from the hospital three
weeks ago.

"I think my mother means to show up." Keil's words
were tentative, his gaze on the coffee in his cup as he
swirled it.

"Some particular reason?"

More in answer to Jessica's tone than her words, he
said, "She's a stockholder, isn't she?"

That much was certainly true, though Claude Frazier

usually ignored the business interest of his nephew's wife so that Jessica had the same tendency. Sea Gull Transport & Charter had been established by her grandfather in partnership with his younger brother Albert, Keil's grandfather, and was still a family-held corporation. Claude was the older brother, the one with vision. It was he who first began ferrying crews, supplies, and machinery to the offshore oil rigs, while Albert had concentrated on pleasure and fishing boat charters. Because Claude had contributed more capital to the start-up costs, he had always held a majority seventy-five percent of the company, while Albert was left with the remaining twenty-five percent.

As the years passed, Albert had been blessed with two sons, a circumstance that Claude had never quite forgiven him, since his only child had been a daughter. Albert's eldest son had been killed in Korea, shortly before Albert suffered a massive heart attack. The younger son, Louis, had married and produced Keil before driving over a seaside cliff on the corniche road east of Biarritz. The profligate playboy of the family, Louis had been drunk and in the company of a buxom blond actress at the time, so he had not been much mourned.

However, the accident had left his widow, Zoe Frazier, in possession of her husband's share of Sea Gull until Keil came of age. Even after he took charge of it and came into the company, she still controlled her widow's portion, which amounted to a twelve and a half percent interest.

Jessica said now, "I suppose you told her what's going on."

"In general, though I sometimes think she knows more about it than I do." Keil did not look at Jessica as he spoke. They were both aware that his mother cultivated a wide circle of friends and acquaintances, some of whom could easily be, and probably were, employees of the company.

Another time, Jessica might have pursued the subject. For now she could not seem to ignore the flowers perfuming the air or all the things they brought to mind.

She glanced around the place that had become her
home away from home, her office with the antique
cherry desk she had rescued from a rummage sale, the
Kurdistan carpet in blue, rust, and gold that lay in front
of a cherry settee covered in blue twill, and the great
philodendron with its slashed leaves that guarded the
window overlooking the Mississippi River. This was
where she belonged, the place where she felt level-
headed, competent, and definitely not the kind of
woman who might succumb to a Brazilian lothario
without a name.

"About the party in Rio," she said, glancing at Keil,
then away again. "Could you tell me again how you
came to have an invitation?"

Keil sat forward in his chair. "Lord, Jess, it was just
one of those things. I was down in the hotel lounge,
talking to this guy on the next bar stool while he waited
for his date. She showed up, and he mentioned they
were on their way to a great bash this couple threw
every carnival, said I was welcome to come along. It
sounded like fun, a chance to get a feel for Rio, meet a
few true *Cariocas*. Nobody said a word about anything
kinky, I swear they didn't!"

Keil had apologized over and over coming home on
the plane. To prevent another round of the same, she
said, "There was nothing at all to make you think this
man might have singled you out?"

"You mean like he knew who I was before he sat
down?" Keil considered a moment, then shook his head.
"I don't think so. It was just a spur-of-the-moment offer, that's all. Maybe I looked like a swinger to him—or
else he thought I would be open to it because I was
American, I don't know. I'm just glad we got out of the
whole thing without anybody getting hurt."

It was Jessica's turn to stare into her coffee cup.
She had told Keil that someone grabbed and kissed her,
but nothing more. It had been necessary to say something to account for how ruffled and upset she had
been. She had not breathed a word about the second
man in the courtyard or the photographs that had been

taken. The main reason had been her overwhelming humiliation; but she had also been afraid Keil might try to confront the man who had made love to her or search for whoever had taken the pictures. All she had wanted just then was to get away from Rio as fast and as far as possible. And to never think of that night again.

The last had been impossible, of course. The patio episode played over and over in her mind in such excruciating detail, she thought she might go insane with it. She would never forget it. Never.

In spite of everything, she had begun to think she had taken the best way out. It seemed barely possible the situation had not been a setup, after all. The person behind the camera could have been just some weirdo who got his kicks from watching and taking pictures, someone who knew what kind of party to expect and had come prepared.

Though she despised the thought of being spied upon, hated the idea of appearing in some voyeur's private picture collection, that explanation had been a relief for two reasons. First, it allowed her to hope that night was an isolated incident without repercussions that might affect Sea Gull Transport & Charter. But most of all, it identified the man who had made love to her as only the chance-met stranger she called him in her mind, something she found much more comfortable to accept. It was bad enough that she had succumbed to the attentions of a masked lover without having to fear he had seduced her in cold blood.

All that had, of course, been changed by the arrival of the orchids.

"Jess? You really weren't—hurt, were you?"

There was concern in Keil's eyes as he watched her. She had been too quiet, lost in her own thoughts too long. Forcing a smile, she said, "No, of course not; I was just—thinking. Has it occurred to you that it could be more than a little embarrassing if anybody found out we were at a party like that?"

Her cousin drained his cup and set it on the desk before settling his rangy, long-limbed body back in his chair. "You mean to the company or on a personal level?"

"Either one. Or both."

"Yeah, well, I certainly wouldn't want Uncle Claude to get wind of it—God, can you imagine? But for the company, I don't see the difference. I mean, people have done worse and shown up among the Fortune 500." A grin lighted his rather square, strong-featured face before he lifted his hands and slapped them down on his knees. "Anyway, not to worry. We got out of the mess, and nobody saw us who matters."

"We can't be sure of that."

He stiffened. "Meaning?"

She picked up a pen and turned it in her fingers, watching it as she spoke. "I've just been wondering about CMARC, since it was their turf. Suppose they wanted an extra bit of leverage to persuade us to be reasonable about the takeover?"

"I guess it's possible." Keil compressed his lips a moment, then shook his head. "But no, I really can't see it. If Castelar wanted to play dirty, he could just buy up our loan. That's Uncle Claude's twelve-million-dollar Achilles' heel."

"Vic Gaddens would never sell it out from under Grandpapa!" she said immediately. "They've worked together for ages."

"And nothing except interest has been paid on the loan in years. Besides which, Vic is only one of the directors at Crescent National, not the whole shooting match, and the rest of the board knows Uncle Claude isn't running the show now, may never really run it again. Bankers are realists; Vic can't be sure you and I are going to be able to keep things going. He might consider selling if offered a high enough premium."

"Pray to God Castelar doesn't realize that." Her voice was tight.

"He'd be a fool to overlook the possibility."

That point was not new to Jessica. She was also acutely aware that Vic Gaddens's opinion of her business acumen would not be improved if the pictures from the patio should happen to surface at the bank.

In an abrupt change of subject, she said, "There's something else that's occurred to me a time or two lately. Sea Gull's problems began with the crew boat explosion in the gulf last year. We could have fought off any attempt to buy in the loan if not for the millions in legal claims and lawyers' fees stemming from it. Have you ever considered how convenient that little accident was for our competitors?"

"A time or two. But bad things happen to good people, as they say, and you can't really blame CMARC or Gulf Stream Air or any of the others for taking advantage of our rotten luck."

"What if it wasn't bad luck? What if somebody wanted to put us out of business?"

"They darn near did it then, didn't they? No, really, that's television drama stuff, way too risky unless they were total crooks who had it in for us."

"Or for Grandpapa."

He shrugged. "Same thing. Hurt Sea Gull and you get Claude Frazier where he lives."

They watched each other a long moment, while between them lay the unspoken recognition that the worry and strain of the gulf accident had contributed its part to the stroke that had felled Sea Gull's founder. Also the fact that if both the company and Claude Frazier had been hale and hearty, there would have been no danger of a takeover by CMARC.

It was Jessica who looked away first. "About Sea Gull, Keil," she began, then stopped.

"Something else on that tiny mind?"

The comment was designed to get a rise from her. She gave him a token smile for the effort before she went on. "I was wondering if it ever bothers you that Grandpapa left me in charge? I mean, don't you sometimes wish you were the one at the wheel?"

He laughed in surprise, though he did not quite meet her eyes. "Lord, Jess, what brought this on?"

She lifted a shoulder. "Thinking about Castelar and

South American attitudes toward women, I guess. Wondering if maybe it wouldn't have been better, all things considered, if you had made the Rio presentation. Some people would consider it natural for Grandpapa to turn to you. You've worked here since you were a kid, one way or another, and you're his brother's grandson, the male heir."

"And two years older, too; don't forget that." He grinned before his expression turned serious. "No, I think everybody around here knew you were being groomed for the top post from the minute the old man sent you off to earn your MBA. You've worked hard since then, doing the donkey work, putting in the hours. The only surprise is the sudden turnover. Everybody expected Uncle Claude to be around forever."

"Including him," Jessica agreed. Regardless, she thought her grandfather might well reconsider his choice if he should catch a glimpse of a photograph of his beloved granddaughter in the arms of some man she could not name. She could not help remembering also, as much as she might hate it, that her cousin Keil had been in Rio, that he had arranged for her to be at the party, and that he had been conveniently absent when the lights went out.

"Anyway, I'm not too sure I'm cut out for the head job," Keil went on as he stretched expansively and clasped his hands behind his head. "I'd much rather be out in a boat than buried in papers or projected earnings. You can have it, honey. If you need me, you can always follow the trail of floating beer cans."

He was only half joking. Keil lived within walking distance of the marina on Lake Pontchartrain, where Claude Frazier had kept a company boat docked for years. The current version was a fifty-foot pleasure craft with a raked hull, flying bridge, and twin Chrysler inboard marine engines. The *Sea Gull IV* was fitted out for the gulf, and had a galley complete with refrigerator and microwave, dining area, living area, two baths, and a sleeping capacity of eight. Though used for business outings and as a floating hotel for guests who came and went in the city, it was recognized as Keil's baby. Summer evenings and weekends usually found him on the water with a revolving crew made up of his circle of buddies and any female they might have in tow.

Yet, for all his relaxed lifestyle, Keil had a good business head. The charter division of the company always showed a handsome profit. Nor did hard work bother him. As port captain for the crew boat operation, he kept their fifty-odd boats in good maintenance and on schedule, and never complained about having to take one out himself now and then on the occasional emergency call.

Jessica didn't doubt for a minute that, given sufficient reason, her cousin would show more interest in the overall operation. Her ouster just might be the incentive needed.

Then there was his experience with women. Though Keil was no playboy like his father, he had been around enough to know how to make love to a woman and see that she enjoyed it. Jessica liked Keil, and certainly took pleasure in his company. Couples more closely related than third cousins had struck sparks off each other before. Was it possible she had also found him sexually compatible?

What a thought, what a terrible thought.

Suspicion. She hated it, hated what that night in Rio was doing to her. She was beginning to think it might well be a relief to know just who had those damned, and damning, pictures and just what they meant to do with them.

"Anybody tell you Madeleine's here this morning?"

"Really? What does she want?" Jessica met her cousin's gaze, her own alert. Madeleine was her grandfather's bride of nineteen months. Hardly older than Jessica's twenty-seven years, she qualified in spades as a so-called trophy wife for a man past seventy-five.

"To meddle, what else? I understand she was in and out the whole time we were gone."

"I can't imagine what she hopes to find." That Madeleine was in the city instead of at the Landing with her husband wasn't too surprising in itself. She was from New Orleans and had family in the city.

"Maybe what she'll have coming if Uncle Claude sails away to that big ocean in the sky?" Keil said in laconic practicality.

"In spite of the prenuptial agreement?" Jessica shook her head. "Anyway, I'm not sure she would recognize a profit-and-loss statement if she saw one, much less be able to read it."

"You never can tell. Sometimes I think there's more to Madeleine than meets the eye."

Jessica had considered Madeleine as one of her grandfather's rare lapses of judgment, a desperate grasping after youth and immortality. The young woman was pretty, a bit plump, and a little mercenary, but not particularly important to the general scheme of things. Certainly she had shown no interest in the company before. If she was going to do it now, however, it might be a different story. With resignation, Jessica said, "Where is she?"

"In the old man's office. Sophie says she was asking for the file on the CMARC deal earlier, but she told her you had it."

"Good grief."

"Right," Keil said in dry agreement.

Jessica got to her feet. "I suppose I had better talk to her. Otherwise, she may run complaining to Grandpapa."

"What do you care? He's not about to pay any attention to her; he thinks she's his little darling with nothing on her mind except her collection of charge cards."

"He doesn't need to be aggravated."

"Yeah, well, don't you let her get to you," Keil recommended with a shading of irony as he unfolded himself from the chair to follow her from the office. "Just remember who's boss!"

Jessica gave him a quick, speculative look as she heard the echo of sarcasm in his tone, but she made no reply.

Keil's smile faded as he watched his cousin stride

down the hall. He was worried about Jess. Not only were there purple shadows under her eyes from lack of sleep, but she was something less than her usual sharp, efficient self. She seemed down, which was noticeable indeed; she was ordinarily the most upbeat person around, always sane, sensible, and in control. Something was on her mind, and it didn't take a genius to figure it out. She hadn't been the same since that damn party.

A scowl settled between his brows as he turned back toward his office. He had passed that night off with a few quick comments, but he'd spent some time thinking about it, too. She had been more than a little upset when he found her, her hair tousled and her lips tender rose red and a little swollen. He'd never before seen her so uncertain or so beautiful. It had been a revelation.

Cousin or not, he'd always had a special affection for her. She had never noticed, as far as he could tell.

Jess seemed to have a blind spot where her looks were concerned. Hell, half the guys in the building would jump out a window if she so much as nodded toward the glass, but did she see it? Not likely. Which was strange, because she was good with people. Everybody liked her, and she seemed to like everybody; she could always find a smile for whomever she met. She understood what made folks tick, but didn't think any less of them for it, no matter what their hang-up.

Being Jess, she hadn't blamed him for Rio. It didn't matter; he blamed himself enough for both of them. He should never have taken her there that night. She claimed nothing had happened, but he knew better. He'd give a great deal to know how she felt about it, but she wasn't the kind to broadcast the gory details of her love life. She had her fences, and nobody got through the gate without an invitation.

He just hoped the damage wasn't permanent. That was the last thing he had intended.

As he slammed the coffee cup he carried down on his own desk, the heavy base hit so hard it cracked the protective glass. Cursing quietly, he threw himself into his chair and squeezed his eyes shut.

Claude Frazier had the largest office in the high-rise, a corner suite of two rooms overlooking the wide river bend that gave New Orleans its title as the Crescent City. It was also the most austere office, done in functional beige and brown and furnished with the same beat-up desk, chairs, file cabinets, and wastebasket that he had been using for fifty years. Even the view was not particularly inspiring this time of day, being mainly the geometric squares of rooftops and, beyond them, the muddy flow of the river where the Algiers ferry was making one of its staggering, diagonal runs for the far bank.

Jessica paused on the threshold to consider the woman who sat behind Claude's desk. Madeleine Frazier was well put together in a glossy fashion. Her hair, a dark brown that just missed being black, was cut short and brushed in a spiky fluff around her face. The true color of her eyes was an indeterminate hazel, which she changed to blue or green with contact lenses as the mood struck her. Her shape was on the voluptuous side, especially at the hipline, though she camouflaged it fairly well most of the time.

The woman also had a vulnerable look about her when she was not pouting or playing the wide-eyed innocent. Jessica thought that might be a part of the appeal for her grandfather; he liked taking care of people. For herself, she had never been able to decide if the impression was valid or just the effect of lashes so long and curled on the tips that they looked like those of a child.

The suit Madeleine had put on for the office was an aggressively businesslike gray pinstripe worn with a white shirt and mannish tie. Seen from the waist up, it made her look as if she had exchanged clothes with a Depression-era gangster. Since she ordinarily favored bright colors, ultramodern chic, and the latest in fads from Saks, the outfit was no doubt designed to make a no-nonsense, all-business statement.

Madeleine looked up at Jessica's mild greeting, returning it with an artless smile before she said, "You brought the CMARC file with you?"

"There's nothing in it that I can't tell you," Jessica countered. "What was it you wanted to know?"

The other woman gave a light laugh. "Everything. And I would really like to see for myself, if you don't mind. Unless there's some reason you and Keil want to keep it from me."

"Of course not, but you have to realize that the information is sensitive. Since I would rather not have the details turn up as common gossip in the break room, I keep close tabs on it."

Color rose in the other woman's face so the powdered cocoa blush she wore looked like a layer of dust on her hot cheeks. "Surely you don't think I would talk out of turn? I know how much Claude hates that kind of thing. On top of which, it could affect me personally when he's gone."

Jessica stood staring at her grandfather's young wife as the words she had heard arranged themselves in rational order in her mind. She said finally, "You will have no right whatever to Sea Gull or any major portion of my grandfather's estate if anything happens to him. You know that, don't you?"

Madeleine's full lips curved in a bright smile. "Oh, I know I signed away all rights. But I am his wife, and he's concerned about what will become of me. Besides, he's a smart old fox. I think he'll leave everything to whoever he thinks will take care of it best."

"He told you that?" Jessica's voice was amazingly calm considering the unease that gripped her.

"He's been drafting a new will since he got home, and intends to give it to his lawyer as soon as he works out a few more points."

"So you might have been left with nothing if the stroke had killed him? That was a narrow escape."

Madeleine gave a small shrug. "A miss is as good as

a mile, as my granddaddy always said." She ran her fingers through her hair, leaving it in soft disorder. "I'm not too sure what Claude means to do, but I could probably handle things here if he makes me a stockholder. All I would have to do is get the rest of the family behind me."

"Including my mother?" Jessica inquired in dry tones.

"Oh, well, she may not care that much for me," Madeleine said with a sweep of her lashes that concealed her eyes, "but when did the two of you ever see eye to eye on anything?"

Jessica did not bother trying to deny something that was all too true. "She'll be out for your hide if you take any part of her interest in Sea Gull."

"Maybe, and maybe not. You and Claude between you have managed to see that Arletta has no say whatever around here. She just might be ready to share—especially if it gives her access to more ready money."

She had a point. Trying a different tack, Jessica said, "And what makes you think you're qualified to manage a company like this?"

"How hard can it be? You send boats out to the oil rigs, and you bring them back. You take people out fishing or cruising, and you take their money."

Jessica laughed; she couldn't help it. "There's a bit more to it than that."

"It doesn't make any difference," Madeleine said carelessly. "I think everybody will be better off if we get serious about this CMARC offer. I'm all for running up the price as high above the outstanding debt as it will go, but the minute it hits the top, I think we should take the money and run."

The woman's words went over Jessica with the heat of a flash fire. "Take the money and run?" she said, walking forward to brace her hands on her grandfather's desk. "Let me clear something up for you, Madeleine. No one is taking anything or going anywhere. Claude Frazier is still in charge here. Keil and I only carry out his orders. Frankly, I think we'll be turning things back over to him soon. That being so, he may be interested to know your future plans for the company he spent his whole life building."

"And you're going to tell him?" Madeleine arched a thin brow. "Come on, Jessica, you and I both know you would never do that. You wouldn't want to be the cause of another stroke."

"Mention selling out to CMARC to him, and you'll bring it on yourself. But then, maybe that's what you want."

"What I want," Madeleine cried with the liquid sheen of angry frustration in her eyes, "is to see the CMARC file so I'll know what everybody is talking about instead of having to sit around and guess!"

Startled by the sudden image of Madeleine revealed by her words, Jessica felt a check in her annoyance. At the same time she thought the other woman had proven effectively that she had a fair understanding of what was happening. She straightened as she said abruptly, "Tell my grandfather to authorize it, and you've got it."

The other woman stared at her a long moment. Voice not quite even, she said, "You don't think he'll do that, do you?"

"I think he'll want to know why you want it. The question is whether you can convince him it's not just idle curiosity."

"I'll tell him you didn't want me to have it, that you don't want me around here at all."

There was a lot of truth in that, Jessica knew. At the same time she had some inkling of what it must be like to be treated like a decorative and brainless toy by her grandfather. She felt an unwilling sympathy for Madeleine. More than that, as irritating as she could be, Claude Frazier had made her a part of the family, a part of their lives. There was no point in fighting it. Sighing, Jessica said, "Come and help us instead of getting in the way, and it might be different."

Shock widened Madeleine's eyes, though there was a shadow of calculation in their depths. "You don't mean it!"

Did she? Would her grandfather allow it even if she did? It wasn't possible to say, and that bothered her. It seemed she had been knocked off balance by the events in Rio, as if she could no longer be certain of anything that involved her emotions or convictions.

"We'll see what Grandpapa has to say," she repeated finally.

Swinging around without waiting for an answer, Jessica strode from the office. In the blindness caused by her inner turmoil, she almost collided with Sophie who was hovering outside the door.

"I wasn't listening, really, I wasn't!" her secretary said as she threw up her hands like a suspect under arrest.

Jessica gazed at her a long instant, her expression clouded by doubts that had nothing whatever to do with Sophie. Then she forced a brief smile. "Don't worry about it. You needed something?"

"Nothing major, only a quick appointment check. I have the executive secretary for the president of CMARC on the line. She needs to know if it will be convenient for you to meet with her boss over lunch on Monday. I looked at your calendar and it's clear."

Since Castelar had refused their request for time, all that could be expected from him now was a demand for a decision on his offer or else a threat of further action. There was no other reason for a meeting.

Her voice tight, Jessica said, "What does he want?"

"His secretary didn't say. All I know is he requested lunch. With you by your lone self; that point was very clear. If you're agreeable, I'm to reserve a table for two at Commander's." The secretary waited with lively curiosity in her expressive face.

Alone. Castelar and herself. Jessica felt distress shift inside her. She didn't need this right now, not with the weekend with her grandfather looming. No matter; refusal was impossible. Castelar had the upper hand, after all.

What if he also had the pictures? What was she going

to do if he took out an envelope and put it on the table, then delivered an ultimatum?

There was only one way to find out.

With a lift of her chin, she said, "You can say I will be delighted to have lunch with Mr.—excuse me, *Senhor*—Castelar on Monday. In fact, I'll look forward to it."

Chapter Four

▦ ▦ ▦ *Jessica sometimes thought the three-hour* drive from New Orleans to the Landing was a blessing in disguise. She needed that time to slow down, rearrange her priorities, change her mind-set so she became a girl again instead of a take-charge business-woman. The process wasn't always easy.

It was a fairly straight shot on Interstate 10 from New Orleans to Lake Charles, skirting Lake Pontchartrain and the Bonne Carre spillway, shooting through Baton Rouge and Lafayette, then skimming along on the road-way built on concrete pilings over the swamplands. She glanced now and then at familiar sights of towering cy-press trees standing ankle-deep in still, dark water, turtles slipping from logs, and egrets and blue herons patiently waiting for a meal. Turning just before she reached Lake Charles, she passed through an area where new rice thrust brave and tender blades above the watery trenches. Beyond that lay stretches of prairie, open grasslands waving as verdant as an inland sea. This was cattle country, land of the Cajun cowboy, where an-imals with bloodlines that included strains from long-horns like those across the Texas border had been tended for more than two hundred years.

The great looping bridge over the Intracoastal Water-way marked the beginning of the wetlands and chenier country. The chenieres themselves were long ridges of land rising from the marsh some two or three miles dis-tance from the gulf. Built up from shell and silt, these landmarks were the sites of ancient beaches left in the retreat of prehistoric seas. The land surrounding them was sometimes called "quaking prairie" for its water-logged, unstable character, though it grew lush grass for cattle grazing even in the driest of summers. Late fall through spring, however, the cattle were moved to higher ground as the marsh was covered by brackish water where saw grass and reeds and bamboo waved in the chill wind from the gulf. Home then to only alligators, turtles, nutria, raccoons, opossums, and the occasional wolf, it became the winter feeding ground of a large portion of the migratory birds and waterfowl of North America.

East of the coastal town of Ombre-Terre lay three chenieres, one behind the other. They dominated the landscape, rising like islands of safety from the marshlands that surrounded them. Closest to the gulf was Isle Coquille, or Shell Island, the largest and most populated chénier and the one that caught the brunt of gale winds. The next was known as Oak Ridge, since it supported the largest and greatest number of the live oaks, which gave the chenieres their French designation. In back was Chenier Diablo, the smallest, also the one closest to the near impenetrable swamplands of the Mermentau River delta.

There had been Fraziers on Oak Ridge since the early 1800s, when a Scotsman of that name had arrived with twenty head of cattle and a Choctaw woman who may or may not have been his wife. The old stories said this first Frazier had been looking for the back of beyond because there was a price on his head. It was entirely possible; quite a few families in and around Ombre-Terre had a felon or even a pirate hidden among the leaves of their family tree. Jean Lafitte had hung out on the chenieres in the old days, so the legends went, and many were the tales of ancestors who had helped to bury, or dig up, pirate gold.

Beyond Ombre-Terre, past the first of a series of metal cattle gaps set in the road, was open range for cattle, some of the last in the state. The cows and bulls, many with the massive size that came from heat-resistant Brahman breeding, thought they owned the road. Few people cared to dispute it, since a charging bull could destroy a car in nothing flat. Between watching for cows, cow patties, and the sudden flights of the big white and blue cranes that stood sentry in the water-filled ditches, this last section of the trip was always an obstacle course.

Once it would have been all Frazier land from one end of the chenier to the other, beginning at Ombre-Terre and stretching twenty miles to the remote back swamps beyond the old Frazier house known as the Landing. A good portion of it still was, even now.

Jessica slowed as she passed the family cemetery and the old home came into view. The main section of the house had been moved bodily to Oak Ridge by river barge sometime in the 1840s and set down in the protecting shade of a live oak grove. With it came a young French Creole woman, for the house had been her dowry brought with her as she wed the eldest son of the Scotsman and the Choctaw woman. The bride gave her husband five children before she died. She was replaced by a buxom German girl who produced nine babies before being granted heavenly rest. A final marriage had resulted in three additional mouths before that much-married Frazier ancestor died of pneumonia and exhaustion.

The Landing had been enlarged over the years as the family increased, additions that engulfed the original walls and spread out to become a rambling structure in the tropical West Indies style. Its deep galleries, or verandas, on front and rear were topped by the overhang of a bungalow roof. With some twenty-five or so rooms, it consisted of a two-storied central structure set above a raised basement that formed a third, lower floor, plus a pair of one-storied *garconnieres* grafted on at right angles in the back. The projecting wings, along with the main house, formed three sides around a back courtyard. The fourth side was enclosed by a brick wall inset with a wrought-iron gate.

Though Frazier descendants had always lived in the

house, the hard times that stretched from the end of the Civil War to the Great Depression had taken their toll. The house had been a virtual ruin when Jessica's grandfather, Claude Frazier, took possession in his turn. That had been shortly after World War II. He had spent years and thousands of dollars restoring it with care and historical fidelity. As a result, it had become a showplace, though the only people who saw it were family and close friends. Claude Frazier had never been a sociable man and felt no need to show off his belongings.

To Jessica, the old house was home, pure and simple. She had lived there most of her life, until she moved into a dorm when she went away to LSU in Baton Rouge. Even then she had come home often. Now she returned for the regular monthly get-togethers, sleeping always in the room that had been hers as a young girl. Because nothing in it had been changed, the room was a part of her transition to the young granddaughter of the house again. The remainder was due in large part to her grandfather's rigid attitudes.

For the Sunday gathering, Jessica put on a shirtwaist dress in flowing aqua silk that came to mid-calf, and buckled on a matching aqua and peach belt. Her grandfather liked feminine clothing that had a defined waistline, a modest neckline, and that covered the knees. He was quite capable of sending any female he considered inappropriately dressed from his presence with orders to change or not come back.

There had been a time when Jessica had rebelled, staying away from the Landing for months on end rather than surrender to his dictates. In the end, that kind of defiance had finally seemed more childish than dressing to please him. It was his house, after all, and she loved and respected him. Why shouldn't she comply with his wishes?

Arletta Garrett, Jessica's mother, had never quite absorbed that lesson. She still skated along the edge of what was acceptable to her father—when she bothered to put in an appearance at all. It was part and parcel of her entire life, one more gesture in a long series of challenges, which included four messy marriages and four even messier divorces.

This afternoon, Arletta wore a black St. John knit sheath a size too small with a scooped neck that just covered her cleavage, and a skirt that grazed her knee-caps. Only its matching jacket made the outfit accept-able, and she spent half her time with that held open by a hand propped on one hip to be sure everyone present noticed.

Luncheon was served family style, at a long table set on the upper gallery at the back of the house. A breeze stirred the corners of the rose linen tablecloth and sent the fragrance of the George Tabor azaleas planted at the end of the gallery wafting down the board with the rich scents of crawfish étouffée, baked honey-glazed ham, chicken dumplings, potato salad, garden peas, and fresh-baked bread.

Arletta, sitting beside Jessica at one end of the long board, leaned close to speak in her contralto made husky by too many cigarettes and too much vodka. "I need to talk to you, honey, when this is over."

"Sure," Jessica said easily, though her smile was a little strained. It would be about money. With her mother it was always about money. "It may have to wait awhile. Grandpapa has first dibs, right after dessert."

"He would," her mother said shortly, and turned away to talk to Nick Frazier, who sat on her other side.

Nick appeared to be listening with one ear while he leaned to spear a deviled egg from a nearby plate. As he caught Jessica's eye, he gave her a roguish smile and a wink. She was unmoved. It meant nothing, she knew, but was only his habit.

Nick's teeth made a white glint in the sunbaked brown of his face. Vagrant gleams of sun slanting onto the veranda shone on the white linen shirt he wore that was a near-perfect match for his tousled, sun-bleached hair. The effect was dazzling, but then it should be since Nick was not only handsome but had a tendency toward the dramatic when it came to style.

Though he and Keil looked something alike, being the same general type, Nick wasn't true family. He was most likely here today because her grandfather had requested his presence for his input on the current situation; Claude Frazier made a point of having a variety of brains to pick. The two men had been shut up together in the study when Jessica first arrived.

Nick Frazier was one of Sea Gull's most valuable crew boat captains, and often had a different, more practical angle on the operation. She spoke to him herself from time to time when he was by the office. It was a matter of trust. Nick, the child of a distant cousin who found herself in trouble, had been adopted as a baby by Claude Frazier in one of his many acts of quiet charity. He had lived at the Landing until he was nineteen, shortly before he started going out as a regular hand on the crew boats. Jessica's grandfather put his faith in few people, but depended on the close relationships he did maintain nearly as much as on ties of the blood.

Her grandfather was much his usual self, Jessica thought, glancing with a full heart to where he sat upright, white-haired and distinguished in his wheelchair at the head of the table. The stroke had left him with little use of his left arm, but the disability was not particularly noticeable, since he held it against his side while he ate. If he was a bit pale and had scant appetite for the bland and easily swallowed special diet on his plate, it was only to be expected.

Madeleine, sitting at the opposite end of the table, paid little attention to her elderly husband. Her infrequent smiles were for Nick, who was dividing his engaging grin and quick sallies between the young wife and Jessica's mother.

Keil sat across from Jessica, on her grandfather's left hand. His expression was grim. The cause might be dread for their coming interview with her grandfather, but could just as easily be irritation for the way his mother, Zoe Frazier, who sat on the other side, kept dragging on his arm and leaning to make sibilant comments in his ear.

Jessica was not the only one to notice the older woman's whispers. Claude Frazier put down his fork and fixed his niece-in-law with a gimlet stare. "If you mean to talk secrets, Zoe," he said with irascible displeasure, "it's confounded bad manners. If you don't, then you should be told that the rest of us can't hear you!"

Zoe ruffled up like a gray pouter pigeon at the attack. Through pinched lips, she said, "I was speaking privately to my son."

"Obviously," the invalid returned. "The question is, about what?"

"Well, if you must know," Keil's mother returned, "I was suggesting a roundtable family discussion of this business in South America. I can't for the life of me see why it's being kept so hush-hush. Why don't we have it out in the open, here and now, instead of you and Jessica and Keil shutting yourselves up in the library or some such place later, while the rest of us are left to wonder what's going on."

Claude Frazier reared his head back before turning his gaze on his nephew's son. "That what you think, Keil?"

The implication was that Keil was allowing himself to be led by his mother, had perhaps been talking to her about company business out of turn. The younger man flushed, his attention directed toward the curled pink shrimp he speared from his étouffée. "It makes no great difference to me either way."

"It wouldn't," the older man said with harsh irony. "Well, I'll remind both of you that business has never been a fit subject for mealtime around here. Too upsetting to the digestion."

"That's old-fashioned nonsense!" Zoe declared with her head thrown back so that the gray bun at the back of her head appeared too heavy for her neck.

"I'm an old-fashioned man." Jessica's grandfather made the point with stiff pride before he went on. "Even if I ignored my own rule, there's no point in a lot of talk. Too many opinions just cause confusion, and nobody except Jessica and Keil will have a say in the final decision."

"And why is that, I'd like to know?" Arletta, seated next to Jessica, straightened in her seat as she joined the fray. "If the company is going to be sold, why shouldn't we be informed?"

"Who said anything about selling the company?" Claude Frazier's thick white brows made a straight line over his nose as he swung awkwardly to face his daughter.

"Everybody knows it may happen." Jessica's mother met his gaze a frowning instant, then added with less certainty, "The CMARC offer is common knowledge."

"Too common, to my mind. Things have got out of hand since I've been under the weather. It's time a stop was put to it."

Zoe drew up her plump form in the gray-black dress that she wore to family get-togethers as a reminder of her dead husband. "I think that you just don't like the women of this family being informed. Your attitude toward the intelligence of every female except your precious Jessica has always been positively insulting."

"That's because not many of you have any," the older man snapped.

"You include your wife, do you?" Zoe inquired.

Madeleine gasped in indignation. Claude Frazier barely glanced toward where she sat. "You can leave her out of it."

"Gladly. Though you might still be married to Maria Theresa if you had paid her an iota of attention. Instead, you're saddled with a child one quarter your age who has no conception of taking care of you, much less tending to business."

"Aunt Zoe, please!" Jessica interrupted, her gaze on the alarming color that had appeared in her grandfather's face.

"Well, it's the truth," the other woman said defensively, though she flung a look of apprehension and lingering rancor in the direction of her dead husband's uncle.

"It's a damned lie is what it is!" Claude Frazier declared in red-faced rage. "Tess had no time for me or anything else. She was too busy chasing after men."

"Really, Father!" Arletta snapped.

"Yes, and you're just like her," he said, turning on his daughter. "An unhealthy weakness along that line runs in the females of this family."

Arletta turned scarlet under the insult. "Whatever my mother may have done, you drove her to it!"

"So what's your excuse?"

Jessica, glancing around the table, saw Madeleine watching Arletta with a small frown on her face. Her own reaction was embarrassment, though it was mixed with a fleeting fear that her grandfather could be right. She returned her gaze to the head of the table as she spoke in compressed appeal. "Grandpapa, please."

The white-haired man met her accusing gaze for long seconds before he swore beneath his breath. "All right, all right, I didn't mean it. But there was no call to bring Tess into this, no call at all."

That much was certainly true. Although Claude Frazier had finally divorced his first wife only a few short years ago, she had not been a part of the family for a long time.

Zoe took advantage of the small lull to renew her attack. "I still think there should be a roundtable discussion on the offer for the company, followed by a vote for or against. Otherwise, the family board of directors is nothing but a farce."

"The farce," Jessica's grandfather said, "would be this discussion of yours. What you want is an excuse to swing everybody to your side so you can tell me what to do with my business!"

"And you intend to make all the decisions no matter what the rest of us want, and in spite of the fact that part of Sea Gull belongs to us!"

"Aunt Zoe! Grandpapa! That's enough," Jessica said in sharp protest, her gaze on the veins swelling in her grandfather's temples.

Her grandfather paid no attention. His gaze fierce as

he stared down the table at his nephew's wife, he said, "You don't own squat. I built Sea Gull from scratch, worked at it night and day, gave it everything I had and then some. If you think marrying my brother's good-for-nothing son gives you the right to meddle, you've got another think coming!"

"My Louis might have been good for your precious company," Aunt Zoe said with her chest swelling in indignation and her eyes turning red. "There's no telling where it would be if you hadn't been so tightfisted, so narrow-minded and lacking in vision. He might still be with us if—if you had given him some responsibility and position like Keil, if you had only let him have a chance!"

The last word was a wail. Hard on it, Zoe shoved back her chair and made a stumbling exit from the gallery into the house. Arletta rose and threw down her napkin before following after the other woman with her face set in lines of angry concern.

It was Nick who stepped into the breach. His face bland, he put a question to Keil about the fishing out on Pontchartrain. After a moment Madeleine joined the discussion. Claude Frazier gave his wife and the crew-boat captain at the far end of the table a long look from under beetling brows before he turned back to his clear soup and broiled chicken.

Zoe and Arletta did not return. The meal wore on, with conversation degenerating into cryptic exchanges about basketball and baseball. Finally dessert and coffee were served and consumed.

Claude Frazier signaled Jessica and Keil, then sent his wheelchair skimming back from the table. Jessica left her place and came to walk beside her grandfather's chair while Keil pushed it. As they moved into the house, heading toward the library, the silence they left behind them was leaden.

The meeting was both exhaustive and exhausting. Nothing new came of it for Jessica except the knowledge that her grandfather was recovering from his stroke. His grasp of the takeover bid and all its ramifications was total.

By common consent she and Keil did not mention the carnival party episode, though she wondered if it wouldn't have been easier just to admit the indiscretion and have done with it. She was even tempted to see what the old man might think about what had taken place. He had endured quite a few attacks from one source or another over the years. The shipping business had attracted a lot of mavericks back in the early days of offshore drilling, and competition to supply the wells had been tough and dangerous. It still was, if the explosion in the gulf that had crippled Sea Gull was any example.

The main reason she avoided the subject was the older man's comment concerning the women of her family. She had realized how he felt for some time, but it was the first time she had ever heard him make an open accusation.

If she wanted to be paranoid, she could imagine he had glanced at her as he spoke. She did her best not to succumb to that temptation. He could not know what she had done. Surely he could not know?

The Monday lunch with Rafael Castelar, when she brought it up, clearly worried him. He fretted over it, giving her all sorts of pointers about what to say and how to say it. She might have been upset over his lack of faith in her ability to handle the situation except that she knew how much it meant to him, realized how it must irritate him to be forced to leave such an important confrontation to her. The most troublesome thing about it was that he seemed to feel Castelar's request was a sign of favor she must somehow exploit. Of course, he did not say how she was to go about it.

Release came at last as her grandfather withdrew for his afternoon nap. Her concern lingered, however. With it so strong in her mind, it wasn't easy to attend to her mother's tirade later in the afternoon as the two of them walked along the path through the side garden.

"Pompous, holier-than-thou old hypocrite," Arletta

said, swatting at a mosquito that buzzed around her face. "What a crock, suggesting I'm oversexed, when he's the one who gave himself a stroke by crawling on top of his child bride one time too often."

"Oh, it was more than that!" Jessica protested. "All these problems with Sea Gull—"

"Yeah, sure, but one of the nurses who works at the hospital in Cameron told me your grandpapa was naked as a jaybird under his bathrobe when they brought him in the night of his stroke. Old fool, playing the stud for that little—"

"How he must hate knowing what people are saying," Jessica commented almost to herself.

Arletta snorted. "Serves him right, he should never have married that silly girl. Certainly he shouldn't say such disgusting things about poor Mama. Why, she hasn't had a man in thirty-odd years at least. And I bet she never came the entire time they were married. If she found somebody else back then who could give her a thrill, it's no more than she deserved!"

"You don't have to get so worked up about it," Jessica said soothingly. She allowed her footsteps to take her farther away from the house, down an ancient walk edged with shrubs ranging from blooming winter honeysuckle to the spireas just budding and on to hydrangeas that would make a display during midsummer. It would be just as well to get away from the house where no one could hear them.

"Why shouldn't I be upset?" her mother said sharply. "Because of him, your Mimi Tess is the next thing to a zombie. The man she was running away with died, you know, and I'm not so sure it was an accident."

"It was all such a long time ago. What does it matter now?"

"Not much, I guess, not to you. So far, you've been his good little princess, doing your best to be what he wants, no life except work and more work—God knows how you put up with it. I blame myself for not seeing it sooner, not doing something about it."

"You were busy with your own problems." Jessica

had heard it all before, the diatribes dredging up the past, the accusations, the self-recriminations. It changed nothing. Arletta always went away again afterward, leaving Jessica with her grandfather just as she had when she was two years old. Jessica hadn't understood then, as she did later, that Claude Frazier had made that a condition for paying her mother's allowance. Knowing hadn't made it any better. She still wondered what her life would have been like if her mother had been around.

"The man's a monster. He took me away from your Mimi Tess, forbid me to see her, when I was barely in my teens, just as he took you from me. And he threw his own daughter away when he found out he could no longer control what I did, just as he threw his wife away. You think he loves you and trusts you, and he does, he will—so long as you do exactly what he wants. But he's a control freak, and the minute you stand up for yourself or do something that doesn't suit his notions of right and wrong, then he'll throw you out, too."

"How can you say that when he's trusting me with Sea Gull right now?" Jessica's protest was strained as she considered how far from right Claude Frazier would consider what had happened in Rio.

"Good Lord, Jessica, don't you know you're just holding it for him until he's ready to take over again? If he had intended anything permanent, he'd have handed Keil the job. As it is, he knows you'll step aside the minute he comes back through the door."

"And if he doesn't come back, what then? I'll still be CEO."

Her mother's smile was crooked. "You might be, if you marry the man he finally picks out for you and give him the proper heir he's been waiting for these fifty years and more. That's your real purpose, along with helping to keep things going until then. Haven't you figured that out?"

"Oh, that's ridiculous!" Jessica said in rising annoyance. "Grandpapa's old and sick. He needs me, needs us all, and he knows I'll do my level best to save Sea Gull."

"Oh, he needs you all right. He needs you to do the things he can't do for himself. But I'm telling you, the minute you look like you might have a mind of your own he'll be through with you. When that happens, he'll hold your child hostage so he's still in control, one way or another. Or he will if he lives long enough."

Jessica looked at her mother, at the bitter lines of her face that were so stark in the bright spring sunshine, at the permed cap of her hair with its dull and dusty look caused by too much brown-red dye. Her eyelids were red, and the muddy whites of her eyes made her irises look yellow-green. It struck her suddenly that Arletta was becoming middle-aged and doing it without grace.

At last she said, "He's your father. Don't you care anything about him? Doesn't it matter to you that he may die?"

Arletta reached into the gilded leather pouch she carried, extracted an engraved silver lighter and a slim cigarette, and went through the motions of lighting up. As she exhaled the smoke from her lungs, she said, "Sure it matters. It means I'll have shares of the company in my name. I'll finally be free."

She didn't mean it the way it sounded, Jessica thought. Her mother would be crushed if Grandpapa passed away. Pretending otherwise was a part of the pose, part of the self-conscious act as the wild and audacious daughter.

What Jessica didn't say, though she had often thought it, was that Arletta had never been a prisoner. All she had to do to break free was to tell her father to take the allowance he offered and shove it. Instead Jessica's mother had left her daughter behind while she went out and married one unsuitable man after another as if to thumb her nose in her father's face. The inescapable conclusion was that getting back at him had been more important to Arletta than having her daughter with her.

"Speaking of the company," Arletta said, "you would be doing me a favor if you could find a reason to accept this takeover offer. The way things stand, most of the family assets are tied up; there's precious little cash lying around that I could get my hands on even if anything did happen. A buyout would be a drastic change."

"Not that much, considering our liabilities," Jessica answered. "We'd still have to pay off the bank loan, you know. Anyway, selling will be the last resort."

"Then, you should see that there is no other alternative, if you can manage it while you're in the driver's seat."

Hearing the suggestion behind the words, she gave her mother a straight look. "I couldn't. Sea Gull is his life."

"You think about it, maybe you'll change your mind. Meantime, since you won't cooperate, maybe you could lend me a couple of thousand."

"Behind on your credit card bills again?" It was a grim guess.

Arletta nodded as she tried a wheedling smile. "And I have an invitation for next weekend in Jamaica. I can't go without a little extra."

"I'd give it to you if I had it, but all I get is my salary and you know I'm still working on the town house."

"Why you want to live there, I can't imagine. The place should be condemned."

Arletta's comment was no surprise. She had never appreciated the property in the French Quarter where Jessica had fitted out one of the two upstairs apartments for herself, with the other usually occupied by her grandfather. It had been in the family for decades as a convenient place to stay while in New Orleans. Claude Frazier had done a minimum to it over the years, even after he began to use it regularly when his crew boat company grew so large he had to shift operations from Ombre-Terre to New Orleans. Jessica was overseeing renovations in her spare time.

"I like being a Quarterite," she said now with a touch of defensiveness, "and I love the walk along the river to the office."

"It's no place for a family."

That was a familiar jab. "Since I don't intend to have one any time soon, that isn't a factor. But if you really need money, Mother, maybe you should ask for an advance on your allowance."

"What, beg like a child? Your grandfather would love that! If you won't make me a loan, I guess I'll just have to miss the trip."

Jessica shook her head in wry disbelief, then opened her mouth to agree to the loan as she had known she would, inevitably. Before the words could be spoken, her mother swung away from her and walked back toward the house with quick, angry strides.

Jessica let her go. The subject of the loan would come up again before the weekend was over, as she knew from past experience. It might be best not to be such an easy touch.

She walked on to where a wrought-iron bench in a design of twining vines sat at the end of the shrubbery border. It was overhung by a pecan tree with sunlight falling through its bare branches to pattern the grass around it. Jessica sat down in a corner of the bench and propped her elbow on the back, holding her head.

It was so quiet here away from the house. Though peace hovered at the edge of her consciousness, she could not quite grasp it. There was too much jangling in her mind.

The bench in the patio of the house in Rio had not been quite like this one. Regardless, it was a reminder.

Someone clamped down with firm hands on her shoulders from behind her. Jessica gave a sharp cry. Tearing free and springing to her feet, she spun around.

"Jumpy, aren't you?" Nick thrust his hands into the pockets of his twill pants as he stepped from behind the bench. "I didn't mean to scare you."

"Where did you come from?"

Jessica closed her eyes briefly, then opened them again as she fought for composure. For just an instant, she had imagined—but no, that was impossible.

"You think maybe I was following you?" Nick

paused, then grinned before turning to settle onto the bench. "Yeah, well, you're right. I was at loose ends, thought I'd join you and your mom. But you were having such a heart-to-heart I decided against it. Until I saw her take off."

Beneath the obvious charm that Nick turned off and on like a faucet was a relaxed, almost sleepy, warmth that could be appealing at times. It was in evidence now as he reached out and patted the bench beside him. Jessica moved to sit down once more, though a little further away than he had indicated.

"So how are things going?" she said as an indication that she didn't object to his presence.

"Keeping busy. Apparently not as busy as you."

She gave him a wary look. "If you're going to ask about the takeover offer, don't."

"Wouldn't dream of it," he said expansively. He stretched in a lazy gesture, crossing his long legs at the ankle and spreading his arms wide, then leaving his right arm lying along the bench behind Jessica's back. "Makes me no never mind what happens. Good boat captains are hard to find. I'm always in demand—one way or another."

His tone suggested something else entirely, as did the slumberous look in his eyes. She gave him a derisive glance as she drawled, "Right."

"You don't believe it? I could do good things for you, maybe get rid of some of the tension that has you tied up in knots. Might even lead to a permanent position, you never know." Settling his hand lightly, almost experimentally, on the back of her neck, he began to massage the taut muscles with slow circles of his thumb.

"Permanent? You don't know the meaning of the word." She shifted from under his grasp, turning a little so she faced him.

He gave her a sleepy look through gold-tipped lashes. "Maybe I could learn, for the right woman."

"Come on, Nick. The only thing right about me

where you're concerned is that I'm the one who got away. You're just curious."

"That's what you think," he said, his gaze narrowing slightly.

"It's what I know." Her words were pointed, but without heat.

"You're wrong. Oh, sure, I was hot for you back when we were green kids. And I stayed mad as hell at the old man for a long time after he chucked me out on my ear for being in your bedroom, where I had no business. But that's ancient history. It doesn't have a thing to do with now."

The incident he spoke of so lightly had been terrible. Jessica had gone to sleep while reading in bed one warm spring night when she was thirteen and Nick six or seven years older. She woke up to find him lying beside her in his underwear. He had kissed her, slid his hand under the top of her shorty pajamas to cup her tender breast.

Before that night, the two of them had been friends and companions, almost like a brother and younger sister. They had chased each other, climbed trees, gone fishing, and nearly drowned together in a clandestine expedition into the swamps; had ridden their bicycles to the gulf shore near Ombre-Terre to play with the kids at the beach houses, learned to drive one of the old farm trucks together. Jessica had been more startled and annoyed than thrilled at the abrupt intimacy. The commotion she made had brought her grandfather running.

The scene that followed had been uglier than anything Nick had done. He had looked so stricken and white around the mouth at the things her grandfather said to him. Jessica had felt guilty beyond words over it, and horrified when Nick had been thrown out of the house with his clothes tossed after him like so much trash.

"Did I ever tell you how sorry I was about that night?" she said now. "I should never have made such a fuss. We could have settled it between us if I had just kept quiet."

"I was an idiot," he said roughly, then sighed. He gave her a direct look. "Of course, if you're really and truly sorry—"

Seeing the expression beginning to warm the blue of his eyes, Jessica said, "Not sorry enough to take up where we left off. It just wouldn't work."

"Now, why not? It wouldn't be because of the old man, would it?"

His long form was not quite as relaxed as he wanted it to appear, she thought. "It has nothing whatever to do with Grandpapa. I don't know why everyone assumes I can't make a move without his approval."

"Because, sweetheart," Nick said in a mocking drawl, "you so seldom do."

"That's not true. If I was that spineless, I'd still be living at home and keeping house for him!"

"Instead you're an old maid living in an apartment next door to him. The most exciting thing in your life is signing checks at Sea Gull."

She gave him a quick look from under her lashes. "Is that so?"

Nick met her gaze an instant. Then he drew back a space, lifting a brow as he studied the hectic flush that bloomed across her cheekbones under his scrutiny. "My, my, little Jessica," he said softly. "What have you been up to that Grandpapa doesn't know about?"

"Nothing that could possibly interest you." Her abrupt recognition of the need for discretion made her tone clipped. She turned to study the fence that surrounded the family cemetery that lay just beyond where they sat.

"Oh, I think you're wrong," he said in soft contradiction. "As a matter of fact, I'm sure of it. My interest is growing in leaps and bounds."

"It's a bit delayed, wouldn't you say?" she suggested in an attempt at self-preservation. "I wonder why, unless it has something to do with Grandpapa's stroke. Can it be I'm not the only person who doesn't have the nerve to go against him—until now when he's down?"

Nick stared at Jessica while the soft blue of his eyes

turned as hard as porcelain. Then he gave a short laugh. "You know, sweetheart, there for just a minute, you looked just like the old man himself."

Heaving to his feet, the crew boat captain walked away. Jessica watched him go, but she was not happy.

Nick hunched his shoulders as he walked. So many years. He had thought he was over being embarrassed about anything, much less a dumb teenage prank. Now the tips of his ears felt like they were on fire. He hadn't meant anything that night in Jessica's room. He had just peeped in, seen her lying there in that little shorty pajama set. She had been so sweet and soft and tender, all white and gold perfection. He had wanted to hold her, protect her, lay down his life for her. The next thing he knew, she was screaming bloody murder and swatting him over the head.

He should never have laid a hand on her; he knew that. Dumb. Pure teenage-hormone-dumb.

But the old man hadn't seen it that way. He thought his precious granddaughter was being molested by the punk kid he had taken in out of the goodness of his heart. Some goodness, throwing him out on the street after bringing him up like a son of the house.

At least the old man had given him a job, trained him as a boat captain. He had often wondered why, unless it was just business. Family was one thing, but a top-grade captain was hard to find. The old man knew he was good, and Claude Frazier had a way of keeping business and family separated.

Funny thing was, Nick had thought he was family for a long time, adopted family anyway. He had felt like it, until it was over.

Dumb. He couldn't have it both ways, couldn't be a member of the Frazier clan and have Jessica at the same time. It just wouldn't work.

Or would it?

Chapter Five

▓ ▓ ▓ *More orchids were delivered to the office* on Monday morning. This time they were rich amethyst with green throats in a vase of Venetian crystal that was rimmed with gold and filled with glass beads to hold the heavy stems upright. Again, there was no card.

The shaky equilibrium that Jessica had managed to regain over the weekend vanished as she stared at them. Against her will, images rose in her mind of a dark patio in Rio and a darker storm of the senses. Her neck and face grew warm and her lips throbbed.

Shuddering, reaching for a sheaf of papers to fan herself, she pushed the vision away. There could be no connection between the orchids and the man who had held her. If she ever heard from him again, it would be with a demand for a payoff. Sending beautiful, exotic, and costly blooms was the last thing she could expect.

Who were they from, then? Keil, possibly, as an apology for deserting her that night? But he had shown no awareness whatever when he asked about the bouquet that came earlier. She might have suspected Nick if this morning's flowers had been the first; extravagant gestures were his style, and he had seemed inclined to initiate some kind of relationship between them. However, there was no reason to think he had started his campaign with an advance delivery, or that he would make a secret of it if he had. The only other person she could come up with was her grandfather, as a way of saying thank you for her efforts. The main thing wrong with that, of course, was that Claude Frazier did not believe in wasting money on flowers.

It was a mystery, one she was not sure she wanted to unravel. She pushed it from her with fierce resolve and plunged into paperwork for distraction. She was only partially successful. The concentration needed to keep on track was impossible while lunch with Rafael Castelar loomed ahead of her.

Sophie put the letters and memos Jessica had dictated through the computer and laser printer, then brought the letters in to Jessica to sign. Short minutes after she took them away, she was back again.

"Carlton Holliwell of Gulfstream Air is here to see you. No appointment, but he's threatening to barge in if you don't give him five minutes. You want me to send for security?"

Gulfstream Air was in the business of supplying helicopter service to the offshore oil rigs. The company was one of Sea Gull's principal competitors, and had tried to muscle in on several of their more lucrative contracts over the years. Helicopter service had an advantage when speed was essential, such as the transport of top brass, delivery service when a rig was down while waiting for a vital machine part, or else when a tropical storm or hurricane changed course without warning and workers had to be airlifted to safety. Still, delivery back and forth to the rigs by air was expensive compared to boat service, with the primary consideration being the greater tonnage that could be transported in a single trip by water. That aspect had kept the game fairly even to date.

"I don't think Mr. Holliwell and I have met," Jessica said with a lifted brow. "Does he look dangerous?"

The secretary pursed her plum-colored lips. "He's got no manners, but I wouldn't call him dangerous. And I don't suppose he can help being a macho redneck honky."

"What did he do? Come on to you?"

"He indicated," Sophie said with great dignity, "that my lack of speed in carrying out his orders was a racial flaw and suggested that I move it. 'It' being a specific part of my anatomy that I waggled as I walked in here."

Jessica gave a disbelieving shake of her head. "I suppose you want him escorted from the building?"

Sophie grinned. "Nah. I figure you can take care of him."

"Right," Jessica drawled with a quick roll of her eyes. "Send him in."

Carlton Holliwell was dressed in pressed khakis that were tailored to his muscular frame and stamped with his company logo on the shirt pocket. Somewhere in his early forties, he exuded confidence and hard-edged masculinity. He stuck his hand across the desk toward Jessica while running his hard, assessing gaze over her.

She gave him her hand, but withdrew it the instant she felt him about to clamp down with a bruising grip. At the same time she noted his rough-cut features with their ruddy color and close-set gray eyes surrounded by sunbursts of wrinkles. Though his lips were full, they had a tightness about the corners that set off alarm bells in her mind.

"Well, now, Miss Meredith," he said with a hint of Texas drawl, "you got yourself quite an operation here, now that the old man's out of the picture."

"It keeps me busy, as I'm sure you can imagine." She allowed him a small smile. "Actually, I have only a few minutes before I have to leave for a luncheon meeting."

"That so?" He looked behind him for a chair and dropped into it without waiting for an invitation. "You might want to stick around a little longer to hear what I've got to say."

"Which is?" Jessica barely glanced at Sophie who was giving her a high sign. As Holliwell turned his head to follow her gaze, the secretary stepped smartly from the room and pulled the door shut behind her.

Carlton Holliwell studied the woman across from him, liking what he saw. At the same time he was uneasy. He wasn't used to dealing with women, and it annoyed him that he was forced to now. More than that, he liked being in charge, and he could feel that advantage slipping away from him. This might not be as easy as he had thought.

With some idea of regaining the upper hand, he decided to plunge right to the nitty-gritty. "I hear you're being sweet-talked by some company down South America way, that the outfit has made you an offer. That true?"

The woman across the desk was not easily flustered; she gave his question due consideration before she spoke. "I can't imagine where you got that information."

"Word gets around, you know how it is." He tried the effect of a sexy smile. She wasn't bowled over that he could see. Too bad. He wondered what it would take to turn her on.

"Not really," she answered in cool tones.

He waved a dismissive hand. "This town thrives on talk; it's the favorite pastime. But you want to watch out for these Latino operations. They're slick, they're sharp, and they play for keeps. They'll tell you a bunch of stuff, then catch you with your panties—that is, they'll catch you napping. This is hardball we're playing here. I'd sure hate to see you lose what your granddaddy built."

"Frankly, so would I."

Carlton Holliwell compressed his lips. The face of the woman across from him was entirely too calm for his liking, her voice too even. She didn't fluster easy. On top of that, she wasn't the kind you could call *honey* and *darling* and jolly along. She had a business head, but was mostly what people would call a lady, he supposed; just the way she looked at him put a damper on his language and cramped his freewheeling style. He purely despised the feeling.

He ground his teeth as he searched for some way to get to her. She wouldn't care beans about his position, he thought, since her own was just as worthwhile. And she certainly wasn't going to be impressed by his armed service background or his early morning, hard-body workout.

Before he could get his thoughts together, she spoke in stringent tones. "Perhaps you could tell me exactly what is on your mind, Mr. Holliwell?"

"I'm about to," he said, allowing his short temper to show in an effort to intimidate. "I don't suppose you've ever heard of a white knight coming in on a negotiation like the one you've got going? What I'm talking about is not some fairy tale, but another guy coming to the rescue, stepping in with money and know-how to cut out the takeover company."

"I understand the term, Mr. Holliwell."

"Yeah? Well, I'm prepared to be your personal white knight. I'd like to make you an offer to merge your crew boat operation with my air company."

He had her attention finally. He thought he could almost see the wheels clicking behind her eyes. She didn't much care for him, from what he could tell, which was a shame. She'd have to learn.

"What makes you think I would be interested?"

"If you're not, you should be," he answered with satisfaction. "You don't know what you're up against here. This business could get messy, real messy."

She placed her hands flat on the desktop in front of her. "What, precisely, did you mean by your suggestion of a merger?"

Something he had said got to her; he could tell by the way her lashes flickered. He wished to hell he knew what it was. Leaning forward, he braced his elbows on the chair arms. "Our two companies put together would be a team stout enough to fight off any threat that might come along. You wouldn't have to worry about a thing; I'd move in here, take over as manager of the whole shebang, take over all your problems and worries."

Her green gaze was clear as she stared at him. "In other words," she said in a voice like tinkling ice in a crystal glass, "you would just—take over."

"You could say that," he answered with a confident nod. "You'd have a nice salary, but wouldn't have to show up more than once or twice a week—or at all if it didn't suit you. That shouldn't be too hard to take."

The woman across from him pushed back her chair and got to her feet. Walking to the door, she pulled it open. "But it would, Mr. Holliwell," she said quietly. "It would be very hard to take. Thank you for your kind offer, but I don't believe I'm interested."

"Now, wait a minute, little lady. I don't think you understand what I'm saying." He shoved to his feet, but hovered there. He couldn't believe she meant to put an end to their conversation. He wasn't even half through.

"You're mistaken," she answered. "I understand perfectly what you mean, and also what you intend."

"No, you just listen, now. What I'm telling you is that you can have it any way you want. I'll be in charge, but I'll sure listen to your input anytime. Our working relationship can be real close, as close as you want it."

He stopped abruptly. Old Frazier's granddaughter was looking at him as if he had just swung down out of a tree. He had thought she might be reasonable after all, had started entertaining all sorts of ideas about the extra benefits of partnership. It made him feel a fool.

"What you don't realize, Mr. Holliwell," she said, the temperature of her voice about fifty degrees colder, "is that as acting CEO, I have no authority to accept or reject your offer. You'll have to take it up with my grandfather. But even if I had the authority, I wouldn't consider a merger. This company means every bit as much to me as it does to the man who built it, and I prefer running it my way. White knight or black, it's all the same difference. I gave up on fairy tales long ago."

Rage washed through him in a wave. He could feel the blood vessels swelling in his head. Voice rough, he demanded, "Are you saying I'm not dealing straight?"

"I'm saying that I want nothing to do with your merger. Is that plain enough?"

"Listen, I came here to talk to you in good faith—"

"Yes, indeed," she took him up, "so long as the discussion went your way. As long as I was a—what was it you called me? A little lady? Well, I don't believe I qualify, something you might want to remember."

"You're a smart-assed little bitch, is what you are," he informed her, grinding the words through his teeth. "You'll wish you had seen your way to cooperating with me before this is over."

"Possibly, but I doubt it. Now, I do have another appointment, if you'll excuse me?"

She was really putting him, Carlton Holliwell, out of her office. He couldn't believe it. Who the hell did she think she was? His face hardened as he jerked into motion, stalking toward her.

As he came closer, she stepped back to let him pass. He swerved, meaning to shoulder into her, let her see just who was pushing who around here. And if he copped a feel at the same time, she had nobody to blame but herself.

From the connecting room beyond the open door, the black secretary had come to her feet. She had heard their exchange, saw what he meant to do. She gave a sharp exclamation as she came from behind her desk.

At the same moment a man stepped into view, moving with swift, easy power to stand just beyond the door. Taller than Holliwell, the newcomer was built solid. His stance was relaxed, and his face was without expression, but the look in his eyes was as steady and lethal as a perfectly aimed rifle. He was ready, he was willing, and he was dangerous.

Carlton Holliwell paused in mid-stride. He clenched a fist as he warned himself to get a grip. Teaching the lady a lesson could wait.

Stepping around her and through the door, he spoke over his shoulder. "You'll be hearing from me."

Jessica did not bother with a reply. She had no breath to waste on the man. A moment later the outer door slammed behind Holliwell. She released the pent air in her lungs in abrupt relief.

Lips curving in a wry and grateful smile, she turned toward the man in the doorway. She stopped, stood perfectly still.

"Forgive the intrusion, senhorita," Castelar said as he inclined his dark head. "I completed an earlier appointment before expected, and thought I might offer transportation to the restaurant for our meeting."

The quiet timbre of his voice set off odd vibrations deep inside Jessica's chest. It was an effort to smile, to collect her wits, to find her voice. "How thoughtful," she managed finally. "I'll be with you in just a moment."

His gaze moved beyond her to her desk, where the bouquet of amethyst orchids occupied one corner, then returned to her face. There was a slight relaxation of the firmly molded contours of his mouth as he said, "Please don't feel you must hurry. I only thought you might be ready because I know the American preoccupation with punctuality. I am perfectly willing to wait in my car downstairs."

Jessica could use a moment to collect her wits, calm her nerves, and pick up her purse. It had also become important, suddenly, to check her makeup. At the same time it seemed bad manners to put him off too long so she could pull herself together. "That's very considerate," she said quietly, "but unnecessary. If you'll have a seat again, I'll only be a second."

Her hands were shaking, she discovered, as she freshened her coral lipstick that matched her coral silk suit. In the fluorescent light of the small rest room attached to her office, her pale face appeared in need of a quick application of blush. That done, she closed her eyes a moment while she breathed deep in one of the calming exercises she sometimes practiced.

It didn't work. Holliwell's suggestion and his patronizing attitude jangled in her mind. She wondered just who had been talking to him and what else he knew about Sea Gull. Or about Rio.

This business could get messy.

Was he, could he, be referring to what had happened in Brazil? Was that what she would be hearing about from him?

She also wondered how long he had been thinking of the merger he had offered, and how far he might go—or had gone—to make sure that it took place.

Holliwell was big and undoubtedly strong. There was a certain familiarity in the way he looked at her. Could he have been the man in the patio? She thought he lacked the lithe grace she remembered, but evening wear changed a man's appearance. Like a uniform, a tuxedo tended to subordinate the differences among men, making them all look like gentlemen.

Was Carlton Holliwell the man who had held her that night? Had his big, hard hands caressed her, lifted her, pressed into her?

Was it possible that he had taken out an insurance policy, so to speak, for the takeover he wanted, one backed by incriminating pictures? Could he have arranged it before he approached her, before she was on her guard?

No, no. That *was* television drama stuff. People didn't really do things like that.

Did they?

Crazy. This business was making her crazy. And she had no time for it. Not now, while Rafael Castelar sat waiting to escort her to the lunch he had requested with her. Her . . . alone.

The Brazilian rose as she emerged. His gaze was searching as it rested on her face. A moment later his stern features softened in a faint smile of approval. Politely deferential, he allowed her to go before him into the hall, moving ahead only as they reached the elevators. Forestalling her instinctive reach for the call button, he performed that service.

She was aware of his gaze on her once more. She turned her head to meet it for a long moment but had to look away again. Sensing it still, she flicked him a glance and raised a brow.

"Was I staring?" he said, his voice deep and low, his smile rueful. "It was unintentional—or, at least, I meant no discourtesy. It's a habit, you know, one I have to remind myself to curb when I'm in the States."

She nodded her understanding. In an effort toward polite conversation, she said, "Do you come here often?"

"A few times a year." He hesitated, then said, "Do you mind if I say you don't look like the kind of woman who would enjoy working in a place where you are insulted and assaulted?"

"I wasn't assaulted," she retorted, a little embarrassed that he would refer to the incident with Holliwell.

"You came close to it," he said distinctly. "A woman like you should be protected, kept from ugliness, surrounded by beautiful things."

"That's very flattering," she said, "but not especially practical in today's world."

"No?" he queried as the elevator arrived and he indicated for her to go ahead of him. "It still happens."

"Where, in a harem?"

He shook his head as the car glided downward. "In my country, in the home."

"Marriage," she said with a slight twist of her lips.

"Is that such a terrible word?" His gaze was serious as he waited for her reply.

"Let's just say it has no particular appeal for the moment."

As they reached the lower floor and crossed toward the wide glass front, Jessica allowed Rafael Castelar to move ahead of her to open the door. She had no intention of competing with him over the old-fashioned courtesies between men and women; she didn't consider them demeaning but only rather impractical in some situations. Still, watching the assurance and determination with which he performed them, she thought she had Rafael Castelar's number.

His car turned out to be a gray limousine. As they left the office building, the uniformed driver standing beside the front fender stepped smartly to get the back door. However, it was Rafael Castelar who offered his hand for support as she slid into the backseat. Ducking inside, he took his place beside her. A moment later the long vehicle moved off into the traffic.

"This is very pleasant," Jessica said, "but I would have guessed you were a man who prefers to drive himself."

Rafael's smile was brief. "I would, under normal circumstances. For now, I prefer to give my attention to my guest instead of watching traffic."

Charming, Jessica thought, but he could not have known he would have a guest when he had hired the limousine. Or could he?

She said, "I'm certainly not complaining, since it brought you to the office at a lucky moment for me. Before we leave that subject, I should tell you that I appreciate your intervention."

"It was less than nothing," he said with a dismissive gesture, then went on after a slight pause. "This man, am I right in thinking he is another suitor?"

"Suitor?" Her uncertainty was caused as much by the inflection he gave the word in his rich voice as by the term itself.

"In a business sense, of course."

"Yes, of course," she echoed with a slight flush. "I . . . suppose you could call him that."

He smiled with a slight twist of his lips. "You are very diplomatic, which is as it should be. I won't pry into this other offer if you prefer not to speak of it."

Oddly enough, his discretion made her feel much more like confiding in him than Holliwell's pushy questions. As there was no reason why he should not know there was another company involved, she gave him a brief rundown on Gulfstream Air and Holliwell's offer.

"This is the first time Holliwell has made advances?" Rafael Castelar said, his gaze intent.

"That I know of, yes," she answered.

"But his proposition was not attractive to you?"

"I wasn't interested, if that's what you mean."

"Nor are you interested in my proposal," he said lightly. "It seems we must both try harder to please."

She glanced at the man beside her, wondering if she was imagining the gleam of pleasure in his eyes. Wondering if she was becoming paranoid.

Proposal. Suitor. Advances. Proposition. Pleasing.

Why was it that the language of business mergers was the same as that describing arrangements between a man and a woman? There should be some less suggestive method of discussing it.

Before she could form an answer to his comment, the limousine swung in a wide turn at an intersection. The movement dislodged her slim leather purse, which lay against her knee, so that it tumbled to the carpeted floor.

As soon as the vehicle straightened, Jessica leaned to try to fish her property from under her feet. Castelar moved at the same time to reach for it. His shoulder brushed hers with a jolting sensation. He paused, his face just inches away.

His dark brows were thick, his lashes thicker. The bridge of his nose with aquiline between the high ridges of his cheekbones. There were slashed lines of ready humor on either side of his mouth, and rich, dark amusement overlaid by concern in the infinite depths of his eyes. His pupils were wide and black in the center of his amber irises, and they widened still farther as she watched. From his skin rose a faint and haunting scent of clean male and some expensive men's aftershave that blended wood notes and musk.

In that instant Jessica was plunged back into a dark courtyard while water trickled musically nearby, mingling with the beat of drums in a samba rhythm. A fresh breeze cooled her heated skin while she was held close and safe in strong, caring arms.

The blood left her face so quickly that she felt it flood downward, suffocating her heart, heating and filling the lower part of her body. Light-headed, she swayed an instant with her gaze fastened on the firm, sensual contours of Rafael Castelar's mouth.

Abruptly she flung herself backward so that her shoulders slammed into the seat. She blinked rapidly as she drew a quick, strained breath.

"What is it?" he said in quick concern.

The words were a release. She moistened dry lips, tried a smile. "Nothing—nothing except we—almost bumped heads."

"Almost," he agreed, gravely presenting the purse he

had retrieved. He glanced beyond her out the dark-tinted window. "Ah. I believe we have arrived."

Leaving the car and walking beside Rafael Castelar under the awning of the blue-and-white Victorian mansion that housed Commander's Palace Restaurant was a strangely remote experience. Her body moved, she seemed reasonably normal, but she felt completely disoriented.

She could not stop herself from watching the man beside her from the corners of her eyes. Had he been the man in the courtyard, or were her mind and her sense of smell playing tricks on her?

It had crossed her mind several times that CMARC, and Castelar by extension, could be behind the incident at the party. She had considered that he might have sent the first man, the one who had attacked her. The man who had saved her she had accepted as probably a chance-led stranger caught in the situation by accident. She had never thought that he might be Rafael Castelar himself.

What did it mean, then? Had the first man been only a guest at the party who had sought her out for purely sexual reasons? Had Rafael Castelar been so quick to the rescue because he had followed her and saw the other man as an unwelcome impediment to his plan for blackmail?

It seemed so unlikely, yet what else was she to think? Assuming, of course, that she was right, assuming he had been there at all.

No, it made no sense. If he was the man on the patio, he would have no reason for polite and courteous gestures such as lunch. All that he would require was to send an ultimatum.

On the other hand, as head of CMARC Castelar had no reason to discuss anything further about the offer he had tendered. It was on the table. He had refused her request for time. The next move, either to accept it or refuse it, should have been hers.

But suppose he intended to bring greater pressure to bear. Suppose he had made this appointment for lunch with the specific purpose of confronting her with the photographs?

That could well be possible. It was particularly appropriate in light of his comment about her discretion. No doubt that was his own private and rather sick joke.

How surprised he must have been that night at her immediate surrender. She had made it so easy for him, so very easy.

The hot, nauseated feel of utter mortification moved over Jessica. She hardly knew where she was going as the maître d' welcomed them and led them upstairs. She thought of cutting and running, but that would not do. Rafael Castelar must not guess she knew, must not suspect she was affected in any way.

If he could play this game, then so could she. She would do it if it killed her.

To smile and take the menu offered her, to pay attention as the waiter asked what she would like to drink, was an enormous effort. She desperately needed the relaxing effect of a glass of wine, but refused it with resolution. Her head must be clear for what lay ahead of her. Anything else would be foolish.

Over the next few minutes, she used food as a subject of conversation, since it was a safe topic and a perennial one in New Orleans. She even went so far as to make a few suggestions for their meal since she was familiar with the menu. That Rafael Castelar accepted them and relayed them to the waiter when the time came was obscurely gratifying.

Once ordering was out of the way and their glasses of mineral water were in their hands, a small silence fell. The man across from her drank from his glass, then set it down and leaned back with one strong brown wrist braced on the table edge. His gaze rested on her face an instant, then shifted deliberately to the curve of her neck, the soft swells of her breasts under her suit jacket, to her hands and the simple yet expensive jewelry she wore—even the clear polish on her almond-shaped nails.

It came to Jessica then that she had his total attention.

He was not looking around the restaurant to see who else was there, was not interested in the decor, the ambience, or the service. That knowledge was oddly gratifying and even seductive. It made her feel that no one and nothing was as important to him as being there with her at that moment.

It also made her nervous.

Plunging into speech with the first thing that came to mind, she said, "I was surprised by this invitation in view of our last meeting. May I ask what it's about?"

"Business at once?" His gaze was quizzical as he smiled. "That's uncivilized, you know. More than that, if we should happen to disagree, then we will still have to endure each other's company until the meal has been eaten. No, no, spare us both, if you please."

The suggestion was made with such civilized good manners, such pleasantness, that she had no choice except to accept it. At the same time she felt a distinct easing of the tension inside her chest.

She was wrong about Rafael Castelar; she must have been. The man who made love to her with such wild and consummate desire could not possibly sit and smile at her across a table without some sign, however slight, of recognition. Nor could someone so obviously cosmopolitan as this man have gone willingly to such a low, repellent orgy as that party had turned out to be. No, it just could not be so. What a blessed relief.

They talked of Rio and New Orleans and the differences between the two cities, of various other places they had traveled, of the cuisine of other countries, and the music. He had an encyclopedic knowledge of jazz, she discovered, and had attended the jazz festival in New Orleans more than once. American movies were also familiar to him, as were the more recent plays from London and New York. From these things they segued easily into books, with a foray into the literature of South America. The last was embarrassing, for though she was familiar with Jorge Amado and had read Rosa's classic *The Devil to Pay in the Backlands*, she could not come close to discussing the authors of Brazil with the authority he showed toward those of her country. When she said something to that effect, he only lifted a shoulder.

"I lived in the States for a time. It makes a difference."

Her gaze was a clear, pure green as she studied him. "It certainly does," she said. "Your English is on the formal side, but you actually have almost no accent."

He inclined his head in wry acknowledgment of the quasi-compliment. "My older sister married an American and moved to Connecticut when I was in my teens. I visited often, and I stayed with her and her husband while I was at Yale."

"Ivy League. I might have known."

"Meaning?" He tipped his head in interrogation.

"Nothing, really. I suppose it's just an attitude."

"Stuffed shirt," he said with a grimace. "You should see me in jeans and sneakers."

She tried to picture it and failed. Still, it was amazing the regret she felt that they were unlikely to meet on such informal terms.

It came to her, then, that he was nothing at all like the remote conquistador she imagined him to be in Rio. He was, in fact, a fascinating companion when he wished to be. The trouble was, she could see no possible reason why he might care to make that effort.

There was one other thing. Seeing this new aspect of him made her realize he could just possibly have been her patio lover after all. From time to time she found herself watching his mouth, or his hands with their strong brown, well-formed fingers. She scanned the width of his shoulders, measuring in her mind. It did not make it easy to concentrate.

Memory could be such a tricky thing. She had thought she would never forget a single instant of that night, and yet bits and pieces of it were slipping away, overlaid by other incidents, other impressions. What had seemed so familiar now seemed impossibly strange, while what had been strange seemed—could surely be—familiar. Horrifyingly familiar.

With their mesclun salad, their chicken and andouille gumbo, their shrimp *remoulade* and blanched asparagus and loaves of crusty bread, they had a half bottle of Chablis Premier Cru. It was just enough to complement the food without muddling the flavors or their heads. Afterward they both refused dessert but accepted coffee. It was when it sat before them, steaming its rich aroma into the air, that they allowed their pleasant small talk to drift into something more serious and even expectant.

"So now," he said with a smile almost caressing in its intensity, "we come finally to business and why I am here—as much as I might want to delay still longer. Say until after dinner."

She would have preferred a longer delay herself, she discovered. Say forever. Dread made her heart jar against her rib cage. With lowered lashes she aligned the unused dessert spoon of her place setting. Voice quiet, she said, "Yes?"

His gaze rested on her flushed face a long moment before he went on. "I must tell you that I was impressed by your approach in Rio. You were knowledgeable and clear in your presentation. It was also obvious that you care greatly for your grandfather and the future of his company. I thought perhaps it might be beneficial to both of us, and to what we hope to accomplish, if we could meet again so I could explain something of my own outlook and objectives."

"I don't see the purpose."

He stopped her with an uplifted hand. "Perhaps you may if you will bear with me." At her slow nod of consent, he went on. "From my point of view, it appears that Sea Gull's base in offshore operations in the gulf is secure. It is an old and respected name in the area, and it would take a concerted and expensive effort to mount a successful challenge against you. Yes?"

"We would like to think so," she said with a wry smile.

His teeth flashed white in the bronze of his face as he reiterated, "Yes. Now. You are not quite so strong along the coast of Mexico, but your grandfather was wise enough to see and take advantage of the opportunity there. The capital investment he made in order to increase your presence in Mexican waters has paid off and will continue to pay off for years to come. And this would, for many, be more than enough."

When he paused, she said, "But not for you?"

"As you say," he agreed with a slow nod. "Or for you, I think, senhorita."

She did not intend to admit he was right. "Then what would be the next step in your opinion?"

"The North Sea."

A short laugh left her. "Speaking of your expensive propositions!"

"That is the weak point, is it not? But Sea Gull has the name, the history, the contacts with established oil companies and their management. If you also had the financing, you could sail into all the cold water ports of the world and annihilate the competition."

The program he had articulated so succinctly was her secret vision, her most closely held dream. For him to sit there and spread it out before her was a subtle form of torture.

"If." Her voice was taut as she picked up the weak point of his scenario.

His dark gaze probed hers. His voice soft, he said, "I can underwrite that expansion."

Anger for his flaunting of his affluence, and for the simple difference made by vast wealth, rose inside her. Voice tight, she said, "Bully for you."

He laughed, the sound of it ringing with rich appreciation and something more that was very like affection. "I don't say this to gloat over you, but only to make you think."

"About what?"

"Possibilities," he answered, his amusement lingering in his eyes. "Do you foresee expansion into the North Sea as feasible for Sea Gull?"

"It's certainly desirable," she said without quite meeting his eyes.

"But not possible under the present circumstances. You do approve of the idea, however."

"How could I not?" There was more honesty than consideration in her words.

"I'm glad." He paused while he circled the rim of his coffee cup with a long finger. "You convince me that my earlier evaluation of your company was, perhaps, too conservative. For that reason, I have reconsidered my initial offer."

He had her attention. "Reconsidered?"

His smile was rueful with understanding for the hope in her voice as he said, "I am not withdrawing it, you understand. I am sorry to disappoint you, but no. Rather, I would like to augment it. I am prepared at this point to increase my original offer by twenty percent."

She stared at him while her mind moved in swift calculation. Finally she said, "That's very generous."

"Not at all." he corrected. "There is a stipulation."

Her chin came up and wariness tightened her features. "Why am I not surprised?"

"Please don't misjudge me." When she made no immediate comment, he went on. "It is my hope that you will also allow time for due consideration before you give me an answer, since the proposition involves yourself."

She was quite still. "Me?"

"Your services add considerably to the corporate bottom line in my estimation. My offer is contingent upon you staying on in a position of management when the purchase is complete."

The heat of fiery anger began in her abdomen and rose to her face with a hectic flush. Her voice compressed to scarcely more than a whisper, she said, "You want to buy my cooperation."

"No!" he said instantly as a frown snapped his brows together.

"Bribe me, then, if you prefer that word; it's the same thing. You think that I'll sell Sea Gull from under my grandfather for a bonus and a grand dream. Well, you've made a mistake on two counts, senhor. Number one, I have no more authority to agree to your offer than I did to that of Gulfstream Air. That's if I wanted to, which I don't. And number two, my services, as you put it, are not for sale!"

He sat forward with his face set in stern, hard-edged lines. "Unlike your Mr. Holliwell, I have tried to pay you the compliment of supposing that you have superior ability in your job—else your grandfather would not trust you to act for him. I also took it for granted that your interest in Sea Gull went beyond mere money. You might return the favor by assuming that I am aware of circumstances at the company I am interested in acquiring. I know, therefore, that you have considerable influence with your grandfather."

"So you expect me to persuade him to do as you want in return for a future position," she said, her voice scathing in spite of its low timbre. "What do you call that if it isn't paying me off?"

"I see no connection. You will forgive me for saying so, but it is unlikely that your grandfather will ever again be able to direct Sea Gull Transport. You are capable of doing it for him as matters now stand, but may find it difficult without him behind you. As for expansion, it is unlikely that you, a young woman without a history of financial responsibility, will be given the chance. That can be changed with my participation. All you have to do is decide if the association appeals to you."

"And convince Grandpapa." There was a stubborn inflection in the words.

"As you say," he acquiesced with tight-lipped control. "I had hoped that the chance to be involved in the development of a company with a larger scope would convince you to approach him. Nothing else has any bearing whatever."

"There is nothing—personal in it?" she said, her gaze steady.

He watched her for long moments, Finally he said coldly, "Miss Meredith, if my interest in you was at all personal I promise you my methods of pursuit would be far different. There would be absolutely no doubt in either of our minds about my emotions or my intentions."

The words had a certain logic. His eyes were steady as he watched her. Yes, she had definitely been wrong.

Heat burned in her face. She said, "Then, why make a point of a private lunch? Why not meet in my office with Keil present?"

"I wanted a chance to know you better, to test any working relationship that might possibly be established between us. Now I think it is my turn to ask why you agreed."

"Curiosity," she said succinctly.

His smile was slow and layered with speculation. The words dropping into a lower timbre, he said, "And is it satisfied?"

How could she say no, when that answer could bring questions it would be impossible to answer? How could she, when it would be so much more comfortable, not to mention convenient, to believe him?

"Yes, I suppose so," she said, though she wasn't sure she meant her own words.

She was definitely paranoid.

Chapter Six

▨ ▨ ▨ *Rafael Castelar, watching the woman* across from him at the table, was uncomfortable with his own duplicity. Contrary to his direct disavowal of interest, he had wanted to be alone with Jessica Meredith since the moment she had walked into his office in Rio. That a table for two in a crowded restaurant was as close as he could come for the moment was a distinct irritant.

It couldn't be helped. He had to move slowly and with care.

All the same, he had trouble keeping his mind on the words she was saying rather than the soft curves of the lips that formed them. He had to guard his gaze to keep it from wandering too often along the line of her jaw and down the turn of her neck to the tenderly shadowed valley where the edges of her suit blouse closed over her breasts. He had to guard against his urge to stare, period; one that had little to do with the national pastime of his fellow countrymen.

It was not his habit to fly thousands of miles and make expensive business decisions based on personal attraction. He had a reputation, not unearned, for clear, nonsentimental judgment and no second thoughts.

Certainly he had not intended to rethink his position on Sea Gull Transport. The reason it had become imperative was sitting in front of him.

Jessica Meredith was as intelligent as she was attractive; she knew very well that his motives were suspect. The question was how long it would take her to understand and accept the strength of the position she now held vis-à-vis CMARC.

Was she capable of using it once she knew? He thought it was possible. Would he allow it? That was also a possibility, depending on the advantages to be gained.

He had other alternatives, other moves to make, before he came to that point. The difficulty was in knowing how she would react to each one, and what its net effect might be. Therefore he needed all the patience he could muster. He required a much better understanding of what made Jessica Meredith tick before he chose a final means of arriving at his chosen objective.

The one thing he was not going to do was go away. Nor would he risk being dismissed like the idiot who had threatened her in her office earlier. A slow and careful campaign, a high order of finesse backed by self-control: these things must be fully exercised to gain this particular prize. He could manage it, he thought. Barely.

One way or another, he was going to own Sea Gull Transport. And he was also going to have the woman who went with it.

One way or another.

The coffee in his cup was exceptional for a restaurant, but still rather weak compared to the brew he drank at regular intervals during every day of his life. The two teaspoons of sugar he had stirred into it had made it barely sweet enough for his taste. Regardless, he had sipped it slowly, making it last as long as he could manage. Seeing her glance at the watch on her wrist, however, he drained the last drops and put down his cup.

"I've kept you from your work long enough," he said, smiling into Jessica's mesmerizing witch's green eyes. "If you are finished, I will see you back to your office."

"There's no need," she said in businesslike tones. "I can take a taxi if you aren't headed in my direction."

"But I am," he said with a trace of dry amusement.

Turning from her, he signaled for the check. As it was brought at once, he closed his credit card into the leather folder and handed it back to their waiter.

Jessica folded her napkin and dropped it beside her cup and saucer. Lacing her fingertips together, she flattened her hands on the table edge in front of her as she gave him a straight look. "About your increased offer, I feel it's only fair you should know it's highly unlikely to find favor with my grandfather. He's a proud man and an independent one. He may have been flattered by your show of interest in what he has built, but he wants no help and would be insulted at the idea that he might need any. He feels that, given time, he can take his company wherever it's possible for it to go. And I'm not so sure he isn't right."

"What if the time is not given to him?" Rafael's words were soft and without inflection.

"I think we can stop worrying about that. He is growing stronger every day, and most interested in what's taking place at Sea Gull." She smiled. "Barring some setback, he'll be around awhile."

"He has no plans for retirement?" Rafael gave his attention to the business of completing the credit card slip presented to him just then, as if her answer had little importance.

"He isn't the type," she said with a decided shake of her head. "You can see, then, that there is no point in further discussion between us. It should not be many more days before my grandfather will be able to give you a definitive and final answer."

"If he is as alert as you say, and as adamant, what prevents him from giving it now?" Getting to his feet, he moved to hold her chair.

A momentary confusion crossed her face, as if she had not, until that moment, stopped to consider that question. To give her credit, she did not try to deceive him. "I don't know the answer to that," she said as she rose and moved ahead of him toward the door. "All I know is, I can't speak for him, and don't intend to try."

With that he had to be content.
At least for now.

Jessica returned to the office, but she did not stay. It
was impossible to concentrate while endless questions
and fears revolved in her brain. Trying gave her a tension headache so fierce she could hardly see.

When she left, she had no particular destination in
mind; she simply walked through the doors and kept on
walking. Winding up at Mimi Tess's house in the Garden District was simple instinct.

Visiting and talking to her grandmother could be a
trial at times. The older woman was vague, dreamy, and
rather fragile. Her attention span was short and unfo-
cused. Far from practical, she never advanced any kind
of concrete advice or tried to find the answers to problems.

Still, her house was a haven of quiet peace, kindness,
and beauty. Mimi Tess always smiled, always had a
warm hug. She never scolded, never judged. And sometimes, when you least expected it, she would come out
with a gentle observation that went straight to the heart
of whatever was bothering you, so the answer to a problem was illuminated with blinding brightness.

The Garden District was a main historical attraction
of the city. It was a section of tree-shaded streets lined
with grand old houses, many built before the Civil War,
and each with its manicured garden, where banks of
azaleas and camellias bloomed and magnolia and sweet
olives perfumed the air. Encroached upon by small hotels and less picturesque commerce in spite of its status
as an historic area, it was yet a bastion of fading, gen-
teel ladies with soft white hair and patrician features
who kept up their mansions as a matter of pride and
duty. They were formidable women in their way, the
backbone of New Orleans society. They had ridden the
streetcars in the old days, or walked along the sidewalks
wearing hats and gloves and carrying silk sun shades to
protect their complexions. They had attended literary
teas, supported the symphony and other cultural icons,

and made their gardens bloom by exchanging slips and roots and information through their garden clubs. Gracious, unselfconsciously elegant, they kept the family silver polished, knew politicians by their childish nicknames, and were walking repositories for the genealogies of generations. As they faded away into nursing homes and cemeteries, a way of life was gradually vanishing with them.

Mimi Tess was one of them, yet isolated from their company by her circumstances. All that busy involvement had been taken from her when she was barely older than Jessica herself, wiped away by a head injury from the accident years ago. To replace it was only an endless succession of days in the care of a housekeeper who also acted as a nurse. The pity of it tugged at Jessica's heart each time she stepped through the cast-iron gate of the old Italianate mansion on St. Charles.

She roused Mimi Tess from her afternoon nap. It didn't matter; Mimi Tess folded her into a gentle embrace scented with White Shoulders and also a trace of vetiver, the eucalyptus-like roots that always freshened the shelves of the armoire where her underclothes were stored. Settling in the front room with tall etched-crystal glasses of iced tea sprigged with orange mint that added a faint taste of bergamot, they took care of the courtesy exchanges about health and family.

In the midst of Jessica's description of the Sunday before and Claude Frazier's progress in recovering from his stroke, Mimi Tess reached out to brush a stray lock of hair from Jessica's face. "You look tired, *chère*," she interrupted in her soft, melodious tones. "Are you all right?"

"Fine," Jessica said at once, since she had no intention of burdening the older woman with her worries. "I just haven't been sleeping well lately."

"You work too hard. It's a shame, when you should be thinking about a young man, about getting married."

"Women have other things on their minds these days, Mimi Tess," Jessica said with a smile.

"Do they?" the older woman said doubtfully, then answered herself, "Yes, I suppose they must. It's all very strange. When I was a girl—" She trailed off into silence as she often did. After a moment she spoke again. "You were never a Mardi Gras queen."

It often worked best if her grandmother was encouraged to follow her own meandering conversational leads. Jessica said, "No. I never had the time."

"You should have been one. The beautiful costumes, the parties, the toasts, the balls. Memories are precious."

"You were a beautiful queen," Jessica said, smiling a little. Looking at the pictures of her grandmother in her costume had been one of Jessica's favorite ways to pass rainy-day visits when she was a child.

"You have none." Mimi Tess's brow was pleated in a frown of concern.

No memories, her grandmother meant. In protest she said, "That isn't true."

"Tell me, then."

Mimi Tess folded her hands and waited expectantly. Jessica, facing her grandmother's unwavering gray-green stare, was uneasy.

Maybe it was true, after all, she thought after a moment. She had been quiet and studious in high school and the same through college. She had attended a few dances, but had never been a part of the fast crowd, had never cared for all the rah-rah activities that went with football and the other sports. Though she had excelled academically, she had shunned the limelight, declining scholarships and honors that might take her away from New Orleans.

Her grandfather had considered all outside activities a foolish waste of time. Knowledge was useful only to the extent that it aided in making money; a liberal education with emphasis on art and literature was the indulgence of impractical eggheads. Popularity benefited nothing; it was only a mindless measure of one person's ability to please other people.

Claude Frazier had claimed that the hard-drinking young men who drove around in fancy sports cars, not to mention the sports jocks in their sweatshirts with torn-out sleeves, were brainless. He thought trendy clothes a silly affectation that lined the pockets of designers and saw shopping as the petty indulgence of females with nothing more important on their minds than looking sexy in order to "trap" a man.

Sexiness, sex in general, was the root of all evil to her grandfather's mind. Dating ran a close second, followed by drinking and drugs. Far from being evil, money was in a separate classification, one on the order of a reward for righteousness.

Such narrow opinions made for a constricted and dull life. Jessica had rebelled once or twice, but the pleasure hadn't been worth the loss of her grandfather's approval. Dullness had finally become a habit with its own comfort quotient, its own built-in safety.

Until Rio. She could tell her grandmother something of her memories of Rio, even if not all.

Trying to keep it simple, she said, "I went to a party last week. There was a man there."

"Oh, *chère*, that's wonderful." The older woman's smile was beatific.

"I'm not so sure." She gave a wan shake of her head. "I did something foolish. And now I don't know what the man looked like or even his name."

"But what you did made you happy? He made you happy?"

Had it? Had he?

"Yes," she said slowly, "at least for a few minutes."

"Then it's all right. Only regret the things you don't do."

Jessica gave a low laugh of surprise as she searched her grandmother's face, wondering if what she had said was just a random comment gleaned, perhaps, from the television soap operas that filled her days, or if it had a reference in her own life. After a moment she said, "But what if it turns out terrible later on?"

A distant look passed over the lined white face. "Hold on to the good time. You need it to help you."

"Mimi Tess," Jessica began, then stopped. No, she wouldn't ask.

Yes, she would; she had to know. "Can you remember the man you went away with that time, Mimi? Do you know what happened?"

Her grandmother's gaze wandered around the room for a moment, then returned to rest on Jessica's face. "I remember."

Jessica sat forward. "What was he like? What went wrong? Why did he let you go?" It wasn't exact answers she was looking for so much as a comparable experience, something to use as a gauge against which to measure her own feelings.

Mimi Tess was silent as her faded gaze delved endlessly into Jessica's. After a moment she smiled. "Arletta has a young man."

Whatever chance there might have been to learn the truth was apparently gone with her grandmother's wandering thoughts. Jessica shook her head a little before she said, "Mother is just a little past that, don't you think?"

Her grandmother nodded. "He doesn't want anybody to know. She doesn't, either."

"You mean—he is literally younger? Younger than she is?"

Mimi Tess said, "I don't think it's right."

"It happens all the time." Jessica's voice was dry. "Who is he?"

"She wouldn't tell his name. But he won't marry her. Young men like him never do. And it wouldn't be right."

The older woman could, on occasion, get an idea or a subject into her head that nothing could dislodge. This seemed to be one of those times. Jessica looked at the soft white skin of Tess Frazier's face and felt the shift of pure sadness inside her.

Once, years ago, the woman next to her had been a fiery redhead with green eyes, a high temper, biting intelligence, and passionate opinions. She fell in love with Claude Frazier the summer after she was Mardi Gras queen and married him in the teeth of her family's opposition well before the fall came around.

The marriage had not been a success. Two people had seldom been such opposites.

Tess's personality was volatile back then, her emotions all on the surface. She was prone to delirious ecstasies of love and also to virulent anger, to wild, plate-throwing scenes that were followed by tearful reconciliations. Her husband was her life; she could not stand to be apart from him for any length of time. She made a home for him, gave him every minute of her time and most of her thoughts, and presented him with a daughter.

Claude was made of different cloth. With the stern blood of his Scots ancestors, he despised any show of emotion, hated any kind of fracas that might draw attention to them and their disagreement of the moment. Love to him was something that should be more felt than talked about; he had difficulty even saying the word. To build something for his wife and his children should be proof enough of his feelings. That he never looked at another woman was solid evidence of his investment in their future happiness.

It was too much for Tess, or not enough. Left alone over too many nights for too many long years, neglected and ignored for the business that occupied her husband's energies, she had looked elsewhere for the life and outward show of love that she craved. She found it in another man.

Or was that the way it had been? Perhaps the man found her? No matter. She and her lover had run away together.

Claude Frazier had been in a cold rage when he found out. He went after his wife to bring her back, trailing her from New Orleans to Atlanta, from Atlanta to Chicago, and from Chicago to New York. He had finally caught up with the two of them.

No one knew exactly what happened then. Apparently there was some kind of accident. The man had disappeared, and Tess had been hospitalized for several

weeks with a head injury. When she and Claude finally
returned to New Orleans, she had been the smiling,
gentle automaton she would be for the next thirty years
and more.

Claude had brought in a nurse to care for Tess. After
a few years, he moved her and her attendant into her
old family home in New Orleans, which had become
vacant with the death of her mother. She had lived there
ever since in an unchanging round of days and seasons.
And if she knew she had been divorced or that her husband had remarried, there was no way to tell.

Jessica had sometimes wondered if her grandmother
was as placid and content as she seemed, if she recognized the passing of the years, if grief or resentment
ever filtered through the fog in her mind. It appeared
that it might from time to time. There was, of course,
no way to be certain.

Only regret the things you don't do.

Those words remained with Jessica long after she had
taken leave of her grandmother and made her way home
to her apartment. They teased at her mind as she
watched the evening news, and later, when she put on a
favorite Julio Iglesias tape, then ran a hot bath scented
with violet bath salts and climbed into it.

Only regret the things you don't do.

The phrase was hardly new. Still, it lingered, possibly
because it just might be another of Mimi Tess's small
gems of wisdom. That didn't make it trustworthy, of
course.

Only regret the things you don't do.

It was possible the phrase could be worth remembering. At least she couldn't seem to forget it.

She couldn't forget Rafael Castelar, either. The songs
on the Iglesias tape, Latin love songs in Spanish and
French and Italian, made her think of him. There was
such passion and desperation in them, such sweetness
and unabashed sentimentality compared to most American songs; they satisfied her in some way she couldn't
quite grasp.

Portuguese, the language of Brazil, was a Latin

language. She wondered what songs of love, words of love, sounded like in it.

No she didn't. Not really. That hadn't been in her mind at all. Had it?

The selection she had been listening to ended. The next had a faster rumba rhythm that reminded her of the samba that had played that night in Rio. If she closed her eyes, she could see the patio again, hear the whisper of palms and water music, feel the heated touch—

The shrilling of the telephone startled her so that she made a tidal wave in the tub as she sat upright. She could let it ring, but it might be important, might even be bad news about her grandfather. Reaching for a towel, she climbed out of the tub and padded across the carpet in a trail of wet footsteps. Before she picked up the telephone, she punched the tape player to the off position with a hard jab.

"Jess, that you?" Her grandfather's rasping voice came strongly down the line. Barely waiting for her answer, he went on, "Madeleine said you left the office early this evening."

The comment was not an idle one, nor did it signal concern about her health. Claude Frazier wanted to know where she had been, and why. Her smile of relief fading, she said, "I went to see Mimi."

His reply was a grunt, which was about what she had expected. He had always made it plain that he considered attention paid to his ex-wife as disloyalty to him. However, his lack of interest was profound, an attitude that could be counted on to end any further inquiry.

He said now, in an abrupt change of subject, "You missed a call from Vic Gaddens."

"Madeleine spoke to him, then?" Jessica's voice mirrored her annoyance even as her nerves tightened at mention of the Crescent National loan director.

"Good Lord, no. Gaddens knows better. He called me here."

He was going to make her ask for the details. That he would resort to that kind of manipulation, all because she had dared leave work, was hurtful. With strained patience, she said, "And?"

"And he claims somebody is nosing around after Sea Gull's loan."

She was silent for long seconds, waiting for more. When it was not forthcoming, she said in strained tones, "Well? Did Gaddens sell it?"

"Not yet. But he felt I ought to know, thought he should give me time to make arrangements, to preempt by paying it off, if that was what I wanted to do."

She could hear the sudden tiredness in his voice. "I wish he hadn't worried you with it, but you don't have to give it another thought. If you'll tell me what you want done, I'll see to it."

He was quiet for so long she thought he wasn't going to answer. At last he said, "The thing is, I don't know. Gaddens said the premium being offered over and above the value of the loan is steep. We'd have to match it, and on short notice. The money would be hard to come by."

"Why can't they just keep the loan the way they always have?" she said, her grip on the telephone receiver so tight her fingers ached.

"They would, if I was up and around. As it is—"

"I know. They don't trust me to keep profits high enough to make the interest payments. But you'll be back. Didn't you tell him that?"

He was silent while minutes ticked by and her damp skin grew cool. Then he said, "I may not."

"What? Of course you will."

"I'm not sure. Madeleine thinks I should retire, and I—Well, I'm not sure."

She couldn't believe he would even think such a thing. She also had trouble accepting that the mood, or whatever it was, would last. For now, she said, "Did Vic Gaddens tell you who was making this offer?"

"No, he didn't. But I don't think it takes a genius to figure it out."

It didn't. She had turned down Rafael Castelar's proposition. This was the result.

"I—I'm sorry, Grandpapa."

"Don't be," he said, his tone suddenly brusque. "It's not over yet."

The phone clicked dead in her hand. She stared at it for long moments before she put it down very quietly and walked away.

Chapter Seven

▦ ▦ ▦ *Sometime during the night Jessica came to* grips, in a small way, with the problems confronting her. By morning, she was feeling decisive. There were obstacles she could not surmount by herself, but also some she could. And she would.

When the daily orchids arrived on schedule, this time an arrangement of pale green cymbidiums supported in a clear bowl by black glass stones, she was able to make it to the front entrance in time to catch sight of the delivery van. She called the flower shop at once to ask the name of the person who had placed the order.

The lead turned out a dead end. The delivery, so the woman in the shop said, was the first and only one they had made to the offices of Sea Gull. It had been a cash transaction with no written record. No one could remember what the person who had placed the order looked like.

Reminded of her suspicions, Jessica instructed Sophie to find out if Rafael Castelar was still in town, and also where he was staying. In less than an hour, Sophie, pretending to be from an upscale jewelry store with an order to deliver, located their quarry at the Westin on Canal Street where he was staying in one of their top suites.

"You want an appointment?" Sophie asked, her liquid brown eyes bright with curiosity.

"No—no, I don't think so," Jessica said. "Maybe later."

"You're gonna wait for him to call you, huh?" The words were dry.

"That's the way it works," Jessica said with a pretense of cheerful acceptance. If the other woman thought her interest was personal, it might prevent questions.

"Not where I come from," her secretary muttered as she walked away, but Jessica pretended not to hear.

In the middle of the morning, when Keil sauntered in with coffee for their break, Jessica moved around the desk and gave him a quick hug and friendly kiss on the cheek. As a test of his suitability to be the man in the garden, however, it was a flop. His aftershave was too spicy, the quick clasp of his arm around her too brotherly, and his body build too lanky. Either he was off her list of possibilities, or else she needed a more intimate trial before she could be certain.

"Now, just what was that all about?" Keil said, puzzled but willing to see the joke as he kept his arm in place.

"You're a nice man, and I like you," she said, her tone light as she smiled into his guileless blue eyes.

"I like you, too," he said, his mobile mouth curving in a grin, "but I have to tell you that you'll get yourself in trouble, throwing yourself at all the nice men."

A shiver caught her by surprise. "Yes, well," she said, her smile dimming, "I'll try to keep that in mind."

"Not on my account. I'll take all the hugs I can get, anytime I can get 'em." Keil, protecting his coffee cup as he released her, did not see her sudden frown. By the time he changed the subject to the number of fishing charters scheduled for an upcoming pharmaceutical convention, she was relaxed and smiling again.

Later in the morning, however, she placed a call to Vic Gaddens at the bank. He was not in, but returned her call a little before noon. He could see her for a few minutes, if she could come in at once.

In the bank manager's office, with its black leather, gray carpet, and brushed steel surfaces, she wasted little time in preliminaries. As soon as there was a pause, she asked flat out how long it would be before a final decision was made on the offer to buy in Sea Gull's loan.

"Now, Jessica, you know how these things are," Gaddens said, his voice smooth and a little unctuous as he leaned back in his chair and clasped his hands across the silky wool of his designer suit. "There's no set time limit, nothing cut and dried about the deal at this point."

"I wish you had discussed it with me instead of disturbing my grandfather." The words were cool in spite of her vow to remain pleasant and businesslike.

The banker pursed his lips. "Actually, I was under no obligation to bring the transaction to Sea Gull's attention at all, but felt I owed it to Claude after all these years."

"You do realize that I am acting CEO?"

"Claude pointed it out. I wish I could say that we here at the bank place the same degree of confidence in you as your grandfather, but frankly, Jessica, we're worried."

Vic Gaddens's eyes, she saw, were as bleak as the little money-lined world he had created for himself. "I can see that. However, I assure you that Sea Gull will go on exactly as it always has until Grandpapa is able to take over again."

"And who can say when that will be? In the meantime, there's talk floating around. We have no choice except to pay attention—and to protect our investment as best we can."

It was the second time someone had mentioned rumors. "What kind of talk?"

"Nothing, nothing," he said soothingly, "just a whisper or two."

"About what?" she insisted as she leaned forward with a frown.

"Since you insist, about management problems, crew problems, a general lack of direction."

"The way I'm handling things, in other words," she said flatly as she sank back again. She hovered between rage and relief, uncertain which was strongest.

"In a word, yes." He steepled his fingers, his gaze on

their polished nails. "You're young and relatively inexperienced. On top of that, shipping is a rough business. Back in the old days, it was really tough: boat crews attacking each other, sabotage, accidental drownings that weren't accidental. It took a man to run things. Times have changed, but not that much."

"You think I can't cut it because I'm a woman."

A pained expression crossed his face. "Now, don't go all feminist on me. What I'm trying to get across is the fact that twelve million dollars plus interest is a lot to wager on you being able to fill your grandfather's shoes. Twelve million. Think about it, Jessica. That's all I ask, just think about it."

Apparently there was not much else she could do. She walked out of the bank with her head high, but inside she felt lost and alone. And no longer in the least decisive.

Still, some time after noon, Jessica got her second wind. Discovering concentration after hours of trying, she worked nonstop until the daylight began to fail.

It was Sophie who broke into her absorption. Her secretary was standing in the doorway with her purse over her shoulder and a sweater over her arm.

"I'm leaving now," the other woman said. "You ready, or you gonna work all night?"

Jessica put down her pen and stretched the kink out of her lower back. Lights were beginning to come on in the buildings that stagger-stepped around the wide crescent-shaped bend of the river, while the sky above them was washed with the pink mother-of-pearl of evening.

"I may stay a little longer," she said. "I'm just beginning to catch up."

The other woman hesitated. "I hate to bother you when you've got so much else going on, but would it be all right if I got my check early?"

"No problem," Jessica answered at once. "Make out the voucher and I'll sign it."

"I knew you'd say that, so I already did it." Moving

into the room, Sophie slid the voucher slip in her hand in front of Jessica.

Jessica picked up her pen again. "This is going to do it? It isn't some big problem?"

"Nothing I can't handle." Her secretary grimaced. "It's that man of mine; I gave him the money to pay the gas bill, and he lost it gambling. Sometimes he's got no more sense than a two-year-old. Why I don't throw him out, I just don't know."

There was wry sympathy in Jessica's voice as she said, "Oh, I think you do."

"Yeah, well, he gives a great foot rub," Sophie said with a grin before she shook her head with a sigh of disgust. "Men. Adam was the only real snake in the Garden of Eden, you know. You're lucky you don't have one of the useless things hanging around, going after you every single minute."

Jessica passed over the signed voucher, then propped her chin on her hand. "I've been noticing how much you hate it, coming in here every morning grinning like a cat that's been in the cream."

"Lord, what you just said, girlfriend!" Sophie gave her a wicked glance from the corners of her eyes. "Just wait till my Zachary hears." Still giggling, she waved her voucher in farewell and moved with long-legged grace from the office.

Jessica stared after the other woman for a long moment, thinking of a man waiting, lazy and relaxed, to give a foot rub. Or something.

She shook her head in an abrupt gesture of disbelief. It wasn't like her to be so sexually aware or so open about it. What was happening to her?

Whatever it was, she could control it. Pressing her lips together with determination, she went back to work.

It was sometime later, perhaps fifteen minutes, maybe even an hour, when she heard a noise. Lifting her head, she listened intently. Everyone else had gone, she thought; she had heard the slamming of file drawers and banging of doors, had noticed with a small part of her attention the gradual quietening of the building. It was only a few minutes, however, since she had heard the last chiming of the elevator as it arrived and departed from this floor.

There had been something familiar about the small scratching sound she had noticed, yet she couldn't quite place it. Too soft for a footstep, it had also seemed too deliberate to be a piece of paper shifting in a draft. Too furtive to be natural, it was yet too natural to cause instant panic and an automatic call for security.

She had to investigate if she was going to be able to get back to work. Rising from behind her desk, she walked into the outer office.

She saw the envelope at once. It had been pushed under the door that Sophie had closed and locked behind her as she left. Plain yellow-brown manila, without address or label, it appeared to glow against the gray-blue of the carpet.

It was just the right size for enlarged photographs.

Jessica stood as if turned to stone. Her heartbeat accelerated, throbbing against her breastbone. Perspiration broke out in the center of her palms. Her stomach muscles cramped.

She could banish the hope that the man behind the camera that night had been a simple voyeur, she thought. He had not been. This was the evidence. It had to be.

Forcing herself to move, she walked across the room and knelt to pick up the envelope. There was no real point in opening the door to look out, since whoever had delivered it must be long gone. Anyway, she could not bring herself to take the risk. Not just now, not yet.

She would take the thing home, would close and lock her apartment door behind her before she looked.

No, she wouldn't. She couldn't wait that long. She had to be sure.

Her fingers were suddenly clumsy as she opened the pronged clasp that closed the envelope. There was only one glossy print inside. She drew it out with shaking fingers.

Her face grew hot, a white heat that spread, tingling,

to every part of her body. She swallowed on a combination of nausea and remembered desire. And she wanted
to crawl under her desk and stay there.

She had once read an article on famous photographs
that had included an outtake from the old silent film *Ecstasy*, starring Hedy Lamarr. The pose and its content
had been considered shocking at the time it was taken,
since it had shown a woman lost in the pure passion of
orgasm. According to the actress, however, the emotion
on her face had not been passion at all but intense pain.
Her director had jabbed a pin into her at the crucial moment.

Jessica thought the expression caught on her own
face was exactly the same. An extreme close-up in
black-and-white, it showed only her face and a naked
shoulder, with just a gray shadow of the man above her
projected like a ghost against the stone wall beside
them. In the photograph, she looked abandoned, glori-
fied, lost in pleasure so fierce it was the mirror of anguish. She looked as if she were dying of love.

With a sharp cry Jessica flung the envelope and print
from her. Pressing her hands to her eyes and mouth, she
stood still while violent shudders coursed over her.

Her chest was so tight she could not breathe. She felt
isolated, stripped of dignity and respect, while her heart
ached with the loss of a lovely and close-held memory.

What a cheap and vulgar travesty that night had been,
after all. She had known, and yet she had not felt it inside until now, had not wanted it to be that way. Somehow she had clung to the wonder and the magic in spite
of everything.

Gone. Gone now.

How accommodating she had been. How the man
who held her must have gloated—or laughed. She
cringed at the very thought of it.

She could not understand what had happened to her.
She must surely have been more drunk than she knew
to so easily let go of the carefully guarded precepts of
years. Or else she had been that most ridiculous of
clichés: the repressed virgin seduced by rum, music,

and a licentious atmosphere, flinging inhibition aside and falling into the arms of the first man to touch her.

Oh, God, and to think that touch, that sweet, mind-drugging seduction, had been deliberate. That was the worst part. Deliberate. No passion, no desire, no shared enthrallment. She had been used, that was all. She had been—

She shied away from the word in her mind. It was spoken so often these days that it had little shock value left, but it had never seemed so ugly or dirty as when applied to what had been done to her.

Fool. Such a fool.

Who had that man been? Who had dared set up that disgusting scenario and entice her into it?

She had to find out. She had to know, because she wanted to kill him. She wanted to find some way to hurt him as he had hurt her, to ruin him, to grind his sleazy ego into dust. She wanted to look him in the face while she did it, to make him know that he could not do what he pleased to her and get away with it. She wanted to make him pay, to have him see and understand that his punishment suited his crime.

She would do it. It was the only way she could live with what happened, the only way she could ever feel right about herself again.

Jessica drew a deep, calming breath and opened her eyes. She lowered her hands, lifted her head.

That was it, that was the solution. She felt better already. All she needed now was a plan of action.

Moving slowly on wobbly and stiff legs, she retrieved the picture and the envelope that had held it. She turned the brown envelope upside down and even reached inside, but there was no note, no letter of demand or instruction—nothing to show who had sent the picture or what they wanted from her.

It was a threat, then, a hint of what might come. There must be so many other shots of her and the man that were far worse. She felt ill just thinking of them.

She was tired of it. She might not be able to stop it, but she was fed up with taking everything like a lady. She'd like to tell these bozos a thing or two and see how they liked it.

She was also sick to death of men, of their superior attitudes and attempts to take advantage of her. She had tried to play by the rules and look what happened: One man thought she was an airheaded shopaholic who wouldn't notice if he took over her company, another didn't trust her to fulfill her financial obligations, and still another thought he could soft-soap her at lunch, then sneak around behind her back to make things go his way. Even her grandfather talked to her as if she were a ten-year-old who couldn't be trusted to cross the street by herself.

A good place to begin would be with Rafael Castelar. How smooth he had been, how courteous. And how two-faced. She would see how his manners held up when his tactics were brought home to him.

Fuming silently to herself, she snatched up her purse and crammed the photograph inside, then searched the top of her desk for the memo sheet with the number of the Brazilian's hotel suite on it. Clutching it in her hand, she slammed out of the office. And she was so enraged that she was outside on the street before she remembered that she had been nervous about leaving her office, afraid whoever had delivered the envelope was still there. Apparently they had gone, leaving the building with the last of the staff.

The Westin Canal, like so many New Orleans hotels, was furnished with massive antiques and reproductions, oversize Victorian prints, and enormous pieces of chinoiserie porcelain. The effect was expensive and colorful without being in the least quaint. Jessica took little notice, however, as she made her way inside from the off-Canal entrance and headed straight for the burnished brass doors of the elevators. The walk from Poydras had done little to cool her temper, and nothing to dampen her resolve.

The first check to her battle plan came when the suite door was opened by a man who could be either a butler, bodyguard, or friend, but was certainly not Rafael

Castelar. Dark-skinned, with a square, impassive face and a massive build, he was plainly of Indian blood. He was just as plainly reluctant to allow Jessica into the suite.

"I am sorry, senhorita," he said with a heavy accent accompanied by a stiff bow. "Senhor Castelar is not here."

"You expect him back this evening?"

The man inclined his large head in confirmation. "I don't know the hour. Perhaps you will return another time."

She was in no mood to accept the dismissal. As he started to close the door, she put out a hand to hold it. "I will wait for him, if you don't mind."

The man wasn't used to women who chose to assert themselves; that much she could tell from the disconcerted look that crossed his copper-brown features. "No, truly—" he began.

"I'm sure Rafael will want to see me," she said, trying the effect of a warm smile as she stepped forward into the suite's small foyer. "There was a matter that came up between us during lunch yesterday that I thought we might discuss further."

The Indian wasn't happy, but he made no attempt to halt her entry. As she walked through the foyer area into the living room, he followed to offer a drink. She accepted, and he moved off toward the kitchen and its pass-through bar.

The carpeting glowed like a green velvet lawn as it flowed under glass and brass tables and in front of overstuffed chairs and sofas striped in subdued green and cream. An armoire in a crackled cream finish housed a television and stereo, but more compelling viewing lay in the lights of the city beyond the great picture windows with their draped and fringed Victorian valances of heavy cream brocade. Pleasant, restful, the room had more character than most hotel suites. The only sign of the man who occupied it, however, was a soft-sided black leather attaché leaning against one leg of the glass-topped desk near the windows, and the papers in neat stacks on its surface.

Jessica turned toward the desk by instinct, then stopped. Snooping was not her style; it went against everything she had been taught, everything she felt about the importance of privacy. To poke around in Rafael Castelar's belongings would be a violation.

But why should she consider his feelings? More than that, what if the rest of her pictures were lying over there in open sight or tucked away in the attaché? Was she going to let scruples prevent her from getting her hands on them?

At the sound of a footstep behind her, she turned with the quickness of guilt. The manservant barely glanced at her, however, as he placed a tray holding her wine and a dish of cheese and crackers on the table before the sofa. Indicating with an oddly graceful gesture that she should be seated, he stood back while she complied.

Regardless, he did not remain with her, but went back into the kitchen, where he seemed to be preparing some kind of light meal. Jessica could hear him running water and opening and closing drawers, could catch a glimpse of him now and then through the pass-through opening between the two rooms. She sat sipping her wine a moment, but was too restless to be still for long.

Taking her glass, she rose and walked to the window. She clasped her arm at her waist as she stared down at the myriad of pulsing lights that framed and emphasized the great sweeping crescent of the river like a scene in some giant electronic game.

The papers on the desk were within her peripheral vision, an obvious reminder and a taunt. She glanced toward the kitchen. The Indian could not see that end of the room while he worked. To look toward the desk area, he would have to step back into the living room.

It would only take a few seconds to sift through the stack lying in plain sight, and one or two more to delve into the attaché. The opportunity was heaven-sent, perhaps even preordained. If she didn't take it, there might never be another chance.

She would do it. So much depended on it.

With apparent aimlessness she drifted down the wall of windows toward the desk. She hesitated with her head cocked toward the kitchen, but the Indian continued with what he was doing. She stepped to the desk.

Nothing.

Though she rifled quickly through the papers, they turned out to be only what might be expected of a businessman away from his office: fax copies of reports and proposals, rough drafts of contracts, letters awaiting answers in English and Spanish, but mostly in Portuguese.

She bent to flip the attaché open. It held an appointment calendar, notebooks and pens, passport, airline tickets, pocket-size dictation recorder—even a paperback mystery. But no photographs, no negatives, no film or camera.

Behind her in the foyer, the suite's outer door opened. The Indian spoke in low tones, a quick phrase in Portuguese. Rafael Castelar's deep tones came in answer.

Jessica straightened, but the attaché fell over as she released it, spilling a notebook from the top. There was no time to put things back the way she had found them. Rafael would walk into the living room within seconds.

Swinging quickly, she picked up her wine and moved to the window to stare out once more. Her heart was pounding and she could feel a flush across her cheekbones. She was not cut out for a life of deceit. Taking a deep breath, she let it out, then sipped her wine as she tried to appear introspective and a little bored with waiting.

"What a nice surprise," Rafael said as he walked into the room behind her.

The words were conventional, but there was an undercurrent of speculation and distrust in his tone. He had seen the attaché, she thought. She might have known he would; he was a man who missed little. That being the case, what did she have to lose?

Facing him with as much poise as she could muster, she spoke in cool tones. "You may not think so when you've heard what I have to say."

Chapter Eight

⊞ ⊞ ⊞ *Rafael studied Jessica while his thoughts* moved at warp speed. There was nothing incriminating in the attaché she had rifled, that much he knew. Few of the papers were of value to her even if she knew his language; they dealt in the main with his far-flung trading ventures. She had refused his earlier offer of a working arrangement, and he had not yet made a countermove. He could think of nothing he had said or done to offend her. In spite of these things, he could see the rage in every line of her beautiful body, see the urge to annihilate him smoldering in her eyes.

He was not easily annihilated. Assuming Jessica Meredith was going to go off like a rocket, he wanted to be on hand for the spectacle. If that put him in the line of fire, so be it.

With a shading of dry humor, he said, "I suppose this is a business call?"

"What else?" she snapped with color flaring into her face. Without giving him time to answer, she went on. "I don't know how you gained your information about our financial position, but it seems you have been doing your best to turn it to your advantage. Did you really think we wouldn't find out?"

"If I did, apparently I was wrong," he said with narrow-eyed caution. He had no idea what she was getting at, but it would be as well if he could discover it.

"You certainly were! My grandfather has done business with Crescent National Bank for decades. Vic Gaddens worked his way through college crewing on one of our boats back in the seventies. These things count in New Orleans."

"And this Gaddens told you that I was inquiring into your finances? I would have expected him to be a bit more closemouthed about it—except that anyone who would let me in on your situation can hardly be trusted not to relay the story of my interest also." Rafael waited with intense curiosity for her reply. At the same time his gaze skimmed her chest, where perfectly shaped curves were rising and falling with her every breath in a way that put a strain on his better intentions.

"He didn't mention names, but there was no need," she said in scathing tones. "I can't believe you would pull such a low-down dirty trick. To try it at this time makes you a miserable, conniving scoundrel. If you had managed to get what you wanted, springing it on my grandfather from nowhere, it might have killed him!"

"But he is all right?" Rafael's inquiry was swift, though he suppressed any outward indication of concern.

"For now, no thanks to you."

He hesitated a moment, then said with compressed irony, "I suppose you have now blocked this move of mine?"

"What a hypocrite! You know very well there's no chance whatever that anyone will trust me with that kind of money."

"So," he said softly. "It seems I may have won."

A spasm of pain and grief crossed her face, and she clenched a fist, holding it at a level with her stomach. Her voice low and vibrant, she said, "You most certainly have not. I'm going to fight you down to the wire. But I warn you. I won't have my grandfather upset again. Any move you make from now on had better be open and above board. And you will go through me to implement them. If you don't, I'll contact Holliwell at Gulfstream Air and throw myself on his mercy. You won't have a ghost of a chance at getting your hands on Sea Gull."

Pepe, soft-footed for all his size, appeared at Rafael's

side with his drink just then. It was none too soon. He took it and swallowed a good portion. With his gaze on the glass, he said, "I don't react well to threats."

"Nor do I, something you would do well to remember."

The lift of her chin exposed the smooth, pure line of her throat. The compulsion to bury his face in it, inhaling her delicate scent, tasting her sweetness with his tongue, came out of left field like an unexpected blow to the solar plexus. The corded muscles of his stomach clamped down like hard steel bands. His brain flashed with the white-hot heat of ground zero. He was not aware of a decision to move, yet he took three long steps toward her before he could even breathe, much less regain coherent thought.

Gaze wide, she backed against the window. Her head bumped it, making it shiver in its frame.

With a wrenching effort he stopped. Voice not quite even, he said, "Why are you afraid of me?"

"I'm not!"

"You do a good imitation, first in the car and now here. Or maybe it's just that all men frighten you?"

Her lips tightened, and she stepped away from the window, skirting him carefully. "Ours is a business relationship, nothing personal—or so you said. I would prefer to keep it that way."

"In that case," he said flatly, "it would be a good idea to conduct our meetings in an office setting from now on instead of my hotel suite."

Her face flamed before she swung and walked toward the foyer. "I will certainly keep that in mind. And I will expect you to remember what I told you about my grandfather, because I don't intend to repeat it."

"I'll do that," he said to her retreating back, "though I don't see the need for such anger over it."

She turned at the outer door with green fire in her eyes. "Believe me, you haven't seen anger yet."

The door slammed behind her. Rafael winced, and his hand tightened on the glass in his hand.

He had not handled that well. He had been too surprised to find her there; the hardball she had thrown him had come too fast for a considered reaction.

Still, the information she had revealed was useful. Or could be if he decided to take advantage of it.

So she wasn't angry yet? He would like to be there when that time came; it should be a sight to remember. What would it take, he wondered, to bring her to it?

Actually he had a fair idea. Taking another swallow of his drink, staring at what remained, he considered possibilities.

It was early on the following morning when Rafael arrived at Crescent National Bank. Vic Gaddens had just arrived and was not yet seeing clients. The CMARC name worked wonders, however; Rafael was shown in immediately.

The banker was accommodating enough during the first fifteen minutes of conversation in his office. Thereafter, he was positively ingratiating. Papers were signed, the electronic transfer of funds completed, and documents presented in record time. Before the first coffee break, Rafael walked out of the bank with the loan certificate for Sea Gull Transport & Charter, Inc., safely in his pocket.

His next move was to have his office make an appointment with Jessica. Here he reached a small impasse. She was not in the office and her secretary could not, or would not, say when she might return. It took some careful digging to discover that she had gone down to the docks to check on a problem with one of the crew boats.

Rafael's brows drew together over his nose as he considered the news. The docks of the world were not known for being safe or hospitable places, especially for a woman. He hoped Jessica had the intelligence to take a man with her who knew his way around. Surely she did; the lady might be headstrong, but she wasn't foolhardy.

He tried to settle to work at the desk in the suite, but was too restless to concentrate. Lack of exercise was the problem, he thought. At home, he swam every morning or else went for a fast canter along the beach. Often on weekends he and his friends gathered for soccer or polo. And sometimes he took off his shirt, grabbed a machete, and waded into the jungle that passed as a garden around the old family place at Recife, hacking back the rampant growth that the gardener was too timid to control.

Any of those things were guaranteed to take the edge off his temper. Even if that edge was caused in large part by physical attraction to the wrong woman. He wanted Jessica Meredith. That raw need was a complication to this deal that had done nothing to improve his disposition.

He could jog or play golf, neither of which promised the requisite exertion or total immersion. The only other possibility that came to mind was to try out a health club. A fast game of racquetball, that second cousin to jai alai, might well give him the workout he needed.

He had the enclosed, brightly lighted court to himself for a time, long enough to limber his muscles and catch his second wind. He was just beginning to break into a light sweat when another player walked in. Big and blond, he carried a ball in one hand and had a paddle in the other with the thong wrapped around his wrist. His rather undefined lips stretched in a smile as he strode forward with the squared shoulders and bulldog swagger of a bodybuilder.

Rafael recognized him at once as the man who had been in Jessica's office the day before. Holliwell, that was the name. Jessica had told him something of the owner of the helicopter service interested in Sea Gull. Rafael had made a point of learning more since then.

"How about a game?" Holliwell said.

The request was polite enough, but carried an undercurrent of cocky challenge. Ordinarily Rafael would have declined. He had no use for pointless masculine competition. However, it was possible to discover a great deal about a man's essential nature from watching the way he played the mock battles of sports. In any case, facing off against Holliwell suited his mood.

With a curt nod of acceptance, he indicated that he would receive the other man's serve. He took up the position.

The ball smacked into the wall and shot straight at his head in a vicious shot designed to demoralize. Rafael slammed it back in hard, swift answer to the unprovoked aggression. Then they settled into the game.

"I hear," Carlton Holliwell said out of the corner of his mouth, "that you bought yourself a loan today."

"Could be." Rafael extended enough to direct his volley at the outermost edge of the other man's range.

The blond man had to stretch for the return. The vicious twist of his mouth showed his dislike of the exertion. He slashed at the hard rubber ball, sending it hurtling past Rafael's shoulder to rebound in another head shot. "Happens I was after that piece of paper myself. You know that?"

"I make it my business to stay informed." Rafael let the ball pass, then smashed it downward on the rebound. It was not returned. His point.

"You went behind my back to snag it." The words were belligerent.

"You should have moved faster." Rafael's comment could serve for the other's play as well as his business tactics.

Holliwell gave him a sour look as he jogged over to pick up the bouncing ball, then snapped it in Rafael's direction as he gave up the serve. "You plan on foreclosing, doing a court takeover so you wind up on the board?"

"That's one of several possibilities."

"It may not be easy going. Old man Frazier is tight with the judge." There was uneasiness in the other man's face as he divided his attention between Rafael's face and the ball he was now tossing in one hand as he prepared to strike.

"The law is still the law." Rafael put a hard spin on the ball as he smacked it.

Carlton Holliwell, busy with the next series of volleys, made no reply. He was laboring, that much was plain from his heavy breathing, but he could still put stinging power behind his strokes and had no compunction about body blows. That suited Rafael fine, since it meant he was free to return the same.

Holliwell missed a close shot that threatened the family jewels before grounding in a corner. Cursing the lost point, he gave Rafael a baleful look. "You're a tough bastard under the polish, aren't you?"

"I have a habit of returning aggression with interest, if that's what you mean."

Holliwell grunted. "Killer tactics, I call it. I'm thinking I'll be lucky to get off the court with my gonads."

"You suggested the match."

"Yeah, well, there's more than one game. We'll see who winds up on top."

Rafael noted the mulish expression on the other man's face, saw the cunning in his eyes, and felt his guard tighten. At the same time he recognized that Carlton Holliwell, for all his bulldog strength and determination, lacked stamina and was low on finesse. Knowing he could take the control of the contest whenever he pleased, he accepted an easy point and allowed the other man a breather in order to discover just what he had in mind.

Chest heaving, Holliwell gasped, "I'd like to make you an offer, buy the loan off you."

"My apologies," Rafael said without noticeable regret, "but it isn't for sale."

"Not even for a hundred grand above?"

Rafael smiled without humor. "Or even a million."

"You might want to change your mind. I got connections, backers with deep pockets."

The look on Holliwell's face carried a silent, if heavy-handed, message. Rafael considered the implications. The other man could be lying to scare off a competitor. He could also be telling it straight: the Cosa Nostra might well be interested in laundering cash through a viable crew boat operation. They could just as easily have an eye to the usefulness to the drug trade of that kind of boat traffic.

If the mob was involved, the stakes had just been jacked up several notches. Getting in the way could well be dangerous. But then, he was used to a high level of risk.

"I back myself," Rafael said in soft, even tones. "Most of the time it's enough. In case of need, however, I can always call on a cousin or two in Colombia."

Holliwell's eyes widened, then narrowed to slits. He gave a wheezing laugh. "The cartel ain't as strong as it used to be."

"No?" Rafael shrugged. "Some say it's like our lizards in Brazil. Chop off its tail and it just grows another one."

Holliwell grunted. "You must want Sea Gull pretty bad. You got plans? Or is the main thing the Meredith dame?"

"It's a matter of business," Rafael said softly. "My business."

"Nah, you got an itch. I saw the way you looked at her the other day. Just don't count on gratitude. She's as cold as a witch's tit; don't put out for nobody."

"Since I don't require it," Rafael answered, the words as slicing as his abrupt serve, "I won't be disappointed."

"I'd still love to see her face when she finds out you've got her where you want her." Holliwell wheezed as he jerked away, diving after the ball.

It was a sight Rafael had been looking forward to himself. Mouth compressed in grim lines, he set himself to exact payment in sore muscles and bruises from the other man for making him feel such a lowlife because of that need.

The crew boat sat alongside the low earthen barrier that served as a levee at the Nashville docks below the city. The berth wasn't the best, being well past the Free Trade Zone and the coffee warehouses. Mighty plans were supposed to be in the works for upgrading the facilities along that stretch. For now, however, it was an area of rusting tin buildings that snaked alongside the river for miles, of ancient facilities once used to store cotton back in steamboat days, of decaying concrete wall, access roads with more potholes than pavement, and bent chain-link fences overgrown with brambles. It was the zone where the tramp ships with registrations from insolvent and barely recognized countries lay dockside to off-load, ships streaked with rust, oil, and other unmentionable forms of dirt, crewed by a gumbo of nationalities. Backing the narrow strip of wharves was a housing project that was jostled in its turn by gray and rotting shotgun houses and beer joints, an area where a night without at least three murders was considered slow and where drug pusher was the career of choice.

That the eighty-foot crew boat, the *Sun Dancer*, had been directed there was a sign of disfavor; Sea Gull's vessels usually docked well upriver, near the Napoleon Street wharves. Jessica had driven down with Keil and the crewman who had been sent to let them know there was trouble, and she felt none too safe even with the double escort. Alone, she would not have ventured near it for all the shrimp in the gulf.

Nick Frazier was the *Sun Dancer*'s captain. They found him in the boat's minuscule lounge, having coffee with the customs agent who had been on board since shortly after the boat docked from a night run.

Introductions were unnecessary, since the agent was no stranger. Problems of one kind or another were always cropping up with the many boats Sea Gull had going in and out. They were settled most of the time with a minimum of fuss and bother.

Nick dragged out a chair for Jessica, waved Keil toward one, then resumed his seat. With the handshaking and general greetings out of the way, they got down to business. As port captain, Keil had a greater knowledge of the crew boats and their operation. By unspoken agreement, Jessica allowed him to take charge of the meeting.

"So what's up?" he said as he settled back in his chair and crossed his ankle over his knee in a relaxed slouch. "Somebody stash their cache in the sugar bowl? We got a stowaway, something like that?"

"You're clean," the agent said with a complete lack of humor. "For now."

Nick shook his sun-bleached head in disgust. "Seems somebody tipped off Customs about one of our boats picking up floating stuff out in the gulf. The tipster didn't say when, where, which one, kiss my backside, so everybody gets searched." He jerked a thumb at the agent. "These guys had nothing better to do."

The agent, a compact Cajun with sun-bronzed skin, dark curling hair, and old eyes, was a Vietnam vet and ex-policeman, a man carefully recruited by Customs. If he had searched the boat, it was because he had reason. If he refused to be riled by Nick's attitude, that was also for a purpose. He said now, "We could have set up a watch, trolled in the perps. But Sea Gull has a rep for policing their own crews. We know we can count on the traffic being stopped, now that it's come to light."

He was right, or would have been in the past. Claude Frazier had once fired a whole crew, right down to the captain, after a drug cache was found on one of his boats.

"You don't think it was an isolated incident, then?" Jessica said.

"Can't really say," the agent answered with a shrug. "God knows, there's enough stuff out there to send the price of Styrofoam floats sky-high. The agency had a cookout on the beach awhile back, and first thing we stumbled across was a bale of weed washed up by the tide."

"But this informant must have convinced you that our boat was something more than just a lucky catch or you wouldn't have moved so quickly," Jessica pointed out.

"Hey, I think I resent that," Nick said in tones of protest.

Jessica, glancing at the customs agent for corroboration, said, "I don't think anybody's pointing fingers."

"Yet," Nick muttered.

"There's something beside a drug charge pending here." Keil's voice carried his authority as he gave the other man a direct look. "If anybody gets caught, Sea Gull pays. And right now, we can't afford it."

The problem Keil had just pointed out was also at the back of Jessica's mind. A hefty fine would be levied against any shipping company whose employees were caught smuggling drugs. The purpose was to encourage the companies to keep a tight security of their own, to post warnings, conduct random searches, check references on crew members—whatever it took to help cut the traffic. The system might be a little screwy, since a company could not always control the actions of its employees, but there was method to it.

Jessica's grandfather had always resented that kind of manipulation. He might be hard on anybody who was caught, and certainly he or Keil vetted every man signed on for every boat, but he refused on principle to do the random searches and post the warnings that Customs wanted. There had been enough erosion of people's privacy, he said, enough interference in their lives. If Customs thought underwear and toilets and grease traps needed searching, they could do it themselves.

The question now was whether she should change her grandfather's policy. Did this new development warrant it?

Keil was apparently thinking along the same lines, for he said now, "What we need to know is how big this thing might be. Are we talking a package or two, or is it a whole damn shipment? Could it be just one man with a little sideline of his own, or is one of our boats rendezvousing in the gulf with some mother ship from Colombia?"

The customs agent pursed his lips. "Venezuela, more likely. With the heat on in Colombia, they've shifted to ships of other registry."

Brazilian ships just possibly? Jessica wondered. It was an interesting thought, one that just might explain why CMARC was so anxious to gain control of Sea Gull.

Of course, one thing did not necessarily lead to the other, but it would be foolish to ignore the possibility. She opened her mouth to make the suggestion. Then she closed it again.

Maybe there was more of her grandfather in her than she thought, because making that kind of accusation went against the grain. Anyway, Rafael Castelar, or anyone like him, was due a chance to defend himself before he was thrown to the lions.

There was one other possibility raised by this incident, though it was not precisely new, and that had to do with the boat explosion in the gulf that had thrown Sea Gull into financial difficulties. Was it drug related in some way? Could there have been some rivalry or delivery failure that had led to the destruction of that boat? There seemed no way to tell, but it was something she intended to keep in the back of her mind.

Jessica had heard enough about the current and rather small crisis, certainly all she suspected there was to hear. Leaving the men to a conversation that had veered somehow to deep-sea fishing, she walked out onto the narrow deck. There was a fresh breeze coming off the river, one she followed away from the landward side and around the prow to the deck overlooking open water.

The river was a great, benign, and muddy flow that barely rippled as it eased toward the gulf. On the far side across its width lay a brown-and-green shoreline that was indefinite with the haze caused by distance, humidity, and air pollution. As she watched, a tugboat pushing barges of coal rumbled past and slowly rounded the next bend. For the moment nothing else moved on the waterway as far as the eye could see.

Jessica lifted her head and let the wind ruffle through her hair to her scalp. The cool touch, the slight movement of the *Sun Dancer* in the water, the vista that was without buildings or boats, ships or people—especially people—was soothing. She could feel herself relax by a few delicate degrees.

It had been a long time since she was on the water. She had missed it without knowing it.

She loved boats, had since she was a little girl. One of her first memories was of going downriver to the open gulf with her grandfather, curled up on the seat behind him while he stood at the wheel. The movement of the waves had been a fierce pleasure; the sounds and smells and changing colors of the sea and sky had fascinated her. Claude Frazier seldom spoke a word when he took her out with him, had never said how he felt or what he thought, but she had known he loved it as much as she did. It had been in his eyes, in his stance and the way he breathed the salt air, as if taking in an element necessary for his existence.

Just as he had never mentioned his love of the sea, he had never said he loved her. She knew he did, though, from the way he watched her and worried about her, the ruthless way he removed anything that threatened her welfare. Those were things she needed to remember. Especially now.

"Want to go for a run down to blue water?"

It was Nick, approaching with quiet certainty, stopping at her shoulder. He had shared her affection for boats as they were growing up together.

"I'd love it, as you well know," she said frankly, turning her head to give him a crooked smile. "But I can't."

"Poor Jessica. If Sea Gull's such a burden that it's keeping you from doing what you want, why not dump it?"

She grimaced. "I may have no choice."

Having said that much, it was necessary to explain Castelar's apparent interest in the loan. Nick listened, at the same time reaching for her hand, where it rested on the railing, playing with her fingers. When she finally came to the end, he lifted a shoulder in a careless shrug. "So maybe you'll be better off."

"I doubt Grandpapa will think so. I see no way to

keep what's been done from him, though. Oh, maybe for a little while, but if I don't tell him, then somebody else just may. He'll be even more upset in that case."

"Right, because he'll think right off that you have all sorts of other deep, dark secrets that you're keeping hidden, things he should know. He's a cynical old bastard."

"Maybe, but you can't blame him," she said. "I'd hate having things kept from me, too, in his place."

"You're such a softy," Nick said, his voice taking on a lazy, intimate timbre.

"I may have been once," she said on a sigh. "Not any more."

"Oh, yeah? You're working yourself into the ground for an old man who thinks you're an extension of his own ego—who can't see, and never could, that you're a beautiful girl with wants and needs of your own."

She recognized the sound in his voice, the heavy-lidded look of his eyes. She could have stepped away from him, made some quick comment to change the subject, alter the atmosphere, deflect his purpose as she had on Sunday. Not now. Now she wanted to be kissed.

His lashes flickered as he saw she was not going to retreat. His breath filled his lungs with a soft hiss, then he reached for her.

His lips were warm and smooth and tasted of coffee with a faint flavor of salt from braving gulf winds during the night. They moved upon hers with sure skill, brushing the surfaces so they tingled from the friction, using pressure to press inside. His tongue invaded her mouth without haste or force, flicking over her teeth, sweeping the fragile lining, tasting her. His hold tightened.

"Ready, Jessica?" Keil called.

His voice came from the other side of the boat. If she didn't answer, he would come looking for her. She would rather not be found there in Nick's arms. She pressed her hand to the warm, firm surface of Nick's chest, using pressure to persuade him to release her. There was the tension of reluctance in his muscles before he complied. She stepped back without quite looking at him.

Was he the one? She couldn't be sure; there had not been enough time. Had there?

Suddenly she didn't like herself much for using Nick and Keil for her experiments. They didn't deserve it.

There was one man who did, however, and she still had to find him.

"Be right with you," she called out to Keil. With a brief brush of her fingers over Nick's forearm in silent apology, she walked away.

Chapter Nine

▦ ▦ ▦ *Jessica turned over in bed to look at the* dim, watery light edging around the curtains. She gave a low moan.

She had barely slept all night, only dropping off for an hour or so toward dawn. Her thoughts had turned in circles as she tried to find solutions to the problems crowding her. Insofar as she could tell, there were none. Now on this rainy Sunday she felt groggy and dispirited, and more than half inclined to flop back over and bury her head under the pillow.

She couldn't do it. As hard as it was to believe, the week was gone. Her grandfather, growing restless so far away from where things were happening, had called late the day before to demand she come to the Landing again to make a full report. More than that, she needed to discuss the incident with the customs agent, had to find out if her grandfather had made any arrangement about the loan, wanted to see how he was progressing with his recovery and when he intended to return to the office.

In spite of what he had hinted, she had no doubt he would soon be back. It was impossible to think of him remaining an invalid forever, impossible to consider that he might never sit in his worn chair in his office again. He had been there, had been exactly the same, for as long as she could remember. White-haired, tanned, and fit, face seamed with lines and scars, stern and pragmatic in his outlook, he had seemed indomitable. Like a monument or a bridge, he should go on forever.

She had tried, after his stroke, to think what it might be like with him gone. She couldn't. So much of her world was built around what he said and thought, what he wanted and expected, that she had little existence without him. It was frightening.

It also disturbed her somewhere deep inside where she seldom ventured. When was she going to have time for herself? When was she going to do the things that she wanted?

Settling to her back to lie staring at the ceiling, Jessica felt an old, familiar despair wash over her.

People thought she was so in control, so together and businesslike. Sometimes she even felt that way herself. But at others it seemed the life was slowly being crushed out of her by the weight of all the things that she must do, should do—or else should not have done.

This wasn't going to cut it. Rolling over and coming upright in a single, fluid movement, she walked toward the closet, stripping off her nightshirt as she went. With the door open, she stood an instant in paralyzed indecision, then reached blindly for a dress of sage green with a cut-lace collar and sleeves. It didn't really matter what she wore, since only family would be there to see her.

She noticed the jade green Lincoln Mark VIII the minute she pulled into the driveway. It sat on the drive before the house, a sleek yet conservative statement, as close as any American car came to having a European attitude.

Nick drove a pickup. Keil tooled around in a Nissan, while his mother, Zoe Frazier, had a sober Cadillac DeVille. Arletta went for the conspicuous luxury of a BMW. None of them, so far as Jessica knew, had changed vehicles. Keil's Nissan sat on the drive that curved around toward the old orchard, but apparently no one else in the family was there.

The Lincoln, Jessica saw, had a rental brochure lying on the dash. A feeling of impending calamity washed over her to settle in the pit of her stomach.

Rafael Castelar rose from a seat beside her grandfather's wheelchair as she marched into the sitting room that connected to the master bedroom. Dressed casually in black pants paired with a gray sand-washed silk shirt, he looked devastatingly attractive, and far too at ease in his surroundings.

"What are you doing here?" she said without preamble.

"Jessica!" Her grandfather's voice, still not as strong as it should be, cracked in his displeasure.

"Your granddaughter and I have dispensed with formality," Rafael said with a smile for the older man before he returned his gaze to her. "Good morning, Jessica."

She distrusted his good humor, his confidence, and especially his presence with her grandfather. Though she had not seen him in the past few days, not since the night at his hotel, she had no illusions that he had been idle. She longed to be able to demand what he had been doing, also what he and her grandfather had been talking about. It would not do, not while her grandfather was looking at her with such amazed impatience.

The older man said now, "Castelar and I are in the middle of something here. Why don't you go and see if you can help Madeleine arrange lunch? She was having a fit awhile ago, trying to find a deviled egg platter or some such thing."

It was a dismissal such as she had not received in years. It hurt. At the same time it made her nervous. She studied her grandfather's face, searching for signs of strain, fatigue, or agitation. There was nothing except a barely contained eagerness to get on with his interrupted conversation.

"I'll come back later, then," she said.

Her grandfather waved her toward the door. "Yes, yes, we'll talk after lunch."

Madeleine was not in the kitchen. It appeared to Jessica, when she put her head in at the door, that everything was under control. Cressida, the cook who had been with her grandfather for years, was humming under her breath while she put fresh sprigs of parsley around eggs in the oval insets on a pink Depression glass egg platter. Jessica returned the woman's cheery greeting and asked about the big meal she was apparently preparing. According to the cook, her grandfather had called everyone in as if it was a regular family get-together. Mr. Keil was around somewhere; she thought she saw him heading out the back. With a quick thanks for the information and a wave, Jessica withdrew and moved on toward the back courtyard.

What was her grandfather up to? Had he invited Castelar, or had the man come on his own? Were they all to gather around to lend support during their talk, or were their numbers designed to lessen the importance of it? She wished she knew.

Catching sight of a flutter of black-and-red print along the path leading through the orchard to the family cemetery, she swung in that direction. The rain had stopped, and a pale sun was alternately coming and going behind drifts of lavender-gray clouds. There was still a mistiness to the air and an unsettled feeling, however. Now and then, thunder grumbled in the distance with a muted threat of more rain.

The winter grass was beaded with water, and puddles stood in the ruts of the gravel trail. Peach trees in full bloom made a bank of pink up ahead, while windblown petals lay like wedding confetti in the wet grass. A cardinal gave its clear call from a perch in the top of a pecan tree. The sound rang so piercingly sweet on the cool, moisture-drenched air that it made Jessica's heart swell.

She had been watching where she was going on the wet track. She looked up to locate the cardinal, then glanced ahead toward the orchard. She stopped.

Madeleine was leaning against the trunk of a gnarled apple tree that had not yet leafed out. Standing close beside her, resting the heel of his hand above her head, was a man with broad shoulders and windblown sandy brown hair. It was Keil.

Madeleine and Keil. Something in their taut stance and absorption in each other made Jessica reluctant to move any closer. Swinging abruptly, she walked away again.

Madeleine and Keil.

She had thought they didn't get along. Had it all been a cover? Madeleine's visits to the office had tapered off; she had come and gone only once during the past week. Keil, Jessica knew, had taken the other woman out to lunch then. She had thought it was to get her out of everybody's hair, but she just might have been wrong.

Madeleine and Keil. It wasn't that surprising, not really. They were near the same age, both young and lively and attractive. Keil was a man who appreciated women.

She really would have thought that Keil had too much consideration to do such a thing. Madeleine was his great-uncle's wife, not to mention the wife of his employer. Wasn't anything sacred anymore?

And Madeleine, what of her? She didn't seem the type to fall under the spell of Keil's charm, as potent as that might be. She liked to think of herself as smart, savvy, and even sophisticated. Before the stroke, she had always been trying to get Jessica's grandfather to take her to New York, Palm Beach, or the Côte d'Azur. As if Claude Frazier could ever be comfortable in such places.

Maybe Madeleine thought Keil would do better. Maybe she was looking forward to being a widow. It would not be the first time that a young woman married to a much older man had found solace with one of his younger male relatives.

Or maybe Madeleine thought that she and Keil, between them, would be able to control Sea Gull. Could be she had figured out that a trophy wife who had signed a prenuptial agreement without coercion would not be in a strong position when it came time to divide the estate. She might think her best bet was to latch on to Keil and his twelve and a half percent.

Jessica shook her head with a sigh. She was being petty and unfair, all because of a brief glimpse of two people talking under an apple tree. No doubt the pair of them were perfectly innocent. She hoped so. She really did, for her grandfather's sake.

The day progressed. Arletta arrived. She was wearing a suit of lavender leather patterned with silver studs in a western motif and matching cowboy boots. Claiming she had skipped breakfast in order to make it to the Landing in time, she stood a stick of celery upright in her Bloody Mary to tide her over until lunch, and even nibbled on it now and then.

Keil, when he returned to the house, indicated that his mother wouldn't be coming this Sunday. She was having a little trouble with her heart. Nothing to worry about, he assured them; according to her doctor, it was only palpitations from nerves.

"From sheer contrariness and spite, more likely," Arletta muttered.

Jessica rolled her eyes, glancing at her mother with a quick shake of her head, though she wasn't surprised. There was no love lost between the two women, hadn't been in years.

"It's true," Arletta insisted, though she lowered her voice so Keil could not hear. "I'll bet you anything she's the one gossiping about my love life. Again."

"Not to me." Still, it was possible Arletta was right, Jessica knew. Someone had told Mimi Tess.

Nick sauntered in just before lunch. During the meal of crawfish bisque and potato salad, barbecue and baked beans, Arletta sat beside him, and found a multitude of excuses to clutch his arm and whisper in his ear. Nick endured it with patience, though his smile was a bit strained as he looked toward Jessica. She, in turn, was reminded of what Mimi Tess had said about Arletta and a younger man. And she wished she could forget it.

Paranoid. She hated it, but couldn't seem to help herself.

Conversation around the table was polite, general, and strained. The main reason was the stranger in their midst. Everybody was busy wondering what his business could be with Claude Frazier, but no one cared to ask. Jessica's grandfather did not make a habit of discussing his affairs even in private, and could be depended on to give short shrift to anybody dumb enough to display public curiosity.

Certainly neither he nor Rafael was giving anything anyway. They spoke affably of the local shrimping industry, a subject Keil and Nick knew well, then moved from there to the pros and cons of draining wetlands and on to exploitation of the Amazon basin.

Rafael was courteous and supremely at ease. He spoke well on any and all subjects, but felt no apparent need to dominate the conversation or insist on his own positions. Claude Frazier listened to him and interjected a comment now and then, but his shrewd old eyes were appraising. With his Scottish heritage, he tended to view any man with suspicion until he proved himself friendly, instead of the usual happy-go-lucky Cajun French habit of taking every man for a friend until he proved a foe.

If Jessica's grandfather had any idea it was Rafael who had been inquiring about Sea Gull's loan, he gave no sign. It appeared that his suspicions had been lulled, or else the two men had come to some accommodation. What the last might be, however, she could not begin to guess.

When the dessert of fresh Louisiana strawberries in Cointreau and cream had been consumed, they retreated to the front gallery. The exception was the invalid, who went to his room for his usual afternoon rest. Keil and Madeleine took the swing on the far end of the gallery, while Jessica and her mother settled into wicker chairs closer to the steps. Nick and Rafael opted for a pair of rocking chairs. Between them, they made an effort at sporadic conversation as they watched the shadow patterns of the rain clouds passing over the marsh.

After a time, Nick offered to give Rafael the full tour of the place, beginning with the old detached kitchen and other outbuildings, including the gazebo-like pavilion over the artesian spring that had taken the place of the old wash house, and ending at the shell road across to Isle Coquille that was used as an airstrip back in the sixties. The Brazilian accepted, and the two sauntered away while Nick regaled him with local gossip about drug drops being made on the airstrip and back in the swamps.

The day had grown oppressive, not really warm enough for air-conditioning, but with so much moisture saturating the air that breathing was an effort. Still, the rain held off. It would almost be a relief, Jessica thought, when it began to fall again.

At least she was able to relax a little now that Rafael Castelar was no longer in the immediate vicinity. She leaned back in her chair and closed her eyes while her chest lifted in an unconscious sigh of exhaustion.

"You look like something the cat dragged in," Arletta said to her daughter with her usual frankness. "Is somebody keeping you up nights, or did you get those dark circles under your eyes from overwork?"

"Neither, Mother," Jessica said with care. "I just have things on my mind."

"Don't tell me, I can guess. Business. Sea Gull." The last two words were spoken with all the loathing she might use in naming Nazi concentration camps.

"What else?"

"Too bad." Arletta stubbed out her cigarette in an Italian pottery ashtray on a table beside her chair. Immediately she lit another one.

"Someone has to do it," Jessica said evenly.

"So let them. Someone like Castelar. Chuck it, honey. Get out from under and get on with your life."

Jessica tried a smile, but it was a poor effort. "It isn't that easy."

"You'd be surprised," her mother said with tart emphasis.

Jessica lifted her lashes as she paused on the verge of asking something she had wondered about for years. It was personal, but then, what wasn't in a family like theirs? She said finally, "Do you ever wish you had hung on to any of the men you married?"

"You asking if I have regrets?" Her mother gave her a straight look as she surrounded herself with a cloud of

tobacco smoke. "Sure. Don't we all? But you don't refuse to go into the water because you nearly drowned.
Failing to ride the merry-go-round because you can't
find the perfect horse is not playing it smart, but just
being persnickety."

"And that would never do."

Arletta shrugged one too-thin shoulder. "You miss a
lot of fun rides that way."

"And a lot of heartache."

"Pain proves we're alive. Haven't you heard?"

Jessica's gaze was steady as she met her mother's
green eyes that were so like her own. "Once I start rid-
ing, I don't ever want to get off again."

"To hell with the brass ring, huh? You want the gold
one or nothing, forever and a day?" Her mother broke
eye contact to stare past Jessica's shoulder. "It doesn't
work that way, honey."

Hearing the bitterness in the other woman's voice,
Jessica wondered if Arletta had ever realized it was
watching the endless game of musical husbands she
played that made her daughter so determined not to repeat the pattern. She didn't want to wind up like
Arletta, alone at fifty-five, still trying to hang on to her
youth to attract the next man, still searching for something she had never found.

Her mother had been unlucky in a lot of ways.
Brought up without a mother's presence and by a father
with no time for her, she had been thrown headlong into
the sexual revolution of the sixties and seventies with
its emphasis on serial partners, experimentation with
drugs, and doing your own thing. Like so many others,
she had discarded the traditions and tenets of duty that
helped build enduring marriages. She had rushed from
one thrill to another, one relationship to the next, always grasping desperately after happiness and never
quite catching it.

Somewhere in that headlong searching, Arletta had
conceived and abandoned a child. She blamed her father for taking Jessica from her, but she could have spit
in her father's eye, taken her child, gone out, and made

it on her own. She hadn't even tried. And now she had to live with the consequences of decisions made at another time, when ideas and feelings had been different.

Jessica had seldom called Arletta mother. Arletta had never wanted it or, at least, never asked it. There had been a time when Jessica had longed for a cookie-baking, hugging mom, a bit plump, a little gray, like those of her friends. There had been times when she had needed someone to talk to, someone who would love her no matter what she did, someone she could always depend on to be on her side. That time was gone. Now she felt sorry sometimes for Arletta, even when she was most irritated with her.

"So," she said to lighten what had become a heavy conversation, "who is this new man of yours I hear about?"

Her mother laughed, a forced sound. "You wouldn't approve."

"Do I have to? It's your life." She frowned a little as she realized, suddenly, how odd it was that their roles were so reversed. Most daughters worried about their mother's approval, instead of the other way around.

"Tell that to your grandfather," Arletta said.

Jessica lifted a brow. "Surely he can't have a word to say against it?"

Arletta stared at her. "You mean because he married a woman young enough to be his daughter? But if you think that, then you must know—I wonder who told you."

"I forget," Jessica said easily. She didn't want Arletta taking Mimi Tess to task, particularly when the older woman would probably have forgotten all about it. "Besides, it's the in thing, these days, isn't it, taking up with a younger man. He'll live to grow old with you."

"What a revolting thought," Arletta said, and took another drag on her cigarette. But she left Jessica's question unanswered.

The sky grew steadily darker as the afternoon crept along. The hush that comes before the rain closed in around the house. Nick and Rafael returned from their explorations. Keil stood talking to them for a few minutes, apparently discussing the old Colonial-era mansion in Recife, or some such place, where Rafael had been born. Jessica's cousin left shortly thereafter, however, saying something about getting the *Sea Gull IV* ready for the wind storm predicted for later in the night. Arletta did not tarry, either; her excuse was the need to make it back to New Orleans before the rain began. Nick did not trouble to give a reason, but merely flicked a final salute before walking out of the house and getting into his truck.

Jessica half expected Rafael to follow the example of the others. She hoped that he would, since she wanted to talk to her grandfather alone. Instead he settled back in his chair, as if completely at home, and proceeded to charm Madeleine with descriptions of the beaches of Brazil and the international crowd that descended on them during the high season.

With little to contribute, Jessica sat listening while at the same time keeping an ear open for the summons she expected from her grandfather when he woke. Finally Cressida came out and motioned her inside. Rising without drawing attention to herself, she slipped away.

"Have they all gone?" Claude Frazier said in a hushed, conspiratorial tone from where he sat in his wheelchair near the bedroom window.

"Everyone except your guest. And Madeleine, of course, though she said something just now about driving to Lake Charles to catch a movie."

She closed the door behind her and threaded her way into the room. It was not unlike entering a minefield, since her grandfather insisted that anything he might possibly want, from his eyeglasses and water pitcher to his collection of magazines and newspapers and small home computer, must be kept on rolling tables within easy reach and plain sight.

"I asked Castelar to stay," he said now. "You'll be needing to talk to him in a minute."

"Will I? About what?" She came to a halt in front of him.

"He has something he wants to say to you." The words were offhand, maybe too offhand, before he went on. "Did you know it was Holliwell over at Gulfstream Air who was sniffing around at the bank, talking to Vic?"

"He came to see me, but he didn't indicate—"

"Why didn't you tell me?"

"There was no need, since I naturally had nothing to say to him."

"Do you think I'm senile?" her grandfather demanded, his face turning an alarming shade of crimson. "Or have you lost your mind? Of course I needed to know! Holliwell is a different kettle of fish from Castelar. He's tricky and he fights dirty, and he's been trying to undermine us ever since he set up shop. If I had guessed he was up to his old tricks—"

"I'm sorry, Grandpapa," she said, reaching out to take his hand and hold it between her own. "Please don't get so excited. It isn't worth it."

He took several deep breaths, staring at her while his chest rose and fell. After a moment he squeezed her fingers. "Yes, well, you weren't to know, I guess, since I never thought about warning you. Anyway, it doesn't matter. I've decided to accept Castelar's offer. That's provided you're agreeable."

Shock rippled over her. Not the least of it was the ease with which the decision had been announced.

"Providing I'm agreeable?" she said slowly. "It's your business, Grandpapa. You can do whatever you please with it."

"No, I can't," he said in testy contradiction as he released himself from her grasp. "I can't run the damned thing now, and I can't make that idiot Vic Gaddens see reason."

"But you will. You'll get better, it may just take awhile."

He gave her a straight look. "I don't think so. Anyway, it's time I slowed down, paid a little more attention to Madeleine. My concern now is you, and maybe saving something of what I've worked for all these years. That brings us to this proposal of Castelar's."

There was no point in arguing with him, since it would probably just make him mad. Thinking of Rafael's suggestion that she become his managing director, she said, "What kind of proposal?"

"Marriage."

Her brows snapped together. "What?"

"You heard me." He waited with his faded gaze resting in intent speculation upon her face.

"You must have misunderstood, Grandpapa. It's just the language of takeovers. Rafael mentioned a position at CMARC earlier in the week, but it was contingent on persuading you to accept his buyout bid." Anger simmered along her veins. She could not believe that arrogant Brazilian had dared mention the possibility to her grandfather after her warning. Even more unbelievable was the fact that the older man was apparently in favor of the proposition.

"For Christ's sake, Jessica, I know when a man is interested in a woman. And I understand when he wants her to share more than just one of his corporate offices!"

Her grandfather's exasperation, and the remote prospect that he could be right, affected her with dread. She forgot caution. With one hand on her hip, she said, "Well, I know when a man wants to marry me! Believe me, Rafael Castelar has not proposed."

"Of course not. Not yet. He had no idea how I might react until today."

"Are you saying he came here to ask your permission like some stupid Spanish grandee in a romance novel? It's ridiculous!"

"Portuguese grandee," her grandfather snapped. "And don't be a little fool. You don't need my permission or anybody else's. This is strictly business—"

Behind them, the door opened. "Excuse me," Rafael said in sardonic tones, "but I couldn't help overhearing. I believe, all things considered, that it will be best if I argue my own case."

The scowl on her grandfather's face smoothed out as he met the other man's level gaze. He gave an abrupt crack of laughter. "Could be you're right. Take my granddaughter away and talk to her before she decides to murder us both."

Jessica didn't like it. She didn't like it one little bit. Still, she could see no way of refusing without upsetting her grandfather. Back stiff, she led the way from the room, then moved ahead of Rafael down the stairs.

She chose the library for the confrontation. It was purest instinct; that room had been her refuge when things became too much as a child. It always had a calming effect that she badly needed now.

The books in the room were encased in glass-fronted antique cabinets, the furniture was rosewood with seats covered with brocade. Tables held collectibles both worthless and invaluable, from penknives of the kind used to trim writing nibs to porcelain souvenirs of the 1984 World's Fair in New Orleans, from wax flowers under bell jars to cigar boxes Jessica had covered with glued-on seashells. Heavy with the scents of old leather-bound books, dust, and furniture polish, it was a room crowded with memories.

The gathering storm made the room dim. Jessica switched on a lamp with a bronze pedestal and a Tiffany glass shade before she turned to face the Brazilian.

Only once before in her life had Jessica been more aware of a man or more embarrassed than now, and that was in Rio. She pushed the memory away as she concentrated on Rafael. He seemed to take up most of the available space and all of the air in the room. It was an effort to keep her breathing even and her voice steady as she hurried into speech.

"Before you say whatever is on your mind, I would like to clear up Grandpapa's mistake. He doesn't hear well at the best of times, but especially now that he's been ill. I suppose something said about my part in this proposed merger made him think that we—that you—"

Rafael stopped her floundering attempt to explain

with a quick gesture. Gaze concentrated and voice quiet, he said, "Your grandfather made no mistake."

She was still for the space of half a dozen heartbeats. They throbbed in her chest with suffocating force while she searched his face. There was nothing to be seen on its strong, sun-bronzed planes except quiet anticipation overlaid by assurance.

"You must be joking. You can't— People don't do that kind of thing these days."

"I have never been more serious."

"Impossible. But even if you were, why would Grandpapa consider it for a minute? What in the world did you say to him?" Comprehension dawned even as she spoke. "No, wait. It was you who told him about Holliwell, wasn't it? Do you realize you might have killed him?"

"I chose my words with the same care that I would use with my own grandparent," Rafael said grimly in return. "There was never a time when he was upset even half so much as when I walked in on the two of you just now."

"Oh, yes, I'm sure," she said with heavy irony. "Everything polite, businesslike, and perfectly normal. But I still don't understand why my grandfather went along for an instant. Or why he thought I might."

"He gave it his consideration because I told him you are the most beautiful woman I have ever seen. Because I said I would agree to anything he asked, do whatever it took, to make you mine."

A soundless laugh escaped her. "And he believed you?"

"I can be very persuasive when I care to be." He shoved his hands into his pockets as if afraid he might otherwise do something he would regret with them.

Some chord in the deep timbre of his voice sent a shiver along her spine. She ignored it. "It makes no difference. Nothing you can say will convince me a man like you would dream of marrying just to take over Sea Gull. It's a strong company, one with a long history of fair dealing, but it isn't that necessary to CMARC."

He watched her for long seconds, his eyes dark amber-gold with consideration. Finally he said, "There is another reason."

"Another angle?" Her distrust was plain in the quick question. "You've discovered that Louisiana is a community property state, have you? In that case, you've made a bad error. It's my mother who will inherit if anything happens to Grandpapa."

"Money or your mother has nothing whatever to do with it."

"What, then?" she demanded.

He made no reply, though his lips tightened, and there was the gleam of hard purpose in his eyes. Holding her clear green gaze, he removed his right hand from his pocket and stepped close enough to place something on the polished surface of the table beside her. It was a moment before he abruptly opened his fingers and took his hand away.

The small object rattled as he released it, rocking a little so that it caught the lamplight with the sudden flashing of fiery rainbows. A moment later it lay still, a tiny masterpiece in gold and diamonds.

It was something Jessica had not seen since that night in Rio—something she had missed, though she had another just like it in her jewelry box back at her apartment.

It was her lost earring.

Chapter Ten

▨ ▨ ▨ *Rage boiled up inside her with the tearing,* cleansing force of an erupting volcano. It burst into her mind with red heat. Without conscious thought or intent, she lashed out at the man in front of her with the flat of her hand in a hard, ringing blow.

His head snapped back with the impact. In the next instant he caught her wrist in a viselike grip, then jerked. She catapulted against the hard wall of his chest. An arm like a steel hawser closed around her, forcing her against his lean body from breasts to knees. Legs braced, he held her in close imprisonment while their heartbeats throbbed in an odd double rhythm between them, and her stomach muscles slowly contracted to leaden stiffness. In the sudden quiet, the boom of thunder could be heard, followed by the sweep and rattle of beginning rain.

His face was pale beneath his tan, so that the print of her hand made a red splotch over the hard muscle ridging his jaw. His eyes were golden and hot, and there was a grim set to his mouth.

"Do that again," he said with lethal softness, "and you may not enjoy the consequences."

She wasn't enjoying them now. She felt sick with her own fury and the sensation of her flesh striking that of another person. At the same time his body warmth and the scent of his aftershave surrounded her, bringing wild, half-forgotten sensations that made her head swim.

She knew him. Her every cell, every atom, every skin

pore, and every nerve ending recognized his touch and responded with mindless acceptance, instant invitation. Her lips tingled, her breasts grew round and full, and a sweet, piercing ache bloomed, incredibly, inside her.

How could she have ever thought that Keil or Nick, or yes, even Carlton Holliwell, might have been this man? The truth was she had not; she had only hoped. The knowledge of his identity had been held in some internal safekeeping, buried deep under terror and reeling disbelief, since the moment she had brushed against him in the limo on the way to Commander's Palace Restaurant.

She dragged air into her lungs, not a smart move since it pressed the tight points of her breasts into his chest. Past caring, she said in virulent sibilance, "Where are the pictures? Did you show them to Grandpapa?"

His face contorted, then she was flung away from him. She brushed against the table, almost overturning it, before she caught her balance and whirled to face him.

"You actually think I would do that?" he demanded.

"Why not?" She clenched her hands into fists as she stared at him. "I get trapped into a party that turns out to be an orgy. You show up conveniently in time to rescue me from some weirdo, and then you—and then . . ."

"Then we made love," he supplied in hard tones. "We. The two of us. Together. I did nothing you didn't permit, or desire."

"I was in over my head, and you knew it," she flashed back at him. "You expected it. That's why you were so quick to take advantage!"

"I was so quick to take advantage because—" Rafael stopped abruptly as he realized he had just convicted himself. And was in danger of compounding the error. His throat burned with the harshness of the breath he took before he made an attempt to rectify that mistake. "It was no coincidence that I was there, true enough. I went to your hotel to talk to you. You weren't in your room, but the doorman remembered the address your cousin gave when you took a taxi. I knew the house, knew the kind of party it might turn out to be, and suspected that you did not. I followed. The rest just—happened."

"So you're supposed to be a victim, too? Since you are a carefree bachelor and head your own company, I fail to see what you have to lose if you're caught in some sordid—"

"Don't!" he commanded with an abrupt, slicing gesture of one hand. "Don't make it something it was not. Tell me instead why you're so sure I'm not married."

Her eyes widened a bare instant at the implication that she had a personal interest, also with the memory of his fiancée who had died. A moment later it turned scathing. "It pays to know your enemy. Isn't that a tenet of war and business?"

"Then you should know that I value my standing in the international business community. More than that, I have personal and family standards that mean something to me."

"Yes, certainly," she jeered, her voice corrosive with pain and disbelief, "and this little episode would be so damaging to your macho ego, I suppose. Why can't I accept that—unless it's because I know too well that the whole point of that party, the whole point of machismo itself, is conquest of one kind or another? Unless it's because I know our every move was caught on film?"

"I realize somebody snapped a few shots," he said, grasping at feasibility, "but that has no bearing—"

She laughed, a brittle sound. "Try again."

He was silent while swift thoughts coalesced in his mind to form a conclusion. "Somebody contacted you."

"You could say so."

Still watching her face where rich red color rode her cheekbones, he said, "You've seen the pictures?"

"One. It was enough."

The rain splattered in on the floorboards of the front gallery beyond the library window. It waved in gray sheets beyond the wide overhang, carrying bits of old tree blossoms and fragile new leaves before it. The wet, muffling dimness closed around them to create a cocoon of soft light and intimacy.

"Show me." It was a bid for time while he tried to see a way to use what she was saying to further his own agenda.

"So you can gloat over it? No, thank you."

"I want only to see how damaging it might be, to discover what we are up against," he said, clinging to his temper with a determined effort. "But we can easily defuse any possible photographic time bomb if you will listen to reason. As an engaged pair, there would be nothing unusual about that kind of familiarity between us."

"Reason?" she said in bitter wonderment. "Tell me what's reasonable about it? Or am I to think you are doing this out of remorse? Well, I know better. You'll stop at nothing, not sleazy entrapment, not checking into our loan, not even marrying into Sea Gull. You know what that tells me? It says you must be pretty desperate. What I want to know is *why*?"

"I could tell you," he said, "but you wouldn't believe me."

"Probably not. Unless, of course, you want to admit to some kind of drug connection."

A short laugh of scorn left him. "The first thought to cross the North American mind when South America and money are mentioned in the same breath."

"With good reason!"

"Oh, yes, just as we have reason to think of money and the Mafia together in the States."

"It's not at all the same!" she said in sharp denial.

"Isn't it?" His hard gaze held hers. He was gratified when she looked away first. That sense of control was premature.

"It makes no difference what you want or why you want it," she said, facing him again with her chin raised in defiance. "You won't get it. I'll see to that, no matter what it takes. Before I let you have Sea Gull, I'll give it away to my very worst enemy. Or yours."

She was too late. He owned Sea Gull, or the nearest

thing to it. Still, he couldn't tell her that, not now. She was so proud, so gallant as she stood there, so full of fight and fire. She made his insides twist with longing and his brain feel as if it were baking in the too-small oven of his skull.

No, he would wait. He would contain himself because he did not want her humble when she came to him.

But she would come. He would see to that, one way or another.

"I take it this means you won't marry me," he said in tight control. "What will you tell your grandfather?"

"The truth," she retorted with a snap.

He tipped his head. "You aren't afraid that might be a bit too exciting?"

"I will say that—that we have nothing in common, that we are too different ever to be compatible."

"You'll lie, then. We have the shipping business in common. Also our dreams. And two people have seldom, if ever, been more sexually compatible in their lives."

"Sex," she said, the single word a scathing denouncement of everything that had passed between them in Rio.

"Don't overlook its importance. Chemistry and mutual benefit are a powerful combination. If you add the incentive of building something together, something strong and enduring, the two of us could count on far more than most couples can claim. Dynasties have been built on less."

"How romantic," she said with a bitter curl of her lips. "But what of trust and respect? Oh, yes, and love. Though I expect the last is something you know little about."

His gaze was trenchant with consideration. "You claim to know more? Is that the reason you haven't married already, the reason you won't consider a merger?"

"We will leave my private life out of this! The reason I won't consider anything more is because I despise your business tactics, I despise your behind-the-scenes maneuvering with my grandfather, but most of all, I despise you."

"Hate rather than love? What stirred it up, I wonder—unless it was some stronger feeling that you refuse to admit, some feeling you would like to deny. But while you're busy hating me, there is something you might like to keep in mind. If you're right and the pictures were no accident, then I was not supposed to be the man in them with you. There was someone else, someone I had to fight to keep from taking you down in the dark."

Her eyes widened, and her lips parted for a shallow breath of shock. An instant later she recovered. "He must have been just another guest, a man who followed me from inside."

"Was he? Are you sure, when he very nearly had you there in front of the glass doors of that courtyard, directly under the camera?"

She clamped her arms around her, holding tight as she swung away from him. "Get out," she said over her shoulder. "Get away from me and stay away."

The dim, watery light beyond the windows gleamed in her hair. It also showed him the slump of her shoulder and the tremors that shook her. Resolve shifted through him, settling in a hard knot in the center of his chest. "I'm going," he said in low tones, "but this isn't over, and that's a promise. It won't be over until one of us gives up or gives in. But you were right about one thing. Conquest could be the point. For me, it may well be the only point."

His footsteps were firm, even as he crossed the polished, random-width planks of the cypress floor. The door closed behind him. Jessica let out a shuddering sigh of relief.

Lies. It had to be all lies. Didn't it?

If it wasn't, it would mean that the most likely reason for the pictures was to remove her from her position at Sea Gull; that was only logical. The person to benefit most from her removal, then, must surely be a member of her own family.

No. She wouldn't even consider it.

She wouldn't.

Oh, God, and neither would she think of Rafael Castelar holding her in a courtyard in Rio, wouldn't remember the piercing wonder of his kiss or his touch. No.

What a fool she had been, what a blind, silly fool. Such a very easy conquest.

Easy, eager, ripe, and ready. What had she been thinking of? Or had she been thinking of anything at all? Had there been anything in her mind or body except a slow, burning hunger such as she had never known, never expected, and against which she had no defense?

Was Rafael right, was hate what she was using now to protect herself? And which did she hate most, him or only her own stupid weakness?

She had wanted him. Then and now. Minutes ago, while he held her against him and she had looked into the dark centers of his eyes, it would have taken very little—a kiss, a soft word of love—to have made her as weak and clinging as she had been that night. She should be grateful he had not seen it, grateful she had the strength to keep that much from him.

Why this man of all men? She had managed to go through her life until now with no more than a teenage crush or two. It had been years since anything in pants had the ability to so much as increase her heart rate, much less cause her to abandon all inhibition, all reason. What was it about him that could do that to her?

Chemistry, he had called it. Apparently he had felt it, too. That was some consolation.

She would control it. She didn't believe in overwhelming passion, didn't accept that desire could be so strong it was beyond resistance. Though she had succumbed in Rio, she knew that it had been a conscious decision made between one touch and another; that was what was so terrible about it. She had allowed her usual good sense to be overruled by rum and music, mystery and an unbridled attraction that she had thought would be completely transitory. She had permitted herself the indulgence of a secret coupling with a chance-met stranger, one she had expected to be without consequences, without regrets.

She should have known better. But it was not a misjudgment she should be expected to pay for the rest of her life.

There must be a way out. All she had to do was find it.

By the time Jessica drove back to New Orleans and her apartment, she was exhausted and it was well after dark. She was also less than happy with herself. She had not told her grandfather that she had refused Rafael. Instead they had discussed the situation, and she had said she was going to think about it. That was only putting off the inevitable, of course, but she had endured confrontations enough for one day. She was afraid that if forced to find explanations again so soon, she might make some slip that would open the door to precisely the revelations she was doing her best to keep hidden.

She had distracted her grandfather as best she could by talking about the possible drug problem aboard the crew boat, discussing their compliance with the safeguards against it. He had been against policing the crew members, as she knew he would be, but had seen the sense of avoiding a fine if at all possible. He had finally agreed to let her and Keil handle it.

There was a car blocking access to her regular parking space located at the rear of a shotgun house on Dumaine. She made a slow block while she sought another one, but nothing was open. Swearing under her breath, she swung over to the Chartres parking lot and left her Saturn there.

It was still raining, a cool, steady drizzle that could last all night. The sidewalks of the Quarter were wet and slick, and channels of trash-laden water made crossing the streets a hazard. Her big doorman's umbrella, the only kind practical for New Orleans downpours, kept her dry, but also blocked her vision as she held it to keep the blowing mist out of her face.

As she neared the great, tall door leading into the lower passageway to her upstairs apartment, she took out her key. Turning it in the lock, she pushed the door inward, then stepped into the darkness of the narrow hall with its staircase winding upward at the far end. She was closing her umbrella when she heard the scuff of a fast step. She swung her head in time to see the dark shape of a man looming up behind her. Then a hard shoulder jolted into her back, flinging her forward. She fell sprawling.

Her umbrella flew out of her hands. Her knee scraped gritty flagstones in sharp agony. The palms of her hands burned as she landed on them.

The man was upon her before she could move. He pushed her flat on her stomach and fell across her with his full weight. She cried out, a choked, gasping sound as the breath was driven from her lungs. Through a red haze of pain, she felt him grab her wrist and twist it behind her back with a cruel wrench that ground her shoulder in the socket. An instant later his weight shifted, and she was dragged over and flung on her back. The man clamped a knee across her thighs while his face hovered above her. His lips, wet and thick, came down to rub across her mouth.

Pain and revulsion flooded her in a sickening wave. She jerked her head up, and was fiercely glad as her forehead came in hard contact with a fleshy nose. Heaving with anguish bursting behind her eyes, she tried to throw the man off.

Impossible. Her pubic bone burned as his knee slammed into her, then he rolled, using his heavy body to force his leg between hers. Reaching down, he began to drag her skirt higher. The talons of his fingers left a burning trail as they raked the tender flesh of her thigh.

She gasped with the harsh sound of extremity. Jerking at her hand trapped between their bodies, she snatched it free. The umbrella was somewhere behind her head. She stretched, flailing this way and that as she searched for it. Touching a scalloped nylon edge, she caught it in a hard grasp. With a wrenching effort, she whipped her arm forward, bringing the awkward, flapping weapon with it.

Her attacker howled as a point caught him in the face. He made a hard swipe at the ballooning umbrella, catching it squarely and sending it tumbling. The backswing he directed downward with malevolent fury, straight at Jessica's face.

It never landed. Behind him, the door, standing half open, crashed against the wall. Dim light from the street slanted through the opening to show a man hurdling in a low flying tackle. He struck the man above Jessica, slamming him across the dirt-tracked flagstones. They grunted, wrestling, heaving this way and that. An arm rose and fell. The sodden thuds of blows made ugly echoes under the high, dark ceiling of the old hallway.

Jessica rolled, dragging herself out of the way, at the same time snatching up the umbrella from where it had clattered against the wall of the narrow corridor. She glanced back in time to see the second man make a hard, jabbing movement. A pent breath hissed, as if drawn through teeth set against sudden agony. The two struggling forms separated. One plunged away, staggering for the door. He lurched out into the street and vanished into the dark.

The other made an abortive lunge after him, then sank back with a hand to his face. Crouching against the wall, he sat still.

Seconds ticked past. The only sound was the soft gasping of breaths. Jessica pushed to her knees. She hovered a moment while she tried to conquer the trembling in her legs. Dragging herself upright then, she felt for the light switch near the door and clicked it on.

She didn't want to see, didn't want to know. Still, it would be cowardly not to look. Brushing her hair back from her face, she turned slowly to face the man who had come to her aid.

He sat on his heels with his back to the wall and his

chest rising and falling with his hard breathing. His dark hair was ruffled, falling onto his forehead. As he lowered his hand, he revealed raw red streaks that angled to cross one bloodshot eye. Still, a wry smile tugged at his well-formed lips as he tilted his head back to squint at her in the yellow light of the bare bulb overhead.

"This could become a habit," Rafael drawled. "But don't feel you have to reward me as before. Unless, of course, it's your—pleasure."

Chapter Eleven

▦ ▦ ▦ *Jessica refused to dignify his suggestion* with a reply. It had been a joke at her expense, that was all. At least she thought he was joking.

She wished that she could accuse him of sending the attacker for the express purpose of saving her from him, but that would not do. The fight had been too vicious, too real. Clearly, gratitude was in order, no matter how hard it might be to find the words.

By the same token, she could not put him out of the town house and slam the door behind him. Ordinary human compassion required some show of concern for his injuries.

"You had better come upstairs into the light where I can look at that eye," she said, her tone something less than gracious.

"No need. Pepe can see after me when I get back to the hotel." He put his hands against the floor and shoved to his feet, but immediately clapped a palm back over his eye socket as if the movement increased the pain.

"There's no reason to play the martyr," she said sharply. "I don't mind having you in my apartment, and I can certainly call a doctor for you."

"Maybe I mind." His answer was clipped before he hesitated. "On the other hand, you may need a witness for the police report."

She swung from him. Picking up her purse where she had dropped it, she retrieved her keys then closed the outer door and tried to lock it. It took three attempts to

156

complete that simple task; her fingers had a tendency to tremble and were without their usual dexterity. She wasn't really upset, however; in fact, she felt super calm, almost numb. Her brain seemed to be working with sharp-edged clarity.

Over her shoulder, she said, "I really don't see what the police can do. Unless you can describe the man, or identify him?"

"I'm afraid I was too far away at first. Anyway, I wasn't paying any attention until he pushed you inside—and afterward I had no time for taking notes."

She turned, her face impassive. "You just happened to be in the neighborhood, I suppose."

"You suppose wrong. I was waiting for you. We have some unfinished business."

"Do we now?"

"Concerning a picture, if you remember? I still intend to see it. I think I have that right."

The keys jangled in her hand as a sudden hard shudder shook her. She suppressed it as she stared at him for long, unblinking seconds. Finally she said, "I suppose that makes two reasons for coming inside, then. Can you manage the stairs?"

Swift consideration moved in his eyes before he gave a brief nod. "Lead the way."

She mounted the curving staircase with its mahogany railing polished to an oiled patina by countless hands through endless years. Inside the apartment, she turned on the chandelier in the small entrance, then left him standing in the living room while she went through the other rooms, flipping on light switches in every one until the last shadow of darkness had been banished. She dropped her purse on the sofa as she came back through, then moved into the bathroom where she found the first-aid kit and a wet bath cloth. As she returned to the living room with them, she indicated with a gesture that Rafael should be seated at the table in the dining alcove.

As he took the nearest chair, she put the kit on the table and stepped close. He spread his legs, guiding her between them with a hand on her arm, so she could reach him more easily. It also made it easier for him to reach her, she noticed, though she dismissed that as unimportant.

The scratches on his face had been caused by fingernails as the assailant clawed for Rafael's eyes. He swore softly as she cleaned and disinfected them, but did not flinch under her ministrations. The corner of his left eye and the outer edge of the ball had been grazed, leaving it bloodshot, but there was no apparent damage to the iris or pupil.

His eyes were even more of a rich amber brown than she had thought, while his lashes were black and thick. His left brow had a slight Mephisto's arch at the center that gave him a quizzical look even in repose. The pulse that beat in the strong brown column of his neck was firm and regular. Curling black hair at the base of his throat hinted at the soft mat that she knew decorated his chest. He was dangerously attractive, altogether too handsome for his own good. Or hers.

As she met his gaze once more, he spoke in low concern. "Who wants to hurt you, Jessica Meredith? Who would dare?"

The calm that surrounded her disintegrated as if he had shattered it with a hard blow. She stepped away from him in swift retreat. As she reached to put the top on the disinfectant, she knocked over the bottle so that the caustic brown liquid poured across the table. Suddenly she was shaking so hard her teeth chattered. Tears sprang into her eyes. She gasped, wrapping her arms around her ribs to keep herself from flying apart.

Rafael breathed a soft oath. Rising in a single, swift movement, he righted the disinfectant, then dropped the bath cloth over the spill to contain it. At the same time he caught her wrist to draw her against him. Closing her into the firm safety of his arms, he pressed her head against his shoulder while he smoothed her hair with gentle strokes.

"It's just the shock, that's all," he murmured against

her ear, "simple delayed reaction. Don't fight it, let it go. It will be all right."

But it wasn't. When the seconds passed and the shuddering that rippled over her did not ease, he let his grasp slacken. Tipping his head to look down at her, he said, "I can think of a tranquilizer with proven effectiveness, but I'm not sure you would appreciate it."

At her stabbing stare of reproof, he shook his head in mock disappointment. "I was afraid of that. The next best thing might be a warm bath, along with something hot to drink."

Turning her in the direction of the bathroom, he led her inside and turned on the hot water. "Let it run as hot as you can stand it and as deep as it will, then get in," he said. "I'm going to make *café diablo*. Unless you need help getting out of your clothes?"

She shook her head, a violent, shivering gesture, though she refused to look at him.

"Too bad." Shutting her inside, he went away.

The hot water helped. The hard shudders subsided, becoming an occasional spasmodic tremor. She was listening to the quiet from the other rooms, wondering if Rafael had left the apartment after all, thinking of getting out to see, when the door swung open.

"I'm not looking, I promise," he said in haste as he stepped inside. "But you need this before it gets cold."

His lashes were lowered, his gaze on the coffee cup he held in each hand. Still, she thought she caught the bright gold flick of his glance before he leaned to place her cup on the rim of the tub. He retreated at once to the doorway, where he nursed his own cup in both hands.

Jessica turned in the water, holding to the wall of the tub for concealment. It struck her as futile to try to hide from this man after everything they had done together, but she could not prevent the impulse. On the other hand, the haze of steam hovering above the water offered some protection, and she felt too drained to summon a proper maidenly outrage.

Not that it was necessary. For all the lascivious

interest Rafael displayed, it seemed he might well spend his waking hours communicating with naked women. She was not sure whether to be glad of his sangfroid or irritated by it.

The coffee was like that extolled by coffee lovers in the famous New Orleans epigram: "As pure as an angel, sweet as heaven, black as the devil, and hot as hell." The addition of copious amounts of rum made it the devil's own brew, but it worked. She drank it in small, reviving sips, feeling its intoxicating warmth spreading through her, relaxing muscles and unkinking nerves as it went. It was enough to make her feel almost normal.

It was also enough to put her on her guard.

Still, there was something she had not yet done, and she had too much of her grandfather in her to shirk it. "Thank you," she said quietly. "For this, and for the other—what you did downstairs."

"I am honored to have been of service," Rafael said in rote formality that seemed a cover for his discomfiture. He studied the reflective surface of his coffee an instant before he went on. "However, there is still the question of a motive for the attack. I could back off because of the disturbance it causes you, but the answer is of some importance."

"You want to know who has it in for me?"

He gave her a direct look. "It didn't have the look of a random mugging from where I stood."

"What else could it be? I don't have any enemies, haven't stepped on anybody's toes particularly. I haven't mortally offended anyone that I know of." She gave him a veiled look before she added, "Except you, possibly."

"Not mortally," he said with a grim smile.

She was relieved, which was ridiculous. She was also nervous with him standing over her. Drinking the last of her coffee, she reached to set the cup on the bath stool nearby, then gestured toward the towel rack. "Would you mind?"

He complied without comment, holding the fluffy rose-colored towel out to her at arm's length. She took it and waited expectantly. His smile was crooked as he turned his back.

She stood up hastily and wrapped the towel around her, half afraid he would find some reason to swing around again. The sudden movement, combined with leftover shock and the enervating effect of a soak in scalding water, made her light-headed. She swayed and grabbed for the shower curtain as her vision went dim.

She didn't make a sound; she would have sworn to it. Yet Rafael whirled and sprang to catch her with a quick arm about her waist. He lifted her, thrusting an arm under her knees as he swung her from the tub. A moment later she was standing on the mat beside him, held against the hard length of his body.

And it was quite hard in places. Mute evidence of his interest, his arousal was also proof that he was not nearly so relaxed, or sanguine, as he appeared.

The urge to push away from him, to assert herself by standing alone, reverberated in her head. The will to move was slow in coming. Before it arrived, he lowered his head and pressed his mouth to her warm, moist lips.

She was flushed with heat, dizzy with a strange mixture of gratitude and doubt, fear and pure attraction. In her veins also was a species of danger-inspired desire. Like a soldier suddenly discovering he has survived a battle, the need to affirm life with sex was a deep-seated ache.

His taste was sweet, his tongue in her mouth a tender yet fervid invasion. She lifted a hand to the back of his head and curled her fingers into the crisp waves of his hair even as she pressed her heated form against him. Lost, she was lost in promise and half-remembered ecstasy, drifting through mists of unimagined contradictions within herself as if they had no meaning. Nor did they, compared to the strength in the arms that held her, the subtle command of his mouth that gave her such pleasure, and took it from her.

The telephone shrilled. Jessica started with a swift-drawn breath. Recognition and self-blame were instant. Her eyes darkened, and she jerked away from the man who held her. Stumbling a little, ignoring his supporting hand, she dragged her towel closer around her and moved swiftly to pick up the receiver.

"Jessica, that you?" Her grandfather's voice came down the line with a strained, almost querulous sound. "Didn't mean to wake you."

"No, no," she said, trying to clear her throat of its misleading huskiness. "Is anything wrong?"

"I wanted to find out again where Madeleine said she was going. I thought you said a movie, but she's not back yet, and I was—well, you know."

She did. Too well. Her grandfather always worried until everyone in his household was inside and the doors locked. Still, she wasn't sure how to answer. The memory of her grandfather's young wife in the orchard with Keil burned in the forefront of her mind. To say where she might be found could help in case Madeleine was in trouble, but it could also be dangerous to her grandfather's health. While she thought about it, she walked into the bedroom with the handset of the portable phone and pulled a housecoat from her closet. Dropping the towel and skimming into the wrap, she said, "A movie is what she mentioned to me, all right."

"She didn't say where it was playing, or what time it would be over?"

"No, no details. I expect she'll be along soon." Jessica tried to keep her voice matter-of-fact, even as she wondered if her grandfather had some reason to suspect Madeleine was elsewhere. At the same time she felt her irritation with Madeleine rising. The other woman should have more consideration than to worry a sick man. Though it was possible, even probable, that she didn't care.

Her grandfather grunted in answer, a sound that could mean anything, including impatience with soothing remarks. After a curt good night, he hung up.

It was only as she heard the click of the receiver on the other end that Jessica's mind veered to a possible connection between Madeleine's absence and the attack on herself. Her brows were drawn together over her nose as she returned to the living room and replaced the phone's handset in its cradle.

Rafael turned from the window, where he had moved to stare out at the street. "There's a problem?"

He had been watching for her return in the reflective surface of the dark window glass, she realized. That was also how he had seen her as she nearly fell in the tub. The bathroom, an afterthought in the old building, faced the windows, and the door had been open. It was a relief to have one small mystery explained.

After a second she said, "Madeleine is missing. You don't suppose something has happened to her, too."

"You think that's possible?"

"I have no idea, but she hasn't stayed out this late before. Of course, I can't suggest to Grandpapa that someone might have followed her and attacked her without telling him what happened here. That would get him in an uproar for nothing if Madeleine is only running late."

"I wouldn't call it nothing." Rafael walked closer with his quick, athletic grace. Catching her arm, he brushed her housecoat sleeve back to expose the livid purple bruises beginning to stain her pale, blue-veined skin.

"Next to it," she insisted as she pulled her wrist from his grasp. "Anyway, he would insist on calling the police, and I don't know if I can face dealing with all that, especially when I have nothing concrete to tell them. But I can't help wondering about Madeleine, thinking what if—"

"You have no real idea where she was going or when she expected to be back, or so I gather from your side of the conversation just now?"

She shook her head. "And I'm not sure the lack of information wasn't deliberate."

"Then, do whatever you think is best for you."

He seemed to be encouraging her to bypass the police. Was that more paranoia, or only wishful thinking? She said tiredly, "All I really want to do is climb into bed and stay there." As he lifted a brow and opened his mouth, she added with more assertiveness than tact, "Alone."

A thin smile came and went on his face. "Which may be the best thing, if you're sure you don't mind."

"Being by myself?" She gave a quick shake of her head. "I'm used to it."

She waited expectantly for him to make some gesture toward taking himself from the apartment. When he did not, she hesitated, then reached for the purse that lay on the couch, fishing her keys from it. "I'll have to let you out downstairs."

He still made no move except to put his hands on his hips. As she turned back with a questioning lift of her brows, he said, "There was a picture you were going to show me, remember?"

She had managed to forget. On purpose. The last thing she wanted was for him to see her in orgasmic transport. It was too embarrassing, and could lead to ideas it would be hard to control.

"There's no need for you to be concerned," she said abruptly. "You aren't in it."

He lifted a brow. "Where am I, then, if this is supposed to be such a damning piece of evidence?"

"Oh, you're there somewhere. Just not central to the—that is, you aren't . . . in focus."

His lips twitched, though the look in his eyes was so intent it was difficult to say whether his basic tendency was amusement or annoyance. "If I'm not in focus, just what is? In fact, what is so interesting about this particular print?"

"Nothing. Nothing at all."

"Then you shouldn't mind if I see it." He glanced around with a speculative look, his gaze flickering from the antique glass-fronted cabinets on one wall to the Italian desk painted with a design of pansies on the drawer fronts. It centered on her purse.

"I don't mind, except—Oh, all right, I do mind. It's not exactly flattering, okay?" Her confused anger mounted as he reached for the purse, then set it aside after a cursory glance inside revealed nothing remotely like a photograph.

"I find that hard to believe, under the circumstances." His bloodshot glance was veiled, as he skimmed her flushed and moist face and tousled hair. Ranging around the room, he opened and closed a cabinet, then directed his attention toward the desk.

"It isn't exactly something I want to hang over the mantel for my future grandchildren," she snapped. "Anyway, I can't imagine why you need to see it. You were there, after all."

He paused in the act of pulling open a desk drawer. "Maybe I need a reminder."

"If you're in danger of forgetting, I certainly am not! It's with me day and night in exquisite and vivid detail."

An arrested expression appeared on his face. He turned his head to stare at her. "Vivid?"

"Intensely," she said, and closed her lips on the word with extra force.

He nodded, his gaze not quite focused. Almost to himself, he said, "That does it."

She swallowed, her gaze on the desk. "What?"

He made no answer. Opening the drawer, he scanned the contents. His face cleared, and he reached inside.

She stepped toward him in haste. As he brought out the brown envelope with the picture, she made a quick grab under his arm for possession. "Don't! Give it back—"

He warded her off with a twist of his body and a raised elbow as he slipped the photo out. His gaze fastened on it. He stiffened to absolute stillness, even ceased to breathe for endless seconds.

Then he spoke, the words soft, liquid, indecipherable, seemingly endless. Portuguese, no doubt, they had the sound of a fervent imprecation, or a prayer.

A small moan caught in her throat, and she spun away from him. Thrusting her fingers through her hair, she clasped the back of her neck while she squeezed her eyes shut. The words strained, she said, "I hope you're satisfied!"

"Never. Not in this life."

The quiet answer brought her around. "What do you mean?"

"I'll never be satisfied until I see that look on your face again." The words carried the low emphasis of a vow.

With a lift of her chin, she said, "It's not going to happen."

"We'll see." His smile was brief before he dropped the photo onto the surface of the desk. Moving to the dining table, he picked up his discarded sport coat and slung it over his shoulder. He walked to the door and pulled it open, then stood waiting.

She didn't want to go anywhere near him, didn't want to look at him. But if she wanted him gone, she had to see him out.

Gaze shuttered, knees not quite steady, she walked forward, brushing past him to reach the staircase. Her awareness of him, of his gaze on her back and hips, was acute as she went down the spiraling steps and long corridor. She used the keys and pulled the heavy door open. He stepped through into the rain-misted night, then turned to probe her features with his intent golden gaze.

He hesitated before he spoke, as if unsure of what he meant to say. "If any more pictures turn up—"

"Yes?" she said tightly as he paused. "You want a private viewing?"

The sensuous lines of his mouth tightened. "It's possible they could be traced, though the contact paper and envelope seem fairly generic."

"Forget it. This isn't your problem."

"Oh, I think it is. The good name of my wife is a matter of supreme importance to me."

"I am not your wife," she declared in hot tones.

"But you will be." Swinging around on the heel of his handmade Italian leather shoe, he walked away into the darkness.

* * *

Jessica had felt safe until the moment she closed the town house door behind Rafael. With him gone everything was far too quiet. She began to think how easy it would be to pick the lock downstairs and force her door, or even to climb up to the ancient second-floor windows with their loose frames and faulty catches. Whoever had been waiting for her before could still be hanging around. If he had seen Rafael leave, he might return.

The man must have been watching for her; it was too much of a coincidence that she should have been selected by chance. Yet what reason could there be for the attack? What would anyone gain by harming her?

There was Sea Gull, of course. She clenched her teeth as she considered that someone might want her permanently out of the way. Yet there was no logic in it even if it were true, not with her grandfather threatening to turn the whole thing over to CMARC. Not that many people knew that, of course.

Driven by nerves and a heavy dose of caffeine, Jessica began to put the apartment to rights. She ran a sink of hot, soapy dishwater and washed the coffeepot and the cups. Putting the first-aid kit away, she cleaned the remains of spilled disinfectant from the tabletop and polished the wood surface with lemon oil to restore the luster. She tossed the towel she had used in the dirty-clothes hamper, then rinsed out the bathtub and fluffed the bath mat before draping it over the tub's rim to dry.

She hardly knew what she was doing, for the thoughts and images that clamored in her head. Foremost among them was that night in Rio.

If it was Rafael who had made love to her, then it was he who had prevented that other man from forcing himself on her, just as he had kept her from being hurt tonight. Who was that other man?

She had thought all this time he must have been the rather coarse-looking Brazilian with the turkey mask she had noticed earlier at the party. It seemed reasonable that he had singled her out for his attention because he had known what was about to take place. Of course, he could as easily have intruded on something already arranged, so that Rafael was forced to fight him off in order to keep her to himself.

But if Rafael had been caught accidentally in the arrangement, as he claimed, then so many things were changed. She would have to accept that he was attracted to her, that he must have followed her out of concern for her well-being, since he had no other reason to be there. In that case his proposals, both of a merger and of a marriage, might have to be reevaluated.

She wanted to believe him; that was what bothered her the most. A part of it was a natural reluctance to accept that she could be the target of such a vile maneuver, but there was something more in the equation that she did not care to examine too closely.

Not that she intended to marry the man by any means. There was a very good possibility that, guessing the kind of party she was attending, he had fully intended to take advantage of the moment when the lights went out. With that scenario, his anger and intense interest in the photos could well be real.

Yet some things about that night in Rio were clear. It was definitely a setup. She was supposed to have been at that party, supposed to have been accosted by a man, supposed to have been caught with him on film. Whoever the photographer had been, he must have known who she was and been able to recognize her on sight. He could have been hired for his role, but it was more likely that he was someone she knew, someone who meant to use what he got against her. Though he had been prevented from carrying out his first plan, it made no difference. For his purpose, the man caught with her could be anybody. He might even have special use for the fact that it was Rafael.

The trend of her thoughts was not likely to help her sleep. In the effort to control them and settle her mind, she switched deliberately to her worry about Madeleine. She considered calling Keil. He might still be at the boat, but there was a cellular phone hookup there. Asking if he knew where Madeleine was might look a little obvious, of course, and annoying if there was nothing between the two of them. Besides, what would she say if Madeleine was with him?

No, it would be best if she checked with her grandfather. If he hadn't heard anything, then she could decide what to do.

The truant herself answered the phone. Madeleine's amusement for Jessica's concern came through loud and clear. The movie had run long, she said, and she had to agree with the critics, but, hey, you couldn't go wrong watching Tom Cruise, could you? As Jessica hung up, she felt she had overreacted in more ways than one, and was relieved on both counts.

She went to bed finally, but still could not sleep. Haunted by unanswered questions, tortured by doubts that she could hardly acknowledge, much less face, she tossed and turned.

The truth came to her at last sometime near dawn. She was afraid.

She was afraid that she had been alone in the whirlwind of desire and fulfillment she had known in Rio, afraid her emotions and her body had been used while the man who held her felt nothing. The thought that he had taken her in cold blood made her feel desolate and lonely inside, and somehow diminished as an individual. Worse still, was the fear that she was still vulnerable to his touch.

Would he attempt to use her weakness against her? Was that what he was doing already with his proposal to her grandfather? Did he think she would fall into his arms in mindless agreement for the sake of a fancy position and nights of stupendous sex?

He was underestimating her. She was not at the mercy of her hormones, and she would not be bamboozled by a show of macho protective instincts, as much as she might appreciate it. She would fight whatever he had planned tooth and nail.

And he had better be very careful. She might not know him well, but neither did he know her.

Chapter Twelve

⧈ ⧈ ⧈ *Keil was late coming in to the office on the* following morning, and looked as if he had partied until all hours the night before. Appearances were deceiving, as he was quick to inform her. He had been forced to take a crew boat out into the gulf on a fast run to deliver a piece of heavy machinery to a rig. Though he had called around all over town, he couldn't scare up another captain to take the job, not even Nick. On the return trip, he had run into a squall that slowed him down so that it was three in the morning before he got to bed.

She and her cousin were nursing their usual coffee cups and having their regular Monday-morning organizational meeting. As they ran down the lists of boats leased, rented, or requested, Jessica noticed the neat stack of her mail that Sophie had opened and left on a corner of the desk. While she listened to Keil, she pulled the pile toward her and began to sift through it.

She discarded an office supply company flier, an offer for an additional corporate credit card, two magazine subscription mailings, and a group insurance offer. As she picked up a letter from Crescent National Bank, she felt an instinctive tightening in her solar plexus.

The information it contained was brief and to the point. The twelve-million-dollar loan outstanding with Crescent National had been transferred. It was now assigned to a Brazilian bank acting for Companhia Maritima Castelar, Inc.

The blood drained from Jessica's face to congeal in a

cold weight in her chest. She ran her gaze over the words twice, then a third time, as if they might change their meaning if she looked at them long enough.

"What is it?" Keil said, an alert light in his blue eyes.

Wordlessly she handed the single page of expensive letterhead across to him.

He skimmed it, beginning to curse with fluency and feeling before he reached halfway down the page. "Why in hell didn't Gaddens let us know before this was finalized?"

"I suppose he thought we'd had our chance."

"He never indicated it was so close to being a done deal that I know of. And he's going to hear about it, I guarantee. When I think of all the years we've done business with him—"

"He thought the loan was in danger," she said as she ran her fingers through her hair with a tired gesture, then propped her head on her hand. "Because of me."

"And me," Keil reminded her in grim tones. "I don't look any too stable, I know, but how was I to guess I would need a buttoned-down image and a bank balance?"

"I'm not sure anything would have helped. Rafael Castelar had the advantage, and he used it."

A small silence settled between them. Jessica glanced at the orchids on her desk, pale yellow ones today, fragile, airy blooms with red-speckled throats. The urge to grab the vase and throw it against the wall was so strong it was a hot pressure in her brain.

Keil sighed and shook his head after a moment. "So," he said, "I guess that's it."

"It seems to be." Her voice was dull.

"It'll be funny, not coming in to work."

"You may be offered a position."

His face flushed. "As if I would take it!"

"Only you can decide that. But CMARC is a big company. You might think about it before you turn anything down."

Keil watched his cousin, noting the too-bright, almost-fevered look in her eyes, the telltale shading of color under her creamy skin. There was something going on with her and Castelar, he was sure of it. Whether it was anything he should be concerned about was another question.

Jessica had always played fair. She was also a beautiful woman; as a connoisseur in that department he had a nice appreciation for her finer points. Attractive females in executive positions sometimes had problems other people didn't, since it was hard to forget what they looked like and do business with them on their merits. They also had advantages. With Jessica, the advantages had often worked to his benefit, but it might not always be that way.

The words tentative, he said, "You sound as if it's not a new idea."

"Rafael mentioned a possible position, though in the context of a direct buyout bid instead of this underhanded kind of takeover."

She called the guy Rafael. Keil filed that away under the heading of Interesting Information. "A position for you, I imagine," he said. "Not for me."

"It would be foolish of CMARC not to make use of your experience and ability." Her gaze was direct even if her smile was wan.

"That's what I like about you, cuz," he said with real affection. "Nothing much throws you. On top of that, you're such a great judge of men."

The light in her face went out as if he had hit a supersensitive switch. Watching it fade, he wondered, but decided to keep his curiosity to himself. Throwing up his hands, he said, "What now? Do we clean out our desks and hand over the keys?"

She gave him a grim look. "We aren't done yet. Before CMARC can take over, they have to put us into bankruptcy and have the judge appoint their officers to our board of directors so they can oust us. That, or cut a deal."

"Like arranging what's laughingly known as a 'voluntary' merger?"

"I suppose that's the best we can hope for at this point."

"And you would accept that?" Doubt threaded his voice.

"I don't know what else—"

She stopped as an arrested, almost smoky look rose in her green eyes. Her lips parted on a sudden, sharp breath.

He frowned. "What's going on in that wicked little mind of yours? What are you thinking of doing?" As she didn't answer, a warning note crept into his voice. "Jessica?"

"I don't know yet," she said, focusing on him after a moment, then glancing away again almost immediately. "I'll have to think about it."

His internal alarm bells were jangling a warning. "You won't do anything foolish, like taking out after Castelar with your trusty pistol?"

"Now, there's an idea. But I don't have a pistol, so I suppose that's out."

"Why am I not relieved? No, really, Jessica, what do you intend to do?"

She stood up, her movements suddenly brisk. "You'll be the first to know when I figure it out. In the meantime I hate to throw you out of my office, but I have things to do."

Jessica closed the door behind her cousin, then stood leaning with one shoulder against it. She felt sick, and was not sure whether it was caused by disgust, terror, or excitement.

She was going to change her mind. It was a woman's prerogative, wasn't it?

But she had to hurry. She had only a few hours, a day or two at most, to act. After that, it would look like desperation. Or else pure self-preservation.

Actually it was both and neither. It was mainly revenge, a way to get back what she had lost. That, and saving something for her grandfather. She could not think what this might do to Claude Frazier otherwise.

At least he had already approved this step—urged it,

in fact. She could almost believe that he had known it would be necessary, which was the reason he had been so insistent. She wouldn't put it past him.

Could she really go through with it?

She wasn't sure.

The Brazilian was a business adversary, a sensual trickster, a sworn enemy who had taken advantage of her. He must have known on Sunday that she would be forced to reconsider his offer; business arrangements such as buying in the loan took some time; therefore the deal had to have been final even then. He could have told her, but that would have been too easy. He had wanted to force her to back down, make her come to him. He had as good as told her it was going to happen before he left her.

She was not going to do that—she just couldn't. Nothing was worth it.

There was, of course, another explanation. He might have preferred that they reach an understanding without the use of pressure. Possibly he had felt an amicable marriage arrangement would be more comfortable, not to mention insuring a better business relationship.

She could wait to see if he really would use the loan now to force the issue. But what if he didn't, what if he accepted her answer as final and forced Sea Gull into bankruptcy? Her grandfather would never survive it. It was a risk she couldn't take.

No, she had to go on the offensive. She needed to make Rafael Castelar repeat his proposal so she could accept it. She would manage it if it was the last thing she did.

The boat sat on its shining platinum reflection, dipping lazily with the wash of the waves that danced around the marina dock pilings. Blindingly white except for sea blue striping at the helm, its chrome rails were polished to a silver gleam and its picture windows had the glitter of cut diamonds. The *Sea Gull IV*, with its raked hull and seagoing air, qualified as a yacht, but Claude Frazier had no use for such titles. It was just a houseboat to him. That was when he wasn't referring to it as *the tub*.

It had been some time since he had taken the boat out, well before his stroke in fact. Madeleine didn't care for the water, not even the relative calm of an inland sea like Lake Pontchartrain.

Over the years, Jessica's grandfather had worn out three other cruisers, spending several afternoons a week and most Saturdays on them. As Nick and Keil and Jessica had reached their teens, he had taught them all to pilot the sleek crafts. He was a surprisingly good teacher, though with zero tolerance for inattention or horseplay of any kind. When he felt they were competent, he went out with one or all of them time and again. Sitting on the bow deck squinting into the sun and drinking beer, he left them alone while they learned to love boating by cruising the Intracoastal Canal and its connecting rivers from one end to the other.

Looking back, Jessica thought the water had begun to lose its attraction for Claude Frazier about the time she and Keil became too involved with hard work and their own lives to go out with him anymore. She sometimes wondered, too, if he hadn't made the decision to marry again about that same time.

A younger wife eased the loneliness he would not admit and made him less aware of his years, no doubt, but there was more to it than that. Marrying Madeleine had been a last-ditch effort for a son and heir; Arletta was right about that much. Like some old patriarch looking around and seeing what he had built, he had felt the urge to perpetuate it. That the plan hadn't worked was not, it seemed fairly certain, Claude Frazier's fault.

The decision to take Rafael Castelar out on the *Sea Gull IV* was either a masterstroke or sheer lunacy, and Jessica had yet to decide which. She had wanted neutral ground, somewhere to be with him besides her town house apartment, his hotel, or, heaven forbid, her office. In the back of her mind had been a vague idea a few hours on the water might help them relax and become used to each other's company. She would then have some basis for pretending to have second thoughts about his proposal. The problem was that there was no place to go to get away from him if things didn't turn out according to plan.

The boat appeared to be in fine shape, washed down, polished, and ready to go. She had asked Sophie to call the marina first thing that morning to have the boat cleaned and serviced and the tanks filled with gas. Basic amenities were always left on board, including a stocked liquor cabinet above the wet bar. All that was required was fresh food and comfortable clothes, and these she had brought with her.

It was a beautiful day. The sunlight was a pale crystalline gold, while the pellucid blue sky was frosted around the lower edge with a meringue of clouds. The wind off the water carried the fresh smell of the not-too-distant gulf overlaid by the rich green fecundity of spring. Jessica closed her eyes and lifted her face to the sun's warmth while turning her head from side to side in an attempt to ease the knots of tension in her neck. With a grand day like this, everything had to go right. She refused to consider anything else.

Rafael would be here any moment, and she still needed to set the table for lunch and change out of her suit. There was no time for simple pleasure. It sometimes seemed there had been none in years.

A short time later, the crawfish dip was heating in the small Crock-Pot; the fried oyster poor boy sandwiches were arranged on plates with potato salad, pickles, and olives; wine was chilling; and the mellow sound of Kenny G. was playing on the tape deck. Her business outfit had been replaced by a more feminine scooped-neck dress of apricot gauze, and she had exchanged her heels for rubber-soled espadrilles.

She was ready. But there was no sign of Rafael.

He had sounded distant on the phone and not particularly anxious to see her. She had given him no reason for this informal meeting, no notion of its importance. His lateness, she assured herself, was probably just a Brazilian disregard for the constraints of time.

In a way she had been surprised to find him still at the hotel. He had other interests and obligations back home, some of which could well be pressing by now. Telephones and fax machines made long-distance transactions easier than in the past, but the physical presence of the person in charge was still mandatory for some things.

The legal arrangements involved in putting Sea Gull Transport into bankruptcy could be the reason he was lingering. As he had not tried to contact her since Sunday evening, she could not flatter herself that his purpose was personal. Apparently he had accepted her refusal of his offer, regrouped his forces, and gone on from there. Which left her wondering just how serious his bid to consolidate their operations by marriage had been, anyway.

She would find out. If he kept his appointment.

An appointment to propose to a man. How had she come to this? It was incredible. It was also necessary.

He was a half hour late. She should eat something, but she couldn't; her stomach was bunched up like a fist. A little wine might help. There was such a tremor in her hands, however, that she almost knocked over her glass as she poured a small amount of the Alsatian Riesling. Feeling both hot and cold at the same time, she took her wine out on the deck and stood at the rail on the port side, staring past the clutter of boats to the wide expanse of the lake that was yellow-brown with spring runoff.

Maybe he wasn't coming. Maybe she should take that as a sign that what she was doing was wrong. But if he did come, then was she to take it as a sign it was right?

One moment she was alone, the next she was not. There was no sound, no alteration in the steady movement of the boat; still, she knew with certain instinct that Rafael was there. She swung to see him leaning with one shoulder against the bulkhead. His hands were in his pockets, and there was careful assessment in his eyes.

It was startling to see him in casual wear. At the

same time there was an indefinable grace about him in his jeans, T-shirt, and sneakers. It was as if the plain white cotton knit had been tailored to his deep chest and narrow waist, the sneakers crafted for his feet. His jeans, though faded nearly white at the knees, pockets, and in an interesting elongated spot near the zipper, had been starched and ironed with a distinct crease down each long leg.

He had such vivid presence, almost as though the life force inside him beat more strongly than in most. She fought its magnetic pull as she studied him. He seemed to have recovered from his fight at her town house. The gouged scratches across one corner of his eye had healed so they were barely visible against his olive-bronze skin.

His eyes were hooded, however, and his face impassive. He looked different: more relaxed but less open, more natural but less congenial. The changes were disturbing.

Still, it was possible the greatest difference was in herself. Before, she had been on the defensive, intent on self-protection. Now she wanted something from him, and must study his mood and disposition for the best approach to getting it. Not to mention being cordial while she went about it.

Trying the effect of a smile, she said, "Are you hungry? We can take the boat out for a run, drop anchor somewhere with a nice view. Once we get there, I'll zap the sandwiches in the microwave and we can eat."

"Shall I cast off, or will you?" he said.

"You, if you don't mind. I'll take the wheel."

Rafael weighed her answer and the intention behind it. Most women he knew would have considered his question the mere politeness he had meant it to be and instantly surrendered the wheel in favor of the less responsible job of first mate. He should have known Jessica Meredith would give up nothing without a fight.

Regardless, she was up to something; he would bet a year of CMARC profit on it. In its pursuit he was to be fed, plied with wine, and softened up by an afternoon in

her company. He couldn't wait to see what she tried
when those time-honored ploys failed.

He didn't feel agreeable. Or lenient. Or helpful in
anything other than a practical, physical fashion. Whatever she wanted of him, she was going to have to come
right out and ask. He was tired of having his every effort toward compromise and accommodation thrown
back in his face, tired of being accused of taking advantage of her. If what she had in mind was reasonable,
then he would decide if it was worth his while to cooperate.

In the meantime it was a real pleasure to know that
she had come to him, that whatever it was about him
that disturbed her could be overcome for the right reason. He thought he might learn to enjoy being courted,
smiled at, treated like a decent human being instead of
as a monster. It was a little like taming a wild creature,
he thought. Suffer enough scratches and bites, and
eventually it would accept your presence. Be patient,
and it might allow a touch. Press a little, and one fine
day it would eat out of your hand.

Lunch was served up as they bobbed at anchor near
the western end of the lake, well away from the causeway and ship channel. It was not exactly a gourmet
meal. Rafael thought the sandwiches would have been
better if he had been on time for the meeting instead of
demonstrating how little inclined he was to jump when
she called. The rest of the food was good in a simple
fashion, but since it had clearly been bought rather than
made with her own hands, there was no need for excessive compliments. That suited him perfectly, as he had
none to offer.

The conversation between them was easier than
might have been expected; he had to give her credit for
that. She accomplished it by asking questions about his
work, where he lived, his family, its history, and his
opinions on soccer, Pelé, and more recent business
shifts in Brazil. It was comical, in a way, her use of
such an ancient tactic of male seduction. Not quite so

funny was how much he enjoyed it, and how difficult it was not to respond more warmly.

He also liked watching her, the way she smiled, her habit of tucking her hair behind her ear in order to have a clearer view of his face, the open warmth of her smile when he exerted himself to make her laugh. He could spend years studying the lines of her face with its lovely symmetry that came from fine bone structure. Her mouth fascinated him, the sweetness and generosity and subtle hint of passion in its delectable curves. He liked the dress she had on, one that flowed around her in soft swirls, conforming to her curves, reflecting just enough color to give her skin a delightful apricot glow that made his mouth water with the thought of tasting it. He wondered if she realized the last, but had some hope that he kept it concealed.

The day, though bright and clear, was still a little too cool for swimming or even sunning. Leaving the dishes on the table next to the lower-level galley, they moved to the sofa on the upper level, near the inside steering bridge. Upholstered in blue and cream, it was deeply comfortable, and had a view of the water through a wide, sliding-glass door.

"Do you have brothers or sisters?" she said as she sat with one foot curled under her, holding a glass of wine that she had barely tasted.

"One of each," he said. "My brother is younger. He's the saint in the family, a doctor with a practice in Rio who donates his evenings to unpaid work in the barrios. My older sister is married to a planter and is very traditional and extremely maternal—she has six children so far."

"Six," Jessica echoed with a rueful look in her eyes.

"Four nephews, two nieces."

She stared at him a long moment. "You sound almost—envious."

"Maybe because I am." He had never considered it in that light, but it was undoubtedly true.

"You like children, then?"

He smiled, thinking of wriggling bodies and tiny,

reaching hands, sweet-smelling little girls with ribbons in their hair and solemn young boys biting their lips over the serious business of kicking a soccer ball across a green lawn. "Who doesn't?"

"A lot of people," she answered with some tartness.

"You included." The words were cooler than he intended.

"Yes—no. What I mean is, I don't know. I've never been around them much. I think I would like them, but I can't be sure."

A sudden theory sprang into his mind. It seemed unlikely, but he decided to test it anyway. "How many would you consider the perfect family?"

"Two at least," she said, not quite meeting his gaze. "I don't think any child should be brought up alone."

"As you were."

She gave a slow nod. "I suppose."

"We enjoy large families in Brazil," he said, his gaze watchful. "Children there are a bit spoiled by some standards. Everybody loves them, plays with them, watches them, and pets them. They can do no wrong until they are old enough to fully understand spoken language. At that time the process of discipline begins, but in the meantime a happy child has been created, one who seldom cries and has the confidence to try any and everything."

A smile curved her lips as she gave him her close attention. There was a soft light in the depths of her eyes. Seeing these things, he felt his heartbeat accelerate in his chest.

Suddenly he knew exactly what she wanted from him. Also exactly what his answer was going to be.

Chapter Thirteen

⊞ ⊞ ⊞ *The man was infuriating, Jessica thought* as she stared at Rafael a long hour later. He smiled, he talked, he was entertaining, but he remained deaf to her hints that she might be willing to reopen the subject of marriage. Nothing she said served to remind him that he had recently sworn to have her as his wife. Each time she turned the conversation in that direction, he diverted it.

He was not stupid, she knew that very well. That meant he either did not want to talk of marriage—or else saw what she intended and meant to make it as difficult as possible.

The urge to chuck it all and let matters take their course was so strong she could taste it. But she couldn't quit now; too much depended on her. Besides, it wasn't really in her nature.

If Rafael was going to be deliberately obtuse, perhaps it was time for a direct approach. She turned to set her wineglass on an end table before swinging back to face him. "You must wonder why I invited you out on the lake this afternoon."

Wry humor flashed in his eyes. "You mean it isn't simple hospitality? I'm amazed."

"I'm sure," she said tartly. "No—"

"Do you smell gas?" Rafael said in sudden interruption, frowning as he tested the air with a deep whiff.

Jessica copied his action. "Not really—at least no more than usual when the generator has been running while at anchor—and I turned it on for a minute to power the microwave oven."

"I suppose that's it," he said, relaxing again. "So where were we? Oh, yes, you were about to tell me, I think, that you know I've assumed Sea Gull's loan."

"I—something like that." She was so startled by the sudden transfer of initiative that she allowed herself to be distracted from her purpose again.

Rafael shifted into a more comfortable position on the sofa and stretched his long legs out before him. "The opportunity was there, and it would have been criminal to let it pass. So I didn't. But you knew that."

"I discovered it. When were you going to tell me, I wonder? Maybe after our supposed wedding?"

"You think it would have been more in character to spring it on you on Sunday, when I could have held it over your head as a threat? What gives you the idea I have any use for a reluctant bride?"

"Oh, excuse me," she said with brightly false affability. "I didn't realize a marriage tied to a business merger was the same as a love match to you."

"It isn't." His tone was as short as the words. "But I see no reason passion and practicality shouldn't be combined."

"Love and passion are not the same thing."

The look he gave her smoldered, or so she thought, before his lashes flickered down to erase it. "I'm aware."

"Then you can see why I was too surprised to even consider the kind of arrangement you offered."

He lifted a shoulder and let it fall. "No duress was intended, as I think I've made plain. You were free to decline, you did, and that's the end of it."

"Yes." He made it sound so final, still there must be a way to revive the discussion. She said, "If it was so simple, then why talk to my grandfather behind my back? Why didn't you mention the idea the night I came to your suite at the hotel?"

"The possibility had not arisen at the time," he said flatly.

"And just when did—" She stopped as an idea hit her with stunning force. Moistening her lips, she said in strangled tones, "You don't mean that . . . it was my grandfather's idea?"

"I didn't object, if you will remember." The comment was as deliberate as the dark gaze he turned on her. "In fact, I can truthfully say the idea occurred to both of us at the same time."

Jessica sank back into the corner of the sofa. "I know he thinks I'm on the verge of being an old maid, but I can't imagine what made him think it would work, with you of all people." Her eyes widened as she stared at him. "Unless—unless you told him about Rio. You didn't. You couldn't."

"Not precisely, no," Rafael answered with a judicious twist of his lips.

"And just what do you mean by that?"

"Without going into details, I allowed him to understand that ours was no longer strictly a business relationship."

"Good grief," she said in blank amazement. "I would love to know how you pulled that off without getting shot!"

"It required considerable tact, I will grant you that. But it seemed best to introduce the idea in case our friend with the camera ever surfaced. I didn't know at the time, you see, that he had already made contact with you."

Her hand, which rested on her knee, doubled into a fist. "No doubt your motives were as pure as spring water. I expect you wanted to protect me."

"There was that," he agreed, ignoring the sharp irony of her suggestion. "More to the point, I had been placed in a compromising position and I didn't like it. It seemed wise to test the likelihood of these pictures turning up in the middle of a bankruptcy hearing."

She watched him an instant before her brows snapped together over her nose. "Are you saying you thought Grandpapa or I might have set you up?"

"Or your cousin Keil, since he was also present. Stranger things have happened."

"That's crazy! There was no way either of us could have guessed you would be there that night, no way we could have known what kind of party it was or what would happen."

"You may not have known. With the others it's not quite so certain. But knowledge of my movements or the situation would not have been necessary to involve me. It wouldn't be the first time I was followed by a man with a camera—as I think you realize."

She did, unfortunately, since she had made a point of looking at the personal file on him in her grandfather's desk. There had been several photographs taken of him in various places, with various people. Much of the information read as if it had been gathered by an information agency. If a private detective had been following him, then it was possible the man had snatched at the chance to film what was undoubtedly a compromising encounter. Such people weren't known for their scruples.

She looked away, her gaze blind with the tumbling of her thoughts. "I didn't order an investigation, didn't know there had been one until after that night."

"Victims together, as you said once before."

There was a trace of sardonic humor in his voice. Hearing it, she turned back to him. "You don't believe me? But in that case, why would you consider going along with my grandfather's suggestion for even a second? In spite of what you said before, there's no real shame for you in what happened."

"But there is for you," he suggested without inflection.

She gave a small shake of her head. "I don't know what came over me that night."

"Nor do I," he drawled, "but I would like to find out. Which is one reason I didn't object, and even cooperated with enthusiasm. For the rest, the idea had certain merits. I went to the Landing to see if your grandfather would agree to my terms, which included working with you. I achieved what I wanted and more. Besides, I was curious."

"Curious?"

"To see how far you would go."

"Even though you suspected I was trying to trap you?" She waited with odd anxiety for his answer.

"The compensations," he said softly, "promised to make it worthwhile."

"Gaining control of Sea Gull without a court fight, yes, I see."

Exasperation rose in his amber eyes. "That wasn't at all what I meant, and you know it."

She had guessed, but that wasn't the same thing. She stared at him while her heart thumped against her breastbone and she swayed minutely to the rocking of the boat on the waves. The sun slanted in glaring whiteness across the deck beyond the windows, glancing off the chrome rails and bouncing dazzling abstract water reflections onto the ceiling. Some distance away a boat motor buzzed past.

Moistening her lips, she said, "Suppose I told you that I have reconsidered."

"You intend to make a sacrifice of yourself, after all? I would have to say I'm not buying."

Heat flared in her face. "Good, because I'm not for sale! Do you honestly think I would do this for money, or even for position?"

"Wouldn't you?"

"Not on your life! The main reason is for Grandpapa, of course. But more than that, Sea Gull has been such a large part of my life that I'd like to see it go on as a separate force, perhaps a separate division, instead of being absorbed into CMARC. And I don't like the idea of all our people being put out of work—especially Keil and Nick, and the older boat captains who have been with Grandpapa for so long."

"All very praiseworthy. Still, I don't think I would be interested."

"Not even if I said that . . . that I have personal reasons, that I've also discovered . . . compensations in the arrangement?"

A diabolical light rose in the dark centers of his eyes. Lifting his arms, he linked his fingers behind his head. "I think I would have to know what these compensations entail before I believe it. I prefer not to risk getting my face slapped again for no reason."

He was inviting her to seduce him. At least she thought that was his meaning. Could she do it? Did she dare?

Reclining there beside her, he seemed so hard and masculine, so distant and dangerous in a quiet, self-contained fashion. Like the jungle jaguar to which she had once compared him, it seemed he might be waiting for his prey to reach the exact point he wanted before he sprang.

It took her breath to think that he had made love to her in the dark, that his firmly muscled arms with their dark glazing of hair had held her. He had touched her with his strong, sensitive hands; the firm and sensual contours of his mouth had been pressed against her lips. She had felt the gold medal of St. Michael he wore below the hollow of his strong throat as it trailed over her breasts.

The flood of memories, heated and carnal, left her tremulous inside. She was attracted to this man in a way she had never been to any other. Yet she had no idea how to convey that to him without leaving herself open to an immediate physical intimacy she neither wanted nor intended.

Oh, but was that true? Was the tension that sang along her nerves from anxiety or from desire? Where did one leave off and the other begin? They were alone, isolated here on the boat by her design. Had she planned for this contingency without realizing it?

He was waiting. Watching. She must take the next step. There was no other way.

If she reached out to touch the lean planes of his face, leaned forward, then she might brush her lips . . .

She sprang to her feet. Whirling away from him, she

came to a halt at the sliding-glass doors. "I can't!" she said in tight distress. "I'm sorry, but I'm just not—not the femme fatale type. I'll marry you, if you really think it will work, but I can't use sex to persuade you that I'm willing."

He came to his feet behind her, then moved close to her side. Though he did not touch her, she could sense the intensity radiating from him. His voice low and deliberate, he said, "I would have been disappointed if you could. But before we go any further, I need to know what kind of marriage you envision."

"Kind?" She glanced up at him then away again. "I don't know. A partnership, I suppose, one of mutual respect for each other's intelligence and opinions, since we would be working together. Something that would allow space for each of us during the time when one of us is in Rio and the other in New Orleans. It could be a fairly open arrangement, if you like."

"I don't like." His words were hard-bitten for all their softness. "What I require is a flesh-and-blood union that will be celebrated in a wide double bed and produce children. It will have its share of arguments and fights, but also a reasonable amount of affection and an extravagant amount of desire. Separations will be few and far between; whatever we do, wherever we do it, the job will be undertaken as a team. This marriage will not be some modern affair that can be terminated with the stroke of a pen, but a lifelong bond dissolvable only by death. I cannot, and will not, settle for anything less."

"You expect a great deal," she said with a catch in her voice as she acknowledged the insidious pull of the future he outlined.

"No more than I'm willing to give." His voice was firm.

"What if one of us falls in love ... with someone else?" She could not imagine the possibility for herself, but he was a virile, handsome man, exactly the kind to attract women by the dozen.

"Then will be the time for sacrifice, if not now. Some

things are more important than personal emotion, personal gratification."

So much for love.

She wondered, briefly, if his relationships with his dead fiancée and his former girlfriend had been on this same order, if possibly the physical closeness combined with emotional distance, that possessiveness without acceptance as a person, might not have driven them to escape him in any way possible. And yet he had indicated, and she believed, that he set no standard he did not intend to maintain.

"Such high principles," she said in troubled recognition. "Are you quite sure you're not doing this because . . . well, because of how I was that night in Rio?"

"Because I was the first man to make love to you?" He reached out to brush a lock of hair back from her cheek. "I won't deny that is part of it. Such things mean a lot to a man, no matter how modern he may consider himself to be."

She grimaced a little, then drew a deep breath. "I can't promise to be everything you want, but I can try."

An instant of silence stretched between them, then he gave an abrupt nod. "I see no reason to delay the wedding. Will a month give you time?"

"Just—like that?" She turned to face him, her gaze startled.

"Swift decisions are my specialty." The planes of his face shifted in a smile. "Having second thoughts already?"

"No. No, not at all. I think the sooner the better. And I would really prefer something simple—because of Grandpapa."

"In New Orleans, of course?"

She nodded. "If you don't mind."

"Not at all. You understand my family will expect to meet you as a matter of tradition."

His family. His traditions. Such things had not even begun to cross her mind. "Won't they be at the wedding?"

"Yes, certainly, but a visit will be expected before then."

It was a small thing, not worth argument. "Fine, if that's what you want."

"I'll take care of it. And if I can help you with the other arrangements, you must let me know. My staff, as well as the company plane, are at your disposal."

"Attendants," she said, lifting a hand to rub at her temple as she tried to think. "Is there someone you can ask to be your best man, with maybe a groomsman or two?"

"Only tell me what is required when you have the numbers."

So polite and businesslike. Wedding planning as a series of problems to be solved with dispatch and common sense. But what had she expected? What else was there?

Jessica suddenly wanted to cry. But then, weddings were supposed to do that to women, weren't they?

With the near future settled between them, there was no point in lingering on the water. While Jessica quickly cleared away the remains of their meal, Rafael saw to raising the anchors fore and aft. She heard the back hatch open after a few minutes, as if he was checking the twin inboard engines. He was probably just curious, she thought, as she completed her tasks and started back up the carpeted steps to the control bridge. He was a boat person; the way he moved about the *Sea Gull IV* made that plain. It wasn't surprising, all things considered.

A couple of minutes later, the hatch slammed shut again and she heard his footsteps coming back along the deck toward the sliding-glass door that stood open for his entry. He was obviously clear of the engines. She adjusted the throttles, then reached for the ignition.

"Don't!"

The harsh command brought her head around, even as she turned the key. The two big Chrysler engines roared into life.

Rafael lunged in that same instant. His hard arm

clamped her waist, jerking her against his hip. Whipping around, he plunged back through the opening of the glass door and across the narrow deck. He did not stop, but stepped over the chrome chain that barred the gangway opening and sprang in an arching dive for the water.

Jessica screamed as she felt herself falling. They hit the surface of the water like striking concrete, then the cold, wet lake sucked her under. Panic and uncomprehending fury clawed at her. She couldn't breathe for the steel hawser of an arm that was cutting off the air to her lungs. She couldn't see, couldn't think as she was dragged down and down and deeper still. She fought, trying to wrench away from the man who held her in a death grip.

Then from far above she heard the booming roar of an explosion. It blasted through the water, sending her and Rafael tumbling, whirling with its concussion. Darkness crashed through her mind. She ceased to fight as shock ripped into her. Time stopped as she drifted on gliding currents.

Then she was rising, thrusting upward in a bubbling, rocket-propelled rush. Her head broke the water. She gasped, choking, coughing, trying to clear her lungs as she clung to the firm support of the man who held her. Finally she lifted a hand to wipe water and wet hair from her face and eyes so she could see.

Rafael's hair was slicked down like a seal's, sticking to his forehead in spiked designs. His T-shirt clung to his wide shoulders as he tread water with waves slapping his neck. His face was pale yet carried a fiery overlay of red and gold, and tiny reflected flames danced in the water beads on his strained features and in the dark pupils of his eyes.

Jessica braced a hand on his shoulder, feeling a rush of gratitude for its strength even as she turned to follow his gaze. Her throat burned with her sudden harsh breath that was flavored with salt water and smoke.

The *Sea Gull IV*, or what was left of her, was on fire. Bits and pieces of the yacht were strewn over the water, smoking as they floated. Flames crackled, shooting skyward from the floating hull. They flared also in iridescent splendor from the slick of gas and oil that lay like a spread fishing net behind the boat.

"We could have been killed," she whispered.

"And almost were." Rafael said. "Think hard, my bride-to-be, and tell me just who wants you dead."

Chapter Fourteen

███ ███ ███ *Jessica's first impulse was to keep the* news of the explosion from her grandfather at all costs. However, it would be worse still if he heard about it from someone else and discovered he had been kept in the dark. Between treating him like a man or an invalid, there could be only one choice.

She need not have worried. He took the news in stride, once he was sure that she—and Rafael of course—had escaped without injury. That the explosion had been an accident he assumed without question. Jessica did not suggest otherwise, to him or anyone else. For one thing, there was no way to prove that deliberate tampering had caused the slow leak in the gas line that, combined with a loose plug wire, had set off the explosion. Even if there had been, nothing whatever was left to show who had set the trap, much less who was meant to be caught in it.

When she informed her grandfather that she and Rafael had settled their differences, he was elated. He had no objection whatever to the proposed visit to meet her prospective in-laws, saying only that Keil could handle things at Sea Gull in her absence. From the tone of his voice, however, she was left to wonder if he wasn't also relieved that she was going. It seemed remotely possible that he was glad she would be out of the way for a while, that he was more worried than he wanted her to know.

Keil was flabbergasted at how close Jessica and Rafael had come to being killed. Over and over he insisted that he had checked the engines just a couple of weekends before with no sign of a problem. The boat wasn't exactly new, he admitted, but it had been maintained in mint condition and had a whistle-clean safety record. A few other people had been on board lately—Nick had hosted a lake party a few weeks back, and Madeleine had slept over one weekend. But Keil himself had been the last person to take the *Sea Gull IV* out.

He had been waiting on the dock when Jessica and Rafael were brought in by fishermen who had picked them up out of the water. One of the rescue party had been an oil executive escaping his office for the day but carrying his flip-out cellular phone in his pocket. Jessica could have done without the marvels of modern communication. Wet, bedraggled, chilled to the bone, and edgy, the last thing she wanted was to participate in an extended postmortem.

Mercifully Rafael kept his theories to himself. She wasn't at all sure he really believed someone wanted to kill her, anyway. It might have been no more than the stress of the moment and the need to find something or somebody to blame.

Or perhaps he did, for he had announced their decision to leave at once for Brazil. Demolishing her objections and clearing away all obstacles with ruthless courtesy, he arranged their departure. As soon as possible after they had given their statements and had been checked for internal injuries, she was on a plane bound for Rio.

It was almost dark by the time they reached the airport. The flight schedule was no problem, however. The CMARC turbo jet had been on the ground in New Orleans for two days. The pilot was on board when she and Rafael, followed by Pepe with the luggage, reached the plane.

"Good evening, senhorita, and welcome." The slender, dark-haired young man who met them at the door flashed a warm smile before turning to the man beside her. "Ready when you are, Rafael. Everything has been checked out."

"Jessica, my cousin Carlos, the son of my mother's

eldest sister," Rafael said briefly as the two men clasped each other around the shoulders in a quick, casual embrace. "My fiancée, Carlos."

"Ah, the lady of the orchids," the other man said as Rafael freed himself and stepped aside. Jessica gave him her hand, but he stepped closer to brush her cheeks with a swift kiss on either side. "You have no idea how glad I am that you have said yes to Rafael. Maybe we can now cease risking life and limb by stealing my aunt's prized blossoms."

She had accepted long ago that Rafael was responsible for the exotic bouquets, but it was nice to have it confirmed. With a swift glance in his direction, she said, "You mean—they weren't commercially grown?"

Carlos, retaining her hand in both of his, looked also to his cousin. "By no means. Only the best and most rare plucked from the gardens of Casa Reposada before dawn would do—except, of course, while we were here in the city. You have no idea how much trouble it was getting these flowers into the States! My aunt, Rafael's mother, is now in possession of a perfectly legitimate license to import tropical vegetation to the U.S. if she ever finds herself in need of one. And I have grown fond of having my morning coffee with chickory, New Orleans style, along with beignets at the Café du Monde."

"*Bom*, Carlos," Rafael said dryly. "Do you think you could release Jessica so we can take off some time this evening?"

"Jealous, cousin?" Carlos dropped an eyelid in a wink for Jessica as he did as suggested, then made a sweeping gesture to welcome her into the plane's cabin. "How romantic. Wait until I tell the family."

"Mention it by all means, if you want to work for the competition."

Carlos was far from repressed. "That would be Sea Gull Transport headed by your Jessica, would it not? When do you think I might start?"

"After your release from the hospital," Rafael said in

a mild threat as he stepped into the cockpit, took the pilot's seat, and placed a set of earphones on his head.

"You're going to fly us?" Jessica couldn't keep the surprise from her voice.

"Nervous?" he asked, giving her a smile over his shoulder before handing a clipboard to Carlos, who had taken the seat beside him.

"Not at all."

It was true, she realized as she settled into a deep and comfortable chair of gray leather set near the door of the cockpit. There was such assurance and casual competence in his manner that she had no doubts whatsoever of his ability as a pilot. At the same time she was obscurely disappointed that she would have only the silent Pepe for company back in the cabin with its scattered seats, low worktables, and general air of a discreet men's club.

"Good." Rafael directed his attention to the bank of gauges, switches, and blinking displays in front of him. "Sit back and relax, take a nap. We'll be there in no time."

She should not have been surprised that Rafael flew himself, she told herself as she buckled her seat belt; it was like him to prefer being in control. Still, the fact that he had not told her made her wonder what else about himself he might be holding in reserve.

The plane took off in a smooth surge of power a short time later. As they climbed into the pearlescent lavender-gray of the evening sky, Jessica's thoughts drifted to her father. He had also been a pilot. Trained by the army, he had honed his skill at flying fast and low during two tours of duty in Vietnam, skills he had used to start a crop-dusting operation when he left the service. The marriage between him and Arletta had survived war but not peace. About the time the divorce was final, he had been killed in a fiery crash in the swamps behind the Landing.

Jessica had been barely two at the time, and living at the Landing with Arletta and her grandfather. It had seemed natural to be there; she and her mother had stayed at the big house while her father was away, and returned there after the separation.

Arletta had gone off the deep end after Jonathan Meredith died, drinking, running around, coming home in the early-morning hours when she came home at all. There had been screaming and yelling between Arletta and Grandpapa that made Jessica hide her head under the covers. Claude Frazier had stood it for nearly three years, then told his daughter to shape up or get out. Arletta had left, leaving Jessica behind.

Until that time Sea Gull had been a small crew boat company operating from the port town of Cameron, not far from Ombre-Terre. With his daughter gone, Claude Frazier, always single-minded about business, had made shipping his life. As his company expanded, he spent more and more time in New Orleans, staying in the old French Quarter town house bought by his grandfather in the 1890s. A dozen years later, he opened an office in New Orleans and moved Jessica and himself there permanently. And Sea Gull had grown still more, though nothing else had been the same.

The big chair Jessica was sitting in reclined, providing a footrest to lift her feet and legs to a more comfortable position. Pepe had already taken advantage of that feature. He was not exactly relaxed, however, as he sat with his hands gripping the arms of his chair so tightly that his fingertips turned white. Nervous perspiration beaded his forehead also, as if he was afraid of flying. That small weakness in the big man made him seem much more human. Jessica exchanged a few comments with him in an effort to distract him. It was tough going, but he unbent enough after a time to release his death grip on his seat and even gave her one of his rare, slow smiles.

The plane droned on into the night, rock-steady and soothing. Her eyes were burning, the effect of dry cabin air, salt water from the lake, and too many sleepless nights. She closed them for a second.

Rafael stayed with the controls until they had skimmed above Miami on a route that would take them out over the Atlantic before turning south for Recife. Leaving it with Carlos then, he went back to check on Jessica. She lay so pale and still that a jolt of alarm shook him even as he realized she was only asleep.

Standing over her, he put out his hand to smooth her hair back from her face. He stopped, closing his fingers in a tight fist. Mustn't touch. She might wake up, and then where would he be?

It was becoming a habit: reaching out for her, then drawing back. Trying to control that impulse only made him more agonizingly aware of his need to put his hands on her. He was a tactile person—*touchy-feely* in the revolting phrase coined by cool-blooded, standoffish North Americans. Still, it was possible they had a point. He distrusted the blood that ran swift and hot in his own veins; once he had her under his hands, he might not be able to stop.

Soon he need not exert such control. He didn't intend to force himself on her in any way, but she would learn that he had his requirements and close physical contact was one of them.

She looked so tired, which was not surprising. The hour was growing late, and she had been through much since that morning. Still, he was troubled by the dark shadows like bruises under the fragile skin beneath her eyes and the faint pucker of a worried frown that remained between her brows. She had shampooed the salt water, engine oil, and smoke scent from her hair, but made little attempt to style it other than drawing it back from her face with a pair of hair clips. The clean, soft strands curved over one shoulder, shimmering with her steady breathing and the movement of the plane.

Dear God, but she had been valiant there in the water after the explosion. Hysterics weren't her style, that much he knew; still she had kept her head, had swam or floated beside him until they were rescued, and never shed a tear. It was not lack of imagination. Horror for the fiery death they had escaped had been in her eyes, lingering long after they reached the dock. He thought, rather, that she had sustained too many blows lately, blows for which she blamed herself far more than she should.

That was his fault, one that he must correct. He would, regardless of the cost. The price, he was beginning to recognize, might well be high.

A crooked smile curved his mouth as his gaze rested on the gentle swells of her breasts under her silk shirt, skimmed the narrow turn of her waist and the flare of her slender hips. There were, of course, those compensations they had discussed. Or would be. Soon. And he would see to it she learned to appreciate them more than she yet dreamed.

Jessica roused when the plane touched down in Recife, disturbed by the slight bump and the lights of the airport shining through the darkness. She felt curiously disembodied, as if a part of her had been left behind so that she must somehow get through what lay ahead without her complete self.

What in heaven's name was she doing here? How had it come to this? She knew of course, yet it did not seem possible that she was to marry Rafael Castelar y Torres and make Brazil her second home. Nothing she told herself about it could make it feel at all real.

If there were formalities associated with their arrival, they were taken care of behind the scenes and by someone else. Moments after the plane taxied to a halt, she was alighting with Rafael just behind her. A stocky man in a white short-sleeve shirt, with the features of a Spanish grandee, the skin of an African prince, and a wide grin showing the split between his teeth, waited to greet them. Introduced as Juan, he was apparently a chauffeur, since he said something to Rafael about a car. Dropping behind with Pepe to help with the luggage, he talked volubly as they made their way through the airport building and out to a parking lot. He spoke at first in Portuguese, but switched to English with profuse apologies at a word from Rafael.

Senhora Castelar, Rafael's mother, had been amazed to hear of her son's coming marriage, according to Juan, though she was also excited about the visit and looked forward to welcoming her future daughter-in-law. She had sent at once to invite all the relatives for dinner tomorrow evening to meet Senhorita Jessica, and of course they were all coming, down to the last small cousin. There had been a great bustle of cleaning and polishing, and much discussion of menus suited to an American palate. A major difficulty, apparently, had been the question of which room to allot the senhorita, but it had been decided, finally, according to tradition.

"What else?" Carlos quipped with a dry glance at Rafael.

"Indeed," the chauffeur said in grave agreement.

Jessica did not quite grasp the significance of that exchange. It seemed her future husband comprehended perfectly, however, for his expression turned laconic.

The limousine that waited was a vintage Cadillac so near a classic that it sported tail fins. Its glossy black exterior, undoubtedly the original paint job, was polished within an inch of its life, while the interior was fitted with mahogany and black plush and had crystal side vases holding nodding orchids.

Rafael arched a brow in Juan's direction. The short man flung up a hand as if to ward off attack, though there was laughter in his eyes. "The senhora insisted; she thought it would be more comfortable for Senhorita Jessica, and that you and your lady might prefer to be private." He shrugged. "You know how it is, Senhor Rafael. One does not argue with your mother."

"*Juan* could have tried," Rafael said with acerbic emphasis.

Juan's lips quirked, and his gaze was bright. "Yes, but it is such a waste of time when she is always right."

Resignation invaded Rafael's face. On a soft sigh he answered, "As you say."

Carlos was not to come with them, it seemed. Since he had been flying in and out on a regular basis, he had a car at the airport. He would take Pepe and the luggage and go on ahead. By the time Jessica reached the house, her things would be unpacked and waiting for her.

Rafael handed Jessica into the limousine and climbed

in after her. Juan got behind the wheel. The glass window between front seat and back slid closed with scarcely a sound, then the big vehicle drove off majestically into the sparse traffic leaving the airport. Wide, long, and heavy, it was doubtless a gas-guzzler of major proportions, but its ride was incredibly comfortable in a way long forgotten in these post-oil-embargo, fuel-efficiency days.

After a few minutes Rafael asked politely if she would mind having the windows down. She shook her head, and he wound down the glass. The warm night wind, smelling exotic yet familiar with its scents of the sea and green growing things, swept inside to blow away the cobwebs from her brain.

They sped past the lively resort area of Boa Viagem with its high-rise beach hotels, outdoor cafés, and night-clubs bright with neon and filled with lively crowds even at this late hour. Ten minutes more brought them to the crowded streets of old Recife, where things were much quieter.

Jessica caught glimpses of baroque buildings heavy with carving, opulent pastel-walled villas behind white stone walls, balustraded bridges and ancient churches. Flowers were everywhere, great masses of bougainvillea, hedges of hibiscus, and walls hung with allamanda with pale yellow flowers shining like miniature moons among the dark foliage. Tall palm trees lined the streets and hung above the houses with their heavy fronds waving in the darkness.

As she sat forward to see better, Rafael spoke. "Not many Americans visit Recife, which is a shame since it's far safer and more beautiful than Rio. The name means 'reef,' because the seamen who discovered the place thought highly of the barrier reef that protects the city from the ocean waves. Of course, their descendants would prefer more action for their surfboards."

"I would imagine."

"We will come back later to look around if you like, but we are heading farther out now. Though I speak of

Recife as my home for a convenient point of reference, I actually live in the country to the north, past Olinda."

It might be her imagination, Jessica thought, but his accent seemed more pronounced, his words and gestures more formal, now that they were in his homeland. The planes and angles of his face, dimly seen there in the interior of the car, also appeared more foreign, less approachable. It was disconcerting. A tight knot of distress laced with inexplicable longing formed under her breastbone.

Grasping for something to say to cover her confusion, she repeated, "Olinda?"

"Another town, one of three that makes up Greater Recife. They say the Portuguese captain who came upon it in the sixteenth century after weeks at sea called out *'O linda!,'* which translates to something like 'How beautiful!' We tend to think he had excellent taste."

"Your family has been here a long time, I think."

"Four hundred years, give or take."

It was said with the kind of careless acceptance that comes from deeply felt roots. Nothing in the words hinted that he realized she had her information from his personal file, though Jessica knew he was well aware of it. She said, "It's strange to realize that people were living here a hundred years before New Orleans was established."

He smiled. "The two places share something of a comparable history. Both endured while cut off from Europe, overcoming great odds to hold on to the kind of civilization the people had left behind them. The people of both built churches, theaters, and opera houses in a wilderness where pirates knocked at the front gates and Indians at the back. We are all children of survivors then. We don't give up easily; it's in the blood."

Was there a warning for her in his words? She could not tell, and it was fully possible that she was growing hypersensitive, hearing innuendo where there was none. Just in case she said anyway, "Some give up more easily than others."

He turned his head to stare at her, but she refused to look at him again.

With Olinda as well as Recife behind them, they traveled inland through forests of coconut palms and a waving wilderness of sugarcane, then past a number of small villages that amounted to little more than thatched huts around a church. They turned off the main road after a time, trundling down a rutted track like two ribbons of silver sand unwinding in front of the headlights. A wall loomed ahead that was crowned by the inevitable mass of bougainvillea. Beyond lay the shadowy bulk of a great house hung with balconies and balustrades, and with palm trees silhouetted against its ancient walls. The big car swung through an enormous iron gate standing open on its hinges, then pulled up on the stones of a courtyard.

The house was mercifully dark and still. Jessica, glancing at her watch as the dome light came on with the opening of the car door, saw that it was the small hours of the morning. She was, apparently, to be spared the meeting with Rafael's mother or any of the rest of the family for at least a few more hours.

A woman wearing an apron, apparently a housekeeper or maid, appeared on the wide steps and came forward to greet them. Rafael gave the quick, light kisses of greeting. The housekeeper bobbed a curtsey and sent Jessica a shy smile as she was introduced. Rafael requested that she show Jessica to her room, and she nodded, then stood back in an attitude of patient readiness.

Rafael turned to Jessica. His face grave, he took her hand and brushed it with his lips. "Welcome to my home, this house which is now yours also," he said quietly. "Go with Maria now, and rest well. I'll see you in the morning."

She was to sleep alone, it seemed; Jessica had wondered. With a few short words he had indicated exactly how things would be while she was here, polite, somewhat formal, warm yet distant. She met his amber gaze for the briefest of instants. It was clear and even compassionate, as if he guessed her doubts and misgivings.

She drew an abrupt breath and let it out in silent acceptance. "Yes. Good night, then. And thank you."

Withdrawing her hand, she followed the maid who had turned and started along a wide hallway. Her words had not been particularly warm or clear or strong. Still, she had meant them. She really was pathetically grateful.

Chapter Fifteen

▨ ▨ ▨ *Jessica woke to the sound of a rooster* crowing. That didn't register as being unusual; there were plenty of chickens at the Landing. Then the rooster was joined in its morning salute by a parrot. Their combined chorus, raucous and determined, assaulted the air in a deafening crescendo.

Jessica sat up in bed, blinking sleep from her eyes. The room came into soft focus. The plastered walls were painted white and lined with portraits of stern-visaged Portuguese ladies and gentlemen in court dress with stiff, gilt-edged collars. A carved wooden crucifix touched with gilding hung above a prayer bench in one corner. Persian rugs in subdued colors were scattered over the cool white and black marble squares of the floor. Curtains of fine-weave natural linen lifted gently in the breeze wafting through open French doors. The tantalizing aromas of coffee and baking bread and flowers drifted in on the morning air in rich, civilized welcome.

Brazil, she was in Brazil.

She shouldn't be here. She should be in New Orleans, hard at work at what she knew best. She didn't have time for this, not now when there was so much at stake.

For an instant the heat and terror of the explosion came back to her, roaring in her head. She forced it down, closing her eyes tightly against the vision. It was an accident, that was all. It had to be an accident because anything else was unthinkable.

Beyond the French doors, the parrot's squawking

quieted to a disgruntled mutter. Mingling with it was a low familiar voice. Jessica slid from the high bed of polished mahogany with its pristine white sheets and reached for her robe of rose satin to cover her matching nightgown. Padding to the French doors, she pushed the light drapes aside and stepped out onto the wide balcony beyond.

The dazzle of sunshine slanting through the palms created slashing patterns of black and gold on the floor and walls of the patio below. It was an instant before Jessica could make out the long reflecting pool that centered the space, the ancient flagstones with their green edgings of moss, the *mandevilla* vine that twisted in fuchsia-pink glory up the columns of the opposite wing of the house, and the table set for breakfast inside the lower loggia. The parrot she had heard walked the loggia's balustrade like a tightrope, flapping his wings in a blur of green and gold.

Rafael was talking to the bird as he tossed a newspaper onto the table and drew out a chair. The morning sun gleamed blue-black in the sculpted waves of his hair and highlighted the starkly handsome planes of his face. Jessica felt her heart lurch into a disturbing rhythm in her chest.

She stepped back, but the curtains behind her wavered and billowed in the draft so she could not locate the opening between the panels at once. Her movement caught Rafael's attention, for he glanced up, then stepped to the balustrade.

"*Bom-dia!* Good morning," he called up to her. "I trust you slept well?"

His voice had a caressing sound that raised chill bumps along the back of Jessica's neck and down her arms. An instant later she realized that the tone of affection must be for the sake of the black-clad servant who had emerged from the house to place a cup on the table and fill it from a silver coffeepot. Her own voice was breathless and a little tight as she answered, "Yes, amazingly well, all things considered."

His brief smile held satisfaction. "Will you join me

for breakfast? I can promise a few surprises, all of them delicious."

"Oh, no," she said hurriedly, pulling her robe closer around her. "Thank you, but I'm not dressed, and your coffee will be cold before—"

"I'll come up to you, then."

The words were polite but firm; it was plain he had no intention of accepting a refusal. Turning to the servant, he gave a few easy instructions, then disappeared through a door set farther back under the loggia. Jessica swung back into the bedroom behind her, one hand going automatically to rake the tangles of the night from her hair. She thought of taking a hairbrush to them, of washing her face, maybe applying a little lip gloss.

There was no time. A knock fell on her door, and it was pushed open without ceremony. Rafael gave her a quick, appraising glance before he closed the door and came toward her. She clenched her teeth as she fought the impulse to back away from his assured advance. He was even more devastating at close quarters than he had been from a distance.

"Don't panic," he said, his gaze on her set features, "this isn't an invasion. I need to talk to you about the family gathering my mother has planned. I should have realized it would happen, so we could be prepared. But it doesn't matter, so long as we settle a few things between us before you meet everyone."

"What things?" She heard the stiffness in her voice, but there was nothing she could do about it.

"What we will say in explanation for our sudden engagement for one," he said with a quirk of a brow. "How we should behave toward each other. What you can expect, and why. You will not be marrying me alone, you see, but also my family; it's the Brazilian way. The number of relatives is not small, and can be overwhelming even to someone used to such things. Matters will go much smoother if the two of us present a united front."

A faint frown creased her brow. "I didn't realize it would be quite so—formal."

"It isn't, not in the way you mean. Still, I am head of the family, and you, as my wife, will join me in decisions that affect the future happiness and well-being of a lot of people. It would be high-handed of me to foist someone on them without warning."

"I certainly don't mind meeting everyone, but I fail to see that it makes much difference."

"How so?"

Disquiet skittered along her nerves at the trace of iron she heard in his tone; still she needed to make her position plain. "I'll be spending much of my time in New Orleans, so I shouldn't affect the situation one way or the other."

"Will you indeed?"

"I have to be there. How else will I be able to run Sea Gull?"

He watched her a long moment, his gaze dark with consideration behind the screen of his thick lashes. Finally he said, "That is a matter we can settle later. For now, we have other things to—"

"I don't think so," she interrupted. "Our agreement was that I would remain in control of my grandfather's holdings. Are you suggesting that I'll be able to do that from here? It's impossible."

"Not here, but Rio. I was thinking of an office for you near mine."

"That won't do at all," she said sharply. "There are problems that come up on the spot, details that have to be monitored, decisions that must be made without delay."

"Keil Frazier is fully capable of taking over immediate responsibility. Cousins do prove useful at times."

The anger of betrayal surged inside her. She had thought he understood, that he had meant their partnership to be equal. She should have known better. "I don't think that will work at all. There can't be two people in charge. Whoever has the final say must put in the time on the job so they know when things are going wrong."

He tilted his head. Voice soft, he said. "I thought you

understood that I have no interest in a long-distance marriage."

"We could commute. Lots of couples do it." The words were defensive and just a little desperate.

"I want to sleep in the same bed every night with the woman I marry, to reach for her when I have need, to be there when she needs me. I want to wake up with her every morning, have breakfast with her, to know that she is near, safe, comfortable—"

"Convenient?" she interjected, reaching for sarcasm to fight the odd pull of his low, seductive tone and the suggestion it carried. "Then you should marry somebody else."

His lips twisted. "I don't think so. We have an agreement. I intend to hold you to it."

"You can't make me marry you," she said with a lift of her chin.

He met her gaze for long seconds, his own dark and fathomless. "Can't I?"

His confidence was chilling. "What do you mean?"

"Think about it," he said, and turned away from her as a knock came on the door, signaling the arrival of their breakfast.

He meant that he could call off the merger and throw Sea Gull into bankruptcy if she reneged. If she wanted to hold on to the company as a separate entity for her grandfather, then she would have to do as he said. Or at least she thought that was what he had implied. It was possible there were other, darker threats beneath the deliberate courtesy of his words.

Rafael Castelar was a pirate in modern clothing, a ruthless competitor who went after what he wanted and got it. His methods might be more civilized, his manners more polished, but the results were the same. He had her where he wanted her, and he meant to keep her there.

She had almost forgotten these things with the explosion of the boat and its aftermath. It was a mistake she would not make again. But there was still a thing or two he might not have taken into account. He was not the only one who wanted something. She would bide her time until she had what she needed, then they would see.

They ate on the balcony overlooking the patio, sitting at a table laid with a cloth of handmade lace and set with antique faience and utensils of old coin silver. If she had doubts about his intentions in invading her bedroom, they were soon banished. The manservant and procession of maids in gray uniforms with black-and-white aprons who served their breakfast made highly effective chaperones.

It was a bountiful meal that began with strong hot coffee foaming with hot milk accompanied by fresh pineapple juice and melon. Dishes continued to arrive, including papaya and newly made cheese, slivers of dry-cured ham tucked into rolls still warm from the oven, tiny bananas fried in butter, baked sweet potatoes, small burritos filled with cheese and coconut, a creamy egg custard draped in a hot puree of pineapple and mango, and coconut pound cake. Each offering was garnished with flowers and presented with a flourish.

Jessica was not at all hungry in the beginning, but ate and drank because it gave her an excuse to avoid looking at Rafael. After a few moments, however, her taste buds woke to the delicious new combination of flavors. Suddenly she was ravenous.

She swallowed a bite of custard topped with mango, then dipped her spoon into the creamy mixture for another. Feeling Rafael's gaze upon her, she looked up to find him watching her while a slight smile tugged at the corners of his mouth.

"What?" she asked, the word sharp as she recognized the amusement in his eyes.

"Nothing, except I'm glad to see that yesterday's ordeal hasn't affected your appetite. Well—there's also the way you eat. In Brazil, we don't keep our left hands in our laps as if they had suddenly become paralyzed. And we don't put down the knife and switch hands with the fork to place a piece of something in our mouths, but follow the European method of helping matters along with the knife held in the right. Your manners are charming but a bit artificial."

"That may be," she said with a too-sweet smile, "but you won't see me trying to peel a boiled shrimp with a knife and fork the way you do. Artificial is in the eye of the beholder. Anyway, you should be used to American manners."

"Of course, and I'm not finding fault but only enjoying how different you are now that I see you here in my home."

There was no heat in his voice, nothing except a supremely assured indulgence that made her want to hit him. "How nice," she said with acerbity. "But I assume your family has higher expectations, since you want to coach me on what to say to them. Just what did you have in mind?"

Rafael was silent while he studied her, then he sighed and used his napkin before dropping it beside his plate. She was going to be difficult, that much he could see. She was a woman of pride being forced to bend to his will. She might accept the necessity, but would make him pay for daring to remove her freedom of choice. Fine. He did not object to paying a fair price for what he wanted. But he did regret the loss of her smiles.

There were women who could be swayed by their emotions, who would follow blindly, regardless of the consequences. Then there were those who would not. If he reached out now and took his Jessica in his arms, would she melt into them and give herself up to his caresses? Or would she spit in his eye instead? He was very much afraid it would be the latter.

She was so delectable sitting there, with her hair tousled from sleep, her robe slipping to reveal the tender white curve of her breast, and the sweetness of mango on her lips. His body ached for her so fiercely he was glad of the overhang of lace tablecloth that covered the signs. He would venture his luck, except he was half afraid that she would surrender to him for reasons having nothing to do with her emotions and everything with what she wanted from him.

Which served him right, he supposed. Some things were better grasped at once and held hard, being too important to risk their loss. Even when chance itself could make them either worth their weight in gold or worthless as the dust of the high Brazilian plains.

Pushing back his plate in sudden repugnance, he said, "There are a few other things you should know about the way we live. Foremost among them is what I mean when I say that I am head of my family. By this I mean not only that I have charge of CMARC and the family finances, but that I am the *patrao*, or patron, the person from whom all blessings flow—and on whom all responsibility ultimately rests."

"The patron? You mean like in *The Godfather*?"

Irritation touched the firm curves of his mouth. "Yes, and no. There's nothing sinister about it, I assure you, though the position is similar. I am, in theory at least, the final authority. I name the babies when they are born, decide the schools each child will attend, approve marriages when they are proposed, use my influence and contacts to arrange jobs, assign plots in the family cemetery, and so on to the last detail for the most distant and laziest of cousins. It also means it's my duty to see that no one goes unchristened, uneducated, unmarried, unhoused, unfed, or unburied—and to pay for these things if no one else feels obliging. You will of course become the *patroa*, my lady who will aid me in all decisions. You can understand that a lot of people will be concerned that a wife who doesn't understand the system may interfere with my duty toward all the others."

"I can see they have a right to be worried," she said with some dryness.

"Yes. That worry may encourage them to make comments and ask questions you consider too personal. It could make them seem judgmental. The best way to combat their curiosity is to smile and refer everything to me."

"Making me seem a quiet little thing with nothing to say and no opinions of my own?"

He compressed his lips, then relaxed them with an effort. "Making you seem gracious and diplomatic, and preventing you from saying something that could set off a family feud."

"Heaven forbid that I should cause any trouble for you. Is that all?"

"No. There is also the matter of public affection."

Her brows lifted. "Of what?"

She knew exactly what he had said, and could guess at what he meant, but was pleased to make him spell it out. He didn't mind at all.

"The best and most acceptable excuse for our coming marriage is a major love affair. We cannot, therefore, keep our hands off each other. I will look at you with my heart in my eyes, and you will do the same. I will kiss you in dark corners, caress you when I think no one is looking—or even when I am certain they are staring. You will press yourself against me, invite me with your eyes, make silent promises with your lips and—" He stopped, clearing his throat of a sudden obstruction.

"I do get the picture," she said, her voice low. "Are you sure this is absolutely necessary?"

The flush across her cheekbones was interesting, but could as easily be from anger or prudishness as from the kind of heated desire that threatened to steam his own brain. Forcing his voice to evenness, he said, "The alternative is to present it as a business arrangement without heart. In that case, my mother will object out of principle if not active concern. The others will fear an expensive divorce at some future date that could affect my ability to provide for them. Because of it, they may freeze you out. It will be much more comfortable for you, believe me, if you can bring yourself to endure my amorous attentions."

He heard the anticipation in his own voice, but could not help it. Let her make of it what she would, providing she noticed it at all. It was possible her mind was elsewhere. She was watching him with intent speculation in the spring green of her eyes.

She said finally, "You have it all figured out, don't you?"

"I've tried."

"I can see that." She lifted her chin. "You are also an extremely conscientious person, aren't you."

"If you mean I have heavy responsibilities—" he began.

"No. I mean you accept them without question because you were born to them and it seems natural, or else because you are so strong within yourself that you feel compelled to lend strength to others. Or possibly because you enjoy the power of deciding other people's lives for them."

He felt the deep crease of a frown between his brows. "It's nothing so complicated, believe me. I have my obligations, and I attend to them."

"And I am one of them." The words were soft, her gaze level.

With a brief gesture toward the room and his home beyond, he said, "You think I am doing this out of duty, because of my actions in Rio? I thought we had settled that it was for our mutual benefit?"

She got to her feet and wandered along the balcony railing to the near corner. With her hands flat on the stone balustrade, she looked down into the patio. "You suggested that before, and I can see the advantages. It will save you time and legal fees, make for a smooth transition. And yet—"

"What?"

"You don't need me."

He allowed his gaze to drift over the slender outline of her body seen in shadow through the satin of her robe. The further hardening of his body in reaction brought a wry twist to his lips. Keeping his voice even with an effort, he said, "Wrong."

She turned to face him, pressing her back to cool stone. "I saw your headquarters in Rio, I've watched how you operate. You could swallow Sea Gull and never notice. And if you think Keil can handle things in New Orleans without my help or my presence—"

"I've told you before, but will say it again if you like. I want you." The truth, he thought, was often the easiest way out of a difficult situation.

"Then why bother with an office, a position—or even marriage? Why not just offer me an apartment and a few diamonds?"

"Would you accept them?"

"Of course not!"

"Exactly." His smile was grim. "But I also want a woman who is more than an ornament, one with something on her mind other than hairstyles and high fashion. I want someone with whom I can discuss business problems and objectives, and from whom I can expect constructive ideas and opinions. I want a woman who understands what I'm trying to build and who will join me in accomplishing it." He paused, then went on deliberately. "I want someone compatible mentally as well as physically. I want you."

She looked away from him. "How convenient for you that your desires and your self-interest lie in the same direction."

"Yes," he said evenly, hiding his desolation. "Isn't it?"

Rafael's mother was a formidable woman; Jessica saw that at once. The impression, however, was not based on size. The older woman was small of stature, though well-rounded, and extremely attractive in the smooth and simple manner of a classic Madonna. There was timeless elegance and style in her black silk, her wide gold hoop earrings, smooth and heavy bangle bracelets that matched her wide gold wedding band, and the polished omega necklace that held a splendid emerald suspended in the hollow of her throat. She sat in her satin-cushioned chair as if it were a throne, and waited for her son to bring his future bride to her. Her dark, magnificent eyes weighed, assessed, while giving nothing away. She was unmoved by smiles and deference, even from her son.

"Go away," she said to Rafael, her gaze intent on

Jessica's face. "I wish to speak to Senhorita Meredith alone."

"Now, *Mamae*, you can't expect me to allow her out of my sight," Rafael said in light protest while his arm tightened at Jessica's waist to draw her against him. "Besides, you will fill her head with all my faults and failures, and then where will I be?"

"Somewhere else," his mother said without noticeable sympathy. "If she is to be one of us she will learn everything soon enough, as we will learn everything of her. We should have no secrets."

Jessica felt definite uneasiness as she met the other woman's gaze. It made her almost grateful for Rafael's arm around her. She allowed herself to be molded against his lean side, and even placed her fingers on his strong hand at her waist for reinforcement.

"Jessica isn't used to our ways," Rafael insisted in answer to that mute appeal. "I would rather you didn't frighten her off with too much interrogation."

The older woman lifted a cleanly arched brow. "I doubt that she frightens so easily, my dear one, else she would not be here with you. Go now and bring us glasses of fruit punch. And make no haste to return."

Rafael met his mother's gaze for long seconds before a resigned smile rose in his eyes. He turned to Jessica and dropped a light kiss on her lips. "Courage, *cara*," he said as he released her. "Remember she loves me as much as you do."

It was a warning, Jessica thought as she watched him walk away, or at least a reminder of the part she must play. She felt deserted and more disturbed than the situation, perhaps, warranted.

"Do you?"

The question was cool and precise. Jessica heard and understood it without any trouble. The difficulty was in how to answer. To gain time to think, she said, "Excuse me?"

"Do you love my son?" Senhora Castelar repeated, waving a graceful hand toward the chair beside her in an indication for Jessica to seat herself.

The chair was deep and cushioned in damask with a cream and gold print. It would be easy to feel indolent and pampered in it, but Jessica felt instead that she might be swallowed by it. She knew how Rafael expected her to answer, knew there would be no repercussions from speaking the words his mother wanted to hear. She said quietly, "Yes, of course."

"There is no 'of course' to it. My son is handsome, much of a man, and easy to love, but he is also wealthy and powerful. There have been many women who have seen one aspect and not the others."

"I'm not particularly impressed by wealth and power," Jessica said with emphasis. "In fact, I distrust it."

"You distrust that part of my Rafael?"

"You could say that."

His mother nodded. "You have reason; it is true these things are of the gravest importance to him. Still, he would never put it before the woman he loves."

"I'm ... sure you are right." The words were compressed because of the inexplicable heaviness in her chest.

"You are not what I would have chosen for him at one time." The older woman let the words stand while she measured Jessica with a fixed regard.

"No, I expect you would have preferred a daughter-in-law more like yourself."

"Do you? I think you are more like me than you know, senhorita. Has Rafael told you of my mother's family who were Confederados from the town of Americana here in northern Brazil?"

"Confederados?" She stumbled a little over the word, despite its familiar roots. "I don't believe he mentioned it."

"They were people who immigrated to this country just after your Civil War, bringing with them everything they owned. My mother's family was once of Texas. She spoke no English, never visited the part of your country known as Dixieland, yet she and my aunts considered themselves U.S. Southerners. I think of myself as such now and then also, when I read of events there. Curious, is it not?"

It certainly helped to explain Rafael's ease among her own relatives. "Perhaps I might visit this Americana one day?"

The older woman inclined her head. "Indeed, you must. You should go there at the time of the yearly reunion of the Fraternity of American Descendants, where you may find relatives, no? But to continue, I think you and I are similar in personality as well as bloodlines, which is good. Once I thought someone sweet and yielding and domestic was required for my Rafael, someone who would make him her world and be a refuge for him from the strains of his position. The young woman he was to have married was of that kind. You do know of her?"

"A little," Jessica said cautiously.

Senhora Castelar nodded. "My son has not been fortunate in his women. When much younger he was so open and tender yet strong inside—this in addition to being handsome and of a certain status—that he attracted many, many women. He easily saw through those who wanted only his manhood or his wealth, but could not resist those who had need of his inner strength. His former fiancée was such an unstable female, and there have been others. He tried to be what these women required, but always they asked more than he had to give them. Never did they see or care that he had needs of his own."

"Unstable," Jessica murmured, and could not help wondering if she qualified for the description.

The older woman regarded her closely. "I see he has not explained these matters to you, after all. It's too bad, but very like him. He would prefer to conceal them, keep the secrets of these women, even when to remain silent leaves a bad impression. The truth is that the young woman he was to have married was addicted to drugs. He tried to help her overcome this sickness, but could not. Her death was from an overdose, though it was called a suicide to save face for her family."

"I see," Jessica said, a little distracted as she tried to readjust her thinking. Then because it seemed she might never have a better chance, she went on, "I believe there was a more recent affair of a similar nature?"

"As you say," Rafael's mother agreed, her voice hardening. "That female was silly as well as weak. She thought the tragedy of his fiancée in the past would make it easy to frighten my Rafael into marriage with a sham suicide attempt. It had the opposite effect. He ended the liaison as soon as decency would permit."

"He would." Jessica could not imagine that Rafael would stand still for that kind of entrapment.

"Because of these things, then, I am ready to admit that someone of your talents and interests may come closer to being a match for him. He needs the stimulation of a strong match, both physically and mentally."

The concession was so unexpected that Jessica was thrown off balance. No small part of that was the realization that Rafael must have discussed her in detail with his mother; there was no other way she could understand so much about her. "It's very kind of you to say so—I think."

His mother's smile acknowledged Jessica's small attempt at humor. "I don't mean to flatter, but only to recognize what may be best for the well-being of my son. Still, is he the best thing for you, senhorita? Can you be happy at his side, sharing his triumphs without striving for your own?"

"I suppose we will have to see," Jessica answered, somewhat at a loss.

"Yes. All the same, you must be sure. Divorce with us is not as convenient as in your country. More, I doubt Rafael will allow it. He does not easily give up his own."

Jessica forced a smile. "If you are trying to scare me away, you're doing a fine job."

"You say so," the other woman said slowly, "but I don't think you frighten easily. I don't think so at all."

There was a softness deep in Senhora Castelar's amber brown eyes, so like her son's, that had not been there before. Encouraged by it, Jessica said, "If you should decide I would not be suitable, what would—happen?"

"What would Rafael do? Or rather, how much would he be swayed by me?" The older woman smiled. "I can't tell you that. Among us, you understand, the mother often rules in the home. She is given much respect, much deference; her word is law for those who live under her roof, particularly when she is widowed. Rafael, being a dutiful and loving son, smiles and kisses me and says, 'Yes, *Mamae*, of course, *Mamae*,' when the decision means little to him. Ah, but when it means much—when he is certain he is right—then nothing, but nothing, can alter his chosen course."

"When he is certain he is right," Jessica repeated thoughtfully. "Do you think he would go against you—even when the thing he meant to do ran counter to his best interests—yet he thought it right and honorable?"

The older woman frowned in quick concern. "What do you mean?"

"I—nothing. It was just a thought," Jessica said, embarrassed by her old-fashioned choice of words. She had been enticed into it by the formal cadences of Senhora Castelar's voice, she supposed, and possibly the air of courtesy and consideration within the ancient walls of the house.

"I believe I understand," Rafael's mother said, glancing away as she was distracted by the sight of her son coming toward them with a servant bearing their refreshment in tow. "The answer to your question is yes, Jessica. Yes, he would. He is nothing if not honorable."

It was the answer she had expected. But it did not make her feel better.

Dinner that evening was a definite trial. Served in a long dining room where double sets of French doors were thrown open to the night, it was an affair of endless courses and furious conversation, most of it in rapid-fire Portuguese. Jessica spent a great deal of time smiling at jokes she did not understand and trying to put names to faces she had never seen before. Mindful of Rafael's warning, she also did her best to copy table manners that seemed both awkward and practical at the same time.

Still, it was as well that she was used to eating without the benefit of her left hand. Placed on Rafael's right where he was seated at the head of the table, she spent most of the time with her left hand captured in his fingers. He lifted it to his lips several times, brushing the sensitive skin above her knuckles with his mouth, sometimes taking a fingertip between his teeth or sucking gently upon it. He toasted her. He drank from her wineglass, placing his lips where she had just sipped. He fed her tidbits. Once he leaned close to her ear as if he meant to translate some bit of conversation as he had been doing all evening. Instead, he tasted the lobe with a warm flick of his tongue so she jerked away in startled surprise. And all the time, there was a wicked gleam in his eyes, as if he knew full well that she was flustered by his attention in spite of his warning that it would be forthcoming.

In an effort to distract herself and allow the heat to die out of her face, she surveyed the guests lined up at the table that was so long it required three centerpieces and held thirty-six place settings. The guests included Rafael's brother the doctor, a volatile young man who talked with wide gestures and spent most of his time making a young cousin blush to the pink tourmaline earrings in her pretty ears, and his sister, who was elegant in turquoise silk and aquamarines in spite of being hugely pregnant. There was also his brother-in-law, the sister's husband, a square and solid man who ate his way with precision through course after course, plus assorted uncles, aunts, and cousins, a great-aunt or two, and an elderly lady who was apparently his grandmother, the mother of Rafael's dead father. At least one priest and two nuns were present, family members who had entered the church, as well as a genial elderly bachelor who had apparently never worked and didn't intend to start anytime soon, and who seemed to be Rafael's godfather. Many of those who were unmarried— bachelor uncles, spinster aunts, and playboy cousins—

seemed to live in the house, including Rafael's cousin and copilot, Carlos.

A second, smaller table was set just behind the first. This one was lined with children, black-eyed imps of all ages who squealed and ate with equal gusto, and were prevented from constant incipient mayhem by the interventions of a couple of bright-eyed and braided maids.

In many ways the evening was like family gatherings at the Landing. It was also very different, being much lighter and more open, with constant talk and bursts of laughter. There was a certain amount of rivalry, but the Castelars all seemed to genuinely like and enjoy each other. Jessica sensed none of the strain, the undercurrents of jealousy and envy, bitterness and old grief, that hung over her grandfather's table.

At the same time she was well aware that she did not belong, that she was a stranger among them. No small part of her self-consciousness was from the close attention she was receiving. From the smallest child to the laughing priest, they stared at her. Knowing that no discourtesy was intended helped not at all; she felt under inspection, like an insect under a microscope. Nor did it make her feel better to realize that she had no real right to be there, that she was not, and never would be, a part of their large, gregarious, and wondrously cordial family. In all truth it made her feel achingly lonely and alone.

It wasn't Rafael's fault. What lay between them was such a sham from start to finish. She wouldn't be there if he was not so determined to force her into partnership with him. His elaborate pretense of love made her feel flushed and feverish while leaving her empty inside. She was tired of being used for his private amusement, tired of accepting whatever he decided was best.

How would he like it if he was on the receiving end of this taunting, spurious passion? It was possible she just might find out.

The cheese and fruit course of the meal was being served. As Rafael peeled a peach and offered her a bite at the end of a fruit fork, she caught his wrist while she took the fruit into her mouth. Meeting his gaze with limpid enjoyment, she savored the peach's flavor, then slowly swept her lips with her tongue to retrieve every trace of its nectar. He swallowed, and his head dipped toward hers. His pulse under her fingers accelerated. For an instant she thought he meant to kiss her full on the lips there in front of his family.

His lashes flickered. A corner of his mouth quivered. "Later," he whispered, a perfectly audible sound in the sudden stillness.

It sounded like a promise and was probably intended to be taken that way. To Jessica, it seemed more like a threat.

Chapter Sixteen

▨ ▨ ▨ *More relatives and friends descended on* the house after dinner. They gathered in chattering groups in the living room that opened on to the patio. Rafael circulated among them, guiding Jessica with a possessive arm around her waist as he introduced her here and there. There was no formal announcement of their engagement, however, no toasts or effusive congratulations. She was glad, though at the same time she had to wonder if it meant she had not been formally accepted as a future bride, that Rafael, most astutely, was leaving himself a way out.

The hour was growing late by Jessica's standards, since dinner had been served around ten o'clock. Still, no one seemed to have any idea of calling it a night. Some of the younger group opened a great mahogany armoire to reveal a sophisticated stereo system, and within seconds the chairs and sofas had been pushed back, the rug rolled up, and everyone was dancing to a rumba beat.

Rafael was summoned from across the room by a soigné cousin who wore her blond hair in a sleek chignon and sported diamonds the size of walnuts. He went at once with a murmured apology and hardly a backward glance.

His place was taken almost immediately by his cousin Carlos, who came to stand beside her with one hand in his pocket and a stiff drink in the other.

"Don't concern yourself, my sweet," he said. "Magda is no man-eater, at least not of such as Rafael. She has a problem with her son who is mad for sport, the *futebol*, and refuses to attend the university. As head of the family, Rafael must naturally talk sense to him."

"I wasn't concerned," Jessica said with a quick upward glance.

"No? Then, you were frowning because you don't like her dress? Or maybe you wonder if her jewels are real?"

She had not realized she was frowning at all. "Nothing like that. But Rafael has a great many people depending on him, doesn't he?"

"Too many." Carlos flashed a smile of great charm. "So it will be my pleasure to take care of you for him for a few minutes. You do not mind?"

"Actually, I'm grateful not to be left standing here by myself."

"Impossible," Carlos said at once. "For one thing, Rafael would not allow it. But if he did, some man must always rush to your side."

Had Rafael sent Carlos some signal she had missed that had directed him to entertain her? She wouldn't be surprised; she was beginning to expect that kind of consideration from him. As for the blatant admiration in his cousin's voice, she put that down to the typical Brazilian man's appreciation for women. Flirting was a national pastime, apparently, not an overture that needed to be taken seriously.

Her tone was wry as she answered. "Yes, I'm sure."

"You don't believe me? You are an exciting woman, so cool and quiet, so different. You don't tease, don't use your eyes to let a man know what is in your mind. You are the enigma, the mystery that must be sought out, the damped fire that smolders but does not burn—until one certain man strikes the spark for the inferno that will consume you both."

"I think," she said lightly, "that you have the wrong woman."

He laughed and shook his head. "No, no, our Rafael does not mistake. That is why he has neglected everything to spend so much time in the States. The challenge is irresistible, the fire beneath the ice, the siren behind the innocence. Even I feel it."

Something in his voice sent alarm skittering along her nerves. "He discussed me with you?"

"A little, perhaps." Carlos shrugged elaborately. "We are friends as well as cousins, almost like brothers—a friendship much closer than is usual in your country, I think. He trusts me as no other, just as I trust him. But you must not think he said too much. It is not his way to speak of what should be private between a man and a woman. It is only that you are so intriguing to him."

"I can't imagine why." The words were short.

"You are a beautiful woman, but you bury yourself in work and pretend it isn't so. You bear responsibility for many things, many people, leaving no time for your own needs. You hold your emotions, your fear and anger and passion, inside while keeping the world at bay. He said to me that there is a tigress inside you trying to get out. He lives for the moment when he may release the tigress."

A challenge. Was that really what she represented to Rafael? She said shortly, "He might want to be careful. He could get clawed."

"Oh, he knows this full well. Being Rafael, it's part of the lure." Carlos smiled down at her, his gaze warm. "But enough of him. Attend to me instead. I would very much like to dance with you."

"To this?" she said, accepting the distraction with thankfulness as she indicated the dramatic tango just beginning. "Oh, I don't think so."

"You don't care for it? Something more American can be arranged in only a moment."

Calling attention to herself by interfering with the music was the last thing she wanted. "It isn't that—"

"Ah, you don't feel the rhythm, don't know the steps." He turned away to set his glass on a nearby table. "Come. I will show you."

"No, really—"

Ignoring her reluctance, he reached for her hand and pulled her after him as he headed toward an open area on the glazed tile floor. Between allowing herself to be led or descending to an undignified tug of war, there was no real choice. In any case, enough people were dancing that no one should pay any attention to her mistakes.

"Now," Carlos said as he turned and pulled her close with an arm firmly around her waist, "all you must remember is that the tango is the ultimate dance of passion in which the man holds and directs the woman. There is nothing for you to do except be guided by me. And we begin."

"No we don't!"

The words, spoken in steely tones, came from just behind her. At the same moment Rafael caught Jessica's wrist, where it rested on Carlos's shoulder, then whirled her around. She came up against him, and his arms closed around her with such hard strength that the breath was forced from her lungs.

"But you spoil everything, my friend!" Carlos said in laughing protest. "And just when I was about to erase you from your beautiful Jessica's memory!"

"Go away," Rafael said, his dark eyes holding Jessica's startled gaze. "You aren't needed anymore."

"I go. But you wound me, and I will not forget it."

Rafael flicked his cousin a trenchant glance. "See that you don't." An instant later he swung Jessica in to the dance.

The hardness of his body, the taut muscles of his arms, were a potent reminder of the night in Rio, especially in combination with the insistent Latin beat of the music. Images tumbled through her mind that she had thought forgotten: the sculpting of his naked body in dark silhouette as he rose above her; the glint of the gold medallion below his throat, the soft tropical heat, the scent of aftershave mingled with night-blooming jasmine. A flush of heat began in her lower body and surged upward to flare across her cheekbones.

In her agitation it was a moment before she realized that she was actually doing the tango, following mindlessly, effortlessly where Rafael led. The ultimate dance of passion, so Carlos had called it. It was possible he was right, for she felt it inside her, saw it burning hot and dark in Rafael's eyes.

"What was he saying to you?" The words were low and edged with roughness as the man who held her spoke at last. "Something pleasing, I think. You were smiling."

What she had seen in his face might well be mere possessiveness rather than passion, Jessica thought, jealousy instead of some deeper emotion. "Nothing special. Nonsense, really."

"You know then to pay no attention? It is his duty to make love to women, to try to seduce them all if he can."

"And yours also?"

"My duty is only to one woman."

Hard on the words, he bent her over his arm in the dance so that the juncture of her thighs was pressed firmly and inescapably against his arousal. She gasped as she felt its straining heat against her softness. And abruptly she was molten inside, malleable to his control in some primitive fashion that she could scarcely recognize, much less combat.

He drew her upright again in a firm, swift move. She clung to him an instant, even as she wanted to push away. She needed to break contact, to put distance between them in order to regain some semblance of composure. That was impossible while the music held them in its sway. Before she could recover, he whirled with her tight against him, then advanced in such stalking closeness that the insides of his thighs brushed hers. She could only hold tight to him with her heart pounding while she moved in sensual counterpoint to the ancient dance of seduction.

Then came the throbbing finale. He stopped with breathtaking suddenness with her caught to him, her breasts flattened against the hard planes of his chest, his mouth inches from hers. His eyes gleamed behind half-closed lids while his diaphragm rose and fell with his hard breathing.

A tremor ran over him, and he stepped back. His lashes came down. Voice not quite even, he said, "We must talk, but not now. I will come to you when everyone has gone."

"To my room?" she said doubtfully.

"That would not be—wise. Just wait for me here, please, before you go upstairs."

It was courteously phrased. Rafael might even have considered it a request. Still, to Jessica it had the sound of a command. In instinctive resistance she said, "I thought we had our discussion."

"One of many. Do as I ask, if you please."

The impulse to refuse was strong, but there were things she needed to clarify for herself as well. She nodded in silent, half-resentful agreement as she turned and moved with him from the dance floor.

It was near two in the morning before the last guests were seen from the house. Rafael went as far as the gate to wave them off, as was customary, and to lock up for the night. The remaining relatives straggled off to their rest. Only Jessica was left, other than the maids who were emptying ashtrays and gathering up glasses as they set the living room to rights. To get out of the way of the cleanup, Jessica walked out into the enclosed patio.

She briefly considered going up to bed, avoiding the proposed conference. But she had agreed to wait for Rafael and would not go back on her word. More than that, she didn't trust him not to invade her room again if she failed him.

"I'm sorry," he said with a rueful smile as he joined her a few minutes later. "You must be tired, so I won't keep you any longer than necessary. It only occurred to me that—well, we could have a problem that should be cleared away before we go any further."

"I'm not sure I know what you mean," she said, trying to read his face in the dimness.

He took her hand and placed it in the crook of his arm, holding it as he led her away from the living room and down beside the reflecting pool. Without meeting her gaze, he said, "We have spoken little about what took place at *carnaval*, but it can no longer be ignored. Neither of us was particularly careful on that night, I think. Certainly I took no precautions, used nothing to protect you—to my embarrassment and regret. And I would be amazed to learn that you were any better prepared."

"No," she said in constricted tones as he paused.

"So I suspected." He took a soft breath. "These things have consequences, sometimes, that are not intended but which must be taken into account. We need not concern ourselves with disease. You have the protection of inexperience and I of—a certain selectivity. You understand?"

"Yes." She could not have said another word if her life depended on it.

"Yes. But another danger exists. If there is anything which would make speed with the wedding plans advisable to protect your good name, then you must tell me."

"My good name," she said, bemused by the curious sound of the words and the warmth they caused, ignoring the rest for the moment.

"I realize this is not a matter of supreme concern where you come from, but among us—"

"You're wrong. It can be extremely important in my part of the States, though we don't talk about it so much anymore."

He inclined his dark head. "Then, you understand what I am asking and the reason for it. I prefer that no shame—"

"That no shame is attached to your family," she finished for him with careful neutrality.

His brief glance was searing. "That no shame comes to you, either among my family and friends or your own, because of my actions."

He meant exactly what he said, she saw. She had misjudged him. In an odd way that made it easier to say what she must. "I—appreciate your thoughtfulness, but you need not be concerned. I'm not pregnant. I've been certain of that since last night."

He gave her a swift look. "It isn't because of the explosion? You weren't hurt, then?"

"No, no. It's just time, possibly a day or so early because of the accident, but still perfectly normal." She could feel warmth in her face, yet was aware of amazingly little chagrin for the subject under discussion. Beyond a certain sensitivity for her feelings, Rafael seemed to view talking of such things as natural so that she was able to do the same. Or she did until he spoke again.

"That brings us to another point, and also takes care of it in part," he said with wry humor in his voice. "You need not worry that I will be creeping into your room tonight or on any other while you're here. The woman I marry is expected to be pure, even in this modern age, and it is assumed I will contain myself where she is concerned. If I violate that expectation under this roof, it will be impossible, living as we do in each other's pockets, to have it remain unknown. No one would be particularly surprised if we ignored this code, since you are not one of us—"

"Being a promiscuous American instead," she offered with acid exactness.

He shrugged a shoulder. "The women of your country have this reputation, unfair though it may be. I know better, of course, and would like to be certain that everyone else understands my respect and protection."

Protection. He used that word often. She could have wished for something a little more personal. Or could she? What did it matter to her, after all, when theirs was only a business partnership?

She said, "You're very considerate, and I thank you for it."

He looked down at her then, and she thought she caught the flash of a grim smile in the darkness. "So polite. How am I to tell whether you are glad or disappointed? No matter. We spoke of being married in a month, but have not settled on a date. Have you decided on one that will please you?"

"Not really." She had tried her best not to think of it

at all, but would not destroy his illusions about her politeness by saying so. She went on, "There has been no chance to speak to a priest or check on the availability of the church. Anyway, what does it matter if it's a month, five weeks, even six? I see no particular reason to hurry."

They were nearing an alcove lined with decorative tiles that held a marble statue of the Holy Mother. Abruptly the muscles of his arm bunched into hard ropes under her fingers, while his grasp tightened on her hand. He swung her around, spinning her into the alcove and following after to press her back against the cool tiles. He pushed his fingers in her hair and tilted her face, then his lips came down on hers.

The heat between them was instant, tropic, and intense. It fired their skins, scorched their minds more surely than the exploding boat they had survived. Jessica lifted her arms and slid her hands along his shoulders to clasp them behind his neck. He crowded closer against her until their bodies were locked together from breasts to knees.

Burning and moist with the hot, honeyed sweetness of desire, their mouths clung. Her lips stung with pressure and swelling pleasure as he stroked and explored them with his tongue. She parted them for his sweet, intoxicating plunge inside. Meeting it, gliding around it, she savored the sensual, liquid slide.

He was magic, an elemental force igniting deep internal fires. She was dissolving in their flames, softening, melting to conform to the hot hardness of him against her. Murmuring wordlessly, she drew closer still.

His low sound of hunger vibrated in his chest. With spread hands he smoothed down her back, skimming the swells of her hips and cupping, grasping the firm, resilient flesh. Lifting her higher against him, he let her feel his arousal, pressing it into the soft, beckoning warmth at the apex of her thighs as he braced her with her back against the alcove's tiles. Caught between hot, hard male and cool, hard ceramic, she gasped in shocked gratification.

He stopped.

For long, agonizing seconds, he was still. Then he released her with the slow reluctance of clenched muscles, shuddering a little as he allowed her to slide down his body until her feet were touching the ground once more.

The sockets of his eyes were dark wells of consideration as he surveyed the ghostly pale oval of her upturned face. Voice husky and not quite even, he said, "Now do you see a reason for haste?"

Chapter Seventeen

▓ ▓ ▓ *To hide away in Brazil forever could have* certain advantages; Jessica saw that well before the end of the first week. The pace was so much slower and more relaxed; the countryside enticing in its lush tropical beauty. The ancient buildings, the beaches, the small shops she and Rafael explored in Recife and Olinda, had such intriguing character. Still, it was not possible to remain. Too much had been left in limbo in New Orleans, too many things required her attention. And that was without considering her grandfather's uncertain health.

Rafael left her in Recife for a couple of days while he flew to Rio to catch up at his office. Complications he found there after so long away made it impossible for him to return to the States as planned. He tried to talk Jessica into waiting in Rio until he was free, pointedly expressing his concern for the danger to her. She would not let herself be convinced. For one thing, she knew her work was piling up in New Orleans in the same way as his. For another, she had a wedding to arrange in a span of time that was daily growing shorter. Mainly, however, she was afraid that giving in to his arguments could become a habit. When he tried to forbid her return toward the last, then, all her instincts rose up in instant opposition. To end the matter she threatened to book a commercial flight if he would not permit Carlos to take her in the private plane.

That, he most certainly would not. Over the half-outraged, half-amused protests of his cousin, Rafael himself flew her home.

It was an uncomfortable journey, since he was grimly silent in his anger that she would go against his wishes. Nor did he linger. Giving her a quick, hard kiss of good-bye at the airport, he took off for Rio again within the hour.

As a concession to Rafael's schedule, the flight had again been made at night. Jessica took a taxi home and went straight to bed to readjust from Brazilian hours. When she reached the office the next morning, there was an enormous arrangement of bridal white orchids with golden throats on her desk. She took it as an apology for ill humor, whether it was meant that way or not. Or at least an indication that Rafael considered her feelings even when she went against him. And she could not prevent the smile that curved her lips whenever her glance touched the bouquet.

By the middle of the week, she was immersed in her old routine once more, arriving early and leaving late, discussing problems with Keil, exchanging quips with Sophie, reporting to her grandfather and checking on his progress at least every other day. The time slid past, becoming a week, then two.

All the same, something was missing. Her concentration was almost nil. She could not recall important details just seconds after hearing them. She misplaced papers, and had to be reminded to return calls or keep appointments. She looked up quickly at the sound of male footsteps in the hall, jumped when her doorbell rang at home, and carried a cellular phone with her everywhere she went. There was something seriously wrong with her.

Rafael. Rafael was her problem.

It was utterly ridiculous, the number of times she thought about him, of what he might think or do or say about some issue; what he was doing in Rio, whether he was at the office, at his Rio apartment, or on the way to Recife. Whether Pepe was looking after him as usual, or if he was eating meals in restaurants and having takeout food brought to the office as she was. She was always discovering things she didn't know about him but needed to find out, such as his date of birth or whether he liked cooked celery or poached pears.

She did her best to prevent such idiocy from taking over her days, but it seemed near impossible. Though the merger of the two business concerns was not yet official, there was constant communication between them. Rafael called at least twice every day with some question concerning procedures, one that usually required that she contact him again later in the day. Their conversations were fairly mundane, but she found herself expecting to hear his voice each time she picked up the phone. Sometimes he called her at home in the evening also. His excuses were not always convincing, and she wondered if he was simply checking to be sure she was all right, as if he had added her to his list of responsibilities. She would not ask, however, so could not know for sure.

Toward the end of the third week, Sea Gull was invaded by accountants. It seemed her grandfather had authorized CMARC representatives to make a preliminary audit of Sea Gull's books. It was a formality only; still it served to make everything seem more definite.

Jessica was half inclined to resent the intrusion, in spite of recognizing the need for it. Her ruffled feelings were soothed, however, as perhaps they were meant to be, by the delivery of a detailed report on CMARC. It was an interesting document, one showing the history of the company along with past and present officers, and listing accomplishments and objectives as well as the usual detailed statement of financial position. Touched by that gesture of trust and implied inclusion in the future of the company, she sat holding it for long moments, smiling a little as she smoothed one hand over the report's leather cover. She handled it with great care as she set it aside for study later when she had greater leisure.

Still, it was when she caught herself doodling her initials entwined with Rafael's in the margin of a list of possible wedding guests that she knew something had to give. She had no time for this kind of juvenile emotional disturbance. The way to fight it was to keep busy with other things. She would clean out her closet, organize the pantry, cook a few things and freeze them for quick meals, maybe align her spice rack in alphabetical order. If that didn't work, she would visit Mimi Tess to soothe her frazzled composure.

It was her mother who opened the door at Mimi Tess's house. Arletta's lips tilted in a thin smile as she waved Jessica inside with the hand that held her cigarette, then moved ahead of her down the long central hall toward the parlor. Though it was the middle of the afternoon, she still wore a housecoat of quilted black silk along with gold leather mules that slapped against her heels with every step.

"So you're back," the older woman said over her shoulder. "Nick said you were, but I couldn't be sure, since I haven't seen hide nor hair of you. Of course, you didn't tell me you were leaving, either."

"I thought you gave up noticing when I came and went long ago," Jessica answered with a wary look at the stiff set of Arletta's shoulders.

"I may not have been a perfect mom, but I care about what happens to you."

"Well, when something does I'll be sure and let you know." Jessica's words were short, caused by too many years of memories of a mother who was never there.

As they stepped into the parlor, Arletta turned to face her. "You call nearly getting yourself blown up or drowned not worth mentioning? You don't think I'd like to hear when some man spirits you away to the ends of the earth?"

"It was hardly that. Besides, Keil and Grandpapa knew, and I called at least half a dozen times."

"Oh, the office, yes. And to your grandfather—as if he wouldn't be more likely to pass any news along to a perfect stranger than give it to me."

A sharp retort sprang to Jessica's lips, but she let it go as her attention was deflected by a shadow at the point of her mother's jaw. With a frown between her brows, she reached to touch Arletta's face, turning it toward the light from the windows. The livid purple-blue of a bruise was plain beneath a concealing layer of foundation makeup.

"Don't!" Arletta jerked away.

"What happened to you?"

"Nothing." The answer was short, Arletta's gaze veiled as she turned sharply to stalk deeper into the room.

"Did you fall? Maybe run into something?" Jessica followed her as she moved away.

"I haven't been staggering around drunk, if that's what you mean!"

"I never suggested it!"

"You thought it," the other woman snapped. "Let it go; I told you it was nothing."

Jessica stared at her, puzzled by her defensive tone. If she had truly not been drinking, then there was only one other possibility that came to mind. Too stunned for subterfuge, she said, "Somebody hit you!"

"No, no, let it go," Arletta answered, but the words carried no conviction.

"Who was it? Did somebody break into your house? Were you mugged, assaulted, what?" Jessica's voice was rising in her concern, but she couldn't help it.

Arletta turned to stare at her. "Why would you think a thing like that?"

Jessica hesitated, not quite certain how much she could say without giving herself away. Finally she described the incident in the hallway of her town house, and how Rafael had come to her rescue.

"My God." Arletta, pale around the mouth, moved to a sofa and dropped down on the cushions as if her legs had no strength. "And you didn't say a word, not to me, not to your grandpapa, not to anybody."

"I thought it was just a mugger at the time," she answered with something less than full truthfulness. "But after what happened with the boat and now this with you—I don't know what to think. It makes no sense; there's no reason behind it."

"I don't know about that," Arletta said slowly.

Jessica watched her with care. "What do you mean?"

"Your grandfather is going down more every day, and there's a multimillion-dollar business at stake. Money—greed—does strange things to people."

"Going down? You don't mean he's worse?"

"He's been having little strokes off and on for the past couple of weeks, didn't you know? That's on top of the one that put him in the hospital. He could go at any time."

"Nobody told me." Distress clutched at Jessica's chest with a hurtful grip so that her voice came out in a whisper. "He seemed to be getting better."

"He'd like to think he's immortal. Too bad he's not." Arletta's lips twisted as she glanced down at her hand that was clutching the sofa arm. Deliberately she relaxed the clawlike grasp.

Jessica was silent for a long moment while pain constricted her throat. At last she said, "So Grandpapa isn't coming back to Sea Gull after all. The CMARC merger will go through, and it's never going to be the same."

"That's about the size of it. And a good thing, too, if you ask me."

Jessica hadn't, but she supposed Arletta was entitled to her opinion. She didn't have the same perspective, of course. To Jessica, it appeared that Rafael had, finally, won. No doubt he had known it at the Landing the day he agreed to Claude Frazier's proposal for his granddaughter's future.

Quiet descended between the two women. A frail voice, half musing, half accusing, came from the other side of the room. "Jonathan never hit you, Arletta. He was a good man, a fine husband."

It was Jessica's grandmother, sitting in quiet contemplation, half hidden in a wing-back chair near the windows. She had apparently caught a portion of their conversation and arrived at her own unique take on it.

"Mimi Tess!" Jessica exclaimed, going forward and

leaning to press a quick kiss to a cheek as fine and dry and fragrant as rose petal potpourri. "I didn't see you there against the light."

The elderly woman's smile was gentle, her gaze a little vague. "How you've grown, child. But you look like your father, you really do. I liked Jonathan. He used to bring me chocolate-covered cherries—he knew they were my favorites. And he was good to my Arletta. He didn't have a mean bone in his body."

"Oh, Mama!" There was embarrassed annoyance in Arletta's voice.

Hearing it, Jessica glanced at the bruise on her mother's jaw again. While it was true that Mimi Tess had only a loose grasp on reality, Jessica knew she sometimes recognized things others missed. And Arletta had not, after all, said she had been attacked. Meeting her mother's gaze, she said in blunt accusation, "A man did hit you, didn't he? Who was it?"

"Don't be silly! You think I would put up with that kind of treatment?"

Jessica gave a slow shake of her head. "Something like it happened, otherwise you wouldn't be staying with Mimi Tess instead of at your own apartment. Are you afraid to go back there?"

"I don't want to talk about it," Arletta said sharply. "It's my business, nothing to do with you."

In the back of Jessica's mind was the memory of the man Arletta was supposed to be seeing: a younger man. Not that the last mattered, of course; there was always a man of some kind coming and going in her mother's life. "You're all right, then?" she said uneasily. "You got rid of whoever did this to you?"

"He won't be giving me any more trouble. You can bet on that."

"You're sure?" She could not keep the concern from her voice.

"Positive."

The resistance in the set of Arletta's body was complete. To press her further seemed like prying, which was a sad commentary on their relationship. Jessica gave a slow nod. "I guess it's all right, if that's the way you want it."

The other woman's smile was tired and a little crooked. "You're a good girl." She drew a quick breath, then let it out. "I think I could use a cup of coffee. Anybody want to join me?"

It was later, as they sat over the crumbs of a butter pound cake while sipping a second cup of the hot, strong brew that was a Louisianian's panacea for all ills, that Jessica returned to the subject of Jonathan Meredith.

"You know, I was thinking the other day that I really don't know much about my dad. I was so young when the two of you divorced, then he died. Grandpapa didn't like me to mention him, didn't want any pictures of him sitting around. There were times when I wanted to ask you what he was like, but it never seemed right."

Arletta pushed her coffee cup away and reached for her cigarettes. Lighting one with her monogrammed silver lighter, she blew smoke toward the ceiling before she answered. "He was a nice guy, a good man, I guess, just as Mimi says. Handsome, of course, and something of a daredevil. He got into planes while he was in the service, flew missions in Vietnam—but you knew that."

Jessica nodded, afraid to say anything that might prevent her mother from continuing.

Arletta took another deep drag and rid her lungs of the smoke, her gaze distant as she watched the gray swirl. "We were fine as long as he was in the service. Sometimes I think I married him because of the uniform and the chance to travel, to get out of the backcountry of Louisiana. After Vietnam, he didn't reenlist, and—well, it wasn't the same."

"What do you mean?"

Arletta shrugged. "The war did something to him, or maybe to us both, I don't know. Anyway, we found a house in Crowley, near the rice-growing area, and Jonathan started his crop-dusting service. He liked to skim the very tips of the rice blades, brush the treetops with his wheels, buzz the egrets in the swamps. He used to chase his plane's shadow down the Mermentau and the Atchafalaya, following all the river bends. Sometimes he'd scare the hell out of me when we flew down to the Landing to visit." She smiled briefly. "You know the old shell road across the chenier? Your grandpapa's daddy built it to check on his cattle, haul them out to high ground during the winter. Jonathan would land on that road like a rough airstrip, set his plane down soft and easy like putting a baby in a crib. God, he loved to fly."

She stopped, the look in her eyes far away and edged with pain. Jessica watched her mother, hearing echoes of a life and love Jessica had hardly dreamed existed. Moisture gathered behind her eyes, and she had to clear her throat before she could speak. "What happened? Why did you break up?"

"Jonathan could get high on flying, but it wasn't enough. He took to drinking, and that didn't mix with airplanes and chemicals. He had a near miss or two, but it didn't stop him; he was always depressed when he wasn't flying, so he drank even more then. And he didn't want me to work. He thought he had to support me, give me a maid and weekly visit to the hairdresser, all that. I was supposed to stay home, take care of our baby—you—and be there when he got home. Never mind that I was bored out of my skull, so at loose ends that I had to take tranquilizers to keep from screaming the house down. Oh, I know it sounds silly, but you had to have been there."

"So there was another man?"

Her mother gave an unhappy nod. "It was your usual story; he was a friend of Jonathan's who started coming around. It was exciting, seemed like it had been years since I felt so alive. Stupid, but I've never pretended to be particularly smart about love. Anyway, by then Jonathan didn't seem to care. So we were separated, and that rocked on a year before I filed for a divorce. I moved back to the Landing while all the legal mess was taking place, and for the twelve months afterward that you used to have to wait for a divorce decree in Louisiana.

The day before everything was final, Jonathan called and said he was coming down to see me, that he wanted to talk. It was raining, coming down in buckets from a tropical storm off the coast. He overshot the shell road in the wind and rain, and crashed in the marsh."

Mimi Tess had been listening, sitting with her empty coffee cup forgotten in her lap. She shook her silver-white head now as she said softly, "No lights."

Arletta gave her mother a quick, almost resentful look. "That's right, there were no lights. Your grand-papa had always rigged a set of guide lights powered by a portable generator for Jonathan. That night he refused to put them out because he didn't want Jonathan to come, had ordered him to stay away. Jonathan was never good enough for me in Papa's eyes, since he had no real family and came from back in the swamps." She wiped a hand over her eyes, then leaned to stub out her cigarette. "I told him Jonathan didn't take orders, but he wouldn't listen. I think he felt the storm would keep Jonathan from flying. He was sorry later, though he would never admit it. But by then, it was too late."

Yes, much too late, Jessica thought. Too late to save her mother as well as her father. Because that must have been the incident that had finally set Arletta against Claude Frazier and started her on her path of self-destructive defiance—flitting to one man after another, to drinking and bars, to pointless spending sprees and useless, empty days.

"So terrible," she whispered.

Arletta closed her eyes, pressing them tight. "Yes, terrible," she agreed on a sigh before she looked at Jessica. "But Jonathan loved you. You were his play-pretty, his baby princess. God, he used to get a kick out of watching you. You would run to him the minute he came home, and he would swing you up high. He'd take you up in the plane with him when you were barely able to sit alone, pretend you were his copilot. Once he told me you were his one, single link with the future. I've never forgotten that because it turned out to be so true."

"I had a baby," Mimi Tess said suddenly, her frail voice reflective. "Such a sweet little thing. But he died. They said he died, and I never saw him again."

Jessica looked from her grandmother to her mother, and raised a brow. So far as she knew, Arletta was the only child born to Claude Frazier and Mimi Tess. Arletta, meeting her gaze, only shook her head with pity threading through the dark remembrance in her eyes.

Still, the mention of babies was a reminder of Jessica's conversation with Rafael. Catching her grandmother's eyes, though speaking also to her mother, she said, "You know that I'm going to be married?"

Interest brightened Mimi's faded old eyes. It was Arletta, however, who said, "So your grandfather informed me, though the whole thing sounds mighty fishy to me. If I thought for a minute that he was sacrificing you to hang on to his precious company I swear I don't know what I might do!"

Jessica hadn't thought of it in quite that light. Still, she didn't intend to go into details now with Arletta. She said, "Rafael and I set a date before I left Brazil. Do you have anything planned for two weeks from Saturday?"

"Two weeks! And I'm just hearing about it? Are you crazy?"

"Probably," Jessica said in wry agreement.

"But we can't possibly pull a wedding together in that time. All the best caterers will be booked. We won't be able to reserve the church or find a good band with an open date. Flowers. They'll have to be flown in special if they're to be worth two cents. And your dress—finding something just right takes forever."

"A big production is the last thing I want," Jessica said firmly. "It wouldn't be right with Grandpapa sick."

"Well, you can't have anything thrown together and tacky, especially if Castelar's people are coming from South America. You don't want them to think we don't know what we're doing. And all my friends will expect something stupendous. Besides, you're my only child, and this is the one chance I'll have to be in the middle of a big wedding."

Jessica saw that she should have kept her mouth shut. Sharing this news, however, had been a way of making up for leaving Arletta out of so much else in her life.

"I'm sorry," she said, "but Rafael and I have already worked out the basics, and his people have everything in hand. It's going to be simple but nice. The cathedral, of course, for the ceremony, then the reception at the St. Louis Hotel afterward. One of the best restaurants in town is doing the food and drink. You really don't have to worry about a thing."

"Just two weeks, the minute Lent is over. You aren't wasting any time."

"There's no reason to wait."

Arletta made no reply, but only reached for her cigarette case again. She extracted one, then sat tapping it on the silver case. Glancing up at Jessica at last, she said, "Have you thought about this, I mean really thought about it?"

Her mother's voice sounded odd, shaded with reluctance that had nothing to do with ordinary reservations over a daughter's choice of husbands. "What do you mean?"

Arletta frowned. "I'm not sure exactly, only somebody has tried twice to hurt you. Maybe that should tell you something."

"Like what?" The question was wary. There had been three times, though Arletta didn't know that. The attack by the man in the dark patio, with the pictures that were taken after, must surely qualify as an attempt at harm.

Arletta glanced at her and away again. "Like maybe getting involved with this Brazilian is a bad idea. Who knows what kind of friends he may have or what he's capable of doing?"

"Oh, please."

"I'm not being prejudiced, if that's what you think. Only it stands to reason. You were perfectly safe until he came along."

"You think the danger has something to do with

Rafael? That it was directed at me because of my association with him?"

"Maybe. But I also think it's mighty convenient that he's always been on hand to step in and protect you—unless he caused you to need protecting in the first place."

A cold chill moved down Jessica's spine, spreading to numb her heart. That night at the town house, Rafael had not gone after her assailant. She had thought it was because of his concern for her as well as his injuries. But what if he had not wanted the man caught, had only wanted to stop the attack because he had just found out he would have what he wanted by marrying Claude Frazier's granddaughter?

Voice stiff, she said, "But he would have died in the explosion of the boat if he hadn't noticed the leaking gas line."

"*If.* But he did get you off, didn't he? And how do you know there ever was a leaking line? The *Sea Gull IV* is in a million pieces; there's no proof. In fact, there's no proof this man didn't set that explosion himself."

Jessica waved a hand in an impatient gesture. "No, really, what possible reason could he have?"

"You're going to marry him, aren't you?"

"One thing has nothing to do with the other!"

"Doesn't it? Are you sure? It must be hard to resist a handsome Galahad who risks life and limb to save you. And in return for his services, he gets a valuable company handed over to him without the delay and expense of going through legal channels—channels that may or may not have given him what he wants."

Jessica had the feeling that her mother was thinking the situation through as she went along, and without full knowledge or proper time sequence. That didn't make it any less credible, of course. She felt like weeping and that interfered with her ability to think. Almost at random, she said, "Whatever is between me and Rafael is secondary."

"Are you sure?" Arletta insisted as she stared at her

with a frown of concentration between her eyes and her
unlit cigarette forgotten between her fingers.

Jessica wasn't sure at all. She wasn't sure because the
fiasco in Rio had certainly been the beginning, and that
had occurred well before she agreed to the marriage.

"Wait," she said in abrupt relief. "Rafael didn't propose this marriage; the idea came from Grandpapa.
Rafael only went along with it."

Arletta gave a sharp laugh. "Did he indeed? And
doesn't that strike you as strange in this day and age?
Why would the wealthy owner of a multinational shipping company meekly agree to what amounts to an arranged marriage? No, I think the idea came from this
Castelar, no matter what you think. Somehow or other,
he got around your grandfather. You've been had,
Jessica. I don't see how he did it, but I would bet
money you've been had."

Arletta might not be able to see, but Jessica could.
The pictures, those damning, eternally damned, pictures. If Rafael had shown them to Claude Frazier, if he
had held them over her grandfather's head, then he
might have cooperated. In the face of such brazen conduct by his granddaughter, his puritanical instinct might
have been to avoid any mention of it to her but push for
the marriage as the best solution to her fall from grace.

She didn't want to believe any of it. And yet, nothing
else had the same relentless logic.

She didn't tell her mother that. What she said, instead, was she wasn't quite sure, but it must have been
acceptable for there was no further discussion. A short
time later, Jessica took her leave with a quick half-
embarrassed hug for Arletta and a warmer one for Mimi
Tess. The next thing she knew she was outside on the
sidewalk.

She decided to walk back to the office in the hope
that the sun and warm spring breeze would help clear
her mind. There was such pain inside her. She felt as if
something had been severed, as if some fine dream had
been cut out and sliced into tiny pieces. Her nose and
throat ached, and she was half-blind with the press of

unshed tears. And she couldn't think, couldn't seem to marshal the arguments that would convince herself that what she feared was not true.

You've been had.

Yes, indeed, in more ways than one.

No, it made no sense. Why had Rafael treated her with such consideration? Why hadn't he tried harder to take up where they had left off in that patio?

Unless he didn't want her?

Yes, but he did; she had proof of it beyond a doubt. More than that, he had told her so.

If she could believe a word he said. Or if it really mattered.

What other explanation could there be? If he hadn't used the pictures as suggested, where were they? Who else had the slightest reason for harming her? What could anyone possibly hope to gain by it?

He's a real lady-killer ...

One woman who was connected to Rafael had died, and another had come close to it. Had they really been so unstable, as his mother said, or had he simply wanted to be free of them?

If she had been killed by the mugger or died in the explosion, then what would have happened? The answer was, nothing much. She had no direct shares in Sea Gull, wouldn't until Arletta was gone, so the percentage of ownership would have remained unchanged. Someone else would have had to step into her shoes as CEO, most likely Keil. Though with the coming merger, there was no guarantee of a permanent position.

Where did that leave her? Still without any real answers.

Nevertheless, her pain and desperate searching for an alternative to Arletta's scenario told her something important. She had been perilously close to allowing Rafael a place in her heart and mind, to letting herself dream that she just might catch a bright gold ring after all while mounting the marriage carousel. Or perhaps she had only been busily fashioning something good and meaningful out of a necessity. That had always been the traditional solution for women in her situation, hadn't it?

She was no clearer in her mind when she reached the office once more. All she had to show for her walk was a blister on her heel and gum on her shoe. Her resulting mood was something less than cheerful.

"Well, girlfriend," Sophie greeted her as soon as she walked in the outer door, "you can stop your fretting and start smiling, for things are about to change."

Jessica gave her a jaundiced look. "Are they now?"

"They are. I've been getting real chummy with a certain secretary down South America way. She checks in regular, keeping me up to speed. I just got off the phone with her maybe ten minutes ago."

Alarm ran like an electrical shock along Jessica's nerves. "And?"

"Her boss man has finally cleared his schedule."

"You mean—?" She stopped, torn between hope and terror.

Sophie smiled with a roguish wink. "Right. Guess who's coming to dinner?"

Chapter Eighteen

▨ ▨ ▨ *Something was wrong, Rafael thought, and* it was more than the quarrel between them before Jessica left Brazil, the awkwardness of the long-distance engagement, or pre-wedding jitters. Her voice was too brittle, her smiles too bright. She accepted his kiss of greeting but moved away at once and had avoided all contact since. He had not been expecting a warm welcome precisely, but neither had he thought to find her so changed.

A possible reason for it leaped instantly to mind. It was not something he could easily accept, since it would brand her a mistress of deceit. Still, he was a realist. He recognized that business was business and people not always as they seemed.

He was aware of a strong and uncharacteristic need to come right to the point, to strike to the heart of what promised to be an unpleasant situation so he could put it behind him. That wouldn't do. The matter needed a subtle approach. Jessica must be given no cause to avoid the issue. Many things he might overlook, but he could not bear the thought of her lying to him.

They had enjoyed a fine meal at one of the better restaurants. He had seen her back to her town house as a matter of course, and accepted her halfhearted invitation to come up for coffee.

Breaking the strained silence that had fallen, he said, "You've had no further problems with your unknown assailant?"

"None," she said. "As a matter of fact, things have been very quiet since I got back."

He had to ask, even knowing how unlikely any disturbance was in view of the twenty-four-hour watch he had arranged for her safety. It would be a relief when he could see to that himself. "No more reports of drugs, then, or difficulties between Sea Gull and Customs?"

She looked up quickly from her contemplation of her fingernails. "You know about that?"

"Your grandfather mentioned it. He wanted to know how we handle such problems at CMARC."

Her attention sharpened. "And what do you do?"

"Our policy is much the same as yours: posted warnings, vigilance, and instant dismissal for anyone caught in the act. Some boat captains may be a bit rougher with offenders because violations reflect on their command, but we can't control that."

"And don't try?"

"As you say." He kept his voice even in spite of his annoyance for the sharp irony of her tone. Pressing his point, he said, "No more trouble, then?"

She looked away as she shook her head. "Either it was a false report or whoever was behind the incident decided to lie low."

"We'll hope it was the first," he said easily. When she made no reply, he went on. "Your only problem, then, has been having our auditors with you. It's a nuisance, I know, but I trust they haven't been getting in your way?"

"Not noticeably. Keil has been dealing with them for the most part."

There had been no particular emphasis to her answer, he thought. "You haven't kept track yourself of where they are in the auditing process?"

"No." She studied him with a look of consideration in her eyes. "Just what are you driving at?"

So much for subtlety. A grimace twisted his lips before he said, "One or two minor discrepancies have come to light. There is also a major glitch."

"Yes?" Her voice had an edge like a piece of broken crystal, but her gaze was steady.

"Two hundred thousand drained from the bank accounts over the past month without appropriate accounting entries."

Shock widened her eyes. "Impossible! That's the major portion of our cash reserves. The only way—"

"The only way it could be missing is if someone with authorization transferred the funds. Such as you or Keil. Or your grandfather, of course."

"There must be a good reason." She put her fingertips to her temple, pressing hard. "I'll look into it. In the meantime, you ... won't mention it to my grandfather, will you?"

Her face was so pale, it matched the white blouse she wore with a severe black business suit. Compared to the bright, stylish clothing he was used to seeing on the women of his country, she looked like a harassed and incredibly seductive nun. He would have preferred seeing her in something more feminine, but it made little difference. He basically wanted her unclothed. And under him, beside him, on top of him. Anywhere, any way she wanted.

He must be going mad.

Concentrating desperately, he said, "I never intended to rush down and present the problem to your grandfather. What do you take me for?"

Her lips compressed, and there was green fire in her eyes as she met his gaze. "I wasn't thinking of you, but of Grandpapa. He may have directed that the funds be moved himself, but I don't know that."

"And if he didn't?"

"Then I'll find out where they went. Though I fail to see that it's CMARC's business at this point."

"Or mine?" he took her up with precision. "It's neither, of course, except for its effect on future management."

She stared at him a long moment before she turned her face away. "I see."

Rafael was aware of an almost overwhelming urge to

reach out, snatch her close, and promise anything if only she would stop fighting him. He was haunted by the image of the sultry, passionate woman in that cursed picture, by the consuming, white-hot oblivion they had shared in a dark patio, and by his escalating need to find both once more.

She was speaking again while she pleated a fold of her suit skirt between her fingers. "It may be that the money was taken as—as a temporary loan. If that's the case, I hope you'll think carefully before condemning whoever is at fault. Sometimes people do things that they wouldn't normally do, things they regret. It would be a mistake to penalize them for a single weak moment out of a lifetime of upstanding conduct."

She was, Rafael thought, referring to herself and what happened between them as much as to the problem at hand. Or perhaps not. She must know very well her grandfather had not transferred the funds, else she would not be concerned with his reaction to the loss. She suspected who was at fault, but was not inclined to admit it to him. Which was not important except that he did not intend to allow concealment in their relationship.

"It was you, then?" he asked in dry reproof.

"No! How can you even begin to suggest—Oh." Her eyes narrowed in resentment. "You wanted to hear me say so. You now assume it was Keil."

"It's logical," he said evenly.

"You can be sure I'll trace it down," she returned in acid tones.

"I expected no less."

She was silent a moment while mutinous anger rose in her eyes. "That's the only reason you came, then, to straighten us out here with this annoying little problem of disappearing assets?"

"By no means," he said promptly, even as he concealed his enjoyment of her show of temper. He thought it was caused by his apparent lack of personal motivation, but would not risk disappointment by asking. Reaching out to where she sat beside him on the sofa, he took a strand of her hair between his fingers, enjoying its hint of her warmth, its silky texture, almost as much as the fact that she did not pull away.

Her voice not quite even, she said, "Well?"

"Well, what?"

"What else did you have in mind?"

He would like to tell her. He wished that she knew Portuguese; then it would be so much easier to say all the things he wanted and needed for her to hear. She must learn; he would see to it. Soon.

He said, "We have a wedding fast approaching, if you recall. You will have questions, details that require consultation. Then there is the marriage contract, which needs to be signed."

"Marriage contract."

The words were flat, but he inclined his head as if they had been a question. "A formality that includes a mutual beneficiary clause between the two of us, among other provisions for your future security. It also includes the details of the merger agreed upon between your grandfather and myself."

"Can such a thing really be necessary?" she said in sharp reproof.

"Not entirely, but it eliminates any misunderstanding. The two corporations will have guidelines for this interim period, and you will be protected should anything happen to me."

"Just as you will be covered if anything happens to me?"

His face tightened at the implied insult. "As you say. We will sign these documents after the wedding, at the same time that we sign our marriage license—which is, you realize, only another form of contract."

"Yes, I suppose so." Her lashes flickered down to conceal her expression.

It was little enough in the way of concession, but he had to be satisfied with it. "We were discussing my reasons for being here, I think. I need to know your preference as to your belongings. It will be perfectly possible for you to leave everything as it is, maintaining

the town house as a convenient address for your visits
to New Orleans. Or you can move into a hotel while
everything is boxed and shipped to Rio."

"I—that's very considerate," she said, glancing at
him for long seconds, then looking away again.

"I hope," he said quietly as he released her hair and
trailed his fingers along the tender curve of her jaw before taking his hand away, "that I am not an inconsid-
erate man."

"I'm sure of it, even if . . ."

"Yes?" His anticipation for what she might say was
less than comfortable.

"Never mind. I'll think about the town house and let
you know in a day or two. But as long as you're here,
I suppose we could discuss what you would like to do
for our—that is, where you want to go after the wedding."

He had thought she meant to suggest that she found
his ultrapolite attention to her needs unsatisfactory. If
so, he must accept disappointment. Just as he must
swallow her reluctance to call their first few days and
nights together a honeymoon. The words even, he said,
"I only require that it be quiet and private."

"You might prefer your hotel suite," she said with a
small nod, as if she had expected no less. "Or we could
come back here if I leave everything in place."

He thought of the bed he could just glimpse through
a half-open door, a big, antique affair with a tester from
which hung draperies of brocade and gauze caught back
with silk cord. "Wherever you are most comfortable,"
he said. "I leave it entirely to you."

Her glance was suspicious. As she opened her mouth
to reply, however, there came a muffled thud from
somewhere in the back of the house.

Rafael made a swift, imperative gesture for silence as
he rose to his feet. Indicating that she was to remain, he
eased from the living room into the dining room, then
through to the darkened kitchen beyond.

Nothing. Nor did anything move on the small enclosed gallery or the tiny back garden that it overlooked.

Inside the house again, he searched the bedroom and connecting sitting room as well as the other rooms beyond that were used by Claude Frazier when he was in town. All were as empty as the dark entrance stair and the hall that lay below it.

"A neighbor's cat, maybe?" Jessica said as he returned to the living room.

"Possibly." He didn't believe it, but there seemed no point in upsetting her by saying so.

Later, when they had hashed out the last wedding details, she walked him to the door. There was nothing in the tense silence that stretched between them to encourage a warm farewell.

It was better that way, he told himself; he needed no tests of his powers of restraint. Yet his urge to touch her was acute, one only whetted by the small encroachments he had made so far. Voice rough with its low timbre, he said, "I won't see you again before the wedding."

Surprise brought her head up. "You're returning to Brazil so soon?"

"I must, if I'm to clear time for later."

"Yes. I have to think about that, too." The reply was hardly more than a murmur.

He reached to close the fingers of both hands on her arms, absorbing the resilient texture of her smooth, warm flesh beneath her blouse, the slender shaping of muscle and bone. He inhaled the delicate, natural fragrance of her at the same time that he drew a breath of purest satisfaction. Her lips parted on a soft gasp. Inescapably drawn, he leaned to taste them, taking their tender sweetness, their satin surfaces and moist adhesion into some deep recess of memory.

She stiffened, began to pull away. A quick tremor ran over her as she tried to control that instinctive impulse.

To have his kiss endured was not what he wanted or needed. Chilled, he let her go and stepped back.

"Call if you need me," he said in tones of careful neutrality. Swinging from her, he went down the stairs without waiting for an answer.

The man assigned to duty outside the town house was easy to find. Too easy. No, he had seen nothing, he claimed. Had there been anything to see?

Rafael allowed the cold anger inside him to surface. When he finally walked away, the man was still babbling excuses. They would not suffice. Pepe must replace such an incompetent guard. Then perhaps he himself could rest easy until his wedding day when it would be his pleasure to assume that duty.

Jessica did not find a dress she cared for at all until three days before the wedding. Everything she looked at had too many ruffles, too much lace, an excess of chiffon, pearls, and iridescent beading, not to mention a supreme surfeit of virginal innocence.

Her final choice was simple and elegant in heavy champagne *peau de soie*, with cap sleeves, a scooped neckline, and a straight skirt that swept into fullness at the back. Even so, she wasn't totally happy with it. Something was missing.

Leaving the dress at the shop to be hemmed, she drove home. Rather than going upstairs immediately, however, she walked over to Napoleon House to recoup her energy with coffee and a pastry. Just inhaling the brew made her feel better. At least that was one thing she and Rafael had in common, she thought wryly, their love of coffee.

She was just taking the first reviving sip when she heard a call from behind her.

"Jessica?"

"Debbie!" she cried, coming to her feet as she recognized the diminutive blonde coming toward her. It was Debbie Ciaccio, a friend from the long summers of her childhood. The two of them exchanged a quick hug even as Debbie launched into speech.

"Lord, honey, I haven't seen you in ages—and that's too long! I went by your office, but you weren't there, so I came on to the Quarter for a little shopping, stopped in here on the off chance you just might be at your old haunt." Debbie dumped the packages she was carrying on the floor, pulled up a chair.

"Oh, Debbie, I'm so glad to see you," Jessica said with heartfelt pleasure as she sank back into her seat.

"Same here," her friend said, her gaze brightly penetrating. "I got your wedding invitation, and you could have knocked me down with a feather. So tell all. Where did you meet a guy with such a fascinating name? What is he like? I want to hear every single detail!"

Jessica had to laugh. Debbie, vivacious to the point of being bubbly yet warm and wise, hadn't changed at all in the years since they had dodged cows and cow patties while picking up shells on the beach near Ombre-Terre. It made Jessica feel better to know that some things remained the same.

Though Debbie was from the northern part of the state, she had spent several summers with an aunt who lived at Cameron and kept a beach house on the gulf. Jessica saw her now only when Debbie came to New Orleans on business with her husband, but they kept in touch. Their friendship was as near as Jessica could come to the kind of relationship that existed between Rafael and his cousin Carlos.

Those days on the beach had been her time of escape, the time when she was most truly herself. Debbie had been a large part of it. She had encouraged her to make her own decisions, her own mistakes, to assert her own personality. She was forever telling her to be herself. It hadn't worked entirely, of course; Jessica could never get over worrying about what her grandfather would think or how he would feel about her actions. Still, she would have been a different person without Debbie.

As good a friend as she had always been, however, Jessica could not tell her the whole story behind her marriage. Debbie would be the last person to understand or approve such an impersonal business arrangement. She would be horrified, beyond a doubt, and probably do her best to talk her out of it. The version

Jessica gave, then, was missing several important details.

"How absolutely romantic," the other woman said. "But I always knew you'd do something wild."

Jessica gave her an incredulous look. "You've got to be kidding."

"Not on your life. You were always one of those quiet, mysterious types that make people wonder. I remember I used to get such a kick out of watching you when we were teenagers. You'd go along in your own private little world, never noticing the way guys stopped in their tracks for a second look, or how they made excuses to come around. There was something about you that turned them on without you doing a thing. I always thought that if you ever woke up and noticed a man, the sparks would fly."

"Oh, come on!" Jessica said with a quick half-embarrassed laugh.

"I mean it," Debbie insisted, her eyes sparkling with enjoyment. "You had some odd power over the poor guys, something inside you that scared them to death, but drew them like flies to honey. I tried to figure it out a hundred times, but never quite got a handle on it. It was as if you had this wonderful animal attraction beneath your don't-touch-me air. I don't know exactly how to put it, sort of like—"

"Like a tigress, trying to get out," Jessica said almost to herself.

Pleasure flashed like a bright light coming on in Debbie's face. "Exactly. Who said that, this Rafael of yours?"

Jessica nodded. "Though not to me."

"Smart man, I'm glad to know he appreciates you. But you'll go easy on him, won't you? You wouldn't want to wear him out too fast."

"I don't think there's any danger." She tried for a tone of dry humor, though she could not prevent the flush that rose to her cheeks. Or the memories that caused it.

"Oh, my." Debbie tilted her head, then gave it a

quick shake. "But no, I won't ask. This time. Tell me about the wedding. I've already warned my other half that we have to come."

Jessica gave a capsule version of the plans for the big event, and even answered a few questions about Rafael and his family. As soon as possible, however, she shifted the focus to her friend.

It seemed Debbie was in town with her husband for a regional meeting of the McDonald's group with which they were associated as owners of several of the fast-food restaurants. In a lull in the round of meetings, she had run out to visit with Jessica, hoping to have her company for a round of the antique stores.

Poking around among all the wonderful old things available in New Orleans was one of their shared enthusiasms from way back. Jessica knew she should head back to work, since she had been out all morning, but was enjoying the relaxed give-and-take of Debbie's company too much to exert the discipline. She mentioned a couple of her more recently discovered antiquing places down on Magazine Street, and they were off.

It was in the third shop they visited, while on the trail of a pair of mantel vases Debbie coveted, that they found the length of silk. Once pure white, it had aged to a delicate champagne color that was a perfect match for the bridal gown chosen by Jessica. Rich, supple, and shimmering, it was brocaded with gold thread in what appeared to be a sinuous and exotic Far Eastern floral pattern. On closer inspection, however, it was possible to discover the tiny tigers hidden among the foliage.

Jessica, holding the heavy, smooth fabric in her hands, could see it as a train attached to her wedding gown. It would be the perfect touch to make the simple gown uniquely her own. The very idea of it made her feel warm and daring and, yes, sexy.

"Go for it," Debbie said in instant approval as she heard what Jessica had in mind.

"I don't know. The dress is nice enough as it is. Maybe I'm being silly. Maybe a train like this would be too tacky for words."

"Nice?" Debbie said in pained accents as she put a hand on her hip. "Jeans are 'nice,' Jess. A comfy T-shirt is 'nice,' for crying out loud. For a wedding gown, you want beautiful. Fantastic. Stupendous. Unforgettable, even. Come on, now! If this is going to make your dress unique, you need it. In fact, you've got to have it."

Jessica hesitated a moment longer, then a small, wicked smile tugged the corners of her mouth. She laughed aloud as she met her friend's gaze. "All right, girlfriend, you talked me into it."

As the evening of the wedding finally rolled around, Jessica was glad she had the tiny tigers. It was doubtful anyone would notice them, but just knowing the small symbols were there gave her a secret pleasure. They also boosted her courage as they hid among the flowers of woven gold.

The dressmaker she trusted with making the addition had done a marvelous job. The modified train draped beautifully behind her in the rich, fluid fabric, for a look that appeared to have come straight from a designer's workshop. An air of unity had been achieved by using a scrap of the same material to cover the bandeau, which held the veil of Alençon lace that was a family heirloom.

Her flowers were pure white orchids with golden throats in a waterfall design complemented by yellow rosebuds and variegated ivy, a gift of the groom. He also sent a necklace of pearls and diamonds with matching earrings. They were lovely, even impressive in their intricate design, but might have meant more if he had waited to present them himself.

There had been no opportunity. Rafael had not even shown up for the rehearsal the night before, but sent Carlos in his place. Her husband-to-be would be arriving at the church directly from the airport, escorting his mother and grandmother.

As Jessica stepped from the car at St. Louis Cathedral, she felt a wave of blind panic. It suddenly seemed impossible that she was going to be married in all religious solemnity, unbelievable that she would be tied to a man she had seen no more than half a dozen times. Worse still was the possibility that he had changed his mind and would not be arriving after all, that she might be left waiting in all her finery.

Then the straggling tourists around Jackson Square, which fronted the cathedral, discovered her and began to snap pictures. Keil, who had arrived with her since he was to give her away, stepped close to block her from view of the cameras, then made a path for her to the great double doors of the church. A moment later she was inside.

The greetings of her two attendants, plus the last-minute adjustments and instructions of the wedding consultant, carried her over the next few minutes. She moved into position with Keil beside her, and was handed her bouquet. Her hands shook as she clasped the ribbon-wrapped holder. She inhaled deeply and closed her eyes, trying to still her fluttering nerves and slow the frantic beat of her heart under her shimmering bodice.

Then she saw Rafael at the end of the long aisle in front of her. He was incredibly, seductively handsome in his evening wear as he stepped forward before the altar with Carlos beside him as best man. Peace and certainty dropped over her like a benediction. She was abruptly, sublimely calm.

Music, candles, sonorous phrases, responses, the ceremony progressed without pause. The only thing that made sense of it was the firm and warm clasp of Rafael's hand. Then it was over, and she and her groom faced the sea of smiling guests. She glanced up at the man beside her, and could have sworn there was pride and satisfaction in his face, and something more that sent a ripple of anticipation over her.

The reception was held in the flagstone courtyard of the St. Louis Hotel, where ordinarily a continental breakfast in the European style was served each morning beneath the overhanging palms. A large table centered by the tiered cake held the place of honor, while smaller tables of food were set up around the center

fountain. Waiters circulated with champagne and more
potent fare. Music filled the enclosed space with its
overhanging balconies, provided by a live band in one
corner.

Jessica and Rafael played their choreographed parts,
dancing the first dance while everyone looked on. The
two of them smiled and exchanged a few strained comments on the food, the floral decorations heavy on
tropical blooms, and the nephews and nieces from both
sides of the family who had joined forces to raid one
buffet table. Afterward Rafael danced with his mother,
while Jessica was led out on the floor by Claude
Frazier, who insisted on leaving his wheelchair to
shuffle a few steps. It was all very correct, very civilized, and heartwarming in its way. Regardless, Jessica
was just as glad when the time came to leave center
stage at last and mingle with the guests at the tables.

A breeze from the river lifted the tablecloths and
wafted the richly combined smells of oysters broiled in
bacon, crab rolls, jambalaya, yeast breads, and the sug-
ary sweetness of cake and wine. The rumble of laughter
and light conversations echoed against the old walls and
under the balconies. The fountain played with the sound
of rain. Palms and banana leaves swayed, casting moving shadows over the gathering.

On Jessica's right side, Rafael listened to his sister
across the table, who was telling him some story about
her children and the flight to New Orleans. Jessica, too
nervous to eat, sat and watched the scene with a faint
smile and intent awareness of a need to imprint it on her
mind so she could always recall exactly how it had
been.

The band changed to a samba in honor of the Brazilian contingent. There was an instant mass movement
toward the small dance floor. In the midst of it, someone stopped beside Jessica's chair and put a hand on her
shoulder to gain her attention.

"Debbie," Jessica exclaimed with a smile of purest
pleasure as she turned. She had given her friend a quick
hug while in the receiving line, but this was the first

time she had been able to speak to her. "I'm so glad you and Mike could make it."

"Oh, we wouldn't have missed it for the world. I just wanted to tell you I approve of your new husband." She sent a quick, laughing glance toward Rafael, where he was busy tieing the shoelaces of a small nephew in knee pants.

"I think he'll do," Jessica said in mischievous agreement as something near joy welled up inside her.

"Yes, and no telling what!" Debbie quipped. "So what did he think of the tigers?"

"He hasn't seen them." Automatically Jessica lowered her voice.

Debbie lifted a brow. "I thought they were for his benefit?"

"A little, but mostly for mine."

"Good grief, honey, all you have to do is let go. You'll be a match for any man."

"Right," Jessica said in rueful disbelief.

"Yes, well," Debbie said with another glance in Rafael's direction, "most any man!" She bent closer to deliver another hug, this time of good-bye, as she and Mike were heading for home. "It was so good to see you again. Call when you can—and you and Rafael come up to Natchitoches to see us."

Jessica agreed, feeling warmth and joy rising like yeast inside her even as she issued her own invitations by way of farewell. As the other woman moved away, she turned toward Rafael once more.

He was watching her, the look in his eyes heated and feral with remembrance. Had he heard what she said to Debbie? Did he recall comparing her to a tigress? Or was he thinking of another samba combined with another courtyard similar in its essentials?

Regardless of the cause, she was startled by the intensity she could feel radiating from him and the knowledge of the tight control he was keeping on his emotions. And an answering awareness sent a shimmer of purest desire down her spine, one so strong that she felt heavy and dizzy with it.

In that moment she was forced to acknowledge a consuming need to discover if the magic she had once found with him might come again. She had denied this part of herself so long, sublimated it to so many other duties and problems. Soon she would know.

But what if the night in Rio had been a fluke? What if she was disappointed? What if Rafael was dissatisfied with her? Yes, and suppose her mother was right, and she had been a dupe from the beginning?

Somehow, in the rightness of the moment and the lovely pageantry of the ceremony, she had lost sight of that possibility.

She couldn't trust the man she had just taken in marriage, and yet the union was permanent. What if she was tied forever to someone who had used her, and who now had the right to do the same again whenever he pleased?

The descent from desire to terror was too fast. She felt sick with it.

It was at that moment that Rafael got to his feet and stepped closer. "Come," he said, taking her hand to pull her up beside him, gazing at her with dark fire in his eyes. "It's time for us to go."

They would be spending the night at the town house apartment. It was a decision made by default. Jessica, unable to decide what would be best or what Rafael really wanted, had let the whole question slide until it was too late to do much else. They would have a few days of seclusion, time enough, hopefully, to work out some kind of future.

Pepe drove them, but did not come inside. Jessica thought he and Rafael exchanged a quick, significant glance before the manservant inclined his head and turned away. As she went up the stairs ahead of Rafael, she heard the car drive off.

"He's no longer on duty, then?" she said as she stepped inside and flipped the overhead light switch, then moved deeper into the room to turn on a table lamp.

Rafael watched her a moment before he turned and locked the door behind him. "You might say so."

"I'm sure we can take care of ourselves without any help."

"Yes."

"I suppose it means, too, that you aren't concerned any longer about safety?" She reached up to remove her bandeau and veil as she spoke. When he did not answer, she glanced at him. There was a slumberous look in his eyes and a pulse hammering in his throat. She felt her heart kick into an answering overdrive.

"It means," he said as he reached to pull the end of his tie free and slide it from around his neck, "that the responsibility for taking care of you is now mine."

"Me?" she said, startled. "I'm—not sure I have any use for a bodyguard."

He slipped the links from his cuffs, then moved toward her to place them with his tie on the table beside her. As he reached to thread his fingers through her hair, lifting the shining strands, his smile was pitying yet warmly promising. "Oh, but you do," he said in low certainty, "and it will be my pleasure to show you some of them."

She moistened her lips with her tongue, a nervous movement that riveted his gaze to her mouth. "We—we should talk about what we are going to do over the next few days. And maybe about when we're going to leave for Brazil . . ."

"Oh, I don't think so," he said, his voice a low rumble in his throat as he began to remove the diamond-and-pearl earring from her ear with gentle yet competent fingers.

His touch was so warm, the attention so intimate as he pressed the long post of the earring farther into the opening in her lobe to remove its back fastening, then slowly began to withdraw it again. Reaching up to catch his wrist, she said in strangled tones, "I can manage."

"I prefer to get these out of the way," he said with a lazy smile as he dropped one earring to the table, then began on the other. "I want no problems with jewelry this time."

Heat flared in her face. Voice breathless even as she released him, she said, "No, really, you don't have to."

"I want to," he said in soft insistence as he began on the other earring. "I want to tend you, to touch and hold you, to put my hands on every single inch of you. I've thought of nothing else for weeks. In fact, I might have finished my work and arrived yesterday or the day before—except for the destruction of my schedule caused by thinking too much about all the things I want to do."

Her skin was feverish with anticipation, and so sensitized by need that she could feel the brush of air currents in the room, the heat that emanated from his body. As he removed the second earring and put it aside, then circled her neck to find the clasp of her necklace, she could not prevent herself from swaying toward him.

He moved nearer, so his thighs brushed hers in tingling contact. His scent of linen and woodsy aftershave and warm male surrounded her like a potent aphrodisiac. Disoriented, oddly weak, she put out her hand for balance.

Her fingertips came in contact with his chest. Without conscious thought she flattened her palm against him, letting it conform to the taut bands of muscle that wrapped his rib cage. Trembling, she abandoned pretense as she pressed her other hand beside the first, absorbing his heat, testing the hard, steady pound of his heart.

He was so alive and so strong. The sheer masculine force of him surrounded her, silently compelled her. She surrendered to it, pushing her hands under his coat, feeling, through the heavy silk of his shirt, the curling resilience of the hair that decorated his chest and the flat, hardened bead of his paps in their silken thicket. He inhaled, a soft sound of tested resolve, as she directed her attention to the small nubs.

Abruptly he pulled her closer against him so her breasts were molded to his chest. With his fingers embedded in her hair, he tilted her head and covered her mouth with his. He grazed the tender surfaces of her mouth with his lips as if imprinting their shape and texture on his own. Brushing over them with moist heat, he tasted their sweetness, their tentative acceptance, then deepened the kiss in mind-swimming incursion.

His tongue swirled, glided along hers, inciting imitation. It was a sinuous dance of provocation, one hauntingly familiar yet new. It fired molten need deep inside her, as well as a shattering craving for the deeper intimacy it suggested.

He found the zipper of her dress and lowered it in a fast, smooth slide. The fabric parted under his hands, then draped forward. He drew it down her arms, one after the other, then released it to let it pool in heavy folds around her feet. Placing his hands on the cream satin of the teddy she wore under the dress, he smoothed them deliberately over the fabric as if luxuriating in the soft texture of her skin, the shaping and firmness of her flesh beneath it. He spanned her rib cage, then circled the narrow indentation of her waist with his long fingers before following the tender contours backward and down. Spreading his long fingers, he closed them gently on the taut curves of her hips, then pressed her closer to let her feel his mounting arousal, moving slowly against her as he had done once before in a darkened patio, forcing her to recognize her own need.

She moaned softly deep in her throat as she passed her arms behind his back under his jacket and eased nearer. His arms tightened. A small cry left her as she felt the dig of his shirt studs into her tender, engorged breasts.

He cursed quietly in Portuguese as he instantly loosened his hold. Then he bent to slip a hard arm under her knees and lift her against his chest. Swinging with her, he strode into the darkened bedroom. The antique bed was lofty with its piled mattresses, and he placed her on the soft surface as upon a high altar. Skimming the studs from his shirt, he shrugged out of it along with his jacket. He dropped both on the floor, then ripped off his cummerbund and let it fall. Unzipping his fly, he kicked off his shoes, then discarded his pants along with socks and narrow black briefs. Naked, he joined her on the bed, stretching out beside her as he supported himself on one elbow.

He was magnificent in the dim light from the living room, as sleek as some great jungle cat, and as powerful. As he shifted, hovering above her, his broad shoulders were outlined in a golden nimbus. He cast a shadow over her, while his eyes gleamed in the dark. The muscles of her stomach fluttered in peculiar apprehension even as she ached to be in his arms once more.

He eased over her, pressing her into the mattress, allowing her to absorb and become accustomed to his weight by careful degrees. Supporting himself on his elbows, he matched their bodies, muscle to muscle, hardness to softness, as if the entire surface of his skin was an organ of touch through which he could assimilate the essence of her. Taking her hands, one at a time, he raised them above her head with her fingers meshed with his and her palms flattened against the hard surfaces of his own. He kissed her then, slow and deep and long.

After an endless time, he released her mouth to trail a careful path with his lips over the tender turn of her jaw and down her neck to the valley between her breasts. He tasted the delicate flesh with quick passes of his tongue, finding the small imprints left by his studs and laving them with slow care. Brushing the tender mounds on either side with his face, he selected one and laid siege to it, climbing slowly to the trembling peak with myriad kisses and delicate, sampling bites. There, he took the nipple into his mouth, wetting the satin that covered it as he tugged gently with his teeth. With that height conquered, he moved to the other.

Pinned in place, Jessica was unable to move, incapable of avoiding his ministrations even if she had wanted to. He was wedged between her thighs, his legs holding her own apart. She could feel his heated maleness carefully, maddeningly nudging the frail barrier of satin that covered her, prodding her moist flesh with his every movement. Half pleasurable, half panicky helplessness rose inside her, along with tingling and oddly exultant expectation. She wanted to remain wary and on her guard against him, even fearful of what he might do to her. Yet somewhere deep inside was an instinctive knowledge that, at least in this way, he would never hurt her. Amazement for that insight touched her, then it was crowded out by the spiraling wonder of the sensations he was creating.

He shifted, loosening and releasing one of his hands before slipping it down to unsnap her teddy. His breath against her skin was warm and moist as he trailed kisses over the skin he bared while pushing the silken garment upward to her waist. With his tongue he dipped into her navel, made wet circles over her abdomen, then moved downward once more to nuzzle the fine curls at the juncture of her thighs.

She made a low sound of surprise, instinctively trying to close her legs in protection. He would not allow it, but pressed them wider as he delved deeper among the tender folds. "Honey dew," he said, the soft-spoken words warm and tickling against the sensitive flesh. "Honey and lemon and nectar of flowers. I could drink you like a sweet, intoxicating *caipirinhas*."

And holding her to him in easy strength, he tasted and explored with careful, searing magic until her breath rasped in her throat. Dazed and pliant, she abandoned modesty to allow limitless access. He took it, using lips and tongue, time and courteous determination to send torrents of hot delight surging through her veins.

Dearest heaven, but she ached with the need to hold, to be close, to be filled. She grasped his shoulders, kneading them, absorbing the essence of him through her palms, before urging him upward.

He released her. Pushing to one elbow, he stripped the teddy from her, leaving only her garter belt of white satin and white hose embroidered at the ankles. With his hand between her breasts, covering her throbbing heart, he traced the miniature cornucopia of her ear,

then flicked inside with his tongue so she shuddered
against him.

"You want me," he whispered. "Say it."

She stilled, reaching to close her hand over his where
it lay just above her heart. Fear skimmed her mind beneath the convulsive craving that gripped her. "Why?"

"Because I need to hear it. Because I require that
there should be at least that much honesty, that much
feeling between us. Will you say it? Please."

"What if I . . . can't?"

He began, with the slow and shuddering wrench of
iron muscles, to withdraw from her.

"No! Wait . . ."

What point was there in denying what was so obviously true, and had been from the first? There could be
no humiliation in simple passion, especially when he
had already admitted his desire for her.

"I want you," she said in aching entreaty. "Now. I
need . . ."

The last words were smothered as he covered her
mouth with his and took the kiss deep. At the same time
he slid his hand under her and lifted her for the hot, liquid slide of his penetration.

That sensation, that abrupt, tight friction followed by
deep filling, was heart-stoppingly exquisite. She could
not breathe, could not move or think as she coalesced
around him in tight, pulsating constriction. He held that
fullness, the wondrous straining pressure, for endless
seconds. Until she caught her breath on a gasping sob.
Then he began to move, in and out, stretching percep-
tion, testing resolve to its outermost boundary.

She flexed her legs, holding to him with quivering
muscles. The change opened greater depth to him, and
he took it in a single plunge, locking their bodies tighter
together. He rocked a moment, giving her the abrasion
of his body against her soft mound, enjoying her shuddering rapture at the movement. Then he took it deeper,
added greater range, eased into a steady and exacting
rhythm that he held with tireless strength.

Perspiration sleeked his skin and gleamed along the

ridged muscles of his torso. His chest heaved as he dragged air into his lungs. A look of fierce, exalted concentration darkened his face. Rocked by his movements, invaded by the hot, slick length of him, she felt such intense, crowding pleasure that it threatened to overflow into something very much like love. The wonder of it crowded her throat with the stinging pressure of tears. They reached her eyes and spilled in wet, hot tracks into the silk of her hair.

And somewhere deep inside she felt a final surrender, as if he had taken, or she had yielded, some last fastness of her innermost self. Her heart jolted, her skin flushed, and her very being dissolved into a release like the unwinding of a tightly coiled spring.

Crying out, she surged upward, moving with him even as she pressed her lips to his damp forehead, tasted his shoulder. She accepted his mouth and the swirl of his tongue while holding him to her with handfuls of his taut, rippling skin.

He whispered soft words in Portuguese that had the sound of prayer, curse, and endearment in one. Never had he sounded more foreign, or more loving. Then he lunged into a hard, fast pace that sounded her, jarred her free of the last tenuous contact with her very soul and sent her soaring with him, above the dark room, into black space.

Chill bumps corrugated his chest, his arms, and his flanks. Abruptly he buried himself in the tightness of her body in a last powerful drive. His body contracted with explosive, throbbing force that wrung a low groan from his throat. She caught him close, cradling him as her own body pulsed in internal welcome, recognizing him, accepting him on some plane beyond resistance or comprehension.

And that deep communication was an ancient riddle. It whispered of both blossoming and future harvest, a beginning that had no end, an ending that had hardly begun. It was a puzzle that could not be solved because they did not dare seek the answer. But it would keep, because one day, if they loved long enough, they might discover understanding within themselves. And dare look it in the face.

Long moments later Rafael released cramped muscles to ease from her. Stretching out on his side, he drew her to him once more with her head resting on his firm shoulder and her leg drawn up across his knees. He stroked her hair with one hand, straightening the shimmering strands, removing them from her face so she could breathe.

She absorbed his tenderness, the steady thumping of his heart under her cheek, the deep rise and fall of his chest. Sighing, she slept with his arms around her, shielding her, claiming her.

The deep darkness of midnight was in the room when she came awake again. His hands were on her, soothing her internal soreness, inciting the banked fires of her desire. As she stirred, he drew her astride him, then released her. He waited.

For an instant she was uncertain what to do. Then sensing his hard heat so close against her, she was galvanized by the rich, sensual impulse.

She eased down on him in slow encasement, taking his entire length within her, and was rewarded by his hissing breath of satisfaction. Pushing erect, she began to move, rising and falling just as he had moved against her. The almost instant blooming of pleasure inside her was unexpected, amazing. She increased her pace, adjusting her seat for a more perfect fit as she grasped his shoulders for purchase. He aided her with hard hands on her breasts, at her waist and hips, while he murmured encouragement in two languages.

And she rode him, wild and strong as a Valkyrie or some mythical witch on a particularly appropriate broomstick. Rode him, surging, glorying in the glide of body against body and the reaching, gathering sensations inside her, rode him until her muscles burned and she gasped for air. Until he took the effort from her and with his sure power sent her hurtling into surcease. And kissed her, murmuring her name, while she dropped into sleep again as into a bottomless well.

Or perhaps it was a dream. She couldn't have done that. Could she?

The answer was in Rafael's jaguar eyes, as gold as the medallion at his neck, when she faced him in the light of day, there in the rumpled sheets. The expression that hovered there was satisfied, warm, lazy with satiation yet glittering with remembrance.

"We are well matched in more than business," he said as he reached to lift the shining bell curve of her hair and let it drift from his fingers to lie across her eyes.

"How?" she asked in a pretense of puzzlement, blowing at the tress that tickled her nose.

He bent his head to take her pursed lips, feathering the bottom one with his tongue through the skein of her hair. When he could speak again, his voice was low and deep. "Guess, tigress mine."

She felt hot all over. It was impossible to sustain his gaze. Regardless, she had never had so bold an impulse or so powerful a need. She turned to face him, a move that pressed the fullness of her breasts to the hard planes of his chest. Her hand grazed the hot hard length of his maleness, and she curved her fingers around it, holding lightly. In breathless challenge she said, "Show me."

He did, though the demonstration took time. Energy. Breath. And repetition.

The evening light was fading by the time they got around, finally, to a real meal, one of salad, cold baked chicken, and hot rolls they managed to throw together in the kitchen between lingering kisses and other more daring caresses. Rafael was finishing his off with rum raisin ice cream, Jessica hers with vanilla draped in hot chocolate sauce, when quick, firm footsteps sounded on the entrance stairs. They were followed within seconds by a sharp knock.

Rafael allowed himself the luxury of a soft curse. Jessica glanced at him and grinned while soft rose mantled her cheekbones. He was still watching that spreading color, thinking of pressing once more into the hot, wet softness of her body when the knock came again.

As she swung toward the sound, rising from her chair, he touched her arm to forestall her. She had on only a cotton terry robe, while he had taken the time to step into jeans and pull a T-shirt on over his head. Smile wry, he said, "Allow me."

She did not object, a fact Rafael fully appreciated given her independence and the fact that it was her apartment, her grandfather's town house. She was learning to rely on him, he thought. That was promising.

It was Keil Frazier who stood on the landing. He looked more than a little uneasy as he stood blinking in the sudden light from inside the room, though he mustered a polite good evening. He started to ask for his cousin, then broke off as his gaze slid past Rafael. "There you are, Jess. Mom has been trying to get hold of you for the last two hours, but your phone is off the hook—not that I blame you."

"What is it?" Her voice was sharp, and her face a little pale as she moved to Rafael's side. In an unconscious movement of discomfiture that set his teeth on edge, she pulled her robe tight around her.

Keil shook his head. "I hate to tell you, but it's Uncle Claude, sweetheart. He and Madeleine stayed in town last night, but he insisted on driving back to the Landing this morning. The trip tired him out, and he lay down for a nap. When he didn't get up after a couple of hours, Madeleine checked on him. It was another stroke. The doctors said to call in the family."

The last vestige of color left Jessica's face, but there were no histrionics, no tears. She had rare courage, but Rafael had always known that. He watched her as she swallowed hard, saw the swift consideration in her eyes before she said to her cousin, "Is he still at the Landing, then, or—"

"No, he's in the hospital at Cameron, ICU."

"You're on your way there now, of course?"

Keil gave a definite nod. "I have to pick up Mom in Lafayette."

"Could I ride with you?"

She had forgotten he was there, Rafael thought. It gave him no great opinion of his place in her world. He stepped forward as he spoke to her cousin. "Is there a helicopter pad at the hospital?"

"I think so, yes, one they use for emergency airlifts to New Orleans or Houston."

"That will do." He turned to his wife. "I'll take you. I can have you there in little more than an hour."

She stared up at him with wonder in her face. "You would do that?"

"It will take only a phone call to have a helicopter ready."

"Keil?" She looked to her cousin in inquiry.

"I still have to pick up Mom. You two go on. Uncle Claude—Well, he won't be holding on for me."

Like the ripple of movement over still water, a spasm of pain crossed the pure lines of Jessica's face. Reaching out, she put a hand on Rafael's wrist that was so icy he covered it at once with his own warm grasp. There was gratitude and trust in her voice, and something more that licked like fire around his heart.

Her smile tremulous, she said, "Then I'll go with my husband."

There had never been any doubt in his mind that she would. Regardless, he felt as if she became his wife in that moment.

Chapter Nineteen

▨ ▨ ▨ *Quiet, efficient, effortlessly commanding,*
Rafael took charge. Jessica considered objecting, but his
orders were too practical for that, and too dedicated to
her comfort and convenience. She could easily become
addicted to the way he made things easy for her, to his
supporting hand on her arm and his calm appropriation
of her every burden from her small suitcase to her
purse. Watching him sling the strap of the last over his
shoulder, she was struck by his easy assurance that indicated plainly that he didn't care who saw him or what
they thought if they did. At the same time she was uncomfortably aware of her instant response to his least
touch, and the odd mixture of pleasure and pride inside
her for the mere fact that he walked next to her.

She did not underestimate the effort he was making.
He was, she had discovered, a deeply sensual man, and
the fact that he would instantly relinquish all claim to
her time and attention because of this crisis was impressive. She would have liked to acknowledge her gratitude and wished she could credit him with the concern
and compassion argued by his actions. She might have,
if she had not been so busy wondering if his interest
in Claude Frazier's health might not equal her own,
though for different reasons.

There were always reasons for the things he did. That
was something she must remember if she was not to fall
completely under the spell of his commanding presence
and sexual expertise.

It would be fatally easy to stop fighting and sink into

the sense of safety and comfort he gave her, the feeling of being wrapped in a cocoon of loving protection. But there was no love involved; there couldn't be. It was merely an attitude, a Latin one, perhaps, of habitual consideration and possessiveness. It could become a smothering trap if she weren't careful.

It was curious, but Rafael reminded her of her grandfather. They were two of a kind: strong, quiet men certain of their place in the world and their ability to arrange matters in it to suit themselves. Impatient with those less decisive or less willing to take risks, they also extended compassionate charity toward those in need as a matter of course. Men of unflinching responsibility, they took what they wanted and paid the price without complaint. The women in their lives were important to them, but were not allowed to interfere with their main objectives.

Comparing the two men in her mind as the helicopter buzzed above the lights of cities and towns and the darkness of the swamps was a way of distracting herself and holding back the fear of what she would find when she reached the hospital. They were both so terribly important to her now that she could not imagine either of them not being there.

Images of her grandfather and herself as she was growing up flickered through her mind. She saw him sitting with her on the long front gallery of the house while a storm came in across the gulf, teaching her not to fear thunder and lightning. Wrapping her in his robe on cold, dark winter mornings while the two of them made coffee in the kitchen before the cook Cressida arrived. Showing her the playhouse complete with tiny working kitchen he had built for her in the back garden when she was ten. Giving her small diamond earrings shaped like flowers on Christmas morning when she was fifteen—how anxious he had been that she like them and how grown-up she had felt. Teaching her to drive on the shell road across the chenier, irascible but painstaking.

She sometimes thought he had tried to correct with

her all the mistakes he had made with Arletta. He had given her more time, more attention, more thought than he had been willing or able to invest in his daughter. And he had tried to restrain her sexual nature in the past because he thought that was the root of Arletta's rebellious defiance through the years.

Another reason, of course, had been his experience with Mimi Tess. Her high temper and demanding love had made him wary of anything other than the most lukewarm of emotions. Jessica wondered if he might not have married Madeleine because she was too cool and self-centered to trouble him with excessive devotion or overwrought scenes.

Still, it seemed Madeleine might be warmer natured than she appeared on the surface, that she could be looking elsewhere to satisfy her needs. It wouldn't be unusual.

The person Jessica was surprised at was Keil. She would have expected him to have more consideration, not to mention more sense, than to become involved with his great-uncle's wife. To carry on at the Landing where anyone might see them had been incredibly dumb. How was he feeling now, after this last stroke?

In less time than she would have expected, the helicopter was setting down behind the hospital. As they climbed out, they were met by cool night air off the marsh that was thick with low-lying fog. The mist wreathed the lights of the parking lot, drifted around the foundation of the building, blanketed the windows. It made the place seem ghostly and insubstantial, as if, like her grandfather, it was barely tethered to the earth.

Madeleine rose from a chair in the ICU waiting room as Jessica and Rafael entered. In answer to Jessica's quick questions, she only shook her head. Claude Frazier was barely with them. He would be gone in a matter of hours, possibly less, according to the doctor. They were not allowed to see him now but could go in during the next scheduled visiting period.

However, Jessica had attended church for years with one of the nurses, while another was the wife of the brother of a Sea Gull Transport boat captain. Visiting hours were waived without her even having to ask. The privilege extended only to closest family, however; Rafael remained behind with Madeleine while Jessica passed through the double doors into the ICU unit.

The section hummed with the quiet machines and low-voiced efficiency of its kind. At the same time there was a hush about it, perhaps from the instinctive reverence in the face of hovering death. Three or four of the curtained cubicles were in use. The one where Jessica's grandfather lay was across from the nurses' station.

Claude Frazier, even in his wheelchair after the first stroke, had always been a large man of overpowering presence. Now he appeared shrunken, as though his spirit was already receding, leaving the husk of his body behind. His face was so gray and waxen around the nose and mouth that Jessica felt sharp alarm. However, there was warmth in his lax fingers as she took them in hers, and she could feel the faint, reedy flutter of the pulse in his wrist.

"Grandpapa?"

The fragile, rheumy line of his lashes quivered, but that was all. When had he grown so frail? How had it happened without her noticing? It hurt her inside to see him. He had always been so indomitable that she had never considered he might die, even after his first stroke. Now she was forced to face it.

"Grandpapa?"

Nothing. The minutes ticked past in endless procession. A nurse came to check vital signs, then went out again. The sound of an ambulance was heard, muffled by walls and distance, until it faded away again. The curtains of the cubicle swayed in the draft beneath them. Drifting on the air current were the typical hospital smells of disinfectant, heated electronic equipment, stale coffee, and human misery.

"Grandpapa, can you hear me?"

Her grandfather's eyes opened with an almost audible

click, but did not focus. His voice rasping, the words slurred, he said, "Jess? That—you?"

"Here, Grandpapa, beside you. I came as soon as I could."

"Knew you would. Waited for you. Had to. Need to . . ." He stopped while a look of worry furrowed his brow, as if he had lost the thread of what he had wanted to say.

Clasping his hand in both of hers, she leaned closer. "Never mind. Don't think about it. You need to rest."

He jerked his head in brief negation while distress shone in his faded eyes. "Can't tell anybody. You. Just you."

"Was it something to do with Sea Gull?" He was becoming so agitated that it seemed best to help him say his piece and get it over.

"No. No, I—" Relief abruptly smoothed his features. "Pictures. That's it."

Jessica stood perfectly still while shock rippled along her nerves. It was the last thing she had expected. Voice hardly more than a whisper, she repeated, "Pictures?"

Her grandfather lay breathing hard, as if the effort of memory had taxed his waning reserves of strength. He turned his head slowly to meet her eyes, and his own were clear when he finally spoke again. "Should have told you. Couldn't. In the safe. Locked away. Didn't look . . . after the first one."

She couldn't sustain his desperate gaze, couldn't breathe, couldn't think. "How—?" she began.

"Doesn't matter. You go. Take 'em out. Understand?"

"Yes, yes I will." She caught her breath against the pain growing inside her while she stared down at their clasped hands. "I—I'm sorry, Grandpapa. I didn't mean it to happen. I don't know what came over me. It was just—" She paused, pressing her lips tightly together. "I'm so sorry."

"Don't," he said as her voice broke. "Just—don't. Should have burned the trash. Too late. Can't let anybody see. You get there . . . first."

"Yes, I will," she repeated while she smoothed her

thumb across the prominent veins of his hand over and over as though she could soothe his hurt and disappointment in her at the same time.

"Castelar. Watch out. Watch out . . . for him."

"Don't worry, don't say any more," she whispered against a shaft of searing anguish. "Just rest and try to get better."

His eyes closed. His breathing was loud in the quiet for long moments, then he spoke once more with thick difficulty. "Proud of you, Jessica. Proud . . ."

It was so unexpected, that approbation, that the ache crowding her chest burned its way upward to press behind her eyes. Tears rimmed her lashes and overflowed in wet tracks down her face, hot rivulets of remorse and love and grief. Searching in her shoulder bag with one hand, she brought out a tissue to mop her eyes and nose. It was soon sodden, and still the tears poured.

Her pain was just as unending. A part of it was recognition of her grandfather's unspoken love, a part was the knowledge of her impending loss. But there was more than that. She could think of only one way her grandfather could have been in possession of the pictures.

Rafael had lied. He had not been an innocent victim caught with her.

It explained many things, but made her grandfather's sudden need to see her married especially clear. He had thought he was forcing the man who had taken advantage of her to do the right thing by her. He had known what had happened in Rio because he had seen the evidence with his own eyes. He had seen it, because Rafael had presented it to him. Rafael had given him the pictures in return for the withdrawal of his opposition to the takeover of Sea Gull. He had not, perhaps, expected to get a wife out of the deal but had accepted the stipulation from—what had been the phrase? Passion and practicality?

It hurt, a rending ache so deep it might never mend. Just as agonizing was the knowledge of her grandfather's shielding concern . . . and his trust.

Her grandfather's hand began to tremble in hers. As her gaze flew to his face, she saw his lips draw back in a grimace while his body shook. Her problems fled as she bent over the bed, calling out to him. His face was pale, graying before her eyes to a bloodless pallor.

"Grandpapa! Oh, Grandpapa!" It was a cry of despair.

And it seemed he heard her, for his facial muscles relaxed by degrees. His shaking subsided. His breathing eased.

The curtain of the cubicle was whipped aside. A nurse entered, her gaze fastened on the monitors above the bed. She pressed a button, began to check vital signs. Over her shoulder, she said to Jessica, "You need to step outside, honey."

"Is he . . . ?" Jessica could not go on.

"Looks like he's okay for now. We'll call you if there's any change."

She nodded, though she still stood gazing down at her grandfather. He had almost died just then; she knew it with absolute certainty. But he had come back, for her. He had come back because he loved her and did not want to leave her. Nor did he want her to watch him go.

Leaning close, she smoothed the fine white hair back from his forehead, whispered near his ear, "I love you, Grandpapa."

She thought she felt his hand squeeze hers, a faint, brief response. But she could not be sure.

It was perhaps a half hour later, as they were sitting in the waiting room, that they heard the announcement of a Code Blue on the intercom. A nurse coming down the hall wheeled around and sprinted for ICU. The doors swung in and out as other personnel entered. Instinctively Jessica looked at Rafael. He took her hand, meshing their fingers, holding tight. Madeleine sat forward in her seat with her arms wrapped around her upper body and her narrow gaze on the pink lady who manned the ICU information desk.

Finally a white-coated doctor emerged from the swinging door. His face was solemn, his jaw firm. They listened politely as he explained what had happened; still it was unnecessary. They knew without being told that Claude Frazier, the head of Sea Gull, was gone.

"I guess it's up to us," Keil said as he stared out over the back garden of the Landing. "I never thought I'd see the day. I mean, I always felt the old man would live forever."

Jessica glanced at her cousin, where he propped a shoulder against the wall of the house beside the gallery railing. Behind them, the noise of women in conversation made a subdued murmur that was like the sound of surf on the beach three miles away. The smell of food, the inevitable offering of neighbors on the altar of family tragedy, hung in the air. A knot of men were gathered at the other end of the gallery, where they could smoke in peace or spit over the railing.

Jessica said on a sigh, "Everything is so different now."

"Yeah. As long as Uncle Claude was around, it was his ball game. Now it's our turn at bat. It's scary, because whatever happens is on our heads."

"Not entirely, not with CMARC's involvement," she reminded him in dry tones. At the same time she wondered if Keil really meant what he said. Once the comment might have seemed natural, but that was before CMARC's auditors had arrived on the scene. Either he was putting a good face on things, or he had some agenda that wasn't immediately apparent. Given what she knew, she was afraid it was the latter.

Her cousin glanced at her with a grim smile tugging one corner of his mouth. "I don't look to CMARC for salvation. From what I can see, you'll still be able to run Sea Gull pretty much any way you want."

"Then you need your eyes examined." The words were short. She had not mentioned the discrepancy in the company books that Rafael had revealed to her, in part because there was little time to think about it in the last hectic days before the wedding, but mainly because she'd hoped the problem would resolve itself. It hadn't.

It was possible that now was as good a time as any to bring it into the open.

She said, "You know CMARC's accountants have found a few problems?"

"First I heard of it," he answered with a frown.

"It seems we are missing cash assets. You wouldn't know anything about it, I suppose?"

His gaze darkened as he stared at her. "Are you suggesting I took them?"

"I don't know what to think," she said frankly, though she was relieved that he seemed as blank as she was about it.

"We're talking actual money, not just a paper loss?"

She nodded. "Do you think Grandpapa moved the funds? He was acting a little strange even before his stroke—since the explosion out in the gulf, really. Can you think of anything he might have done with the money, anywhere he could have hidden it if he had thought . . ."

"If he had an idea Sea Gull was going under?" Keil continued, completing the thought. "Anything is possible, but I'd have said he'd fight to the last ditch."

"Well, we'd better find out, because Rafael is going to want answers."

"I got you," Keil said, giving her a straight look. "My backside is in a sling because I'm the most likely culprit. God, I don't know what's happening here. I feel like somebody's out to get me."

"You?"

"Crazy, huh?" He ran a hand over the short sandy waves of his hair then clasped the back of his neck. "But hey, it should have been me taking the boat out the day of the explosion, you know, since I'm the one who uses it more often than not. Then that business down in Rio? I've been thinking about what you said—about me being targeted in the hotel bar—and you just may be right. Another thing is this business with Customs. You know somebody tipped them off to search that crew boat? Makes you wonder, doesn't it?"

"But why you?" she said in tight perplexity.

He gave a moody shrug. "Beats me. Of course it could be they're just out to get Sea Gull, so anything or anybody standing in the way are natural targets."

There was an irresistible logic to that. The attacks on her in Rio and at her town house, as well as the rest, could be part of the same effort. But what did anyone hope to gain? Who would benefit if the shipping company went under?

She could think of one person.

Rafael had been in Rio.

Rafael had been at her town house, conveniently, when she was attacked.

Rafael had been on the boat.

Rafael had convinced her grandfather that a merger would be of mutual benefit, and he'd accepted marriage to her to seal the bargain. Between that personal arrangement and buying up the loan, he had taken over Sea Gull without so much as a skirmish, much less any real battle.

Had that been what it was all about, a wide campaign to discredit Sea Gull and its acting management so that Claude Frazier would give up without a whimper?

She had heard of some underhanded business maneuvers, but this took the prize. Once she might have doubted it was possible. Not now. Given what her grandfather had said to her, it made perfect sense.

Still, she would like to be sure. If only there was a way to be absolutely sure.

A group of people walked out onto the gallery from the house. Among them were a couple of neighbor women, as well as Madeleine and Zoe.

Keil's mother detached herself from the others and came to join Jessica and her son. With a jerk of her head back over her shoulder, she spoke in low-voiced scorn. "Just look at the grief-stricken widow, in black from top to toenails, playing the lady of the manor to the hilt. It's enough to turn your stomach."

Jessica barely glanced in the direction indicated. "Somebody has to do it."

"Then, it should be you or your mother. Or better yet, Mimi Tess, seeing that she's here."

The older woman was indeed on hand, thanks to Arletta, who appeared to think it would be a disgrace if her mother was left out. Jessica had wondered privately if the ordeal wouldn't be too upsetting for her grandmother, but so far Mimi Tess had held up well. She grasped the situation perfectly well when it was explained to her, and spoke of Claude being gone with soft and tearful regret, but with no great anguish. It was enough to make Jessica wonder if Mimi Tess wasn't more rational than everyone gave her credit for.

Nevertheless she thought her grandmother would be much better off sitting upright and regal in the living room, accepting condolences and talking to old friends, than playing hostess in a house she had not entered in ages. She said so.

Zoe's agreement was grudging before she went on. "But Madeleine is an embarrassment to the family. I mean somebody should tell her that you don't wear a cubic zirconia necklace big enough to choke a mule before five, much less to your husband's funeral. And does it seem to you she's put on weight since Mardi Gras? You don't suppose she could be pregnant?"

"Mom, really!" Keil said in pained protest.

Zoe glared at her son. "You think it's not possible because Claude was laid up in bed? Don't kid yourself; he was a randy old goat. Besides, nobody said it was his."

"Nobody said she was pregnant at all." Keil's tone was acid. "She's always been, well—curvaceous."

"Hippy, you mean," his mother corrected.

"Pleasingly plump," Keil insisted.

"We'll hope you're right," the older woman said dubiously. "Because it would be the absolute last straw if she produced a brat at the last minute." Malicious amusement crept into her eyes as she glanced at Jessica. "Just think what our dear Arletta would say!"

Jessica shuddered at the very idea. It would, of course, be Arletta who would lose the most if there should be a new heir. At the same time there was something ridiculous about the image of a baby brother for her mother, a tiny uncle for herself. She had trouble entertaining the possibility for more than a second.

Zoe caught sight of the family lawyer just then and moved away in pursuit. Jessica watched her solid and rather dumpy figure recede while a frown drew her brows together. She could not help remembering Keil and Madeleine together under the peach trees.

With a quick glance at Keil's set face, she said, "It was nice of you to take up for Madeleine."

"She hasn't had an easy time of it." His scowl was moody as he shifted to put his shoulders against the house wall beside him. "Anyway, she's all right, once you get to know her. She grew up poor, you know; her dad was on disability, her mom worked in a beauty shop. You can't blame her for marrying money when the chance came along. Whatever the bargain between her and Uncle Claude, she kept her end of it."

"She said something a few weeks ago about another will. Do you know what happened with that?"

He shook his head. "I guess there'll be a copy of the final version around some place, if you know where to look. I wouldn't worry, though. Uncle Claude may have changed things a bit to provide for Madeleine, but I expect that's all."

He was probably right, Jessica thought. In any case they would find out in due time.

"I was surprised at Castelar sticking around; I half expected him to leave you to it, maybe fly back for the service. Seems he's taking his duties as a husband seriously."

She made a sound that might be taken for agreement as she looked around for Rafael and discovered him down in the courtyard talking to the local priest.

"You think he means to finalize this business with Sea Gull while he's here, before he takes off for Brazil again?"

"I've no idea. He hasn't confided in me."

She heard the bitterness in her voice but could not help it. In truth, she had hardly spoken to Rafael at all.

There had been so much to do, making calls, choosing a casket, deciding on the suit and tie her grandfather would wear, directing the grave diggers to the proper site for the grave in the family cemetery. She would have to face the man who was her husband eventually, but the pain of betrayal was too new, too raw, to even think about it now.

Keil did not comment, though he gave her a doubtful look. "I'd like to hear from him where I stand, once and for all. If he doesn't want me around, that's fine. I've been thinking about maybe starting a little charter boat business of my own."

"Oh, Keil, no!"

He gave her a wry smile. "Yeah, well, I'd miss you, too, kiddo. But Sea Gull isn't exactly my life. I've got other options."

His words remained with Jessica as the interminable day wore on. It was as if everything was changing, now that her grandfather was dead. That could only add to her sense of dislocation, and her pain.

Still, the rituals of death carried her forward. The kindness of friends and neighbors nearly overwhelmed her: the hugs, the memories, the tales of her grandfather's generosity. Tears came again and again, until she was afraid to stray too far from a box of tissues. She grew used to turning and finding Rafael somewhere near, to looking to him for advice or an escape from a sticky situation, even as it made her uncomfortable. He expected nothing from her, did not pressure her in any way, and she was grateful. At the same time she knew it could not go on forever. There were many things that would change when the funeral was over.

Mimi Tess cried at the Requiem Mass held at the small chapel where the family had gone for years. The sight was heartbreaking as the quicksilver tears rolled down the fine silk-crepe of her face and desolation shook her thin, bony shoulders. It seemed so tragic, the barrenness of the years that lay between Mimi Tess and Claude Frazier. Jessica could not help wondering at the wounded pride, the hurt and anger, the doubts and fears that had torn two people apart when there had been so much love between them.

The sight of her grandmother was blurred by her own desolate tears then. And she knew she cried for something more than the death of a loved one.

Finally it was done. The last prayer was made, the last pallbearer's boutonniere placed on the casket, the last platitude spoken. The family returned to the house while the people from the funeral home completed their job. Then the last cup of warmed-over coffee was poured out and drunk, the last plate of food pressed on a feebly protesting mourner, the last distant cousin waved away, finally, down the drive. Only the immediate family was left. Most would spend the night, since it was late for setting out on the drive back to Lafayette or New Orleans.

It was the need to escape the lowered voices and oppressive air of final moments that drove Jessica from the house. Dusk was falling in lavender stillness across the chenier as she left the back garden and walked down toward the cemetery once more. The crew from the funeral home had finished and gone. The grave was mounded with earth and covered with flowers.

A cool wind off the gulf sighed through the oaks and cedars on the perimeters of the rusty Victorian iron fence and flicked at the stiff ribbons on the wreaths of carnations and mums on their wire stands. Jessica took one of the yellow roses from the casket spray for remembrance, then stood turning it in her fingers.

She felt as if a large chunk of her life was gone, the chunk that had kept her afloat. How peculiar it was to realize there was no one left to disapprove of what she did, no one to blame her for what went wrong. Also no one to praise her or stand behind her. No one she could trust.

"I'd like to spend eternity with you, Jessica. Would you mind?"

Jessica whipped around, startled as the words came so low and deep from behind her when she had thought she was alone. It was Nick who lounged close by with his hands shoved in his pockets and a whimsical smile curling his lips.

"I mean it," he said when she made no answer. "I'd like to be buried here at the Landing one day. Since you'll own the place eventually, do you think you could mark off a spot for me?"

"But—why?"

He looked away beyond the fenced enclosure toward the green sea of saw grass that stretched into infinity toward the gulf. "It's so quiet and restful. Private." He looked back at her. "You'll take care of me, I know. Besides, I've always felt like I belonged here, whether I really did or not. I'd like my own piece of the chenier, even if it's just three by six."

She watched him for a moment longer, absorbing the sincerity in his sky blue eyes. Some in the family might not like it, but all they could do was complain. Abruptly she smiled. "Sure. Why not?"

"I knew you'd understand. You always do."

She watched the wind ruffle the sun-bleached fairness of his hair and flap his collar against his lean brown jaw. Tipping her head, she said, "You don't expect to need it anytime soon, I hope?"

"Lord, no! But it doesn't hurt to get these things settled."

That was true, she thought, it was always best to settle things. Swinging from him, she turned back toward the house.

Nick didn't move, but stood with his gaze on the grave at his feet. As she paused to look back at him, he said, "He was a tough old geezer, but he was fair, I'll give him that much."

"Why do you say that?"

"He didn't have to take me in way back when. And he had his reasons for throwing me out. I just wish—" He stopped, closing his lips tightly on the words he had meant to say.

"What?"

"Nothing important." He looked up, then moved to join her. "I'll walk with you back up to the house—I was coming to get you, anyway. Your grandpapa's lawyer is here to talk about the will."

"You're joking," she said in blank disbelief.

"Nope."

"But why? It's too soon to even think about legalities. He should have more tact."

"Actually, I think your aunt Zoe arranged it yesterday. Hebert says he intended to get everybody together anyway, though, before they got scattered."

"Just like in the movies." Jessica's tone was caustic. She had expected to get together with Arletta, suggest that the two of them visit the lawyer's office in a few weeks to discuss the provisions made by her grandfather. The last thing she wanted was a public reading with all the petty wrangling that would follow.

"Buck up, honey," Nick said with his flashing grin. "Louisiana law is pretty well cut-and-dried when it comes to a man's last will and testament. How bad can it be?"

She didn't answer.

It was just as well.

Anson Hebert was no dry stick of a lawyer. Round and balding, bluff, hearty, an avid duck hunter and devoted family man, he had sent five sons to LSU and still took his wife of forty-odd years dancing every Saturday night. The law was a sacred trust, in his view, but could still be fairly elastic, depending on the requirements of intrinsic justice or, on rare occasions, the needs of friendship. He was a great talker, but a secure repository of secrets. He slept well at night.

Regardless, Hebert seemed nervous as he stood reading Claude Frazier's will. The papers rustled and quivered and stuck to fingers that were damp with perspiration. His voice was low and hurried, and he ran his words together as if he hoped to get everything out in the open before anyone realized what he was saying.

The gist of it was instantly clear, however. Claude Frazier's former wife, Maria Theresa Frazier, nee Ducoulet, would continue to receive her present support and maintenance payments from the settlement made

and held in trust since the time of her divorce from
Claude Frazier. His current wife, Madeleine Kimbal
Frazier, would draw an allowance from a second and
separate trust for life or until she remarried, but would
not participate directly in the division of the estate and
its assets. Arletta Frazier Meredith Weber Cavour
Garrett, his only child, would receive the Frazier family
jewelry, the collection of rare coins, and any other items
of intrinsic value presently residing in private keeping.
In addition, she would take possession of one-third of
the seventy-five percent interest in Sea Gull Transport
& Charter, Inc., currently held by Claude Frazier. These
shares would be reserved in trust under the control and
administration of his granddaughter, Jessica Meredith
Castelar. This said granddaughter would additionally receive one-third of the seventy-five percent interest, as
well as the New Orleans town house and the land and
residence on Oak Ridge Chenier known as the Landing.
The final third of Sea Gull owned by the deceased
would be inherited by the natural son of Louis Frazier
and Maria Theresa Ducoulet Frazier, a child legally
adopted at birth by the deceased and given the name of
Nicholas Frazier.

Stunned silence lay over the room as the lawyer finished reading and began to shuffle his papers back into
order.

Nick. Nick would also inherit an interest in Sea Gull.
Nick was the son of Mimi Tess and Louis Frazier. Since
Louis Frazier was Zoe's late husband and Keil's father,
that meant Nick was Keil's half brother. He was also a
half brother to Arletta, therefore Jessica's uncle. As the
relationships clicked into place in her mind, Jessica
drew a breath of shock and forgot to release it.

Abruptly Zoe gave a shrill scream and fell back in
her chair with a plump hand pressed to her chest. Her
round eyes glared and her face turned as white as if she
had been visited by a ghost.

"What in the name of heaven—" Keil growled as he
came up out of his chair, while Madeleine, beside him,
turned dark red and silent.

Mimi Tess, blinking and pale, shrank into the corner of the sofa and clenched her quivering hands in her lap. Not far from where she sat, Nick leaned back grim-faced, his gaze averted in a manner that indicated plainly he was not as surprised as the rest of them.

Only Rafael remained relaxed and watchful as he waited for what would happen next.

"I knew it!" Zoe cried on a shuddering moan. "Oh, I just knew it, but could never be sure because nobody would breathe a word. No, and why not?" She looked around, her gaze malevolent. "Because of Claude's precious ego, that's why! He couldn't stand anybody knowing his wife had been fooling around with a man ten years younger, and her husband's nephew at that!"

Jessica's grandmother gave a soft cry and put her hands to her face. Keil glanced at her and away again as he spoke with bewilderment roughening his voice. "I can't believe it."

"Well, I can!" his mother cried. "I've always known, deep down in my soul, that my husband died because he had the nerve to run off with his uncle's wife!"

"Was Mimi Tess with him when he was killed in France?" Keil gave a dazed shake of his head. "But I thought—I always understood it was some actress."

"A likely story! Where would my Louis have met any actress? No, it was just a tale made up to protect the guilty. Especially Claude, because he was the one who ran them off the road and killed Louis."

"That will do!" Arletta snapped. "It's all lies, and I won't sit here and listen to such slander a minute longer."

"Slander, is it?" Zoe gave a sharp laugh. "If you think so, then just look at your darling mother."

Mimi Tess was crying, her silver-white head bent forward on her neck like a rain-ruined lily while tears leaked through her thin fingers. The soft sounds she made as she struggled with her grief were indescribably poignant. Arletta shifted awkwardly, as if she would like to go to her but did not know how. Jessica, being closer, simply slid along the sofa and wrapped an arm around her grandmother's thin, shaking shoulders.

At the same time Nick came and knelt in front of the older woman, taking her hands. "Don't cry, *Maman*," he said in low, vibrant tones, giving her the title of mother in French that could also be a diminutive and an endearment. "Please don't cry. It's all right. There's nothing to cry about now."

Zoe, glaring at him, gave a harsh laugh. "No, I guess there's not, now you've got your foot in the door at Sea Gull."

"Oh, shut up!" Arletta said, turning on her. "What's it to you, anyway? You're not losing anything!"

Zoe's face turned purple. "I lost a husband, didn't I?"

"Which is no great wonder if you were as tightfisted then as you are now, not to mention as tight-assed. For God's sake, Zoe, stop bitching and whining and get on with being alive!"

"And maybe get myself another half-dozen husbands, or at least more men, like somebody else we could name?" the other woman said at once in vicious sarcasm. "Excuse me, but I don't think you're much of an example."

Arletta gave a dry laugh. "As if you could follow in my footsteps!"

Zoe's face flamed. "As if I would want to! I hope I have more dignity than to run after younger men like you and your slut of a mother. It's plain pitiful. Too bad you can't see yourself the way other people see you!"

"Ladies, please!"

It was the lawyer who spoke in some haste as Arletta began to get to her feet with fury in her eyes. After a moment the two women subsided to tight lips and stiletto glances.

Jessica was uncomfortably aware of Rafael watching from the sidelines with what appeared to be impassive distaste. She resented it, but was also embarrassed that he should see her relatives in such a bad light. What must he think of her mother and grandmother? She could not begin to guess, since it was so hard to know what she felt herself.

Nick. The son of her grandmother, brother to her mother, therefore her uncle. But son of her great-uncle, so her second cousin. No wonder her grandfather had been so horrified at finding the two of them on her bed together all those years ago. It had not been their half-innocent exploration of sensual possibilities that had caused him to eject Nick from the house back then. No, not at all. It had been the specter of possible incest.

It was a relief to know the truth. She could sense the internal unwinding of twisted guilt and shame as she realized she was not to blame for Nick's expulsion, that she need no longer feel besmirched by her grandfather's attitude.

At the same time she could see why he had considered the women of his family unstable and even insatiable. First his wife had betrayed him with his own nephew, foisting a child on him who was not his in the process. Then his daughter had gone through man after man, husband after husband, in search of the love and acceptance that was always beyond her reach. From his point of view, there seemed cause to suspect inherent weakness.

Yet Claude Frazier, never an introspective man, had been unable to see his own faults and weaknesses. All that the women in his life had needed, Jessica suspected, was to be loved by him and to know it. In his concentration on boats and business, he had never given them that certainty, had allotted them only a small portion of his thoughts and his time so that they felt of little worth to him. He had handed them the security of money and had expected them to accept it as a symbol of his love. When they did not, he had felt rejected and had retaliated in kind.

She knew these things because she had watched them unfold for years. She understood because love was her own greatest need, and no money, job, or corporate entity was ever going to take its place. Nor would a marriage based on these things suffice, especially when it was undermined by deceit. This she also knew. Now.

Beside her, Mimi Tess reached out with pale, trembling fingers to touch Nick's face. Her features twisted with joy and grief as she brushed over the strong contours as if learning them by heart. "Oh," she whispered. "Oh, my baby. Where did you go?"

"Nowhere," Nick said as he caught her hand and pressed a kiss into the palm. "I'm right here. I'll always be here."

"They took you away. I missed you so, *cher*. But it wasn't wrong, what I did. It wasn't." The elderly woman looked into his face with beseeching appeal while tears slid unheeded into the lace at her throat.

A muscle jumped in Nick's jaw, but his gaze did not leave his mother's face. Voice firm yet husky, he said, "No, it couldn't have been."

Jessica, watching them, felt sharp pain for the things that people do to each other in the name of love. Mimi Tess had been in a coma when she was brought back to Louisiana by her husband. There had been months shut away in a hospital, with a series of operations to relieve pressure on the brain caused by her head injury. Or so the story went. She must have also had a child, Nick, that her husband had taken from her. But was that done because she was incapable of caring for it? Or was it a punishment?

The answer might never be known. It would be best that way.

"Such a beautiful baby," Mimi Tess whispered as she touched Nick's hair, "so like my Claude. I never told him about you, though, my sweetling. That was wrong, too. But I was so angry, and he had no right to say such things to me."

"Tell who, Mimi Tess, Grandpapa or Louis?" Jessica put the question in some confusion as she leaned forward to see her grandmother's face. "What are you saying?"

Mimi Tess turned her head, her gaze searching.

"Louis was my friend. He made me laugh—we made each other laugh. Was that so bad?"

Did she, could she possibly, mean that she and Louis had never been lovers, that Nick was, instead, Claude's own son?

He might well be; his age was right. And according to the story, Claude had followed close on the heels of his runaway wife, chasing the couple down after less than two weeks. Her grandfather could have guessed, or else merely been afraid it could be true, and so had adopted Mimi's child later. But if Nick was really his own son, then what had been done to him was so much worse. The shares of Sea Gull, then, could have been left to Nick as recompense for that old wrong as well as a birthright.

Yes, but what could repay Mimi Tess for a lifetime branded as a wayward woman and an adulteress? What could make up for years of being something less than fully alive?

"No," Jessica said softly. "It wasn't that bad."

"Claude should have known. He should never have said such things. Never." Her grandmother's voice drifted away on a sigh with the weariness of a thousand regrets. "So sad. All that temper." The faded gaze clouded, and she looked again at Nick, searching his face.

"Senile," Zoe said under her breath.

"Keep your opinion to yourself!" Arletta snapped with a sharp gesture. "She's just tired and—and has had too much to bear." She glanced at her mother and away again with discomfiture that was more from her own partisanship than Mimi Tess's vagueness.

Her gaze stopped on Madeleine, then suddenly narrowed. Diving forward, she snatched up the younger woman's hand and turned it toward the light. An exclamation of fury left her. "That's what I thought! My grandmother's ring! My father never gave it to you—he wouldn't! You took it. You've been in his safe!"

"I have a perfect right," Madeleine said, her face flaming as she jerked her hand free. "I'm his wife!"

"Were his wife," Arletta corrected. "But you aren't an heir. You had no business prying into what doesn't concern you. What I want to know is what else you found? And what you've done with it!"

Jessica stared from her mother to Madeleine as dismay moved over her. The safe. The pictures from Rio that had been handed over to her grandfather were in there. She had thought they would be secure enough until she could find time to dispose of them.

It was possible she was wrong.

Chapter Twenty

▨ ▨ ▨ *It was later, creeping toward midnight,*
when Jessica made her way in the dark to her grandfather's bedroom. She didn't need lights to see where she
was going, certainly didn't want to advertise what she
was doing or attract company. She knew the exact loca-
tion of the great four-poster bed used by her grandfather
and his father and grandfather before him. The maze of
chairs and tables on which her grandfather had kept his
belongings was achingly familiar. She knew which faded
watercolor of ducks on the marsh hung over the wall safe
to conceal it.

She didn't consciously recall the combination for the
ancient black iron box, but still it came to mind as soon
as she touched the dial. She spun through the cycle,
then pulled the door open.

Sheafs of papers done up with rubber bands, an old
journal closed by ribbon, two or three jewelry boxes of
worn velvet, a collection of old coins in a tin: Jessica
could tell what the safe contained by touch alone, and
because she had seen most of it many times. Taking the
things out by handfuls, she set them on the nearest table
then reached to turn on a small lamp.

"Is this what you're looking for?"

Rafael.

She flinched with her heart beating high in her throat.
To follow through with switching on the light was
purest reflex action.

He was standing at the window, where the drapes
provided camouflage for his tall form. In his hand was

a thick manila envelope. His gaze was somber as he met hers across the room.

She had left him reading downstairs over an hour ago when she came up to take her bath before bed. That he was here was a betrayal. It was not surprising, of course, as she thought about it.

Voice brittle, she said, "If those are the pictures, they're what I wanted."

He hefted the package. "I think it may be, though I haven't investigated."

"And finding where they were, I suppose, was just a lucky guess?" She knew perfectly well how he had known where to look, but wanted to hear him say it.

"I saw your grandfather put the envelope away after he showed it to me," he answered in even tones. "My mother has a safe fairly similar in her bedroom, one installed by my own grandfather when they were popular back in the thirties. I could open it without any problem by the time I was ten."

"Congratulations." Moving closer with determined steps, she held out her hand. "I'll take those, if you don't mind."

"Maybe I do," he said with a judicious twist of his lips as he held the envelope beyond her reach. "After all, I have a stake in them, too."

"Which can hardly matter to you."

"It matters." The words were edged with steel. "Besides, it's my responsibility to protect you, and I can do that better by keeping them."

"I am perfectly capable of protecting myself."

"By destroying them?"

She hesitated. "We could burn them together."

"We could," he said before his lips twisted with sardonic humor, "and no doubt we should. But it seems a shame."

"In fact, you would rather keep them as a lever until everything is over. I understand."

His eyes narrowed with cogent thought as he studied her taut features. After a moment he said softly, "Or maybe as proof?"

"Proof of what?" she demanded, her face flaming with shame and indignation. "That I was careless and stupid, and all too susceptible to Brazilian charm? It certainly proves nothing else."

"Rather that you are warm and giving and passionate, or can be when the mood takes you."

"Or when I've had enough to drink," she said tightly.

"You knew what you were doing." The words carried quiet precision. "You knew it that night in Rio, just as you knew it three days ago when you came to me as my wife."

"Yes, and I know what I'm doing now," she said in chill disdain as she lifted her chin. "You wanted me to think my grandfather used those pictures to blackmail you into accepting marriage, that he was the one who ordered and paid for them. Well, I refuse. It was you. You had them done. You brought them here. You used them—and me."

"No!" he said, his brows snapping together over his eyes.

"Oh, yes. It fits right down the line. You knew Keil and I were in Rio, knew where we were staying. You sent the man and woman to set us up, then kept watch at the party to be close by when the lights went out. If you saved me from the cretin on the patio, it was only because you had plans of your own, plans that involved a camera."

"You can actually believe that?"

The dark blood of rage shadowed his face in the dim light. He had been found out and didn't like it, she thought. "Why not, when my grandfather told me so on his deathbed. I can't imagine why you agreed to a marriage to cement the merger between CMARC and Sea Gull, but this much I do know. It's over. It ended when my grandfather died."

"Because you don't care what anyone else thinks now that he's gone," he suggested in compressed tones.

"Because I can't stay married to a man who could do a thing like this."

"And what kind of wife," he inquired in trenchant irony, "condemns a husband without a hearing?"

Her smile was grim. "What could you possibly say? The evidence is too strong against you."

"Many things, if I thought you had the will to listen."

"Not likely." She couldn't hear him out, being far too susceptible to his persuasion. Even the rich, low timbre of his voice made her feel less decisive, less certain.

He watched her for endless seconds while swift consideration moved behind the dark gold of his eyes. Then his features hardened. "I still have the pictures."

The suggestion sent shock and anger along her veins. "So you do. Am I supposed to prefer being married to a blackmailer to enduring a smear campaign? That's even if you could expose me without damage to yourself? I don't believe so. But here's a deal for you. Give me the pictures and I'll be gone out of your life. You can do as you please with Sea Gull. You'll have won."

"No. I can't allow—"

"Try and stop me! Anyway, I don't think you really want to force a woman like me on your mother or your sister after all. Think how disgusted they would be if they found out what I was really like."

"Jessica, please, I never intended . . ." He stepped forward with one hand outstretched.

"Don't!" She retreated, though the effort it took to make her tense muscles move left her trembling. "I've heard all I want to hear. I don't doubt you meant to be a fair husband, at least by your lights, once you had your way over the merger. But that isn't enough for me. I need something more than mere respect or protection, or even passion. Now, if you will hand over the pictures, I'll say good night and good-bye. If you have any decency left, you'll leave this house now."

Rafael made an abortive movement toward her, then stood perfectly still. The golden glow of the table lamp slanted across the planes of his face, giving them the metallic hardness of bronze. His eyes seemed to hold dark torment overlaid by anger, though that could be no more than a trick of the dimness. Somewhere a dog barked, then was quiet again.

"Oh, I'll go," he said at last in virulent derision, "but the pictures go with me."

"No!" she said before she could prevent the protest.

"Try stopping me," he recommended, flinging her own words back at her. "But don't worry. No one will see them except me. Though, of course, I hardly matter, do I?" He swung, moving toward the door. Reaching it, he looked back, his gaze opaque, unreadable. "At least I'll have a souvenir."

He was an idiot; Rafael knew that much if little else. First of all, he was crazy for refusing to hand over the pictures. Then, like a fool, he stopped long enough to look at them after leaving the Landing. As a direct result of that moment of brain-damaged weakness, he picked up a speeding ticket on the trip back to New Orleans. Then he was so cutting with Pepe that the big Indian refused to speak for hours. Moreover, his attention had been so fractured during the safety check for the plane that he had to stop and start over twice, then repeat the whole process a third time to be sure.

Jessica was a woman of such passionate responses, so much warmth and lovely abandon. The memory of it crowded his mind and thudded in the hot cauldron of his brain until he felt delirious with it. She was angel and siren, kitten and tigress, cool lady and hot woman, hard businesswoman and soft female—everything he needed or had ever wanted. He could not stop thinking of how it had been and might never be again.

The primary damage was to himself, of course, for he knew full well now what he had lost. It hurt with a deep, enduring ache that disrupted his temper and threatened his sanity. It made him wish he had more gall and fewer principles, more macho arrogance and fewer scruples.

He should have made love to Jessica in Brazil and bedamned to the maids, his cousins, aunts, uncles, grandmother, and even his mother. He should have picked her up tonight and carried her kicking and screaming with him back to Rio. Or to bed. He should have made love to her until she couldn't think, then forced her to listen to him.

There were a lot of things he should have done.

This wasn't the end. She couldn't get away from him; he would insist that they work closely to mesh Sea Gull's operation with CMARC's. She was angry now, but she would get over it. Any appeal to reason would have a better chance of being heard at a later date. Still, it infuriated him to be forced to leave her behind, even temporarily.

He would have to start all over. How, exactly, he wasn't certain, but he would work it out. He had not handled the situation well back there at the Landing. He was usually more adroit, better able to deal with anger and surprise. Instead he had been caught off guard, stunned into incoherence by the accusations and Jessica's rejection after the incredible closeness between them. This time it mattered too much for smooth reasoning or facile arguments. Unable to marshal a reasonable defense without causing her grief by condemning her grandfather, he had been forced to stand on pride and dignity alone. For what good it did him.

There was much to be said for the old ways. The arranged marriages of times gone by had been ironclad, as certain as any relationship between a man and woman could be. A couple endured their enforced intimacy as best they might and sometimes, surely, managed to work things out. At least there was a chance.

Some might say he had gotten what he deserved for taking part in such a cold-blooded arrangement as the one between Frazier and himself. He wouldn't argue with them. Yet it had been impossible to resist. She had needed his protection as much as he had needed to give it. If the opportunity came again, he was afraid he would act in exactly the same way.

Now what?

She would call him; she would have no choice. Responsibility to Sea Gull, to the other stockholders and her grandfather's memory would force her back to the office. Once there, she would have no authority without his sanction, no way to work except through him.

So he would wait and try not to think of what might be happening to her in New Orleans without him at her side. If anything. He was, just possibly, the main source of her danger.

In the meantime he must decide what he was going to do when the summons came. Certainly he would not drop everything and return at once. He really didn't trust himself if he saw her again too soon. She might cool off, but he didn't hold out much hope of it for himself. Another angry scene would not be helpful, and, torn between a strong need to wring her neck and the violent inclination to kiss her senseless, he might well say or do something that would be fatal.

No, he would not go.

He had done everything he knew to convince her he wanted this marriage. Now she must decide once and for all exactly what she wanted. If she made the right choice she would call, or maybe even come to him.

When that happened, he would force her to listen to reason. She was intelligent and fair-minded; she would understand and accept his version as the truth. She must.

In the meantime he would wait and see.

Chapter Twenty-one

■■■ *The old man was dead.*

Carlton Holliwell smiled in satisfaction as he read to the end of the obituary. Tossing the paper to the table beside his breakfast plate, he leaned back in his chair.

It was about time. These old geezers had been running things too long. Now what did it mean for Gulf-stream Air?

Castelar still had a stranglehold on Sea Gull because of the loan. His grip was even stronger now Frazier wasn't around. Being married to the granddaughter didn't hurt, any way you looked at it.

Too bad the old man hadn't croaked a couple of weeks sooner. He would've had a foot in the door himself.

Never mind, he could still get around Arletta again, no sweat. She had a weakness for tough guys like him. On top of which, he was enough years younger that coming on to her flattered the hell out of her. Funny how well some things worked out.

If Arletta could manage to get her hands on her share of Sea Gull now, it just might be up for grabs. He might buy it or talk her out of it. He'd be in a position then to cause Castelar grief, cost him plenty to get rid of him. He liked that idea. He liked it a lot.

Christ, but that Latin lover boy got on his nerves. He'd enjoy rearranging his face if he thought he could get away with it. He wasn't sure he could. But he had friends who would be glad to see CMARC and it~

owner cut down to size. They might even contribute to the cause.

He'd have to think about that one a little more. In the meantime he had better make up to Arletta. Mouthy witch, trying to tell him what to do. Suspicious, too; he'd had to backhand her last time he saw her. She hadn't been too happy with him about it, but he could talk her around.

She'd hinted once or twice about getting married. Could be it would come to that; a wedding ring excused a lot for her kind. For all her free and easy ways, she was pretty damned conventional. Anybody who kept getting hitched that way had to believe whole hog in wedded bliss. Yeah, she'd marry him and like it. He had what she wanted and then some.

There was plenty for Arletta's little girl, too. She was another one that needed to be taken down a notch. He could get off on that idea. Hell, he might get more kick out of being a family man than he thought.

Right, but little Jessica might not be around. Castelar would want to keep her under control down in South America while he took over. Didn't seem likely he'd manage it, though. She wasn't the type to give in without a whimper, and she'd had a taste of being the boss under her old grandad. With a company the size of Sea Gull Transport at stake, she'd stick around. He'd bet on it.

So what was the plan?

He'd missed the funeral yesterday. Would have been a nice touch to show up, but he could still send flowers. Then he'd run by and see Arletta, say how sorry he was to hear about her old man. Offer a little comfort. Yeah, that would make a good opening. Once he got his hands on the old broad, he'd have her where he wanted her in no time flat.

It was late afternoon when he pulled into the parking lot of Arletta's apartment building on St. Charles. He'd been by earlier, but she wasn't at home; he figured maybe she was still at the home place over toward the

Texas line somewhere. This time her BMW was finally back in its slot.

He got out of the car and used the reflection in the window glass to smooth his hair, then tugged his belt back up where it belonged. He was halfway to the front entrance when a car pulled up into the parking lot behind him. Looked to be a taxi come to pick up a fare.

The door of the ground-floor apartment opened, and a woman stepped out. She was willowy, honey blond, and in a hurry. Little Jessica, as he lived and breathed. She looked wrapped up in her own thoughts until she caught sight of him. The she turned downright unfriendly.

"Well, well," he said at his most genial, "if it isn't the competition. I wasn't expecting to see you here."

"I could say the same," she returned, her voice as chilly as a winter wind off the lake.

"Guess you must have been down at your grandpa's, maybe drove back in with Arletta. Sorry to hear about the old man."

She didn't look particularly impressed by his somber tone or his sentiments. With a glance at the apartment building behind her, she said, "You know my mother?"

"We go back a piece." He shrugged a beefy shoulder. Let her make whatever she wanted out of that.

Amazement and suspicion chased themselves across the pale oval of her face. "How far?"

"Few years. We make the same bars and clubs. What's it to you?"

"Nothing whatever," she said with precision. "Only it seems odd you didn't mention it when we met."

"It wasn't exactly a sociable chat." Hadn't been anything to tell, either. He'd only put a move on good old Arletta after he'd run out of maneuvering room.

Jessica said, "Maybe that's what bothers me, all this sociability between competitors."

His upper lip curled. "Guess you don't want anything that might cause problems for Sea Gull, especially now when you think you've got a free hand."

"I feel a greater responsibility, if that's what you mean."

Her calmness got his goat. "Yeah, well, don't let it go to your head. You won't be able to pick up a pencil without Castelar looking over your shoulder."

"You would know, of course," she said in derision.

"You bet I would. Castelar and I had us a little talk. He has plans, big plans. You can go along or you can get hurt. Me, I decided not to mess with him and his crowd. Just didn't seem smart."

She favored him with a narrow look. "You sound as if he warned you off."

"You could say that. But first the bastard stole your loan right out from under me. I was all set to sign the papers, but he got to Gaddens, offered more."

"He knew you were after the loan?" Her voice was tight beneath the surface doubt.

"Damn straight, he knew. Must have had a strong notion to be your boss." He shook his head, enjoying her amazement and close interest. "It cost him plenty."

"What do you mean?"

His laugh was short and sarcastic. "CMARC doesn't need Sea Gull. Hell, Castelar could have put us both out of business if he wanted. Talking merger with your grandpa was just being polite, a way to salve the old guy's pride and save a little time while CMARC moved in on him. The only reason he did anything more was because of my bid for the company. But I guess maybe it was worth it to him. I saw where the two of you tied the knot."

"We'll be untying it."

"Yeah?" Carlton raised a brow. "What happened? He get frostbite trying to mix business with pleasure?"

Jessica's lips thinned with distaste. "You'll have to excuse me. My cab is waiting."

Before she could move away, the apartment door swung open. Arletta stepped out, giving him a jaundiced smile. Voice gravelly from too much smoking, too much crying, in the last few days, she said, "Looks like she's following in my footsteps, wouldn't you say?"

How long the old girl had been standing there listening behind the door, Carlton had no idea. Fact was, he'd forgotten about her.

"Let's just say it didn't work out," the younger woman snapped.

"I'd rather say you're too picky." Arletta took a draw on the cigarette that trailed smoke from between her fingers.

"It's better than having no standards whatever."

The last sounded like a shot in a battle that had been going on a while, Carlton thought, though it was also directed his way.

Arletta exhaled, watching her daughter. "So people aren't perfect? Big deal. If you'd open up, I might could set you straight about a few things."

"Thank you so much," Jessica said stiffly. "But I told you it's a private affair, and I'd rather keep it that way. I've got to go. I'll call you."

She swung and stalked to the cab. Stepping inside, she slammed the door. As the vehicle pulled away into the flow of traffic, Carlton stared after it, wondering.

"So are you coming in, or just going to stand there?" Arletta said.

He turned, allowing a crooked smile to work its way across his mouth. "What you think, baby?"

Jessica stood with her shoulder to the window in the town house apartment and her temple resting against the cool glass. It was raining, a slow, steady drizzle of the kind that could last the rest of the night or all the next week. The raindrops hitting the other side of the glass made a musical, repetitive sound that should have been relaxing. It wasn't.

She had a headache that three pain tablets and a cup of herb tea had so far failed to relieve. She felt so keyed up she thought she might go straight up the wall at any unexpected sound. Her thoughts revolved in her head with such speed she had difficulty sorting them out, much less making sense of them. And beneath it all was a deep, aching loneliness that nothing could soothe.

A part of the last was grief and loss, legitimate and to be expected. A part of it wasn't. She refused to think about what else, or who, was missing.

Had Rafael really used the photos to trap her into marriage, or had he been trapped himself?

If it was her grandfather who had dictated the marriage, then why had Rafael agreed when he had no need for Sea Gull?

If Rafael's interest in her grandfather's shipping company was merely a courtesy, then what could be behind the harassment of its crew boats and the violence directed against her?

If he was not involved in any way in these things, had no inside knowledge of them, then why hadn't he defended himself against her accusations?

Nothing added up.

She tried to be methodical about it, to start at the beginning and reason it through to this afternoon when she had spoken to Carlton Holliwell. She couldn't seem to manage it. For one thing, there was no natural progression of events that she could see. Then she kept getting bogged down in the time she had spent with Rafael, the things they had said and done. Especially the last.

Maybe Holliwell was right, maybe she had no business trying to run a shipping company. She lacked balance and perspective, and she was a terrible judge of men. Every time she had to make a tough decision, her emotions got in the way.

And she couldn't see what was in front of her nose. Take Nick, for instance. She'd always known there was something odd about her grandfather's attitude toward him, had always thought he and Keil looked something alike. Still, it had never occurred to her that he could be so closely related. One reason, of course, was that she could not imagine her grandpapa refusing to publicly acknowledge anyone who was a bona fide member of the family. She should have realized that he had his weaknesses just like other men.

And just where did Nick fit in? How long had he

known he was her uncle? Was it possible he had been told as far back as when they were kids growing up together? How had he managed to live with the secret? What had it felt like, and how had it affected him?

People aren't perfect.

Her mother had said that a few hours ago. What kind of comment on her own humanity was it when it took Arletta to point out that particular truism to her? Was the fact that she could be surprised a sign that she had perhaps misjudged her mother along with all the rest?

Oh, but had she misjudged Rafael? Could the reason he had let himself be trapped into a marriage agreement have more to do with a private meeting in a patio than it did with a public merger?

The discreet yet piercing chirp of her telephone broke into her thoughts. It was Madeleine calling from her car phone. She was on her way into the city, and wanted to know if she could put up for the night at the town house. She would be there in ten minutes, give or take.

Another round with her grandfather's wife was the last thing Jessica wanted. She thought she had managed to avoid that kind of thing by her early departure yesterday from the Landing. Wrong again.

She put on decaffeinated coffee, since it was fairly late, then set out old Haviland china cups and saucers, a silver sugar and creamer set, and a pink crystal platter of bakery cookies. As she took lace-edged napkins from a drawer, a rueful smile curved her lips. It seemed she was turning into a typical Southern female, automatically falling back on the forms and displays of tradition when she was uncertain.

If she expected Madeleine to be impressed with her show of hospitality, it was wasted effort. The other woman barely glanced at the cookies and refused the coffee outright. Requesting a glass of water, she paid no more attention to the delicate crystal glass she was handed than if it had been made of cheap plastic.

"You probably think I shouldn't have come to New Orleans," Madeleine said, leaning back against the chintz of the sofa with its muted rose pattern, and balancing her water glass on her knee.

"No, why?" Jessica might wish she hadn't, but that was another thing entirely.

"Oh, everybody pretends widows don't have to go through official mourning like in the old days, but they gossip like crazy if you get out too soon. I don't care. I stayed cooped up out there in the back of beyond while Claude was sick, but I can't do it anymore. I've got to get away, got to—to find a life for myself."

"Somebody objected?" Jessica suggested as the other girl faltered to a halt.

"Zoe. She seems to think I should follow her example, cut myself off from the world on account of my perfect husband—though from what I've heard about hers . . . Well, no matter. The point is, I could use a job. I've got to get away, off the chenier, before I go crazy."

As much as Jessica might resent the implication that living with her grandfather had been a kind of imprisonment, she could understand the other woman's urge to take off on her own.

"I'd like to help you, really I would," she said slowly. "But you know how things are at Sea Gull just now. I'm not sure I have the authority to hire a new janitor, much less create an executive position."

"It doesn't have to be anything fancy. I could be somebody's assistant, a secretary, anything."

She meant she would like to be Jessica's assistant. Or someone else's in the company.

Jessica said slowly, "This wouldn't have anything to do with Keil, would it?"

"How did—What makes you think that?" Madeleine's deep breath made her large breasts swell under her silk chemise dress.

"I saw the two of you together at the Landing."

Madeleine was silent for long moments, then she moistened her lips. "I don't know what you saw, but it can't have been much because Keil wasn't having any—if you know what I mean. Oh, the feelings were there, and I was willing." She gave a small, embarrassed laugh. "Maybe too willing. Anyway, it didn't happen. I . . . don't think he likes me all that much."

"I doubt that's it," Jessica said with abrupt insight. If Keil was trying to keep his hands off his grandfather's young wife, it explained much about his inability to settle down. Or attend to business lately.

Madeleine refused to meet her eyes. "Anyway, I wouldn't object to being close enough to see Keil every day, but that's not the main thing. I need something to occupy my time and, believe it or not, I don't like taking the money Claude left me."

"You don't?" Jessica could not prevent that question.

Madeleine shook her head so emphatically, her short hair ruffled like dark brown feathers. "Makes me feel cheap, like a kept woman. More than that, I don't think he should have siphoned it off like that in the middle of all this takeover business."

"What do you mean?" Jessica said sharply.

"Well, I don't know too much about these things, but the way Claude explained it, he made an electronic transfer of the money from Sea Gull to a Cameron bank. I think he knew he wasn't going to make it—all those little strokes, you know. Anyway, he said that you and the others were settled, but he wanted to be sure that I would be okay. He didn't think I had a right to expect part of the company, but this lump sum would be put in a trust account of some kind, and the interest paid to me every month. But I know he couldn't afford it, and it just—doesn't seem right."

Sea Gull's missing funds. This was where they had gone, then. It made perfect sense, now that Jessica knew.

She said, "But if you don't take the money, then that's where the job comes in."

"That's about the size of it." Madeleine straightened her shoulders. "I don't mean to move in on you and Keil, never did, but I'd really rather work for what I get."

Jessica gave a slow nod. After a moment she said,

"Grandpapa wanted you to have the money, so it's yours. What you do with it is up to you. If you're serious about working anyway, I can check with personnel, but can't promise much with things so up in the air."

Madeleine nodded, then gave her a quick look through her long lashes. "They'll calm down now, I expect, with Claude gone and Rafael taking over. You got your photographs back, so that's all right."

"You saw them." Jessica had known it was possible but having it confirmed gave her a winded feeling.

"Don't get all bent out of shape; it's no skin off my nose. I like you better for it, if you want to know. Makes me feel more like I can talk to you."

A short laugh escaped Jessica. "I guess that's one way to look at it."

"Before, you always made me nervous—though I admire you, really I do," Madeleine said earnestly. "All this business with CMARC, well, it's been over my head. I hate being treated like a brainless doll, but maybe I'm more of one than I thought because I don't get it, all the legalities and shouting over who's in charge. It's just a business, not some life-or-death thing. I even hate it in a way. Claude would still be alive if he hadn't got so mad about it that he gave himself this last stroke."

"What do you mean?" Jessica sat forward, her gaze sharp.

"You don't know? He had a call about the crew boat that exploded in the gulf back last year. Seems it wasn't an accident. He got to thinking that somebody meant to put him out of business, and damned near succeeded."

"Who?"

Madeleine gave a quick shrug. "I've no idea, and I don't think Claude knew. The man who called didn't give a name, just said he had a hot tip for him. Claude would have looked into it, but he got so upset that, well . . . you know."

Her grandfather had died before he could follow up, before he could learn who had set out to ruin him. "Did he have any ideas? Did he say anything at all that might show what he thought about it?"

"He mentioned that drug business a few weeks back, like maybe there was a connection. Nick was on his mind, too. And Vic Gaddens; I heard him call the bank, trying to talk to him." Her face clouded with bitter humor as she added, "But I'm only guessing. Claude didn't say much. He never told me much of anything about his business."

"I have a feeling," Jessica said slowly, "that might have been a mistake, not to mention a terrible waste of woman power."

Color rose under Madeleine's clear skin. She started to speak, hesitated, then said in a rush, "I did think one time that Claude knew more than he was letting on. On the way to the hospital, he kept trying to say something about Brazil. It may sound silly, but I think he was afraid for Rafael."

"Or afraid of him?" Jessica suggested in compressed tones.

Madeleine looked disconcerted. "Maybe. Claude mumbled something about him being in the way so they would have to take care of him, but I'm not sure. He wasn't making himself very clear."

"Yes, I can imagine," Jessica said on a sigh. Running her fingers through her hair, she clutched a silken handful as she leaned back and propped her elbow on the top of the sofa cushion beside her. "Anyway, I'm glad you came, glad we were able to talk."

Madeleine gave her a smile that was almost shy. "So am I. I'd have done it sooner, you know, but I don't think Claude would have liked it. He didn't much want the people close to him having friends. He seemed to think it was disloyal in some way. You know what I'm saying?"

"He needed to be the most important person to them," Jessica answered, her smile wan.

"And if he couldn't be that, then he didn't have much use for them anymore, kind of like you and Rafael. You made your choice to his mind, so he intended to see you lived with it. If you wanted the man, then you would get him."

Jessica gave her an arrested look. "He said that to you?"

"Not in so many words; you know the way he was. But he stayed up all night after he got those photographs, figuring all the angles, trying to see the advantage to himself and to Sea Gull. He thought what he finally decided was best for everybody."

"Rafael didn't bring the photographs with him that day he came?"

"No way," Madeleine said definitely. "Claude had them several days before then."

"You wouldn't happen to know where they came from?"

Madeleine shook her head. "They just showed up for all I could tell."

"So you think Grandpapa did actually suggest the marriage to Rafael?" She waited with a knot of fear in her chest to see what Madeleine would answer.

"Why else would he invite him to the Landing?"

"But you don't know it was the reason," she persisted.

"It makes no sense any other way, does it? I mean there were the photographs and all that, but Rafael already had the loan. He didn't need you."

No, he didn't need her, but he had still agreed to the marriage. Why, unless it was for reasons seldom recognized these days, much less mentioned. Honor. Responsibility. Compassion. Or maybe because two women in his life had already turned self-destructive, and he couldn't risk it happening again.

He had felt sorry for her, obligated toward her, and so he had added her to his list of dependents. It was also possible he felt he owed that gesture to Claude Frazier for all he was taking from him.

"Yes," Jessica said in hollow tones, "I suppose that was it."

"It doesn't mean Claude didn't love you, him arranging things that way. He did."

Distracted, Jessica only made a soft sound that could be taken for acknowledgment of the observation.

"You didn't mean to desert him, I know, or grow away from him, but that's the way he looked at it. It pained him less to send you away than to have you around as a constant reminder that you were no longer his little girl. I think maybe women with minds of their own scared him. It was too easy for them to decide to leave him for good."

"I know," Jessica said, her voice fretted with grief. And she did, she really did. People weren't perfect, but instead were scarred and twisted by the happenings in their lives. They did things they regretted, things that could not be undone.

Herself included.

Chapter Twenty-two

⊞ ⊞ ⊞ *The orchids on Jessica's desk were such a* pale, unblemished violet-blue that they bordered on gray. The vase was of silver in a heavy and rather barbaric design that might well have been taken as a Mayan antique. The presentation was beautiful and unusual, but lacked warmth or vitality. In all truth, its somber heaviness and colorless perfection were depressing.

No card was in sight, but then, none was needed. The flowers had been delivered in person by Rafael's cousin Carlos. He sat beside them on the desk corner, flirting outrageously with Sophie, who was returning the compliment with enthusiasm.

As Jessica stepped into the room, the smile of Rafael's cousin faded and he slid from the desk to greet her with a quick kiss on either cheek. "Senhora Jessica, good morning."

She was oddly touched by his gesture with its connotations of affection and acceptance. At the same time she was wary of it and of his visit. Her feelings were not helped as she saw him glance at Sophie with a significant nod in the direction of the outside office. The secretary gave Jessica a wink as she turned smartly and walked out, but what it was intended to convey was a mystery.

"How is everyone at Casa Reposada?" Jessica said as she closed the door, then moved around to seat herself behind her desk.

"Well enough." Carlos studied her with minute attention. "I see you are also in good health."

Her glance was pensive as she heard the odd emphasis in his voice. "I'm fine."

"I am delighted. So it isn't illness that prevented you from returning with Rafael to his country."

"Heavens, no. Didn't he explain?"

"You were detained, I think he said, by the business of your grandfather's estate."

"And that isn't good enough?"

"It doesn't account for his temper," he answered simply. "Rafael has been such a bastard to live with—if you will forgive the expression—since his return that we would not be surprised to learn you had been left for dead."

"I'm sure," she said with dry skepticism. "And who might all these concerned people be?"

"His mother and the rest of the family, of course." Carlos smiled with a rueful shrug. "Even I felt a few qualms."

"You can all stop worrying. There's nothing wrong." She straightened the edges of the already neat stack of papers left ready for her signature.

"So you say. Why, then, must I be the one to arrange orchids for you? I ask this in the quest for knowledge, you understand, not from mere curiosity."

She looked up quickly. "They aren't from . . ."

"No, I regret to say. Well?" He quirked an eyebrow.

She had given herself away. In some annoyance she said, "You want to know why there are no longer regular deliveries of orchids? That's easy. Because Rafael no longer needs to bother for a mere wife."

"No, I don't believe that is the problem."

"Then I haven't a clue. You'll have to ask him."

His grin was deprecating. "I would do that, if I did not have this enormous fondness for my head. Instead, I will tell you what I think. You have had words, the two of you. Rafael, being a man of pride, would not defend himself as he felt you should know his high regard for you, therefore should accept that he would never willingly cause you pain. You took his silence for indifference, or perhaps worse, guilt. Perhaps you told him to leave you. To protest would have been to reveal how much he cared, therefore exposing his weakness where you are concerned. So in his anger and pain he obeyed your command. Now neither of you can unbend enough to reach out to the other."

"A typical lovers' quarrel, in fact," she said, her smile tinged with irony. "I'm sorry to disappoint you, but it was a little more than that."

He made a sound between a hum and a grunt. "It is serious, then."

"You could say so. Look, Carlos, I appreciate your concern, and I'm sorry if the others are upset, but some things just don't work out. Can we please let it go at that?"

He was silent while he considered her. Finally he said, "I'm not sure that is possible."

"I don't see why not."

"You think to continue here at Sea Gull, yes? You will be working with Rafael, speaking to him constantly on the phone. How will you conduct yourself? What will you do or say when the two of you are alone? Can you put aside everything that has been between you and act like a businessperson who has no thought except for the good of the company?"

Jessica had asked herself these same questions. Unfortunately she had found no answers. She looked away. "I don't know. I can try."

"Fine. And what do you expect from Rafael?"

"I don't know what you mean."

He tipped his head as he watched her. "He is no bloodless American, no businessman with a computer chip for a heart. One day he will look at your lips, or perhaps touch you by accident, and his patience will be at an end. He will reach out for you, and nothing will stop him. What then?"

A warm sentience moved over her, lingering around her heart. Jessica, recognizing it as incipient hope, stifled a moan of despair. She didn't want to feel it, didn't want to feel anything. "Why," she said unsteadily. "Why are you doing this?"

"Because Rafael is my friend, my *compadre* who is closer than a brother, and I cannot bear to see him hurt. More, I have seen you with him, and know that no other woman can be so perfect a match for everything that he is, for all the fire and passion he has inside him."

She gave him a skeptical look. "You're certain we're talking about the same man?"

"Don't!" Carlos said in pained rebuke. "You, of all others, must know how he can be when he loves from the heart."

"Why would you think so?" she said in bitter denial of the images that rose warm and sweet in her mind. "He married me for money and duty and, just possibly, fear of what I might do if he failed me. Oh, yes, and I mustn't forget desire, though it didn't last past the wedding night."

"It lasted," Carlos said with a crooked smile. "Why else is he in so foul a mood? As for the rest—never. He is a man of compassion but would not tie himself to a woman for such reasons as you give. Not again. You are the mate of his soul. To deny it is foolishness."

She needed the armor of suspicion, needed it desperately. "He didn't send you to say that, I suppose."

"He doesn't know I am here." He shrugged.

"Then it's only your opinion."

"It's what I know to be true," he insisted. "If I thought that it would make things better between you, I would pick you up bodily and take you to him. That I do not is more because I fear he would take me apart for touching you than from doubt that it would be useful."

Jessica gave a mirthless laugh. "Caveman tactics. It wouldn't work, I promise you."

Carlos smiled, but there was dark consideration in his eyes and he made no answer. A short time later, he said his good-byes and left the building.

The day wore on. Jessica tried to work, but it seemed impossible. She picked up folders and put them down again unopened. She sat taking the cap off her favorite pen and putting it back on again. She got up from her chair to walk toward Sophie's office, but forgot what she intended to say or do by the time she reached the door.

Rafael's face kept slipping into her mind: the dark gold of his eyes, the shape of his jaw, the lines of his mouth. She could almost hear the rich tones of his voice echoing in her head, feel his touch drifting over her skin in languorous, endless appreciation.

With the aid of fierce determination, she managed to concentrate two whole minutes, and even actually accomplished a little. Afterward it was easier. Afraid to stop then, she continued through the lunch hour; food was the last thing on her mind in any case, and she really needed to catch up.

By midafternoon she had waded her way through most of what was piled on her desk. It required such teeth-gritting effort, however, that tension knotted the back of her neck and her head pounded with every throb of her pulse. She was just about to call it a day and go home to a hot bath and two aspirin when a call came through.

Sophie took it, spoke briefly, then got up and walked to the door of Jessica's office. "You have any idea where Nick could be about now?" she said, standing with a hand on her rounded hip.

"Not the faintest," Jessica said with exasperation. "Who wants to know?"

"The assistant crew boat captain for the *Sun Dancer*. Nick was supposed to take her out at two o'clock on a regular run delivering men to a rig. He hasn't shown up at the dock."

Jessica propped her head on her hand and closed her eyes. It wasn't like Nick to be so irresponsible. Was this an indication of the way things were going to be from now on? After a moment she said, "Are we sure he didn't cancel the trip or delegate it to one of the other captains?"

"If he did, nobody got the message. And the boat is cleared and ready to go right now."

She considered a moment longer. "Crew boat operations are Keil's department. Let him handle it."

"He's not in his office, or so the assistant captain says. I swear I heard him come back after lunch, though. Hold on, let me see." Sophie was back within a few seconds. "His secretary says he had a message from his mother. He took off like a bat out of hell for places unknown."

Jessica frowned, then sighed, sat up straighter, and spread her hands flat on her desk. Firming her mouth, she looked up. "Call the assistant captain back and say he's authorized to take the *Sun Dancer* out, but to be sure he brings it back in one piece. Tell Keil's secretary to put off anything and anybody until tomorrow, or, if that doesn't work, route the important stuff through me. Then check Nick's apartment. If he isn't there, leave a message saying he's to call me."

"Right," Sophie said with a snappy salute and a cocky grin. "Welcome aboard, sir."

"Go soak your head," Jessica answered with sour humor.

"And ruin my new hairdo? You gotta to be kidding!"

"So much for the captain's orders," Jessica muttered in mock despair.

Her smile faded as the secretary went away. What had taken Keil from the office in the middle of the day? It must have been important, or he would have stopped to let her know. Or would he? The two of them had not had one of their coffee sessions in a while, several days in fact. Well, they had talked a few minutes the day before the funeral, but that didn't really count.

She had no idea, for instance, how Keil felt about Nick and the changes caused by the will. He had not looked particularly happy at the time; still, his reaction had been overshadowed by his mother's tirade and the business with Mimi Tess. Since their return to New Orleans, Jessica had been so preoccupied with her own problems that there had been no time to seek him out. It had crossed her mind that they might have time for a talk session this evening after business hours. That was before Carlos had shown up.

A churning sensation in her midsection was a reminder that she had not eaten since breakfast. On impulse, she stood up and reached for her purse. Her mother lived less than ten minutes away, and it was possible she could provide a sandwich and a cup of tea. She might even be able to shed a little light on what was going on with Keil and his mother.

Arletta was making a chicken-and-sausage gumbo. The great pot of it that barely simmered on the stove's back burner filled her kitchen with the smoky scent of andouille combined with the richness of onion, celery, green pepper, garlic, and chunks of white chicken meat in stock. The gumbo was thoroughly cooked, but had not quite reached its peak of flavor. The rice was done, however, sitting white and fluffy in a blue earthenware crock. Jessica did not wait for either perfection or an invitation, but went straight to the cabinet and took down a bowl. Filling it with rice, she then covered that with the savory cross between soup and seafood stew.

Her mother smiled a little at Jessica's obvious hunger. Reaching to pour herself a cup of coffee from the pot on the warmer, she said, "To what do I owe this pleasure? It must be important, since you left the office early."

Jessica said, "I'll have to go back to lock up my office. But I wondered if Aunt Zoe is sick, if maybe you'd heard from her today?"

"You think it's likely after what she said at the funeral?" Arletta inquired as she joined her at the table. "I wouldn't call her if I were gasping my last, and she certainly wouldn't call me. Anyway, Zoe's too ornery to be sick."

"But she acted as if her chest hurt when she heard about Nick."

"Pure nerves. The woman's as strung out as a pair of cheap panty hose."

Jessica gave her mother a quick look, wondering if her lack of sympathy came from honest knowledge or old animosity. "I don't suppose you've spoken to Keil since lunchtime, either?"

Arletta made negative sounds, while her gaze narrowed. "So what's this about?"

"Probably nothing," Jessica said with a shrug of indecision before she went on to explain.

Her mother heard her out in silence. After a moment she said, "You don't really know that Keil didn't leave to check on this business with Nick and the crew boat."

Jessica shook her head as she spooned up aromatic, dark brown gumbo. "Ordinarily he would have said something."

"Things aren't ordinary just now," Arletta paused, then went on. "It will be like pulling teeth, but I suppose I could find an excuse to call Zoe."

Jessica was touched at the offer, though she couldn't help grinning at her mother's obvious reluctance. "Never mind. I'll do it."

"Let me know if you find out anything," Arletta said at once in relief.

No more was said for a few minutes while Jessica finished her gumbo. It was her mother who broke the silence.

"Honey, about Carlton Holliwell . . ."

Jessica looked up inquiringly.

Arletta huffed a sigh as she looked away. "I'm truly sorry about the way he mouthed off when he came by. After you left, I told him not to come around again. I'd already handed him his walking papers once, but apparently it didn't sink in."

Embarrassment mixed with sadness made a heavy weight in Jessica's chest. She pushed back her bowl before folding her arms on the table. "If you're doing this for me, Mom," she said, feeling her way slowly, "I wish you wouldn't. I may not care for the man, but as long as you're happy with him, I really don't have anything to say about it."

Arletta stared at her for a long moment. Then she gave a slow shake of her head. "You called me Mom. I don't remember ever hearing that from you."

"If you don't like it . . ."

"I didn't say that. I do. Really. I was just surprised, since I've never been much of a mother."

That admission almost took Jessica's breath. Flushing a little, she said, "I suppose I haven't been much of a daughter, either. But I've been thinking a lot lately, about you, my dad, Grandpapa—and everything that has happened. I think I see now why you had to get away."

"Do you really? I used to think it was a big deal, used to feel it was the only way I could be myself, keep from turning into the empty-headed, boringly virtuous female your grandfather thought he wanted for a daughter." Arletta's lips curled with weary derision. "Might have been nothing except self-indulgence, start to finish."

"You had the right to decide your own life."

"Maybe. But by hanging around and thumbing my nose at Claude Frazier, I lost the chance to make something of myself, to go someplace else and do something on my own. See what I mean?"

"You weren't trained for anything."

"Oh, that's just a cop-out. I could have got training somehow. I think I might have, if your father had lived. Instead, I drifted from man to man and wound up letting them push me around, tell me what to do. Then they would remind me too much of your grandfather, and away I'd go."

"The times were different." Jessica didn't know why she was making excuses for her mother, since she never had before. It was just that she suddenly felt sorry for her, and for all the wasted years between them.

Arletta lifted a shoulder and let it fall. "Doesn't matter now, I guess. But I worry about you."

"Me? What for?"

"I think sometimes that you paid for all my mistakes, that your grandfather kept such a strict watch over you and everything you did because he wanted to make sure you didn't turn out like me. In the process he turned you into a . . ."

"Empty-headed, boringly virtuous female?"

Arletta gave a hoarse chuckle as her own words came back at her. "Not exactly. On the other hand, are you sure you're doing what you want by working for Sea Gull? Or are you only doing what he wanted? Are you still trying to make him happy?"

"I wish I knew."

"Well, think about it," Arletta said, "because you don't have to stay if it's not what you want."

"What else is there?" Jessica asked in quiet desolation.

"Anything. Everything. Don't you ever think about what you might like to do if there was no Sea Gull Transport?"

Jessica's smile was wry. "Oh, I've thought about it. Trouble is I never came up with an answer."

"Well, think about it until you do. When the CMARC takeover is final, you can leave it to them with a clear conscience, if that's what you want."

Jessica looked down at the table, following the pattern in the cloth with a thumbnail. "Actually, I like business. I enjoy being on top of things, watching something grow, coming up with ways to make it work better. I'd love to see Sea Gull expand, and I'm curious to know what will happen. Some of the ideas Rafael discussed with me—well, the times ahead should be exciting."

"That's all right, then," her mother said doubtfully.

It could be, Jessica saw that. She had meant every word she said. For the first time, she could admit to herself that maybe there were advantages to the merger.

She said, "That's always supposing I get to keep my job."

Her mother nodded. "I'm not going to pry into what happened with you and Rafael. That kind of interference never set well with me. I just want you to be happy."

"Yes, I know. I suppose it will work itself out, one way or another."

Arletta met her gaze an instant then. "Just don't wind up like me, thinking you're a free spirit, but really so dependent on men to feel good about yourself that you fall for any dumb line. Even when you're old enough to know better."

Hearing the corrosive humiliation in her mother's voice, Jessica said quickly, "If you're talking about Holliwell . . ."

"In a way, but it's all right. I don't really need him, don't need anybody. Zoe had a point, you know. Maybe it's time I stopped trailing around after anything in pants, time I started thinking about how I look to other people."

"Don't!" Jessica said in low anger as she recognized her mother's pain and embarrassment. "Don't let anybody, *not anybody*, dictate how you live. That would be like substituting other people for Grandpapa, don't you see? Forget Zoe, forget me, forget everything except what makes you feel good about yourself."

They watched each other, green gaze meeting green gaze, while something warm and powerful passed between them. It felt elemental, a bond that could not be easily broken.

Then in the midst of the moment, Arletta's face twisted. Tears filled her eyes, and her lips began to tremble. "Oh, God," she said. "Oh, Jessica, honey . . ."

"What is it? Tell me!"

As Jessica reached out to take Arletta's hand, her mother clutched her fingers in a tight grip. "I didn't realize—never intended—" She broke off, then tried again. "I only wanted what was best for you. Oh, God!"

"Mom, you're scaring me to death. What are you trying to say?"

Tears glistened along the reddened rims of the older woman's eyes, then spilled down her cheeks. "I thought you were being used, that your own grandfather was molding you into something as stiff and coldhearted as he was himself. You worked so hard, never had any fun; it seemed like you had never been young. You had no use for men, and I thought—It seemed you were never going to find anybody to love. And then—then I saw the pictures."

"Pictures?" Jessica's heart began a hard throbbing that pulsed upward into her head with sickening force.

"Of you and Rafael. I was so surprised, shocked, really. But you looked so gorgeous and warm and alive."

As Arletta paused, Jessica gave her hand that she held a small shake. "Where did they come from? How did you get them?"

"They came in the mail," Arletta said with an echo of bafflement in her voice. "No explanation, no return address, just a plain brown envelope. I couldn't believe my eyes when I opened it."

"And what did you do with them?" Jessica asked, her voice tight in her throat.

Arletta drew a deep, hiccuping breath. Pulling her hand away, she wrapped her arms around her chest as she rocked back and forth in her chair. "Oh, honey, don't hate me. I've wished a thousand times I hadn't done it. I know how it's going to look, but I wasn't jealous of what your grandpapa had done for you, really, I wasn't. I thought it would help break the ties that held you if he saw them, that it was the only way you could be free. But it didn't work, and then . . ."

"Grandpapa?" Jessica whispered in horror as she sat back in her chair. "You gave the pictures to Grandpapa? It was you?"

Arletta swallowed, a gulping sound. Her face a mask of grief and her words so thick they were almost incoherent, she said, "Yes, it was me, and now he's dead. Do you think I helped kill him?"

"Oh, Mom," Jessica said, and reached out for her mother, her own pain no longer important. "You didn't cause his death, you couldn't have. I don't know who did, but it wasn't you."

Chapter Twenty-three

Sophie was covering her computer keyboard for the day when Jessica returned to the office once more. She looked up with worry in her golden brown face. Relaxing into a smile as she saw Jessica, she said, "I was hoping you'd get back before I had to leave. The phone has been giving me fits. I've got half a dozen messages . . ." She broke off, then said in an entirely different tone, "What's the matter?"

"Nothing, nothing," Jessica answered without meeting her assistant's gaze. "You heard from Keil?"

Sophie wasn't fooled, but she allowed herself to be distracted. "No, not him. But Cressida down at the Landing called. If I understood her right, there's some kind of weird activity going on at a place she called the old shell airstrip. She wants to know if she should notify the police about it. Then a guy named Pepe, who has something to do with Rafael—"

"Bodyguard, chauffeur, cook, general factotum."

"Yeah, him. He wanted to know if you had faxed a message to Rafael. I told him you hadn't, as far as I knew, so he says fine, no problemo—or words to that effect. End of conversation. And then—"

"What kind of message was I supposed to have sent?"

"Didn't say, and I didn't get a chance to ask. The guy was all business and none too friendly about it. So then I heard from the dock, where it seems the *Sun Dancer* went out as instructed under the assistant captain. After that, just a few minutes ago, Keil's dear old mother called. Didn't say what she wanted, but left a number where you can call her back. I think that about covers it."

"Thanks," Jessica said, accepting the slip with her aunt's telephone number that Sophie held out to her. She glanced at it, then stood holding it as if uncertain what to do with it.

"You want me to get her on the line for you?"

Jessica summoned a partial smile. "No, no thanks. I'll take care of it."

Sophie took her purse out of the bottom drawer of her desk and slid the strap over her shoulder. Her dark gaze concerned, she said, "You sure you're going to be all right? I could stay if it would help."

Nothing might ever help again, but that wasn't Sophie's problem. Turning toward her office, she said, "I'm fine. Really."

"You're sure? I could get you a cold drink, maybe an aspirin. Cup of coffee?"

"No, no, you go on home to your Zack."

Sophie looked unconvinced but dutiful. "I guess I'll see you in the morning, then."

"Yes, in the morning."

The secretary hesitated a moment longer. When Jessica did not look toward her again, she swung and let herself quietly out of the office.

Jessica sat down behind her desk and put the card she held on the surface. Reaching for the phone, she pulled it toward her, then sat with her hand resting on the receiver.

Rafael. She had accused him of giving the photos to her grandfather, and he had not defended himself. He had let her rant and accuse and never said a word.

Why?

That question was the single coherent idea in the jumble of her mind. If she knew the answer to it, everything else might fall into place. Or maybe not. It certainly made no sense that her mother had betrayed her. Jessica would not have believed it if she had heard it from anyone else, but there could be no doubt. Arletta had given her grandfather the photographs.

Regardless, Rafael had known her grandfather had them, had known where they were kept. It followed, then, that her grandfather must have used them to convince him to marry her.

Or did it?

Wasn't it possible that Rafael had sent the pictures to Arletta himself? He was a good judge of character; he might have suspected what she would do with them. Afterward he had only to appear at the Landing to achieve what he wanted.

No, that didn't compute, either. He could have had what he wanted without marrying her at all. Sea Gull had been his, for all rights and purposes, from the moment he bought the loan.

But if he hadn't kept his silence from guilt when he was found with the pictures, then what was the reason?

Pride. That was what Carlos claimed. Was he right?

Or could it be that Rafael knew who had taken the pictures or had commissioned them, knew who had given them to Arletta. If that was it, he might not have spoken because he wanted to avoid questions that might implicate them. He could have failed to defend himself in order to protect that other person.

Was that why?

Or was there, just maybe, something he intended to do with those photographs that was more important than proving his innocence, something he still meant to carry out.

Could that be it?

Then there was also the chance that the pictures might show something he did not want her to see. What could it be? No one else had been present beyond the two of them and the hidden photographer. Had they?

Oh, but what if there had been an audience, hidden watchers behind every window and door? Voyeurs, watching her initiation like some virgin sacrifice to an ancient and cruel god.

Ridiculous. Crazy, even. Shivering, she rubbed at the

goose bumps that prickled along her arms. The whole thing was making her crazy.

No. Totally impossible.

The man who had indicated so delicately that he would not touch her while she was under the roof of his family house could not have indulged in such a public display of machismo. The man who had protected her from harm, not once or twice but three times, could not have exposed her to such humiliation and danger.

Watch out for Rafael.

Her grandfather had said that to her. He had known something, suspected something that made him think she required the warning.

Oh, but had he really? She had taken it for granted he was trying to put her on her guard against Rafael. What if she was wrong? Rafael was her husband, the man her grandfather had arranged for her to marry. Claude Frazier had met, judged, and approved him. It didn't make sense for him to suddenly suspect him of harmful intent.

Suppose her grandfather had been trying to tell her something else entirely, as Madeleine had suggested? What if he had really meant she was to guard and protect Rafael, rather than be wary of him?

But how could her grandfather suppose that she was capable of that? Why would he think it was necessary?

Unless . . .

Unless it was someone in the family who was the source of danger?

It was not an entirely new thought, but neither was it a comfortable one. It had been far easier to suspect the stranger among them, the man who had pushed his way into her life and changed it beyond belief.

So he had become a scapegoat in her mind. Was it possible he had been that for someone else as well? Had he been someone conveniently close at hand to point to with suspicion, someone to shoulder the blame because on a dark, hot night during *Carnaval* he had allowed passion to overrule logic and good intentions?

Rafael would not defend himself, and so she had

judged him guilty and sent him away. Now, she was glad. If he was in South America, then he was out of the way, out of danger. It was possible they would all be safe so long as he remained there.

The piece of paper Sophie had given her was still in her hand. As she focused on it, her mind cleared and she actually saw it. The phone number scribbled there was not one she recognized. She thought, rather, that it might be for a cellular phone. Brows lifted in amazement, she began to dial.

The phone buzzed importantly, then rang again and again. Jessica was expecting at any second to hear an automated voice explaining that no one was available. Then her aunt was abruptly on the line.

"Good grief, Aunt Zoe," Jessica said, "a car phone? I didn't dream you had joined the twentieth century."

"Well, I did, last Christmas," the older woman said, huffing and puffing as if she had run to catch the call. "But never mind that. Can you come to the Landing? Now?"

"But I only just got back from there," Jessica protested. "Is something wrong?"

"Indeed there is, though I really can't go into it on the phone."

"Is this about Keil? Is he with you?" Mention of the Landing had made her think the call must be concerning something else entirely, but now she wasn't so sure.

"Oh, Jessica, it's so awful. You've got to come right now, you hear? Don't bother going to the Landing, just turn and come out the road across the marsh to Isle Coquille. You know where I'm talking about?"

"Yes, of course, the old airstrip road. But Aunt Zoe, is Keil okay?"

"I really can't go into the details, Jessica! They say people can pick up what you say on these things on any radio, you know." Her aunt's voice was shrill with anxiety as she added, "You get yourself on over here! I'll be waiting."

Jessica rose to her feet with the phone still in her hand. "Should I call the police, or—Aunt Zoe?"

There was only a dial tone for an answer. Her aunt had ended the call.

Lock the desk. Cover the computer. Close the office door and lock it behind her: The routine was so automatic, Jessica didn't have to think about it. On her way to the parking lot, she reviewed the amount of gas in her car. She had filled the tank two days before, after her return from the Landing. There was no reason to stop, then, no reason for delay of any kind.

Keil had been like a brother to her in the last few years. They had weathered so much together, from her grandfather's shouting and ill humor to business discussions that lasted far into the night. They had joked and laughed over a thousand cups of coffee, helped each other out with paperwork, covered each other's mistakes. Then had come the takeover bid followed by Claude Frazier's stroke and also the mess in Rio. Things between them had grown a little strained. Still, it was a minor problem when weighed against everything that had gone before.

The stretch of I-10 on the bridge-like causeway skirting the Bonne Carre spillway had never seemed so endless before, nor had the curving leg into Baton Rouge. Her car felt as if it were crawling, though she had to ease back on the accelerator continually to keep her speed to a range of minimum safety. She thought of the last time she had made this trip, its unimpeded progress in the helicopter with Rafael, and her chest ached with gratitude for his understanding that caused him to offer the flight.

Past Baton Rouge and Breaux Bridge and Lafayette. Over the waters of the swamps where duckweed floated in a lacy green veil. Along the miles of highway on pilings where the sections made a continuous thumping under the wheels that assaulted the eardrums. Then heading south this side of Lake Charles, down into rice and cattle country. Flying like a duck homing for the marshland in fall, zinging over the Intercoastal Canal, winging with the wind blowing backward through her hair and the salt smell of the gulf strong in her nose.

It was dark by the time she reached Ombre-Terre; lights were on in the houses of the town and among the ranches on the narrow road out to the chenier. Slowing her speed, she kept close watch for free-ranging cows, for straying nutria or opossum or the flapping flight of a crane or heron disturbed by her headlight beams. Finally she spotted the Landing up ahead, rising among its oaks with a single light burning in a back room. Seconds later she turned off onto the old airstrip road with its scattered piles of cow manure. That track of rutted shell reflected the light of a pale yellow half moon as it ran straight into the dark marsh and the night. On either side the brackish water shone like stretches of murky mirror.

For a moment she thought nobody was there. Then she saw the two vehicles, a Cadillac DeVille and Bronco, parked just off the straight stretch of roadway that served as a landing strip. They were out of the way on the high ground that surrounded a big oak. Already slowing, she eased off the gas even more. Something about the darkness, the quiet and lack of movement, was disturbing. She could feel the hair rising along the back of her neck.

The driver's door of the Cadillac opened, and a dumpy figure climbed out and stamped into the open. Aunt Zoe. With a short breath of relief, Jessica wheeled cautiously off the road. Pulling in just behind the other vehicles, she cut the engine.

"It took you long enough!" her aunt greeted her in querulous tones.

"I came as fast as I could. Where's Keil?" Jessica's gaze lingered on the Bronco as she got out. She thought she had seen a man behind the wheel of the four-wheel-drive vehicle just before she turned off her headlights. If so, he was making no move to join them.

"He isn't here yet. Oh, Jessica, I've been so worried." The older woman looked toward the Bronco, then away again.

"He's all right, isn't he?"

"I don't know. That is, I'm not sure."

Her aunt's face was pale, and she seemed to have lost her usual overbearing assurance. She plucked at her dress with agitated fingers before clutching her hands together over her full stomach so hard that her knuckles creaked. Doubt and distress made Jessica's tone sharp as she asked, "So what is it? What's going on here?"

Her aunt's gaze flickered over to the Bronco again. "I don't know how to tell you. It's all so complicated; you've no idea."

"Tell me something, for heaven's sake!" she demanded, setting her hands on her hips. "I've been imagining all sorts of disasters with Nick missing and now Keil going off Lord knows where. Is it something to do with drugs? Is that why we're here? Has somebody been using the shell road to bring them in again? Please don't say Keil has anything to do with this, because I won't believe it!"

"No, no, not my Keil. But I think . . . I'm almost sure it's that foreigner you married."

Pain squeezed Jessica's heart, but she pushed it from her. "Oh, come on! The man's a multimillionaire."

"Yes, and how do you think he got that way?" the older woman said in triumph.

"Hard work and the intelligence God gave him!" Jessica took a sharp breath to calm her rising anger even as she recognized the truth in her own words. That she could ever have considered for an instant that Rafael had drug connections seemed unreal. She went on in quieter tones. "Look, Aunt Zoe, I don't know why you got me down here, but if you think a drug drop or anything like it is really going to take place here, then we have no business standing around waiting for it. Let's go to the house where we can talk sensibly."

"No! I'm going to show you I'm right and you're wrong."

"You're going to get us killed is what you're going to do if something really is going on!" Jessica said in frank exasperation. "Good Lord, don't you know these people don't play games?"

"Neither do I! I'm going to show you what a stupid

mistake Claude Frazier made by not letting my Keil take over at Sea Gull long ago."

"If that's what this is about, you might ask your son if he wanted the job."

"He's a man, and his grandfather, not to mention his father, helped build the company. There should never have been any question that he would take over. But oh no! Claude couldn't stand it that his brother and his nephew had sons when he didn't. He had to bring you in and set you up as a figurehead, let you pretend to manage everything instead of my Keil."

"None of which makes a hill of beans, now that CMARC is taking over," Jessica pointed out as calmly as she could manage. "Anyway, this is no place to discuss it. If you want to stay here and watch the dew fall or get yourself shot, that's fine. Do it. But I don't think I'll join you, thank you very much. I'm going back to the house."

"You can't!" Her aunt shot out her hand to grab Jessica's arm.

She pulled free of the clammy grasp with a single jerk. "Watch me."

The door of the Bronco opened with abrupt force. The compact form of a man stepped into view. He moved from the darker shadows, and moonlight slid in a faint sheen along the dark metal barrel of the pistol in his hand. His voice was snide with his self-satisfaction as he said, "I don't think so."

It was Carlton Holliwell.

His voice echoed in her mind. She saw his thick-shouldered, bull-like shape with short legs that made him appear squatty there in the dark. And abruptly she recognized him for something more than a competitor, knew him with instinct made acute by suspicion and memory of a brief and vicious fight in a dark patio. With that knowledge came cold, stalking fear.

"You," she said softly. "It was you in Rio."

She did not realize she had spoken until he laughed. "Right. This time there's nobody around to help you out. Ain't it a shame?"

The night air was damp and cool with spring, and carried the fetid hint of marsh gas. Insects sang in raucous symphony, inviting love, chancing death. Somewhere a cow lowed, a warm and homely sound. The stars overhead in their moist blanket of black glittered and winked in unconcern. Their light silvered the wings of a white crane that rose majestically from the swamp, then skimmed over the tall cypress trees with their branches almost raking its belly and wheeled away into the night.

She could not fly away. Pinned by the threat of the gun, she waited. The numbness of shock began to recede, leaving her alert, watchful.

"Mr. Holliwell, I don't think—" her aunt began with a quiver in her voice.

"We need her. Don't lose your nerve now."

There was contempt beneath the warning. Jessica wondered if her aunt heard it as plainly as she did. And if it mattered.

She didn't know exactly what was going on, but it seemed this might be her only chance at the answers she needed so badly. Her gaze intent as she tried to see Holliwell's face, she said abruptly, "If you were the man in the patio, who was behind the camera?"

"Guess." He slanted a glance at Zoe Frazier.

"Somebody had to catch that disgusting display," the older woman said in macabre primness.

"Did they, now?" Jessica said as illness and anger spiraled through her. "How can you stand there calling what I did disgusting when you set me up to be raped while you recorded it for posterity? Dear God, Aunt Zoe, what were you thinking?"

"Keil, I was thinking of Keil," the older woman returned, breathing heavily through her nose. "I did it to get back what you stole from my son."

"Besides that," Holliwell said on a sneer, "your own mother thought you needed a good lay."

"That's a lie!"

"Think so? She said you were going to die an overworked virgin, told me so herself during one of our after-the-loving talks. That's what gave me the idea, baby, when I found out you were going to be in Rio at *Carnaval* time."

"Sick." The word was clipped. She didn't trust herself to elaborate, for fear of what she might say.

"Effective, you mean. Or it would have been if Castelar hadn't stuck his nose in it. I can't figure out what tipped him off."

"Something you wouldn't understand, the simple concern for another human being."

"I'll bet. A regular Galahad, ain't he, always charging to the rescue? Well, I hope you're right. Matter of fact, I'm depending on it."

Jessica was silent while her thoughts gathered in swift, horrified order. Watching her still face, Zoe said defiantly, "It was my idea to send the pictures to Arletta. I knew she would hand them over to Claude. For one thing, she wouldn't know what else to do to protect Sea Gull and the family, but mainly she couldn't resist showing him how wrong he was about his sweet little Saint Jessica."

Sparing her a brief glance, Jessica said, "But it backfired on you, didn't it? Instead of throwing me out, Grandpapa took Rafael in with him. You had to deal with a high-powered Brazilian who preempted all moves and wound up owning everything. Maybe I should thank you."

"Don't," Holliwell recommended with ugly emphasis. "It ain't over yet."

"No?" Jessica's gaze was dark with consideration there in the shadows. "I think it is. One of you faxed a message to Rafael in my name, didn't you? You think he's going to come flying in here. And then what? You'll shoot down his plane? Wait until he lands, kill him, then plant cocaine the way you planted it on Sea Gull's crew boats?" She laughed. "Sorry, but you're going to be disappointed. In the first place, Rafael doesn't come running when I call; we're separated, in case you didn't know it. But the main thing is that one of his people phoned the office to confirm this mysterious message of yours and was told I didn't send it."

Holliwell glowered at her a stunned instant, then began to curse.

"What are we going to do?" Zoe asked in panicky dismay as she turned toward him. "If Castelar doesn't come, everything will be ruined."

"Shut up!" The command was vicious. "Shut up and let me think."

"What about Nick?" the other woman cried as she waved in the direction of the Bronco. "He won't stay out forever. How can you handle him if he comes to? And what in God's name is the point without the plane or that husband of Jessica's?"

Holliwell swung on Zoe with the gun raised to strike. "I told you to shut up! Keep yapping and I'll leave you here with the rest!"

Zoe fell back, her breath wheezing in her chest, mouth quivering with her terror. "You ... you can't do that."

"Like the lady said, just watch me." The look he gave her was malevolent.

Jessica stared hard at the Bronco. Did her aunt mean Nick was lying unconscious in the vehicle? What could the purpose be, unless that they were all to die? All of them who had a stake in Sea Gull. All except Keil.

The night stretched around them, relentlessly benign in its empty quiet. The polished green leaves of the oak above their heads whispered with the passage of a wind gust, then hung still again, shining like black glass triangles in the moonlight.

Abruptly the last pieces of the pattern fell into place, forming a quilted whole in Jessica's mind. In the gratification of discovery, she whispered, "That's it. It has to be."

"Figured it out, have you?" Holliwell swung, glaring at her from under his brows without appreciation. "Too bad. You might have been better off more stupid."

She gave a quiet laugh. "You'd have liked that, wouldn't you? You might have switched your attention to me from my mother and saved yourself a lot of trouble. But I didn't make it that easy, so you decided to get rid of me. Permanently. That's what this has all been about from the beginning, hasn't it—getting me out of the way so Keil could take my place. You thought with his laid-back attitude, it would be easy to persuade him to agree to the white knight merger with Gulfstream Air. At the very least, the pictures from Rio were supposed to give my grandfather such a disgust of Brazilian ways that he would abandon the CMARC venture."

"It would have worked, too, if it wasn't for that damned Latin pirate."

"But it didn't. So you fell back on buying up our outstanding loan, or at least you tried. Only Rafael got in ahead of you."

"Hell, he got in ahead of me before that," he said, his face set in a snarl. "I was supposed to take you on at that party, get down and dirty with you so the old man would shove you aside and promote Keil to CEO. It was days before old Zoe, here, got around to telling me I was too late because Castelar had already done it. Guess you were more ready than Arletta thought."

Aunt Zoe made a squawking sound of protest. "You ran off and left me at that party in Rio, or you'd have known."

Jessica ignored the byplay, keeping her gaze on Holliwell. "That was why you jumped me again at the town house, wasn't it? You didn't know Zoe already had the pictures you needed. Besides, you couldn't stand being beat out of your dirty fun so you meant to set it right by finishing what you started. Only Rafael was there that time, too."

"I nearly got him on the boat, interfering son of a bitch," Holliwell said in vengeful cruelty.

Jessica tipped her head as she turned to her aunt. "Yes, but it might have been Keil just as easily, since he's the one who usually took out the *Sea Gull IV*. Would that have been all right?"

"Oh my God," Zoe Frazier said, holding her breastbone. Eyes wide, she turned her gaze on the man beside her.

"Don't be a stupid fool," he snapped.

"Is it so foolish?" Jessica asked, willing her aunt to listen. "What's one more life, then or now? Or later on for that matter, after he decides it's too risky to let you—and Keil—live when you can tie him to this?"

"The boat was a professional job," Holliwell said in grating explanation as he stabbed a glance at Zoe Frazier's distraught face. "A favor from my friends, nothing to do with me."

"The kind of friends who may not be too happy to miss their chance at having their very own crew boat company as ready-made drug transport?" Jessica suggested. "You must be desperate to make good on your promises. However, I'm afraid this isn't going to work for you. What will happen to your grand scheme, then?"

"It'll work."

"You think so?" She was all serious consideration. "Say you kill Nick as planned, what then? Mimi Tess will inherit as his next of kin, I imagine, which means Arletta will eventually get his share plus my grandmother's on Mimi Tess's death. Which is fine if you think you can talk Arletta around. But kill me, and then what happens? I'll tell you, since I don't believe you saw my marriage contract. My husband becomes my beneficiary, so he takes charge of my shares of Sea Gull. With those, plus his ownership of the loan, he will become the official CEO under the CMARC umbrella. And there will go all hope for you."

Holliwell snorted with savage humor. "You think you're so smart, don't you? You got it all figured out."

"I know you can't win this way. It might be wiser to let both me and Nick go. Then you had better head for parts unknown before your friends or the police catch up with you."

"Wrong, bitch. I talked to your South American, saw him lose his cool when your name came up. He's coming, honey. He's coming, even though he may guess it's a trap."

"No, he won't—"

"Oh, yeah, he'll come. He would do it for any single one of that bunch of relatives of his, even that big stupid ox who guards his back. It's a thousand times more likely he'll do it for the woman he married. And when he gets here, I'm going to shoot him down before he sets foot on the ground, make it look like some drug drop gone sour, or maybe a Mafia hit to keep him from horning in on their territory here. Then I'm going to kill you, after a little while, after I've had that fun I missed down in Rio. Because if you die first he inherits, just like you said, after which that bunch of vultures that's his kin come into it when he passes on. So we can't have that. But if he dies first, then you afterward, Jessica baby, guess what? His part comes to you plus a South American fortune besides. All that lovely loot will fall on Arletta like manna from heaven. Hey, and you don't have to be a genius to know who's gonna to be there to make sure she takes good care of it, now do you?"

The look Jessica gave him was caustic. "She broke off with you. She wouldn't think of letting you near her again."

"No? Not even when she's so broke up about the terrible death of her gorgeous daughter? Hey, I think she'll be glad for a shoulder to cry on, not to mention a man to tell her what to do with her business. Oh, yeah, she'll come around for her Carlton. You can bet on it."

It was just barely possible he was right, though Jessica didn't want to think it, would never admit it. She said in chin-tilted bravado, "All that doesn't matter because it won't happen. Rafael will never leave Brazil."

"Think again," he said, and laughed as he cocked his head and turned his malignant gaze to the night sky.

She followed his line of sight toward the southeast, searching the dark heavens above the swamps while hope and dread swelled in her chest. Then she saw it, the wink of a moving star, a pinpoint of light that was fiery white and escorted by a smaller spark of pulsing green—the lights of a plane, gleaming brighter by the second.

A moment later she caught the sound of the plane. It grew, a deep-throated and powerful roar that changed to a lower rumble as the craft lost altitude with its firm and deliberate descent.

Rafael.

It was Rafael, coming in at treetop level, searching for the Landing and its airstrip. Rafael flying into ambush.

Rafael.

Coming for her. After all.

Chapter Twenty-four

▧ ▧ ▧ *Terrible, aching joy surged through her. In* its wake, the moment, the night, the place became surreal even as her every sense tingled into exquisite life. She drank the soft, moist air, felt the intermittent caress of the wind from the gulf, heard the blended insect songs like a symphony, recognized the scent of grass crushed by car wheels as she might some exotic perfume. She was hyperaware of her aunt's nervous jittering—and also the threat of the pistol in Holliwell's hand. Though terror and rage simmered below the surface of her calm, she stood poised and rock steady while her brain began to function with piercing, absolute clarity.

Something must be done. She refused to stand there and allow herself to be killed, or to permit Rafael to die before her eyes. It was up to her. There was no one else.

Her best chance might come from being a woman. Holliwell considered her weak and defenseless, so he was supremely confident of his control of the situation. That meant the element of surprise would be on her side.

Another thing was his divided attention. He needed to cover her while keeping an eye on the plane to judge its moment of arrival.

On the other hand, she had so much to lose. She could not afford to make a mistake.

What was Rafael thinking? Could he see the vehicles and people where they waited there in the darker shade of the live oak? Could he even see the straight stretch of shell airstrip reflecting white in the moonlight? It must be possible to land in such places, since drug drops coming out of South America were often made under such conditions. But could Rafael chance it when there was so little activity, and no preparation for his arrival in the way of lights or markers?

Surely he wouldn't land if he saw a problem. Or would he? He was a careful man but, once committed, did not agonize over details. And he was daring when circumstances and his own will made it necessary.

She wouldn't think about the dangers.

He was coming . . . for her.

In spite of everything.

Steadfast, infinitely competent, and caring in his own dark and dangerous way, he had not failed her, nor would he, ever. The love she felt for him was a deep, eternally silent passion. Knowledge of it was not new, nor was its slicing edge of pain.

The plane skimmed toward them, as steady as the great white crane that had passed overhead moments before. Its landing lights came on. In the bright, steady beams, the twin lines of the shell road shone like rivers of molten silver.

"Get out there where he can see you," Holliwell growled, directing his weapon at Jessica. "Wave like you're glad to see him."

There was hatred in the glance she flung at him, but she did as instructed. The plane dropped lower, coming in incredibly fast. Bathed by the beams of its lights, she waved with tears rising in her eyes, waved with both arms high above her head, waved until they ached.

The plane bore down on her while its engine roared in her ears. Now she was caught in the full glare of oncoming headlamps. And abruptly, deliberately, she changed to the high, overhead signal seen in a hundred movies, the wild gesture that said, *Keep going! Don't land!*

Dust and ground shell swirled into stinging grit, whipping with dried grass and leaves to make a battering whirlwind. Jessica squeezed her eyes shut and ducked instinctively as the plane zoomed past overhead.

Blinded, coughing as she tried to breathe, she could not see who sat behind the controls. There was no way to tell if Rafael was alone or if Carlos was with him as copilot. There might have been time for his cousin to make the return journey after the delivery of orchids that morning. It could possibly make a difference, since Holliwell had indicated no plans for a second man.

As Rafael's plane banked into a steep turn, Jessica stumbled from the strip. Deliberately she came to a halt beyond her aunt, closer to Holliwell. He gave her a hard glance, but immediately returned his attention to the aircraft. His grip on the pistol he held was lax as he followed Rafael's progress across the sky. A sneering grunt of triumph left the burly executive of Gulfstream Air as the plane completed its swing, then lined up for the runway once more.

Jessica knew an instant of bleak defeat. She had hoped that Rafael would wing away back to Brazil, or at least to New Orleans. It hadn't worked. Now there might be one last chance if she dared take it.

Carefully she edged closer to Holliwell, her gaze on the weapon in his hand. She could try for it now, or wait until Rafael was on the ground. The last was safest, for Holliwell would be most distracted then. But what if he opened fire the instant the other man set foot on the plane's steps? If Rafael was caught unprepared, without cover, he wouldn't have a chance. She could not let that happen.

Yes, but could she prevent it? Possibly not, but what did she have to lose? If she couldn't, and still managed to live herself while Rafael died, would anything ever matter again?

The answer was no, nothing. The only thing to do, then, was try.

Courage and desperation, what was the real difference between the two? The question drifted across her mind as she stood with the high-pitched drone of the approaching plane in her ears and the wind lifting her hair. No answer came. She shivered once, then was still.

The insect song faded, blending with the engine roar. The moonlight and stars dimmed beyond the stabbing brilliance of the lights. The night eased away, leaving them all half-blinded, white-faced in the glare.

Closer, closer. The incline of descent was perfect, steady. The landing gear had been lowered so the black circles of tires looked like the claws of a giant bird reaching for earth.

Muscles tense, feet set, Jessica concentrated on Holliwell. The target was not the man, however, but the weapon. She must not lose sight of the pistol.

Nearer the plane came. Wingtips swinging delicately for balance. Saw grass bending with the wind of passage like a wave coming toward them over the marsh. Mist boiling up from the water of either side, trailing in twin comet's tails of spume.

Soon, soon. Wheels hovering, engine noise dropping, whining. A whirling cyclone of debris. Wind noise shifting, declining. Closer. Closer.

Touch down!

Jessica lunged. Heart and mind, bone and sinew in grim concert, she plowed into Holliwell with every ounce of force she could muster. Her fingers spread like talons, she ripped the pistol from his grasp even as he twisted away with a hoarse oath.

She couldn't stop her plunge. Her legs tangled with his, and she stumbled, falling. He clutched at her. Snatching her hair in a cruel grasp that made tears spring into her eyes, he jerked her around to grab for the pistol.

But she saw what he meant to do. Using the momentum as she swung in his grasp, she flung the pistol from her. It landed with a solid clunk somewhere beyond the light. The next instant a hard fist connected with her jaw.

Pain exploded in a burst of red inside her head. Spangled darkness closed in around her, and she fell, arms outflung, sprawling like a rag doll in the grass.

Dimly she heard curses and cries and the ungodly thunder of an engine. She rolled, half-blinded, and pushed to her knees in time to see the plane sweep past.

The steps formed by the lowered door were hanging down so they nearly touched the ground. Rafael stood on them, leaning out as he clung to the support strut. He dropped to the road bank, hit it rolling at a spot just behind and beyond the oak's deep shade. Then he was swallowed up by the sudden darkness as the plane sped on.

It kept rolling, braking only when it was several hundred yards down the track, almost back to the chenier road. Its lights were twin beams boring across the waving grass and into nothing. Abruptly the engine was cut. It wound down into silence. Then every light was extinguished and the night went black.

Holliwell bellowed with rage. Swinging this way and that, he searched wildly for sight of the pistol. At the same time he peered beetle-browed into the surrounding blackness or flung quick glances over his shoulder as he looked for some sign of Rafael. Neither pistol nor man was to be seen. He spat out an obscenity, then jerked around and plunged toward the Bronco. He reached for the handle, snatched it open.

The vehicle door was rammed wide from inside. It slammed into Holliwell and sent him staggering back. Nick half fell, half lunged out of the Bronco. Eyes livid above the duct tape that slashed in a silver streak across his mouth, he reached with bound hands for the other man. The two went down in a flailing mass of arms and legs.

It was then that headlights appeared, drilling the night as a car swept down the main road and swung onto the track. Traveling at speed, it swerved around the parked plane, then bounced its way over the rough shell strip. A Nissan, it barely slowed its pace as it barreled down on them, then slewed to a halt in a spray of gravel and ancient seashells.

Even before the engine was cut, the driver's side door

flung open. Keil sprang from the vehicle and sprinted toward them, a fast-moving silhouette in the delayed brightness of the car's automatic headlights.

"No! S-stop!"

That shrill, quavering command came from Aunt Zoe. She narrowed her eyes, blinking rapidly against the dazzling brightness of the Nissan's headlamps, as she held the missing pistol in front of her with both hands. She was trembling like weak gelatin, though she stood braced with her short, stout legs wide apart. Her frenzied gaze swung from Nick to Holliwell, around to Keil, then on to Jessica who was just pushing to her feet.

"S-stop," she repeated on a ragged gasp. "Stop it now or I'll shoot."

Holliwell struggled upright like a bear heaving to its hindquarters. She jerked back around to cover him. Catching a movement to the side then, she whipped in that direction to point the pistol at Nick. He ignored her as he dragged himself upright to lean against the side of the Bronco, blocking the door and access to whatever extra weapon might be inside.

There was a whisper of sound. Zoe twitched in that direction with frantic haste. Rafael, no more than a moving shadow drifting in from behind the older woman in the oak's deep shade, halted at once.

The assembled company hovered, teetering in their places as they recognized the danger in a trembling, inexperienced finger on the pistol's trigger. Zoe Frazier might well fire, but was just as likely to shoot one of them by accident. Tense, expectant, they waited to see what she would do.

It was at that moment that the automatic lights of the Nissan blinked out.

Keil's voice, sounding rough and strange, ripped into the darkness. "What on earth are you trying to do, Mother? Give me the gun."

"No!" Zoe drew a hiccuping breath that turned into a moan. The trembling in her hands became a shudder. "You don't understand."

"I know whatever is going on here has to stop." He eased closer.

"Go away," she pleaded, then turned abruptly petulant. "You're just like your father! No ambition, no thought in your head except drinking and women, always taking sides against me. You let Claude run over you just like Louis did, let Jessica get in ahead of you. But I can fix it. Everything will be all right if you'll just leave it to me."

"This is crazy, Mother. Nothing's going to happen here; I won't let it." Voice positive, soothing, Keil kept his gaze trained on his mother's face in the darkness.

"I'm not crazy, I'm not! I can do this, but not while you're watching. Just go away. Please, darling. You're not supposed to be here."

"But I am, in spite of the wild-goose chase you sent me on. Now, come on, let's go home."

"Oh, Keil—"

"Shit!" Holliwell ground out as he pinned the older woman with a fierce stare. Jabbing a finger toward Rafael, he commanded, "Shoot Castelar there first. *Do it now.*"

She twisted her head from side to side on her thick neck. "I can't, don't you see? Not yet."

"Then, give me the gun!" Stalking toward her with arrogant assurance, the burly man held out his hand.

"No!" Keil shouted.

"It's too late," Rafael said at the same time, his tone slicing in its quiet authority. Easing around the oak, he moved forward half a dozen steps. "You've put your son in danger, Mrs. Frazier."

As Jessica's eyes adjusted to the moonlight dimness once more, she saw there was dried grass in the ruffled waves of Rafael's hair and mud stains on the pressed perfection of his brown linen shirt and trousers. His face appeared stern in the faint glow of distant starlight, and the dark sheen of his eyes was searching.

His shift of position, she saw, placed him between her aunt and herself, so that his broad shoulders shielded her from the line of fire. It also brought him within a long arm's reach of the gun in the older woman's hands.

Holliwell's eyes had a hard glitter as he flicked a glance at Rafael. He stepped forward in his turn. Directing his attention to Zoe as if he could command her by the force of his will, he said, "We can take them, you and me. Just hand over—"

"He'll kill Keil along with the rest of us." Rafael's warning cut across the other man's cajoling words. "Then he'll kill you. It's the only way he can be safe."

A rough laugh came from Holliwell. "Lord, would you listen to that? But don't you believe it, lady. He's just trying to save his own hide, and his precious Jessica." He took another step and his voice hardened to a threat. "Now, quit fooling around and give me that pistol!"

The weapon in Zoe's hand shuddered around to center on Holliwell's navel. "I don't know . . ."

A quiet, musical note came from the darkness beyond the tree shadow. It might have been a hunting owl, a bat on the wing, or even a nutria surprised in his nightly rambles. It fit none of these precisely, however, having instead a foreign, tropical sound like a birdcall Jessica had last heard in Recife.

Holliwell whipped his head around to stare into the night. Then he looked at Rafael with rage and chagrin twisting across his face. "Bastard."

Rafael faced him, at ease yet with hard purpose in his stance. "Did you really think," he said softly, "that I would risk my wife's life by flying in here at night alone? There are men armed with heavy weapons moving into position on either side of us. Give it up, Holliwell."

"So you called in help from your drug-running cousins down in Colombia, huh? I might have known."

"My cousins in Colombia are just relatives, no more; I leave consorting with the cartel to you," Rafael said with irony strong in his voice. "I did call on my *com-*

padres for aid, and they will be more than enough to take you down. Let it go. It's over."

"The hell you say!"

Hard on the words, Holliwell sprang to snatch Zoe's pudgy wrist. He twisted the weapon from her weak grasp and spun her around. Her despairing scream gurgled abruptly into silence as he clamped a powerful arm around her neck. Dragging her in front of him, he brought the pistol up and pointed it at her temple.

He didn't count on Zoe's son.

Keil, already plunging forward to disarm his mother, rammed his shoulder into Holliwell's ribs. The three went down in a violent sprawl of arms and legs. There came a muffled snap, plainly audible amid the grunts and curses.

Rafael leaped to the heaving pile. As Holliwell whipped the pistol around, beating at Keil's head, trying to bring it to bear, Rafael grabbed his wrist and wrenched the weapon free. Hovering on one knee, he shoved it in Holliwell's face, pressing the bore between his glaring eyes.

"Hold it there, or die," he said in lethal command.

Holliwell made his choice in the space of half a breath. Face twisting with hatred as he stared up at Rafael, he spread his fingers and lifted his hands to the level of his face.

Keil rolled away from the downed man and shoved to his knees. He reached then to put his hand on his mother's shoulder. She did not move, but lolled across Holliwell with her heavy legs spread wide.

Nick reached up and pulled the tape from his mouth with a rasp that was obscenely loud in the sudden quiet. Swinging to the Bronco, he opened the door with awkward movements of his bound hands, then reached in to turn on the headlights.

In the sudden, brilliant glare, they saw Zoe's head tilted far back, lying at a too-cozy angle against Holliwell's shoulder with her cheek nestled intimately into the turn of his jaw. Her mouth was a bloodless circle of horror, her plump features were cut by grooves of old bitterness, old grief. Her eyes, reflecting horror and tragedy in their fast-clouding surfaces, were open wide in the final stare of death.

Chapter Twenty-five

▨ ▨ ▨ *Keil covered his mother's eyes, closing* them slowly with fingers that trembled. His soft breath of pain mingled with the sighing of the wind in the leaves overhead. Motionless, he knelt in the strong beams of the vehicle lights while moths and gnats, drawn by the brightness, fluttered around his head.

"I'm sorry," Rafael said, reaching across the sprawled forms to put a hand on the other man's shoulder. "Her neck must have been broken in the fall."

"I killed her." The whispered words carried the recognition of unbearable guilt.

"Get her off me." Holliwell growled the request from between them as he squirmed under the inert weight.

Rafael's gaze was meditative as he glanced at the other man, then back up at Keil. He said, "Not you. You didn't harm your mother."

Keil met Rafael's steady gaze. He looked down at Holliwell, then back up again. His eyes were red-rimmed, his thick lashes spiked by unnoticed tears. He chewed a corner of his mouth, said in tentative understanding, "You mean . . . ?"

Rafael gave a slow nod.

"Hey! It was an accident!" A species of panic filtered through the belligerence of the man on the ground.

"I think," Rafael continued as if Holliwell had not spoken, "that your mother was an elderly and misguided lady who wandered into something she didn't understand. She came here tonight thinking she might protect her niece and her son. And she was killed for her pains."

Holliwell clenched and unclenched his fists. "I tell you I didn't mean to do it!"

Nick pushed away from where he leaned against the Bronco. In hard tones he said, "Tell it to a judge, my man. I know what I saw."

It was a courteous and humane fiction the men were fabricating between them. It would be a kindness to Keil if it was believed, no doubt, but Jessica did not think that was the whole reason for it. Rafael, with his strong family roots, was whitewashing the Frazier name. The fact that this version of the events might also lessen the damage to Sea Gull was not, perhaps, incidental.

In all truth, however, Rafael was not so far from wrong. Without Holliwell, her aunt might never have done anything more dangerous than fret and fume with her resentment and bitterness.

"Poor Aunt Zoe," she said in tones of quiet, reflective pity. "She had no idea of the meanness in people. I'm sure she would have done everything in her power to keep me from being hurt."

At that moment Carlos lounged into the light with an semiautomatic weapon held casually at his side. Behind him came Pepe, who was also armed and had bandoliers holding ammunition crisscrossing his massive chest. They were, apparently, the only members of the armed force Rafael had mentioned. Certainly they had been more than enough.

In a voice of elaborate innocence, Rafael's cousin said, "Is Louisiana not one of those states which has reinstated the death penalty for murder?"

"And Grandpapa's old friend is judge for this district," Jessica said in agreement. "Even if the death penalty isn't applied, I expect the trial and appeals will be so long and expensive it will use up whatever Gulfstream Air might be able to beg or borrow from its backers. If, of course, these mysterious backers contribute anything."

Holliwell jerked as if he meant to get up. The pistol in Rafael's hand did not give, but pressed deeper into the engorged flesh of the man's brow. Holliwell cursed, a long and virulent spewing of fury.

Rafael listened for a few seconds only. Speaking over his shoulder then, he said, "Nick, is there any of that duct tape left?"

Nick gave a hard laugh. "Plenty."

The funeral was not large or well attended. There was no outpouring of floral offerings. Still, it was decent and mercifully short. It was also depressing.

All that hatred, jealousy, and scheming caused by misplaced love, and what had it come to in the end? Jessica thought. Nothing except wilting flowers, damp earth, and a long, long sleep. How much better it would have been to let it go and find some other joy, some other manner of loving. That might not have been easy, but could it have been any harder than a lifetime of keeping humiliating memories alive?

No, better to start over again, make use of the past to create a better future. At least, the good moments would not be eaten away by the acid of regret. Perhaps there was a lesson here she should take heed of, also.

As before, with her grandfather's funeral, Rafael remained for the service. He gave no explanation, nor did Jessica ask for one. Soon enough, he would be gone for good. She was only glad of his presence while it lasted.

She thought once or twice about suggesting he stay, perhaps to fill in for Keil for a few days, to help with the CMARC transition, give his advice in the continuing untangling of her grandfather's estate—any excuse would do. She refrained. He might oblige her from mere courtesy, and that would be too painful to bear.

Keil went back to New Orleans the day after the funeral. Nick drove him, since he had no other transportation of his own. He was also loathe to see him go alone. It was time the two of them talked, as well; they were cousins at least, if not half brothers, and had Sea Gull and its welfare in common. They had gotten along fine as kids and as young men out for a good time on the boat. Surely they could do the same now that they were partners.

Keil's leaving signaled a general departure. Arletta, who had spent the morning going through Claude's closets and sending things to the church rummage sale, began to cart boxes of items she had selected for herself out to her car. Pepe and Carlos helped her, then afterward ambled off down the road to the airstrip to check out the CMARC plane. Rafael shut himself in the study to make a series of phone calls, including one to arrange for a fuel truck from Lake Charles for refilling the plane's tanks before he took off again.

Jessica knew she should also get ready to leave. However, she was too restless and, in truth, too reluctant. She could not go until after Rafael left in any case. That was only polite, for she was his hostess, wasn't she?

Arletta suggested that Jessica might want to look around the house and choose a few things she would like to take as keepsakes. She tried, but could not settle her mind to the task. It would all be there next time she came, anyway, for there was no question of selling the Landing. It would become a getaway place, available for whichever Frazier needed it most. Like the birds of autumn, someone among them would always be returning to the marshlands.

Leaving the house, she wandered down the steps and out onto the lawn. Across the road was a path that led to the edge of the marsh. The small pavilion at its end had been built on the foundation of what had been the washhouse in other times. A purely decorative structure these days, it was a good vantage point for looking at the marsh, a pleasant place to sit. Jessica turned in that direction.

The rays of the sun slanted low across the saw grass, gilding the tall blades and casting swordlike shadows. The grasses, waving in a gulf breeze, made a soft clattering whisper. Flocks of red-winged blackbirds fluttered here and there, perching at awkward angles on the

blades, impervious to their sharpness. The briny tang of
the gulf swirled in the moist air along with the marsh's
own scents of green growth and muddy fecundity. Frogs
and insects sang their spring songs that were interrupted
as she scattered them from her path. Near the watery
edge where the grassland turned to soggy marsh, a
small herd of cattle grazed. The graceful white shapes
of cattle egrets hovered around them, stalking their
tracks or sometimes using the bony ridge of a cow's
back for a perch. On a distant stretch of open water,
brown pelicans paddled and dove. They were joined by
a flock of roseate spoonbills that dove for the blue-
brown water surface with the sunset flashing rose and
pink on their wings.

She could see no ducks and geese. Most were gone
by now, winging to northern nesting grounds. Soon the
drying heat of summer would be upon the marsh; there
was more grass and less water than the last time she
was here. The ranchers would be bringing the main
herds of cattle over from the winter pastures any day
now.

Farther out across the wet prairie, she could see
where the old shell road cut across the land, with the
plane that was parked on it half hidden by the waving
grass blades. It looked like a mirage in the uncertain
shimmer of moist air, as if it might be gone next time
she looked.

Green velvet moss grew on the steps of the pavilion
and around the wood curbing of the spring in the center
that had once supplied water for black iron wash pots.
The temperature under the spreading roof was several
degrees cooler than in the sun. Along the open sides,
the benches were damp to the touch. Jessica did not sit
down, but moved to lean one shoulder against a post
made from a tree trunk. Turning her back on the pavilion and the big house, she stared out over the wetlands.

Behind her, the water of the artesian spring pooled
cool and clear before it overflowed, running under the
pavilion's cypress wood floor and into the marsh with a
soothing, trickling noise. The warm breeze brushed

across her forehead like a gentle hand, while the warm sun striking under the shelter felt good. She closed her eyes. If there was peace to be found anywhere, then surely it was here.

The sudden fluttering of a bird frightened into flight jerked at her attention. She squinted against the sun as she looked toward the sound.

A wolf, gray, rangy, and raw-boned, stood poised at the edge of the marsh. It was perfectly still, ears pricked, scenting the wind. As she lifted a hand to shield her eyes from the sun's glare, he turned his wary, feral appraisal in her direction.

Jessica smiled with the shift of poignant pleasure inside her. She felt little fear; the wolf was no more anxious to interfere with her than she was with it. Yet it was good to know that there was wild, free life being lived among the tall saw blades and watery pathways of the marsh.

Abruptly the wolf wheeled and vanished into the grass. Jessica heard no footsteps, nothing unusual, yet, like the wolf, she knew she was no longer alone. She spun around. Rafael stood, relaxed and patient, beside the spring.

"I must have scared off your friend. Sorry."

As startled by his nearness as she had been by the wolf, and also as irrationally pleased, she said, "He was nervous of me anyway."

"Wise animal." The words were dry.

What reply could there be to that? Frowning a little, she glanced away. "You took care of refueling?"

"Yes, no problem."

"So, I suppose you're ready to go."

When he made no immediate answer, she looked back at him. There was intent speculation in his amber gaze before his lashes came down to conceal it. He answered then, "As soon as the fuel gets here."

He was wearing the shirt of fine nut brown linen in which he had arrived, and which Cressida had laundered and ironed with painstaking care that morning. The gulf breeze molded it to the hard planes of his chest. She had traced that same firm musculature with the palms of her hands. Its every line was imprinted on her mind. Unforgettably.

Her voice was abrupt as she said, "I apologize for what happened here. You should never have been dragged into such an ugly family squabble."

He would know exactly what she meant. They had discussed the whole thing at length over the past two days, including all the pitiable, vain, discordant reasons.

"Is there any other kind?" he said. "But don't be too contrite. I pushed my way into the middle of it when I went after Sea Gull. Or if you prefer, when I followed you to the party in Rio."

"I'm glad you were there. I'm so grateful that it was you—or rather that it wasn't ..." She drew a deep breath, closing her eyes. "Anyway. I do appreciate it, even if I never thanked you."

"But you did," he said with low consideration. "More than adequately, if my memory is correct."

"That was another thing altogether," she said with hot color rising to her cheekbones.

"Was it indeed?"

Ignoring that quiet comment, she went on. "I've been wanting to thank you, too, for coming to the rescue the other night. I don't know how you managed it so quickly—but I know I might have died if you hadn't. I value the fact that you risked your life for no real reason."

"There was every reason. You are my wife."

He said those last words as if they explained everything. Perhaps they did. She was his wife, therefore it was his duty to cherish her as he had sworn before God and man. And he would, no matter the cost.

"I didn't intend to be such a heavy responsibility," she said evenly. "In any case, I'm sure a divorce will be a relief. I promise not to make it difficult for you."

"There will be no divorce."

"An annulment, then, if that's easier."

"It isn't. As I told you once before, with me marriage is forever."

His features were set in implacable lines. His eyes were black with their relentless integrity. In confusion she said, "You will want a family. Sons."

"And daughters. Yes."

She made a brief, helpless gesture. "Surely you know a priest or bishop who can arrange a dispensation from the Vatican then—one who has a church needing an altar or roof? It's been done before."

"Not by a Castelar."

She felt as guilty as if she had suggested some grievous sin. Back stiff and chin high, she said, "You may change your mind one day."

"I doubt it." His gaze drifted over her face as if memorizing it. It touched the gentle curves under the bodice of her gold silk shirtwaist, then shifted to the horizon. His features hardened. "But perhaps you have had a change of heart; perhaps there's someone else you want to marry?"

Her smile was brief and wan. "No."

"It's as well. Just as there's no reprieve for me, there will also be none for you."

She turned her head to consider him. "Isn't that an unenlightened attitude for the head of a multinational corporation?"

"I am also a man," he said, the words vibrating deep in his chest, "one with no need for 'enlightenment' if it means going with the trend rather than fighting for what is right. Nor do I have any use for an 'enlightened' woman. I require one who is strong in heart and mind, a woman of passion who knows what she wants and goes after it. And in return she will have my heart and my soul and the last ounce of strength in my body. I will love and cherish her above all others, will make of her the bright burning candle in the darkness of my world, the orchid of my soul that stuns with its beauty and haunts with the rare sweetness of its fragrance. One day, she may come to me. Who knows? But until then, it suits me to be tied to you with this unbreakable bond. It will keep us both—safe."

The look in his eyes, the timbre of his voice, the

solid foundation of his words, coalesced in her brain to form a single conclusion. Before she could voice it, he leaned swiftly to place his mouth on her parted lips.

It was a sweet, familiar magic of taste and touch. Invading the senses, it promised and cajoled even as it fired her blood. Warm and smooth, the surfaces of his lips caressed hers. Their pressure brought pulsing heat. The sweep of his tongue was a beguiling abrasion that lulled thought, incited imitation, and also other less languid inclinations.

Swaying, she lifted her hand to his neck, trailing her nails through the thick silk of his hair to clasp his neck. He caught her hard against him so the points of her breasts prodded his chest and the sensitive surface of her abdomen was imprinted with the shape of his zipper and the firmness beneath it. He inhaled with the sharp sound of tried control.

Abruptly she was free. Rafael's gaze burned into hers for a single second. Then he walked away with his steady, long-legged stride. The sun canting down the sky gleamed in his dark hair, turned his linen shirt to bronze-gold. Slowly he grew indistinct, his outline shimmering as she watched him go through the prisms of her tears.

"Did you tell him you loved him?"

It was Arletta who asked that question perhaps an hour later as she stood with her hands on her hips and her bottom lip thrust out in disapproval. She was upset by Jessica's wet eyes and thick voice, but had no patience with her urge to hide until Rafael had gone.

Jessica answered her question with a quick shake of her head.

"Whyever not?"

"I can't be sure how he feels about me."

Arletta raised her eyes to the beaded ceiling of the long back gallery with a long-suffering sigh. "The man wiped out his accumulated assets to buy a company he didn't need, let himself be blackmailed into offering marriage, flew thousands of miles on the off chance that you were in trouble, and tackled a Mafia front man and a raving lunatic to save your neck. What more do you want?"

Rafael had performed a few other miracles her mother had not enumerated, but Jessica saw no need to remind her. Her smile a bit damp, she said, "I don't know, now that you mention it."

"So, do you?"

"Do I what?"

"Don't be dense, this is your mother talking."

Jessica tried to stare down the woman who had borne her, but it was no use. "Oh, all right. I think I've loved him since the moment I walked into his office in Rio. Or since the first time he kissed me, anyway."

"Then why in the name of heaven are you letting him get away? Again?"

"I can't just go running after him!"

Arletta's look of tried patience did not change. "Why not?"

"All the usual reasons," Jessica snapped in reviving defensiveness.

"Women are supposed to wait to be asked? Horse stuff."

"Pride, then. Doubt about what he might say or do. The absolute terror of looking like a fool."

"Honey, there are worse things, believe me, than looking like a fool. You can be one."

From the heavy irony in her mother's voice, Jessica knew she was thinking of Carlton Holliwell. If Arletta felt any regret for the way things had turned out, however, she gave no sign.

Jessica pushed a hand through her hair in distress. "I know all about being foolish; I've certainly had my moments." As Arletta raised a questioning brow, she added, "I'm the one who sent him away the last time."

A troubled pause descended while her mother looked at her more closely. "Why would you do a thing like that?"

"Because I misjudged him, thought I couldn't trust him. Because I was afraid he would see how I felt.

Because—oh, a dozen reasons, but mainly I suspected it was what he might want."

"And now you're miserable and so is he."

"Now, after some of the things you told me, I think maybe I was wrong."

A slow smile came over her mother's face. "I'm glad to see I accomplished something worthwhile. So what are you going to do about it?"

"I don't know." Her original action of choice had been to do nothing, allowing Rafael his freedom. But he had thrown that back in her face, and she wasn't so sure anymore.

"You'd better decide fast. Rafael is down at the plane, and I saw the fuel truck turn off in that direction a good half hour ago."

Jessica rubbed her hand across her face, then pressed two fingers to the ache behind her eyes. "I guess I don't know what to do because I don't know what's best for everybody. Most of all, I don't know what Rafael wants from me."

"That's always the way it is, don't you know that?" Arletta said. "But listen, whatever you come up with to do will be fine with me. You don't owe me anything, and I don't want to run your life. All I want is for you to be happy."

Jessica's smile was wry. "Yes, well, I'll try. I will try."

Arletta left her alone then, which was amazingly intuitive of her, all things considered. Jessica sat watching the light turn lavender-blue as the sun sank into the tree line. Her mind turned to another evening, another moment of truth—the instant when she had found herself alone with Rafael on her wedding night. She had survived that one, and even found it glorious.

Tigress, Rafael had called her, his tigress. It was fair enough; she had been less than tame. Yet how graceful and sleek and powerful she had felt with him. For those brief, wonderful hours, there had been loving acceptance, and a communication of mind and body that went beyond her most fervent dreams. It had been everything she had ever wanted.

A woman who knows what she wants, and goes after it.

She knew what she wanted now. Could she go after him? Did she dare to let herself go and become the tigress again?

Only regret the things you don't do.

Mimi Tess had said that. Mimi Tess who, like her daughter Arletta, had made a wrong choice, had left the man she loved and paid the price.

But if she dared, if she went to Rafael, would he want her? Could she become the things he seemed to need? Was that what he really wanted from her?

She saw the fuel truck leaving as she started down the steps of the house and turned toward the airstrip. She had cut it close, so close.

Rafael and Carlos would be making their final check. Pepe would be strapped into his seat, quietly sweating as he waited for the plane to lift into the air.

She didn't even think of getting into her car. There was no time to find her keys. In any case there was a shortcut across the marsh that would be faster, or so she thought, especially if she ran.

It was farther than she remembered. Or maybe she wasn't as good at finding a dry path through the grass and reeds as the thin young girl, all eyes and legs, who had raced over the chenier with Nick and Keil.

Back then she had been wild and unfettered, supremely certain of her strength, her competence, the rightness of her wants and needs. She could be that way again if she tried. She could.

The plane's engine kicked over and wound itself up to a rich idle. They were getting ready to take off.

Jessica broke into a run. Her feet pounded the earth, following the faint trail where no saw grass grew after more than a decade. The arching blades that leaned over it snatched at her, leaving long red stripes on her face and arms. She winced but did not stop.

Then the plane was just ahead of her. The door was

closed. Silver-white in the waning light of the evening, it shivered as it prepared to launch itself into the purple sky.

Carlos was in the pilot's seat; she could see him with the headphones on, checking switches on the panel above him, marking off items on his clipboard. He set the board aside, reached for the controls. He was going to take the plane up. Rafael was leaving it to him while he worked in the cabin. Slept. Talked to Pepe. Anything. Nothing.

The plane began to move.

She motioned, calling, screaming above the engine's gathering roar. Carlos saw her and gave her a thumbs-up signal. He thought she had come to wave good-bye.

Now the plane was rolling faster. It trundled past her and accelerated with a power surge, picking up speed. Faster, smoother, ever more steady, it sped down the shell track with dust blowing out behind it. The engine's whine increased. The wings wavered, found air currents. The wheels skimmed the ground. Left it.

The plane was airborne. Lifting up and up and into the gathering darkness. Going. Going.

Gone.

She let her arm fall to her side. Slowly, half blinded by the rush of tears, she turned away.

Rafael was standing under the oak. His face was still, his eyes darker than the coming night as he watched her.

Rage and joy clashed in her mind. She took a deep, glorious breath of relief and reached to dash the moisture from her lashes. Then her mouth firmed. Her gaze narrowed. She started toward him.

It was a stalk, a glide with a determined, predatory edge of angry grace. The gulf wind rippled the tawny bell of her hair and flattened her dress to her strong, lithe form. Her breasts were high and proud, her hips moved with careless sensuality.

Rafael stepped forward. His smile started in his eyes, lighting them, making them gleam, then curved his lips into a smile of satisfaction.

"You didn't go," she said, the words clear, almost threatening, as she came closer.

"I couldn't," he said simply.

She reached him and put out her hands. Snatching his shirt in a tight grasp that twisted the fabric, she jerked him down until his face was within inches of her own. "Don't ever," she said with soft, sibilant emphasis, "*don't ever* do that to me again."

"If I did, what would happen?" Twin devils danced in his eyes as he wrapped his arms around her with care, then tightened them to hard, suffocating closeness.

"I would track you down," she murmured against the column of his neck, reveling in his strength and the stronger purpose behind it. "Then I would do desperate things to you. After I tell you how much I love you."

"Mamae de Deus," he said on a low groan as he sought her mouth. "Kiss me quick, so I can signal Carlos to return. Then you can begin."

Jennifer Blake brings you
all the passion and drama
of TIGRESS in

Spanish Serenade

When nobleman El Leon is doomed to an impoverished, miserable life by the evil machinations of the powerful Don Esteban, he vows to reclaim his wealth and honor—at any cost.

Pilar, Don Esteban's beautiful stepdaughter, is withering away under her stepfather's tyranny. To escape, she turns to the handsome Leon and offers to pay him to kidnap her. And when he does, both discover they will never be free again. Bound by desire, they become slaves to their hearts....and to their revenge.

Don't miss this enthralling tale of love and retribution.